THE L

"HAYNES JOHNSON AND HOWARD SIMONS HAVE WRITTEN A HOT BOOK—AND ONE THAT DESERVES TO BE. *THE LANDING*: A TIGHT, TAUT THRILLER."

—Dan Rather

"What sets *THE LANDING* apart . . . is not so much the plot—fast and tense as it is—but the lovingly re-created portrait it paints of the nation's capital in the frenetic days of World War II . . . The story races along, gaining momentum as it winds its gripping way through all strata of Washington society. Tight and suspenseful, vivid and thoughtful, *THE LANDING* is a fine debut."

—*San Francisco Chronicle*

"A TRIP, COMPLETE WITH HEAT, CONFUSION AND TERROR, TO WARTIME WASHINGTON, A CHASE PLAYED OUT IN THE SUMMER OF 1942 . . . FAST MOVING AND EXCITING . . . DISTURBING AS WELL AS ABSORBING."

—Heywood Hale Broun,
Washington Post Book World

"An extraordinary history of the most dangerous moment our nation has known in this century . . . Fascinating: it *has* to be read."

—Senator Daniel Patrick Moynihan

THE LANDING

"A PANORAMIC THRILLER ... fleshed out with canny sketches of real people—Roosevelt, Hoover—and trenchant observations of the seething social and bureaucratic fray. A neatly plotted confrontation, set squarely among genuine events yet always crackling with suspense."

—*Kirkus Reviews*

"*THE LANDING* is about W.W. II Washington, wily spies, super-duper sabotage and enough chills and thrills to permanently punk your hair."

—*Boston Herald*

"A riveting new political thriller ... *THE LANDING* has more twists than a box of pretzels as it accelerates toward an incredible climax."

—*American Way* Magazine

"Everything one wants and expects in a suspense thriller. It is exciting ... The characters are believable, the situation intriguing, the backdrop fascinating."

—John Katzenbach

"PLENTY OF ACTION AND INTRIGUE ... HAYNES JOHNSON AND HOWARD SIMONS CERTAINLY KNOW THEIR STUFF."

—*New York Daily News*

THE LANDING

"AN ABSOLUTELY CRACKING TALE OF TER-
RORISM AND INTRIGUE . . . In any context this
chilling spy yarn would be a reader's delight. But
what these two authors have done—and it is where
they reach another level of success—is tell the tale
against the backdrop of an overcrowded, over-
worked and overheated city struggling to become
the cogwheel for the Allies' arsenal of democracy . . .
SUBTLE AND GRIPPING."

—Toledo Blade

"The history and the memory [of W.W. II] are
brought to vivid life in *THE LANDING* . . . The
reader experiences the war itself as well as all the
things that went with it—rationing, long lines at the
theater, overcrowded trains and buses, uniforms
everywhere and always the fear, fear that just possibly the Allies might not defeat the Axis . . . An
excellent story."

—Associated Press

"TOTALLY BELIEVABLE. A BRILLIANT JOB
OF RESEARCH, A GOOD SOLID STORY AND
A REAL PAGE TURNER."

—San Francisco Examiner

THE LANDING

**Haynes Johnson and
Howard Simons**

POCKET BOOKS

New York   London   Toronto   Sydney   Tokyo

Dodd, Mead and Company: Excerpt from the poem "We Wear the Mask" from *The Complete Poems of Paul Laurence Dunbar*. Used by permission of the publisher, Dodd, Mead and Company.

Harper and Row, Publishers, Inc.: eleven lines from "Heritage" from *On These I Stand: An Anthology of the Best Poems of Countee Cullen*. Copyright © 1925 by Harper and Row, Publishers, Inc. Renewed 1953 by Ida M. Cullen. Reprinted by permission of Harper and Row, Publishers, Inc.

Life Picture Service: Excerpt from a *Life* editorial dated July 6, 1942. Courtesy Life Picture Service. Used by permission.

POCKET BOOKS, a division of Simon & Schuster Inc.
1230 Avenue of the Americas, New York, N.Y. 10020

Published by arrangement with Villard Books, Inc.,
a division of Random House, Inc.
Library of Congress Catalog Card Number: 85-40736

ISBN: 0-671-63037-7

First Pocket Books printing June 1988

10 9 8 7 6 5 4 3 2 1

POCKET and colophon are trademarks of Simon & Schuster Inc.

Printed in the U.S.A.

For Tod and Marcia

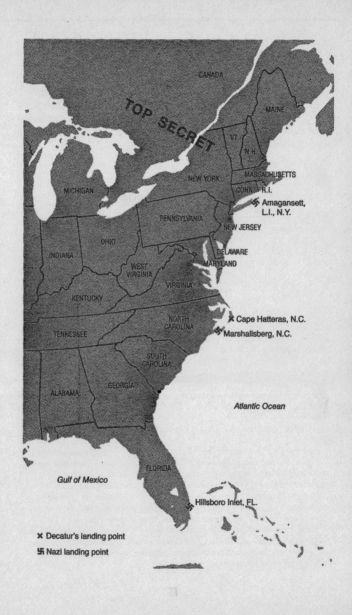

TOP SECRET

CANADA

MAINE

VT.

N.H.

MICHIGAN

NEW YORK

MASSACHUSETTS

CONN. R.I.

⊞ Amagansett,
L.I., N.Y.

PENNSYLVANIA

NEW JERSEY

INDIANA

OHIO

DELAWARE

MARYLAND

WEST
VIRGINIA

VIRGINIA

KENTUCKY

NORTH
CAROLINA

✗ Cape Hatteras, N.C.

⊞ Marshallsberg, N.C.

TENNESSEE

SOUTH
CAROLINA

ALABAMA

GEORGIA

Atlantic Ocean

FLORIDA

Gulf of Mexico

⊞ Hillsboro Inlet, FL.

✗ Decatur's landing point

⊞ Nazi landing point

FOREWORD

Among the official documents relating to German saboteurs and Pearl Harbor stored in Box 3, File No. 383.4 at the National Records Center of the National Archives of the United States, just across the District of Columbia line in Suitland, Maryland, are a map of the Eastern coastline of the United States marked SECRET showing three landing sites and the following memorandum, declassified from "Secret" to "Confidential" and now open to the public:

JOHN EDGAR HOOVER
DIRECTOR

Federal Bureau of Investigation
United States Department of Justice
Washington, D.C.

June 22, 1942

SECRET

MEMORANDUM

The Federal Bureau of Investigation has definitely established that two groups of trained saboteurs have been landed on the shores of the United States from German submarines since June 13, 1942. One group landed on Long Island at Amagansett and the second group in Florida near Jacksonville. Each group brought with it supplies of high explosives, detonators, and timing devices, all of which have been specially designed at a special sabotage school in Germany.

Each of these groups upon arriving in the United States was well supplied with funds and available information establishes that one group had in its possession some $83,000.00, while the second group had approximately $50,000.00 in its possession.

Information has been developed indicating that an additional group will be sent from Germany to the United States approximately every six weeks and that these groups will initiate a wave of terror within the United States by the commission of acts of sabotage against key industries, factories, electric power systems, and waterworks.

Data have been developed indicating that on approximately June 13th a third submarine landed Naval officers somewhere in the vicinity of Cape Hatteras. These officers were equipped with shortwave equipment.

On Saturday morning, August 8, 1942, after a trial from which the public was barred and upon the personal orders of President Franklin Delano Roosevelt, six Nazi saboteurs captured from the two German submarines that landed on Long Island and Florida were executed in Washington, D.C., and buried there in unmarked graves.

Thousands of pages of stenographic transcripts of the trial of the saboteurs, which began on Wednesday morning, July 8, 1942 and was held behind guarded doors and drawn curtains in Room 5235 of the Department of Justice, are now declassified and can be found in the National Archives, Record Group No. 319, Records of the Army Staff. They also make reference to the existence of a highly secret training camp in Germany and contain photographs of explosive devices, tin containers, and German charts "showing areas comprising Eastern Sea Frontier [of the U.S. Navy's officially designated wartime Atlantic coastline] June 12 to 18, and paper describing area by metes and bounds."

Included in the National Archives file on German saboteurs is another secret document, now declassified: a lengthy message from James J. Maloney, Supervising Agent of the United States Secret Service's New York office, dated June 24, 1942, to Frank J. Wilson, Chief, U.S. Secret Service in Washington. It informs Washington Secret Service headquarters of the discovery, "from a confidential source," that a German submarine landed on Long Island sometime in the early-morning hours of June 13; that a great deal of material was captured; and that based on further confidential information furnished the New York Secret Service office "it is our understanding at this time that all the evidence in the case, as heretofore mentioned, has been turned over to the Federal Bureau of Investigation . . . and is now in the laboratory of the Federal Bureau of Investigation in Washington. . . ."

In the newspaper collections of the Library of Congress, copies of the daily Washington papers—the *Evening Star*, the *Times-Herald*, the *Post*, and the *Daily News*—contain brief accounts of the multiple random assassinations of blacks that took place in the streets of Washington early in the summer of 1942, including the report of the arrest of a white man that supposedly solved those murder cases.

Volume Four, *The Hinge of Fate*, of Winston S. Churchill's memoirs of World War II, describes his second visit to Washington beginning on June 20, 1942, and recounts the deliberations about approving the "Tube Alloys" project during his long sessions with President Roosevelt while he was a guest in the White House at that time. Churchill also relates, in cavalier fashion, the attempt to assassinate him when a man "was caught fingering a pistol" just before the Prime Minister boarded the seaplane that carried him back to England on Thursday, June 25.

In his diary, William D. Hassett, the President's private secretary, records Roosevelt's reaction to Attorney General Francis D. Biddle's evening phone call that June, informing him of the arrest of the Nazi saboteurs and of the President's reply to his Secret Service chief's anger "because [FBI Director J. Edgar] Hoover's boys hogged all the credit" and refused to cooperate with other intelligence agencies.

Hassett's diary for July 2, 1942, later published in his *Off the Record with FDR: 1942–1945*, describes President Roosevelt's remarks about Americans being "always too soft in dealing with spies and traitors" and of the "efficacious example" of hanging as he signed the orders appointing the military commission "to try these dastards." In his memoirs of the Roosevelt years, *Working with Roosevelt*, Samuel Rosenman reprints his wife Dorothy's account of the President's trip from the White House to his mountain retreat of "Shangri-la" in Maryland on the day the German saboteurs were executed in Washington. She also recounts the uncharacteristically bloodthirsty stories which the President told with gusto over cocktails later that afternoon.

To this date, no records have been found and nothing else appears to be known about the two naval officers who were reported to have landed in North Carolina from a third German submarine on or about June 13, 1942.

Haynes Johnson
Howard Simons

December, 1985
Washington, D.C.

part

1

THE
FARM

1

He glided alongside the lake, carefully slipped by the small fishpond, darted in a half-crouch between the pines, skirted the open park and garden faintly illuminated in the moonlight and saw dimly the high fence topped by barbed wire that encircled the grounds. There he was. He held his breath, dropped silently to the sandy soil, and froze. Easy, easy. No false moves. He waited, his muscles tense, his heart pounding, as the guard passed slowly by. The veins on his neck throbbed, and a wave of dizziness swept over him. His heart was beating so fast, he was certain it could be heard in the still night. Damn, I'm losing control. He inched up, eased into his crouch, and moved forward. One step . . . two . . . three. Now, now, remember, *remember*. Quickly, hand over mouth. Ram it home. Hard now. In, up. Rip! There, it's done. Quick, catch the rifle before it falls. The roaring sound inside his head grew louder. His breath rattled in his throat and his chest hurt as though iron bands had been clamped around it. God, I can't breathe. He felt faint. Suddenly, he was far away. It was clammy, cold, and wet. The drumming in his ears intensified. Something was trying to reach him. Was it a voice or a signal?

"Lieutenant . . ."

He didn't want to be disturbed. The numbness felt good. Never had he felt so drained.

"Lieutenant . . ."

He shuddered to consciousness. A knife was in his hand, a sack of a body at his feet. He looked down. On the coat, around the heart, a large dark stain was spreading. Next to it he saw a small red triangle. The mark of the dead man's prison caste. Political.

3

"Lieutenant . . ."

He shivered. Damn, it was cold. Why was he so wet? Now he remembered.

"Lieutenant . . ."

So, he had done it. His first one. He couldn't bring himself to say murder. Some throw up afterward, his instructor had said. Others faint. Still other soil their pants, or wet them, as he had done. A very few have orgasms, or so they claim. "Most get to enjoy it after their first," he remembered his instructor saying.

"Lieutenant . . ."

"Yes," he answered.

"You did very well."

2

From Berlin, their bus wound south and west for thirty-five miles through the heart of the ancient Kingdom of Prussia. It crossed the sandy plain that once caused the province to be called the "sandbox of the Holy Roman Empire," rolled past fertile fields watered by the Elbe and Oder, and moved through stretches of deep fir forests set among hundreds of lakes dotting the countryside. Finally, they reached their destination, the last stop, inside the walled city of Brandenburg, nestled along the Havel.

They all made that trip alone, wearing ordinary workmen's clothes, caps tugged slightly down over their foreheads, and all arrived at dusk when shadows from the Gothic cathedrals, with their gargoyles and knights, saints and monks, fell over the marketplace. They carried nothing with them. Their orders were direct. They were to talk to no one, remain as inconspicuous as possible. Once inside Brandenburg, get off the bus and stroll toward the Neustadt. When they reached the Rolandssaule, that colossal old Germanic figure hewn

4

from a single block of granite and towering eighteen feet above the square, they were to take the first cobblestone street to the right and walk casually, beyond the walls, out of town.

It took them only half an hour to move down that dark lonely road to the lake, but it always seemed longer. They passed isolated old estates, many dating back centuries to the warrior princes of Prussia. Behind the massive stone walls they saw outlines of chimneys and turrets dimly silhouetted against the tall pines. Then the road turned and they were in open country along the lake leading to the main gate of the farmhouse.

Wilhelm Canaris, the short, stolid, impassive genius of German intelligence, characteristically had searched the Brandenburg countryside painstakingly before settling on the farm for his most secret of all training bases. It pleased him that he had found the perfect place, and one that proved his many enemies wrong.

They had all been against him, from the High Command of the General Staff down, especially those fools Himmler and Heydrich, whose Gestapo so hated and distrusted him. Unlike them, he was not some emotional fanatic; he did not believe in training suicide squads or murder teams merely for the sake of murder. He didn't even despise the Jews, though he had no compunction about using them, or any group, to achieve his purposes. At the farm, Jews were indispensable—and disposable.

It pleased him, too, that he had been able to establish such iron control over the farm operation that even Himmler could not penetrate his organization, or find out what happened there. "Don't worry, Heinrich," Canaris had said coldly to the SS chief when questioned about why he needed so many prisoners, or what they were for. "Just keep supplying them. I will take care of them. They will find themselves right at home."

That was one of Canaris's few attempts at humor, although, typically, nothing in his austere manner let Himmler know it: until Canaris took over the farm and sealed it off so securely to outside scrutiny that few among the Führer's top echelon even knew of its existence, the farm had been the country estate of a wealthy Jew who manufactured shoes. To any passerby, it still retained the look of a prosperous absentee owner's weekend place of leisure.

The narrow dirt country road that wound its way through the forests and fields banked sharply once it reached the main entrance of the farm, and then headed directly away. A stone wall, of the kind common to medieval monasteries in that part of Northern Europe, encircled the grounds. Rising above it, shielded by a stand of firs and massive old hickories running alongside the smoothly mortised stone of the inner wall, stood a cluster of smaller outbuildings with sharply high-pitched roofs covered by dark red tiles. Small chimneys broke the steep slope of the roofs. With the exception of small dark block-like boxes cut into the ends of the buildings, each appeared to be without windows. Barely visible from the road were the thick gray sandstone walls that encased each building.

They appeared unoccupied. In fact, they were filled with security guards, electronic and infrared sensing devices, and ultrasophisticated radio equipment. Immense care had been taken to give the place the look of casual attendance. In daylight, no guards patrolled the outer wall. Each morning plainly dressed workmen moved out from the outbuildings to a small, well-stocked pond off the main road that ran back from the gate into the estate. They cast their lines without an obvious care for the problems of the faraway war. Others, similarly dressed, moved about on what seemed routine chores. They were anything but inattentive and casual. Their training and their record of performance ranked them among the world's best, and deadliest, security forces.

A glance through the main gate showed a road winding through the grounds and by the fishpond, toward a dark, lonely, extensive body of water, inky-black in color, set against what appeared to be a vast expanse of deep, unbroken, dense forest. This, too, was an illusion, for within that forest, near water's edge and hidden from daylight view by an ingenious series of camouflage nets, were squat gray buildings, cleared grounds, a compound surrounded by a high barbed-wire fence, and even an aerodrome.

Beyond the main gate, among the many outbuildings, rose the solid stone structure of the principal farmhouse itself. To all appearances, it was a substantial two-story mansion of many large rooms, and nothing more. It was, in fact, the heart of Canaris's Abwehr.

Canaris was a professional who handled his job as coolly and as well as anyone alive. Better, in fact, for no other intelligence chief in the twentieth century had so formidable a task or performed so brilliantly against such a complex of odds and opponents. Not only was he charged with outwitting the British, French, Polish, Russian, and American intelligence services, all the while controlling a worldwide network of stations and agents, he had to fight constantly against highly placed enemies at home. He knew their jealousies and assaults on his service. He also knew that success was his only shield. Canaris and his men could not fail.

His own authority had grown in direct proportion to his many successes. And he succeeded because he left nothing to chance. That was why Ausbildungslager Quenzgut, at Quinzsee in Brandenburg, was so special an operation. There was no other place like it in the world, Canaris knew. It was the headquarters for his Section II.

The organizational charts described Section II merely as being assigned "sabotage and special duties." Its "special duties" included training for missions that could determine the fate of the war and the future of the thousand-year Third Reich. So far, Section II had accomplished every mission, but the greatest of all was now before it.

Normally, several Abwehr Section II units underwent day and night training simultaneously at Quenzgut farm. But now, in the early spring of 1942, the grounds had been cleared. Only a handful of instructors occupied the farm.

"Admiral," Captain Erich von Hagen of the old Colonial East Africa Corps reported to Canaris, "they are ready, and they are the best."

"Best is not good enough, Captain," Canaris replied. "They must be better than that. This one comes personally from Hitler. I can only tell you that the outcome of the war depends upon how well we train them here now."

3

The prisoners picked up the body sprawled on the ground, carried it over to the shallow grave they had dug earlier, and tossed it in. It hit the bottom with a hollow muffled sound. Strange, the lieutenant thought, I feel nothing, absolutely nothing. He stood silently, drawing on a cigarette. Then, on impulse, he moved to the edge of the hole and looked down.

The body lay on its back, the right leg twisted at a sharp angle, the left flexed slightly, the arms askew. The face was clearly visible directly below. A blond. Very young, very pale. The eyes were closed, the mouth open. The lieutenant stared down intently as the prisoners began throwing earth on the body. He noticed they had small purple triangles on their gray prison coats. So, Christian Fundamentalists, not Jews, gypsies, Communists, or criminals. The Fundamentalists would live longer than the others.

They worked quickly and silently. The only sounds breaking the stillness of the night came from the scraping of their shovels and the soft plops as the earth hit the body. He watched as the prison uniform was covered; then just part of the face was visible. Remarkable, absolutely remarkable, he thought. I'm not even curious about him. How could I have been so emotional a moment ago and now feel nothing?

He swung sharply about, and strode away. His instructor fell in beside him.

"Your next game is tomorrow night, Lieutenant."

"Yes, thank you. Good night."

"Good night, Lieutenant."

He continued on to the farmhouse. A guard with a German shepherd passed and saluted. He returned the salute.

8

Another guard, with his automatic rifle also slung upside down, snapped to attention as he walked up the steps to the massive door fashioned of oak. Again he returned the salute. "Good evening, sir," the clerk said as he entered. "Another delivery, sir." He handed over a bundle of newspapers and magazines. There were five papers, the *Times* and the *Herald-Tribune* of New York, the *Evening Star*, *Times-Herald*, and *Post* of Washington, and four magazines, *Colliers*, *Life*, *The Saturday Evening Post*, and *Time*. Each was stamped, "Property of the Oberkommando der Wehrmacht, to Return." The lieutenant glanced at them and, as always, was impressed. They were only a week old. God, they're good, he thought. I wonder how they do it. He reached out to take his key and suddenly stiffened. Damn, he'll see my pants, he thought in disgust. He turned aside abruptly from the clerk and moved toward the stairway leading to the second floor. As usual, he didn't notice the clerk press a small button under the front-desk counter as he walked upstairs.

He reached his door, took a deep breath, put the key in the lock, turned it, and went inside. Thank God, it was empty. *He* wasn't back yet. He fumbled with his belt, unbuttoned his fly, and started to pull down his heavy wool pants. In his haste, one pants leg caught on his combat boot heel and he almost fell in the middle of the room. Damn these uniforms! Why did they give us these? They had been Polish, and were now dyed blue to distinguish them as special trainees. Christ, can't I do anything right tonight? He took another breath, straightened up, moved to his bunk, and sat down. Methodically, he unlaced his boots, rapidly drew off his pants and undershorts, and quickly stuffed them at the bottom of his green laundry bag slung at the end of his bunk. He sighed slightly, sat back heavily on his bunk, and ran his hand over his forehead. For the first time that night he began to relax. There, no one will know. He held out his hands, looked at them, and flinched. The heel of his palm was covered with blood. It still felt damp. He got up and went to the toilet and briskly washed his hands. Then he stared intently for a long moment into the mirror.

I wonder if anyone could tell, he thought. He pulled the

skin slightly around his eyes and turned his head from side to side, studying the reflection before him. Nothing. He looked the same: the skin smooth and unlined, the features regular and earnest, the hair wavy and brown, the eyes as dark and coolly appraising as ever. Why should I think I'd look different? He looked at himself again, shrugged, and turned away.

The Abwehr psychiatrist stifled a chuckle. He and his orderly had both been smiling as they watched the lieutenant struggle to free himself of his wet pants. They had resumed their post before the one-way mirror after the buzzer alerted them that someone was returning. The orderly had his earphones on, ready to take down in shorthand everything he overheard. Seated next to him at the short table placed directly before the mirror was the psychiatrist. He picked up his pen and began making notes on a long yellow pad.

After he finished a cigarette while lying on his bunk, the lieutenant turned off his light and tried to sleep.

It was almost two o'clock when he heard the sound of the door opening. Gunther. The lieutenant's mouth was dry and he felt as though he had been running, running until he was about to drop from exhaustion. It was not a new sensation. He had been experiencing it ever since childhood when he had that high fever, and it was always the same: the same long, long plain covered by deep, thick clouds speckled throughout with spots of black and he had to keep running and running and running to get out of the banks of clouds, but he never could. It always troubled and angered him: it was a sign of weakness and fear. He was too old for that kind of thing, and he was ashamed to admit to anyone that it kept coming back whenever he got too tired or too emotional.

He shook his head sharply and bolted upright in his bunk.

Now he was fully awake. He snapped on his light, reached for a cigarette, lighted it, and let the smoke out slowly through his nostrils.

"Sorry, Willi," Gunther said.

"No matter," Willi replied.

"How did it go tonight?" Gunther asked.

"Well. I killed a man tonight. One of the prisoners working around here."

"First time?"

"What?"

"Was that the first time you ever killed anybody?"

"In person, yes," Willi said, drawing deeply again on his cigarette and looking directly at Gunther. "I've killed in combat but it was always at a distance and never this way."

"But before that, Willi. How about rabbits or squirrels?"

"No, nothing, I grew up in the city."

"Pity," said Gunther.

"How about you?" Willi asked.

Gunther got into his bunk and turned the light back off. From the darkness, Willi heard him say, in a dispassionate yet strangely proud voice, "I have killed animals and humans."

4

He lay on his bunk playing Mozart in his head. He used to play Mahler in his head, but Mahler's work was forbidden. Mahler was a Jew. No one could hear what he was playing in his head, but he still reacted as if they would know. A few months ago some Mahler passages intruded. He tried to get rid of them, but the more he tried the more they repeated. He was finally able to suppress them but he lived in fear they would return and he would be discovered. It was another weakness. Even if no one else knew about it, he was disgusted with himself. He had to be stronger.

It had been ten weeks since Willi Gradison, as he was known there, came to Quentz. For the last week he had killed a man each night, three times with a knife, twice with a garrote, once with a club, and, finally, with his bare hands. He did not get to like it, as his instructor said he might, but he became coldly proficient. Slashing the jugular and stabbing in the throat were the worst. God Almighty, there was a lot of blood. He didn't think he'd ever get used to the way the blood spurted and how it smelled sweet and musky and felt thick and hot. God, it was so different from what you'd think. But killing would be no problem later, he was now certain. The problem was Gunther.

Gunther Haupt. Willi didn't know his real name, of course, but he knew enough to be deeply troubled by him. Except for the last week when they went out alone on their nightly "games," they had been inseparable. Gunther is good, Willi thought. He's even better than I am at some of the things we've learned. That wasn't what bothered him. The problem wasn't how well Gunther performed, but the way he was. Gunther really enjoyed the killing. More than enjoyed—he lived for it.

From the beginning, there had been something unnerving about Gunther. He spoke little, but every now and then he would interrupt his words with a peculiar high-pitched laugh. When he laughed, his ruddy face flushed to a bright red. He had a habit, too, of thrusting out his jaw and drawing his lips back over his teeth whenever he got excited. It was unsettling.

Gunther was extremely strong. At night, in their rooms, he amused himself by bending iron bars with his bare hands. The hands were huge and covered with freckles. He was about ten years older than Willi, a heavyset man of 210 pounds, standing just under 6 feet, with powerful shoulders, pale blue eyes, thin lips, and a long, narrow, slightly hooked nose. He combed his dark blond hair straight back. If you looked closely, you could see a faint scar, about an inch and a half long, curling from behind his left ear to the line of his jaw. He spoke English well, though not as well as Willi, with just a trace of a Midwestern accent. Willi thought he had been in Chicago and Milwaukee, but wasn't sure. He didn't really know much about Gunther, any more than Gunther knew about him. They were not supposed to; V men were trained to be silent and not ask questions. They didn't use their real names, and even at the farm they continued to sign for equipment by placing a V, for *Vertrauensmann*, or confidence man, before their false first and last names. But by now Willi knew enough about Gunther to form a picture, and it bothered him.

Unlike Willi, who had moved with the Wehrmacht through the lowlands of Belgium and Holland and on into France, Gunther had been in Norway and on the Russian front. He liked to talk about it, especially about Kiev, where they drove all the Jews together and executed 35,000 of them. The first time they really talked at night, Gunther told two stories about Kiev that Willi couldn't drive from his mind.

"We marched the Jews in groups of two and three hundred at a time," Gunther said, "and made them dig these big holes. Then we marched them to another big hole that the last group had dug. The SS *Einsatztruppen* officers were shooting them in the back of the head and in the neck and then kicking them down into the hole as fast as they could pull the trigger. Their trigger fingers got so tired they had to be rotated every few minutes."

Gunther laughed piercingly. Willi felt the skin on his neck tingle.

"I remember a dirty old Jewess sat on the road near the body of a young Jew woman who happened to be her daughter, and she refused to leave that dead body. She just sat there, rocking back and forth, holding the young Jew in her arms. The only way they could get that old woman away was by shooting her right there in the road."

He laughed again, and again his face flushed.

"I tell you something else, Willi. We captured this Russian artillery officer, and he wouldn't tell us where his battery was located. He was a big, big son of a bitch, and he wouldn't even talk when we held his hand over burning candles. He screamed and screamed but he still wouldn't talk. You could smell the flesh burning and everything. When he finally told us a place we knew was wrong, we ripped off that bastard's clothes. Then we threw him naked into the snow and poured water on him."

Gunther broke into his sharp laugh again, and his teeth flashed.

"In less than a minute," Gunther went on, his face flushing again, "the swine was frozen in a lump of ice."

From a casual remark he let slip, Willi knew that Gunther

had met Hitler years ago, but he quickly changed the subject as soon as it came up. Gunther also mentioned Röhm's name once, and as swiftly dropped it. Willi suspected Gunther had been an old SA man. If so, he must have been one of the only survivors of the massacre. Röhm, that stocky bull-necked Nazi leader who had proudly carried the awful scars of 1914 when half his nose had been shot away, and most of his Sturmabteilung (SA) brown-shirted Storm Troopers were slaughtered by Himmler's Schutzstaffel (SS) men after they caught Röhm in bed with his blond male lover. Once, when Gunther was packing a duffel bag, Willi had seen him putting back a dagger. It had a strange design and appeared to have a name engraved on it, with some words below. Willi remembered hearing that Röhm had had special daggers made for his top aides, and wondered if that was one of them.

To hell with it, he thought. I don't know him, and he doesn't know me. What does it matter? All that matters is that we are very good together, and we had better be. He didn't want to think about the mission. It was not helpful. But like Mahler's music, it kept intruding. Damn, I shouldn't have thought about it. He forced himself to start playing Mozart in his head again. He had just finished the first movement of the D minor of the string quartets when there was a knock on the door.

He sat up and straightened his officer's blouse. "Yes."

"Orderly Clerk Steiner, sir. Mail, Lieutenant." Then a pause, and loudly, with just the trace of a sneer: "Another letter from home."

The little bastard, Willi thought. Every day he tries to taunt me like this. "Come in, Steiner."

Willi had a way of staring down people and making them feel uncomfortable when he wanted, and he wanted to now. He drew himself up to his full height, stood silently for a moment, and looked coldly and deeply into the orderly's eyes until he saw him quickly glance away. Then he reached out for his letter. "Thank you, Steiner," he said slowly. "You may go."

"Yes, Lieutenant."

When the door closed, Willi opened the letter and read:

May 19,1942

Dearest Liebchen:

I trust this letter finds you well. We are. Your cousin Eric is home on leave from France. Oh, how I wish you could come home now, too. It has been so long. Hans Greider is home, too. He lost an arm at the front. He, too, asked for you, and I told him you were still somewhere in France. I received a letter from Anna and she wonders why you don't write her. I wish you would write to your sister, also. We never hear from you. Please write, even a line. It would mean so much. We are short on potatoes now, but other than that we are well. Your father thinks the war will be over in less than a year. Not everyone agrees but, as you know, he is never wrong about these things. Do write us, and take care of yourself. Your father sends his love, and you know you have all of mine.

Be careful, Liebchen
Mother

Willi crumpled the letter, put it in the ashtray, struck a match, and set it afire as he did with all his mother's letters. Willi's father had died in France in 1917.

5

Gunther was crossing the explosives field, where they practiced on the wooden posts, iron railroad tracks, and steel girders set out across the grounds. One hundred parts saltpeter, ninety parts sulphur. Either ignition formula, he found himself reciting mentally. Dr. Koenig had taught well. He recited another: Two hundred parts saltpeter, one hundred parts sawdust. Dampen dust, mix with peter. Dry.

Either ignition formula. And another: One hundred parts plaster of Paris, one hundred parts aluminum powder.

No problem, he had them all. But for what?

He walked beyond the gymnasium and laboratory, past the pistol and rifle ranges, the jump tower and small aerodrome, and toward the lake by the woods, concentrating intently on what he had learned. Whatever else, we've got to have rubber boats. Those damned kayaks. We will surely drown in them.

They went out in them night after night in pitch-black darkness, lighted only by the blizzard of stars always above in the northern skies. And each time they capsized in the freezing lake.

It was strange, this place. All those empty buildings, no planes at the aerodrome, no trucks in the motor pool, no one but the doctor at the laboratory, no lights, no radios in the low stone structures that normally serve as barracks for the regular training groups, no sound even. They shut down everything just for them. Only the constant sighing of the wind stirring the firs in the deep forest encircling the lake broke the stillness. Even the prisoners' compound, set far back in the woods behind a high barbed-wire fence, was unnaturally silent. You wouldn't know anyone was there, and yet they had to keep bringing new prisoners in. He wondered how they kept them so quiet. It reminded him of those nights in the seminary when they all meditated in silence and it was a sin to utter a word. As always, he angrily pushed aside that memory. It's even getting to me, this place.

He thought of Willi. Capable enough, and he seems reliable. Smart, of course, and his English is superb. He learns easily. I gather he did well in combat, and he's not as squeamish as I thought. Nothing I say bothers him. But weak, somehow he's weak. Most of them are. Young fools, filled with nonsense about glory. What do they know about glory? Like those young zealots after the purge who came to their meetings, snapped to attention, shouted "Long Live Röhm," and shot themselves. For what? Willi reminds me of them. At least he doesn't talk, and he's not emotional. He doesn't show any feeling at all. *That's* what bothers me. He's not real. There's something about him that isn't right. I'm not sure I trust him.

Gunther was approaching the woods when he heard a familiar birdcall. His face flushed in anger. They always broke his concentration. He had hated their sound ever since that first time, years ago in the summer, when he was with a girl. They had been on the ground. She let him open her blouse and fondle her breasts. He forced his hand under her dress and between her legs until he touched inside her underpants where he could feel she was slick and wet, then the sharp scolding sound of that bird ringing in his ears ruined everything. He threw her aside roughly and stalked off, furious. He hated birds. He didn't really like women, either. He used them as diversion when he wanted. Nearly always afterward, though, they made him feel unclean and impure. He thought again of the seminary and those days when he had studied for the priesthood: so innocent then, so serious, so ecstatic at times, so transported with rapture by the sounds of their evening chants, so close to being one with God. Then always those dreams about women. They tormented him, made him feel unworthy, and finally forced him to succumb and fail. He shook himself slightly. Well, he had found God, and God was German, and he wasn't in the seminary. He was in the brotherhood with Hitler and the rest.

Gunther smiled grimly. Too much, this place. He strode purposefully on.

"Good morning, Lieutenant, you're late. Shall we begin?"

His instructor stepped from the edge of the woods and onto the field. "Only the hands today, Lieutenant." He held up his bare hands and smiled slightly.

Although he spoke only in English, as did all the others, Gunther suspected he was Ukrainian. Of all his instructors, this was the only one Gunther personally wanted to hurt, but never could. It was a matter of pride. Gunther was much bigger and immeasurably stronger, yet he always wound up beaten. He could never get his hands fully on him.

"Ready," Gunther said.

They circled each other. Gunther lunged, and was chopped to the ground by a sharp blow on the side of the neck. He got up, feinted to the right, and threw the full weight of his body toward the instructor's legs in a sudden feet-first dive. The instructor spun around, and slammed the toe of his combat boot on the side of Gunther's face before he hit the ground. He moved lightly to the side, quickly delivered a paralyzing kick to Gunther's kidney, kneeled, planted a knee harshly on the small of the back, drew Gunther's right arm sharply up behind him until it felt as though it would snap, and, with the left hand, reached under Gunther's chin and jerked it sharply up.

Gunther groaned. "Enough," he said. He staggered to his feet, his head down, his right arm dangling. "Look what you've done."

As the instructor moved forward, Gunther suddenly rose up and kicked him as hard as he could in the groin. He could feel a crunch as his foot struck the testicles. The instructor doubled over in pain. Gunther moved again. With both hands, he grabbed the instructor's head and smashed it into his uplifted right knee, cracking the nose and drawing a jet of blood. Gunther dropped beside the man crumpled on the ground. "If you report anything more than the fact that I beat you this morning," he hissed into the instructor's ear, "I will kill you."

He got up, brushed himself off, and began walking back to the farmhouse. When he heard the birdcall this time, he smiled.

6

A pool of light from the small lamp fell on the walnut desk in the office behind the classroom. Laid out across the desk, in neat horizontal rows, were stacks of paper, each weighted down with a smooth round piece of white marble.

Dr. Werner Ungerheur, a slight sallow man with rimless glasses, thin graying hair, and a wispy mustache, bent wearily over the papers again, and then glanced down at the long yellow pad before him. On his pad he had carefully printed, in small block letters, the general heading of each round of reports. Already, he had laboriously worked through thirteen of them: GENERAL CHEMISTRY. LIGHT-BURNING MIXTURES. HARD-BURNING MIXTURES. IGNITION FORMULAS. EXPLOSIVES. PRIMERS. FUSES. TIME AND ELECTRICAL DEVICES. SECRET WRITING. PLANT, CANAL, LOCKS, RAILROADS. FIREARMS. COMBAT. "Games." As he finished each category, he added his own comments in his precise hand on the yellow pad. Then he placed the latest set of reports beside the others on the desk, anchoring them with another piece of marble.

He took off his glasses, wiped them with his handkerchief, rubbed his eyes, and picked up a large manila folder. It was marked: PERSONAL BACKGROUND/ANALYSIS. Again, he began to read. I must have gone through this a hundred times, he thought. Why do I have any doubts at all?

For nearly three years Dr. Ungerheur had passed on all the senior agents dispatched by the Abwehr around the world. As the Abwehr's chief psychiatrist, he personally observed and assessed them before signifying their readiness for missions to Cairo and Port Suez, to Syria and Turkey, to the Far East and England. He certified the Indian, Arab, and Ukrainian teams trained for "special operations," the euphemisms for sabotage strikes designed to sow mass terror among civilian populations and for removal of civilian leaders. He helped select the very first Abwehr commandos, the Kampf Trupps, that slipped across the Polish border disguised as coal miners and workers in the early hours just before the Wehrmacht struck three years ago in September; and he oversaw the training of the first of the Brandenburg units, the Lehr und Bau Kompaignie zbV 800 (Special Duty and Construction Company No. 800). But of all the groups he had observed, the one before him now was the most difficult to judge.

It wasn't lack of competence. By any normal measure, they were superb, the best by far to be trained at Quenzgut. But the Admiral had made clear their mission would be anything but ordinary. It bore the highest state priority, and, more than any of the others, he had been made to feel a sense of extraordinary urgency about this one. He moved around the desk and began pacing slowly back and forth, his head bowed deep in thought.

There *were* problems. But every time he examined them, he was left with nothing specific, just a gnawing sense that something was wrong. Burning the letters? No. The way they talked to each other? No. They obviously didn't like each other, but that was natural. These kinds of men had to be on guard about everyone and everything. To be successful they had to be coldly self-sufficient; if necessary, they had to be capable of going it alone. How they had performed? No. So what was he troubled about? Maybe they were almost too perfect, too machinelike, too cold, too lacking in any real human emotions. But wasn't that good? He would be held at least partly responsible, Ungerheur knew, if they failed. But what if they succeeded? And where would they find two better ones?

He walked back behind his desk, took off his glasses, wiped them again, sighed slightly, picked up his pen and began to write: "I find that V. Willi Gradison and V. Gunther Haupt are mentally stable, psychologically fit, and ideally prepared, physically and emotionally, for any . . ."

7

He stood in the shadows, among the pines by the lake, watching as the prisoners came forward on their burial detail. Good, he thought, they have yellow triangles on their prison uniforms. Jews. They will not talk. The prisoners bent over the body lying beside the shallow pit they had dug, and rolled it over.

"Great God!" one of them gasped as he saw the face.

"What the hell do we do?" the other whispered hoarsely.

"How the hell do I know. But keep your damn voice down."

He motioned over his shoulder to where the lieutenant was standing.

"Well, we have to do something." His companion sounded terrified.

"No, we don't. It'll mean trouble, believe me. If they see it's one of them instead of the prisoners we always bury, *oy*! God help us!" He shivered, and reached down to grab the body.

"Jesus, they'll blame us," the younger prisoner whispered, desperately. "What are we going to do? What the hell are we going to do?"

"Nothing," the older prisoner said. "We are going to do nothing."

"Nothing? How can we do nothing?"

"I tell you," the older one said urgently, "something will get us in trouble. Nothing gets us nothing. Shut up and bury the damned Nazi. Now! Quick! Let's get it over with!"

They grabbed the dead man's feet, dragged him to the shallow pit, and rolled him in. The lieutenant, still watching silently, turned quickly and disappeared back into the shadows. The prisoners picked up their shovels and started to cover the body. Though each of them recognized the dead man instantly, neither noticed the thin line around his neck where blood had oozed and dried into a necklace of small red beads.

Two days later Orderly Corporal and Mail Clerk Helmut Steiner was listed as absent without leave.

8

It was after eleven o'clock when Willi entered the front door of the narrow, darkened *Gasthof* at 6 Rankee Strasse, just off Kurfürstendamm, and began to climb the stairs to the third floor. As well as he knew Berlin, he still stumbled around in the blackout and was late. Gunther was waiting inside Room 333. They nodded warily at each other. Another man, dressed in a gray gabardine suit, white shirt, and dark blue tie, was seated in one of the straight-backed chairs across from Gunther.

"One moment," the gray-suited man said, as he stood up, walked across the small unfurnished room, knocked on a door, and entered. "Come," he motioned a moment later, upon returning.

They followed him into a small, dark, windowless room. It was the nerve center of the Schriftleitung der Kaukasus, or the blind house, Berlin headquarters of the Abwehr, though it didn't look it. Against a paneled wall, facing the door they entered, was a desk, its top bare as the walls around it. Behind it sat a short stocky man with a piercing direct gaze. Willi stirred uncomfortably; he found himself glancing momentarily from the man's startlingly cold blue eyes to his own reflection cast by a large wall mirror behind the desk. With his dark business suit, thick dark eyebrows, and snow-white hair, the man seemed to blend naturally into the darkness of the room. Both Willi and Gunther stiffened in recognition.

Canaris.

They had never met the man, few V agents did, but they knew the legend: a tiny, soft-seeming, nondescript man with prematurely gray hair ("Old Whitehead," they called him)

22

and disturbing blue eyes, scarcely taller than Napoleon; a hypochondriac who wore the thickest of overcoats even in summer and heavy sweaters on tennis courts in broiling sunshine; an insomniac who existed on scant amounts of sleep and who urged his staff also to take the same quantities of Phanodorm and Bromural and other pills as he did to keep themselves always mentally alert; a silent man who moved so softly it was said you never heard him and who always had his two dachshunds by his side. Only seven years before, in 1935, this same man had taken the extremely small group divided into Sub-Sections East and Sub-Sections West and expanded them into the all-encompassing intelligence service with its three main sections and their multiplicity of sub-sections serving all German military services, Army, Navy and Air; gathering and assessing all economic, commercial, and technical information; overseeing all intelligence photography; running the wireless networks for agents around the world; supervising the secret inks, personal documents, and passport departments; establishing elaborate military security and counterespionage operations; placing agents in foreign intelligence services and training them with daring ingenuity to transmit false and misleading information to the heads of their rival enemy secret service branches.

So, Canaris himself. And this must be his "Fox's Lair" that they had heard whispered about. Whatever they were involved in, Willi realized, had to be even bigger than they had suspected.

The Admiral measured them carefully, looking at them up and down, and then fixed on their faces.

"Good evening, gentlemen," he said gravely in a low, soft, melodious voice. "Make yourselves at ease. I congratulate you. It is given to few people to do what you will do for your country."

He shifted in his chair, and paused in thought as if carefully choosing his words.

"It is said that sometimes little groups of men can do more than entire divisions. In your case two men alone will affect history more than armies."

9

Canaris fell silent, still gazing directly at them, watching for their reactions. Aside from a flicker in their eyes and a faint flush in the face of the shorter, heavyset man, he found none. He nodded silently, then turned toward the tall, thin, middle-aged man in a dark business suit standing quietly beside him. "Colonel."

The colonel, wiry, with razor-sharp features, high cheekbones, and dark hair flecked with gray, half snapped to attention. "Excellency!" He moved to the mirror, lifted it from the wall, and pressed a button. "Please," he said, motioning them through a panel that had swung open in the wall before them.

This second room was larger and brightly lighted. Phosphorescent tubes encircled the ceiling, casting a bluish light. A long conference table, covered with papers, maps, and glossy photographs, stood in the center of the room. One wall was taken up with floor-to-ceiling maps. They were nautical charts of the United States Atlantic coastline, and bore the legend: United States Eastern Defense Command. Large red circles had been imposed on three locations of the map.

On the other walls were more maps, blue photostatic copies of water lines and water systems, and blowups of glossy photographs. The pictures showed bridges, railroad tunnels, and aerial shots of what appeared to be large industrial installations. One, clearly, was of Niagara Falls. Another showed the Panama Canal.

"Be seated gentlemen," the colonel said, gesturing to two chairs set at the long table.

As they pulled back the chairs, they noticed that each

paper before them had been stamped with red capital letters. They spelled out the world GEHEIM, or secret.

"If you will pick up the folders with your names on them, we will dispense with the paperwork first. You will find three cards. The first one is your draft registration. Examine it carefully. Then sign on the back as indicated."

Willi picked up the card and read:

Registration Certificate. This is to certify that in accordance with the Selective Service Proclamation of the President of the United States,

And in ink,

William Peter Grant, 1443 East Jefferson Avenue, Detroit, Michigan, has been duly registered this 16th day of October, 1940.

Below that was the signature of the Registrar, Tenth Precinct, 15th Ward, City or County of Detroit, State of Michigan, and the words:

Be alert. Keep in touch with your local board. Notify local board immediately of change of address. Carry this card with you at all times.

Affixed to it at the top, in the right-hand corner, Willi saw a small thumbnail photograph of himself. He signed his name on the dotted line at the bottom.

On the back, under the heading "Description of Registrant," he found his height listed at 6 feet 2 inches, his weight at 185 pounds, his hair and eyes, brown, and, for "Other obvious physical characteristics that will aid in identification," the word "none." In small print below he read: "U.S. Government Printing Office, Form 16-17105."

They both examined, and signed, the next two cards, one for Social Security, the other for their driver's licenses.

The colonel picked up a pointer, moved to the large wall maps, and spoke again. "Gentlemen, two other groups will go after you. They will land here—and here."

He quickly swung the pointer high up on the map to one of the large red circles in the north and then far down to another in the south. "You will land here, as naval officers to all who see you from now on." He tapped the third circle in the center of the map.

"You do not need to know who the others are. They will know nothing about you. Not even that you exist. All you need to know is the general outline of their mission. You have before you descriptions of the targets they have been given."

He pointed to one of the large photographic blowups. "The northern team will strike here, at the main water line near the railroad station at Scarsdale, New York, just beyond the Bronx River Parkway. And here."

He tapped another blowup. "The Hell Gate Bridge. This carries the main traffic into New York City from the north. And here." Again, a sharp point on the wall. "The creolite plant in Philadelphia. And here." A tap. "The Horseshoe Curve Tunnel on the Pennsylvania Railroad."

He paused, and for the first time smiled slightly.

"We also have some other plans for them. They will plant detonating bombs inside the major railroad stations, and they will also plant them in all large department stores owned by Jews." Again, he paused.

"Something else you should know. As you are aware, the best elements want the Jews out of power in America. And they do not want to see the white race desecrated. They want to be rid of the filthy Jews and all their tribe and the filthy Negroes—and we are ready to help them. The colored people have rioted before, and we will help them do so again. Killing a few of them should provide the spark, especially if they think it's the white people who are doing it."

He smiled. "You remember the Führer has taught we must be the hammer, not the anvil. The hammer is ready to strike. The Americans are not united. They are divided. All it takes is something to turn them against each other. We will provide the match. We will strike the Jews and the Negroes and when those sparks ignite there will be a civil war unlike anything the Americans have known before. Then we will proceed with the Germanization of the United States and complete the Führer's dream of a real Anglo-Saxon state of the New Germany in America. Everything we have worked for, every group we have set in place, all our friends already in America, are ready."

Willi stared at the colonel. He remembered the day his mother brought him the card to sign in Detroit, making him a member of the League of the Friends of the New Germany; he could still recite it word for word:

"The aims and purpose of the League are known to me, and I pledge myself to support them without any reservation whatsoever. I acknowledge unconditionally the leadership principle upon which the League is formed. I belong to no semitic organization (Freemasonry, et cetera). I am of Aryan stock and have neither Jewish nor colored blood in me."

They assigned him to stand in front of Jewish stores, distributing copies of Streicher's *Stürmer*, with its call to "oust the Jew from political power, take over complete control of politics, economics, and culture, and institute a real American government." He also passed out pamphlets from their adjunct, The White Man's Association, with its appeals to fight against "the race desecrators of Aryan culture."

God, it seemed a thousand years ago. What was he really like then, when all this began? Could he have been so innocent? Everything had seemed so simple. He had no questions then about what he should do; he knew what was right. Now nothing was simple. He had to force himself to stop thinking of what he had become—a killer—and how he had changed and what he would have to do next. A vague ripple of doubt swept through him. His eyebrows knitted slightly in an involuntary frown. No, I cannot show doubt or betray emotion. He willed himself to relax. There, that was better.

The sudden flashing of the colonel's pointer brought him instantly back. The colonel swung the pointer around and moved it far inland.

"Our second team will strike magnesium and aluminum plants here, and here." He indicated points on the map around East St. Louis, Illinois, and Alcoa, Tennessee. "They will also attack the inland waterway and the sluices between

Cincinnati and Louisville." He looked at them. "Do you understand? Any questions?"

Gunther spoke. "What makes you think they can do all these things? Surely you don't believe the Americans are that incompetent?"

He was clearly scornful. The colonel didn't seem to mind.

"You are right to ask," he said patiently. "Let me say this: the teams we are sending are the best we have ever trained. We have every confidence they will be successful. Each man has lived in the United States at least ten years. They are dedicated and resourceful. In addition, I will only say this: when they finished their training, we gave them one final test assignment. They were ordered to infiltrate and plant dummy packages of explosives inside the I. G. Farbenindustrie plants at Bitterfeld, Dessau, and Aachen. You know what that means? Those are our most heavily guarded aluminum installations. They knew they would be shot instantly if detected. All of them carried out their assignment. Not one was detected. As for the Negroes and Jews, do not concern yourself. Our plans for them are already in place. Does that answer your question, Lieutenant?"

He smiled, set down the pointer, stepped closer, leaned over, placed his hands palm down on the table, and said, in a calm, conversational tone: "Before you begin to study your orders, there are other things you must know. From this moment on you will not exist. Your families will be informed you are missing in action. We will take care of their needs.

"Now, listen carefully to what I say: After your mission is fulfilled, under no circumstances—none, ever—will you go to any German embassy, or German official, of any kind, in any country you may happen to be in—even after the war is over. If you wish to return to Germany while the war is still on, you should go to a neutral country in the Western Hemisphere, like Chile or Argentina. How you do that is your affair. You will receive no help from us. But you are absolutely forbidden to contact any Germans there, or to ask for any assistance of any kind. Do you understand?"

They shook their heads silently in assent. He continued: "If you reach the German border, or any countries occupied by German naval or military forces, you are to present yourselves to the first officer you encounter. You are to tell him only that you wish to be sent to C-1. Only that. You are to say nothing else. No explanations, no reasons. Is that clear?"

He watched them closely. Again they nodded.

"Gentlemen, I remind you of something else. You have sworn a solemn oath never to disclose your activities to anyone, in any fashion, as long as you live. As you know, the penalty for breaking your oath is death. You should be aware that we have placed V men inside the American Secret Service and their FBI. We have all the offices of the FBI under constant observation. We know what is going on there. At all times we know who is going in and out of those offices. So we will know if you enter there. Do you understand?"

The colonel stepped back from the table, stood fully erect, and looked down on them. "Gentlemen, you may now begin to read your orders in the folders before you. I envy you, and I salute you."

He raised his arm sharply, wheeled, and walked briskly away. The door closed as they broke the seals and tore open the folders.

10

"You told them?"

"As you ordered, Admiral."

"You did not indicate what would happen?"

"No, sir."

"Good."

The colonel pursed his lips, hesitated, and then spoke. "Your pardon, sir."

"Yes?"

"May I ask why they should know about the other missions?"

Canaris stared at his aide. "Do not worry, Colonel. We are spinning our little web. The minute those secondary teams land in America, the FBI will be informed. The Americans will think they have got them all."

It was the first time the colonel had seen the Admiral smile.

11

Willi lifted the curtain and glanced out the window. Nothing. Only a dim gray line on the distant horizon broke the blackness. The countryside was invisible.

He glanced at his new watch. Only Canaris's people could make such a thing, he thought. No one could ever tell. On the face of the crystal opposite six o'clock, a small hole had been drilled. Through it a metal screw, bearing an electrical wire, was inserted. Another wire had been attached in the main stem of the watch. Inside, the normal spring had been removed from the thirteen-jewel movement and an extra-heavy one put in its place. The winding mechanism was actually a firing pin, and the small lever on the notched wheel served as a safety pin. It could be set for as much as fourteen days and three hours before exploding.

Willi reached inside his gray Army fatigue coat and closely examined one of the three new pens. It was gold in color, had a metal clip, and a fountain-pen point. On the nib he could read, in English, "warranted chrome tin iridium." You could barely see the timing device behind the tip of the pen. There was no way to tell that inside, instead of ink, the capsule was filled with concentrated sulphuric acid.

"You have to give them credit, Gunther," he said. "It is quite remarkable."

Gunther sat across from him, his back against the upholstered material of their compartment, rocking slightly with the motion of the train. They were the only passengers on their car. When they boarded at the Zoo Station in Berlin, signs had been posted outside each door leading to the first-class compartments: "Reserved, by Order of the High Command."

It's strange to see Gunther in a German uniform, Willi thought. Especially wearing the gray regular Army cap, with its eagle and triangle and cokardee button and swastika they had been issued for this part of the trip.

Gunther shifted. He fingered the stainless-steel watch chain he now wore. He patted his waist and felt his canvas money belt containing $4,000 in American money. "Is yours comfortable?"

"Fine," Willi said. "Can you tell?"

Gunther shook his head.

Odd, Willi thought, his strong sense of distrust rising again. We've had hardly anything to say to each other since our briefing. Maybe that's just as well. "I'm going to try to sleep," Willi said, and felt foolish the moment he spoke. "We've only got a couple of hours before dawn." No reply. Why did I say that? he said to himself in disgust. He turned his head away and started to stretch out on his seat. His eyes closed, but he couldn't sleep. Inwardly, he was churning.

So he was on his way, back to America. He thought of where they used to live in Detroit, of his sister—he no longer knew if she was still there—and of his mother, his pathetic mother, still locked away in Germany in her false world of pictures and imaginary conversations with his father. And he thought of his last visit to America. Great God, that was only three and a half years ago; it seemed like thirty at least. But he remembered every moment of that trip. He was certain he would recall every detail as long as he lived.

God, I missed so much. Hank Greenberg almost broke Babe Ruth's record. And while I was conquering France and avenging the father I never knew, the Tigers went all the way to the World Series. France lost to Germany and the Tigers lost to Cincinnati. I wonder if we would have won if I had been on the team. *We.* Do I still think that way? They said I was good enough; I could have been playing shortstop alongside Gehringer and Greenberg. Would that have made the difference? Did I make a difference in France for the Wehrmacht? He shifted uncomfortably in his seat. What nonsense. What childish drivel. Sometimes I don't even

31

know who I am. And what have I become? Good now only for cutting throats instead of catching line drives.

The clacking of the train wheels over the expansion breaks in the tracks was mesmerizing. He thought again of the mission and felt a tightening in his stomach. They still didn't know what it would be, or when they would be told. Or how. Probably not till they reached America. *If* they reached America. He stirred uneasily. No point thinking about that. He had to be coldly fatalistic, the more so the better: worrying only led to mistakes, and mistakes, for him, would be fatal. He had to survive this mission. Too much depended on it. On him. His entire life, all that he was, all he had become, were bound up in it. What if he didn't survive? What if—he moved and stretched his legs and made his mind a blank. A peculiar thought intruded, at first pleasant, then disturbing: What if he met his sister once they were back in America? Stranger things had happened. What could he say? How should he act? How would *she* react? Christ, it could be awkward. It could be devastating. It could ruin everything. He tried to imagine what she looked like now, but her face was a blur in his mind. He was nodding into a fitful state of sleep when he half dreamed she was running toward him with her arms wide open. He tried to motion her away, but she kept running, faster, and started to call out his name. No, he heard himself shouting at her. No. A trickle of sweat began to form across his brow and his mouth felt dry.

He shifted again, barely opened his eyes, and saw Gunther sitting straight up, looking directly at him. For a moment, he felt a sense of panic: he believed Gunther knew just what he was thinking. Had he really spoken aloud? What had he said? No, of course not. He just imagined it. Then he turned away, cradled his head against his arm by the window, and tried to sleep.

Their train clattered on through the night.

12

They left again at dusk. After changing into their dungarees, Navy pea jackets and caps, they moved out through the back door into the alleyway. The black Mercedes was there, the engine running. They got in, and sat back as the driver pulled away down the alleyway, out into the street, and sped off into the traffic.

Eleven minutes later they pulled up to a pier in the harbor of L'Orient, west by southwest of Paris, in the province of Bretagne, on the far west coast of France, where in centuries past French merchant vessels set sail for the Far East in search of fame and glory and riches for their king.

They got out, slung their sea bags over their shoulders, strolled toward a freighter tied up to the quay, and walked up the gangplank. The piercing but brackish smell of the ocean hung over the pier. They crossed the deck to the other side, and began climbing down a ladder. Below, lying alongside the freighter, hidden from view of the shore, was a long gray submarine rising and falling with the evening tides. They could hear the waves slapping rhythmically against the hull. A seagull shrilled overhead.

Around the conning tower, facing them in the darkness, they saw the figures of four men holding what looked to be submachine guns.

They stepped lightly onto the deck, walked quickly toward the tower, climbed another iron ladder, and then went down into the submarine to the control room.

A slim man with a closely trimmed dark brown beard and full round face, wearing an officer's cap, stepped forward.

"Welcome aboard, gentlemen. We get under way immediately. Please join me."

He issued a curt command and headed toward the ladder leading back up the conning tower. As Willi and Gunther followed him up past the first section housing the steering mechanism and through the open hatch onto the tower platform, the engines coughed into life. *U-204* began slipping away into the harbor, out into the Bay of Biscay, and on to the open sea.

The captain pointed beyond the cannon mounted before him on the turret. Several hundred yards away a large steamer was moving slowly ahead of them. On either side they could make out the shape of smaller vessels.

"Those are our minesweepers," he said, gesturing to the smaller ships, "and that is our punch absorber." He pointed toward the steamer. "It is built with separate airtight compartments. Even if it hits a mine, it will not sink, and our way will be clear."

He stood silently, staring ahead, his lean hands grasping the tower railing.

"You are special passengers," he said quietly. "We have never had such an escort before."

13

He squinted as he entered the giant cargo plane, its dark interior a sharp contrast to the brilliant sunlight outside, and counted seven other passengers. Captain Taylor Bates USN nodded at them and moved toward a bucket seat in the center of the aircraft. It's going to be an exhausting flight, he thought, as he wriggled his long lean frame down into the bucket seat, especially with these damned things. They're more like instruments of torture than seats—and this case won't make it easier, either. He jiggled his black leather attaché case, handcuffed to his right wrist, and arranged it so that it rested across his lap.

Not that physical discomfort mattered to Bates, particularly now. This time, even more than usual, he was anxious to get back as quickly as possible and report.

Bates took off his officer's cap with his left hand, revealing a thatch of wavy iron-gray hair, and glanced around the cabin appraisingly through steady deep-blue eyes made even more vivid by his thick black eyebrows. With his craggy features, strong jawline, cleft chin, and unmistakable air of command, "Spud" Bates was the epitome of Old Navy, the black-shoe Navy, formal, stiff, and proud. He came by this naturally; Bates was the third generation in his family to graduate from the Academy, and his service background was unmistakable to everyone else aboard.

Seated opposite him, his left arm in a sling, his head swathed in bandages, was a seaman first-class. Three young sailors were in the bucket seats alongside him. An ensign, pudgy, Bates noted critically, and another wounded sailor occupied the seats on his side of the aircraft. They settled back and gazed out the windows as the old DC-4, now designated C-54 by the military and known as the "Skymaster," lumbered down the runway, lifted off, its four Pratt and Whitney radial engines groaning loudly, and slowly rose above the green fields of England on a perfect day in early June. It banked steeply left, and then climbed until it left British airspace and leveled out across the North Atlantic on its long flight path to Washington, D.C.

The attack came where no German pilots were supposed to be. It ended as swiftly and shockingly as it began.

A Messerschmitt BF 109F dove out of a cloudbank, all four machine guns blazing. The first thirty-nine bullets ripped through the fuselage across from Bates, tearing gaping holes in the C-54's thin aluminum skin. Bates saw the young seaman sitting across from him wave his bandaged arm and then slump into his harness, dead. The pudgy ensign died of massive wounds to the head. The two other sailors sitting on that side died instantly.

Before the second barrage of bullets struck, Bates unbuckled his seat belt and threw himself face-forward onto the metal aircraft floor, instinctively covering his head with his attaché case. Smoke filled the aircraft and made him

35

choke. He was conscious of the sound of groans around him and the even more terrifying whining noise as the plane dipped sharply forward and began to plunge toward the sea.

The Messerschmitt circled and dove again at the crippled Skymaster, firing all its guns in a last vicious burst; then, as the smoking American craft headed downward in a lazy spiral, the German plane broke off the engagement and disappeared.

In the cockpit, the pilot was dead and the co-pilot mortally wounded. Before the plane crashed, the co-pilot succeeded in regaining the controls. He fought the machine down to the ocean, where it belly-flopped with a sickening thud into the Atlantic; then he died.

There were three survivors: Bates, the navigator, and one of the wounded young sailors returning home. They managed to get a raft out the cargo door and, amid the heaving seas, clambered into it from the smoldering aircraft. Desperately, Bates and the navigator paddled away from the plane. Fifteen minutes later and 500 yards distant they watched numbly as the C-54 sank beneath the waves.

"Did they have time to get a radio message off?" Bates crisply asked the navigator.

"I think so, sir, but I don't know if they did."

Bates nodded grimly and continued paddling. He didn't express his other concern. Suppose it was the Germans who radioed their position?

"See if you can make him more comfortable while I check what we've got here," Bates said, gesturing to the young wounded sailor lying glassy-eyed and limp in the raft. He stowed his paddle and began to rummage around the raft. His attaché case slapped against him as he moved. He grasped the handcuff to steady it and cursed to himself. Damn this case, he muttered. What a helluva mess. The key to the handcuff wasn't even in London; it was locked inside a constantly guarded safe back at his Office of Naval Intelligence headquarters in Washington. Under normal conditions, their security procedure made sense: not until a courier's run between Washington and London had been completed and he was back in the American capital would the cuff be removed. But now ... He shook his head in disgust, and continued to search for whatever implements were aboard the raft. He found a small first-aid kit; shark repellent; a flag that said sos; and a small knife.

Bates picked up the knife, checked the position of the sun on the horizon, estimated they still had several hours of daylight, and then sat calmly in the center of the raft. Methodically and laboriously he cut into the attaché case. After repeated slashes, he had a large enough hole from which to extract the papers inside. His first thought, as always, was to go by the book: burn the papers whenever faced with imminent capture. On second thought, the idea of striking what few matches they had on a bobbing raft somewhere in the North Atlantic made no sense. So he deliberately began to rip the documents, one by one, into shreds. He sprinkled them, confettilike, upon the ocean. It was only after he deposited the last fragments of his secret papers onto the waves and glanced behind him that he became aware of a sickening fact. They were not sinking. Quite possibly they might not sink. They were, instead, floating serenely off in a steady stream behind the raft, pieces of crucial intelligence information maddeningly still afloat in the shape of rectangles and squares and rhomboids. If recovered, conceivably they could be pieced together to disclose the vital knowledge they contained. Bates's heart sank; but he betrayed no emotion. He kept rowing on, stoically. There was nothing else he could do.

It was nearing dusk when the wounded sailor, now propped up inside the raft facing Bates, rose up and cried out, "Jesus Christ, will you look at that fucking thing!"

Bates turned quickly. He saw a periscope rising at a steep angle from within the wavelets that washed around it. His heart skipped a beat as he stared at the conning tower pushing upward through the sea. "Oh, shit," he said. Painted on the tower was *u-507.*

The next hours were a blur in his mind, but with one constant nagging concern and puzzlement about the actions of his captors: from the time they were brought aboard the submarine until their separation upon landing, when Bates was placed alone in a shed near the submarine pen and the other two sailors were escorted away by German Army

37

guards, no one had attempted to remove his attaché case. Even now, hours later in the small, narrow, windowless cell where they moved him again, the torn and empty case still dangled from his right wrist. He couldn't figure out why they made no attempt to examine or remove it. It made him uneasy. At first, he tried to make the case inconspicuous. Once, in the submarine, he even sat on it. But that was preposterous. He couldn't hide it. Yet there seemed no interest in it at all. He paced back and forth beside the iron-framed cot and waited. The long minutes dragged by. Nothing happened. No one came. It was unnerving. He wanted to face whatever it was that awaited him.

He lost all sense of time. It must have been night, but there was no way to tell, when he heard footsteps coming down the corridor toward his cell. Eyes peered at him through the slot in the upper half of the iron cell door. A key clanged in the lock. The door opened. Bates instantly recognized the SS officer's insignia as that of a full colonel. It was going to be serious. He stiffened, squared his shoulders, and faced the German.

"Ah, Captain," the SS colonel said pleasantly, in perfect English. "I am looking forward so much to our conversation. You will be cooperative, of course."

Bates braced himself. "I am an American naval officer. Bates, Taylor. United States Navy. My Officer's File Number is 7925. I expect to be treated as a prisoner of war strictly under the accords of the Geneva Convention."

"Very good, Captain," the colonel said, interrupting him. "Most impressive. We can learn that much about you from your dog tags, and your religion and blood type as well. I had in mind having a little deeper conversation."

Bates flushed. He felt foolish. He reached up toward his open collar with his right hand, dangling attaché case and all. The dog tags were still there. Why hadn't he disposed of them? Then he remembered: after shredding the documents, he almost did; but then he decided not to. No one would know who he was if he died without his dog tags. He didn't like the idea.

"Come, come, Captain Bates," the colonel continued, "let us not play games with each other. I know your rank—I can see the four gold stripes of a captain—just as you, with your intelligence background, can see that I am a colonel in the SS. Really, Captain. Your attaché case and handcuff are a dead giveaway. Surely you know we operate the same way. We chain our intelligence couriers to their documents, too. But you are obviously something far more important than a mere courier, no?"

Bates's mouth tightened. His throat constricted. The colonel seemed bemused.

"You know, it's interesting," the colonel said, in a confiding tone. "We both use couriers regularly in our line of work, but I believe it is very rare for captains, especially captains with Annapolis rings, to play the part of the messenger. Very, very rare."

He stared reflectively at Bates. "Oh, yes, Captain, we have much to talk about. You will make it a lot easier on all of us if you will be cooperative."

Bates threw back his head and spoke, quietly but firmly. "My name is Bates, Taylor. Captain, United States Navy. File Number 7925."

The colonel sighed and shook his head sorrowfully. "I am sorry, Captain, truly sorry. You leave me no alternative. Perhaps later you will be more realistic." He stepped forward, pulled out Bates's dog tags, quickly made some notes on a small pad he held in his left hand, and then turned away.

"Think about what I say, Captain," he said from the doorway. "I assure you, believe me, it is in your best interest to be cooperative."

The door clanged shut. Bates was alone.

Less than half an hour later, after Bates's name, rank, and naval officer's file number assigned upon receiving his commission at Annapolis were telegraphed "Top Priority" to Abwehr headquarters in Berlin, a senior intelligence officer on Canaris's personal staff was carefully reading Taylor Bates's dossier.

Most of it consisted of American newspaper clippings that chronicled Bates's naval career beginning in 1912 when he graduated from the United States Naval Academy with the rank of ensign; but the file also contained photocopies of pages from Annapolis yearbooks and biographical data about Bates and his family, both his father and grandfather. Canaris was proud, and rightly so, of the biographical files his Abwehr had compiled in the late 1930s on senior commanders of virtually every potential enemy country. Already they had provided invaluable information to German field commanders, in all branches. They formed what amounted to a psychological profile of the officers who opposed them in the war. The American military biographical file had required painstaking effort by Nazi sympathizers and Abwehr agents operating out of the German embassy in Washington and their missions in other large cities; but compared to the security of other nations, the U.S. file was by far the easiest to establish. The American habit of openness, of publicizing all, made the basic task simple. Agents clipped newspapers and magazines whenever they noticed the name of an American military officer. Especially helpful were the hometown newspapers published in communities near military bases and college towns with military units assigned to campus and recruitment duties. Those local papers uniformly published news releases furnished by the Army and Navy departments about the promotions and career achievements of officers and servicemen with relatives there. Harder to come by were the class yearbooks from the military academies at West Point and Annapolis; but diligent searching through used bookstores and libraries in the United States provided them, too. Every few months, entire yearbooks, or biographical notations from them, were sent by diplomatic pouch to Abwehr Berlin headquarters. There, Order of Battle specialists matched the material to dossiers already established or began new ones.

As Canaris said to his aides on more than one occasion, with a manner of open contempt, "We should thank the Americans, they do our work so well for us."

So it proved in this case. Bates's file was rich in military service detail and personal background. Included were citations from books on American naval engagements published in the nineteenth century that mentioned exploits of some of his family. From his 1912 Naval Academy yearbook, the *Lucky Bag*, they learned his nickname was "Spud," that he played football and baseball, that he was a member of the French Club. From the Ithaca, New York, *Sun*, they learned where his father lived in retirement and that he had taught mathematics at Cornell University. From other material in the file they learned that in World War I Bates had served on a destroyer that never saw action; that at war's end he held the rank of lieutenant junior grade; that he married Sallie Westmore of San Diego when he was stationed there in 1919; that they had two sons and a daughter; that he served with the fleet that carried U.S. Marines to the Dominican Republic and Nicaragua in the 1920s; that he was a naval attaché in Paris in 1927; that he was promoted to full lieutenant in 1932; that he served in China; that (and this was most interesting) he rose unusually rapidly in rank after serving as a staff officer at the Naval War College and became a lieutenant commander in 1938 when he was assigned to the Department of Navy in Washington. In 1940, again in an unusually swift rise for that prewar period, he was promoted again to full commander. That is where the file biography of Captain Taylor Bates, USN, ended.

Bates had fallen into the deep sleep of the exhausted when his cell door opened and the light snapped on. He opened his eyes groggily, but didn't budge from his prone position on his stomach.

"Good evening, Spud," he heard a voice say, "were you having good dreams of Sallie and the children?"

Bates raised his head and stared up at the German officer. This one was a major, regular Army, not SS. His manner was friendly, affable almost, but Bates felt even more alarm than previously.

"Here, Spud, have a Chesterfield. You like them, I believe."

He stepped forward and held out an open pack of cigarettes. Bates rose, shook himself awake, and sat on his cot. "No, thank you," he said, as the major moved the cigarette package closer.

The major drew up a chair and faced him. "I am impressed, Captain. You have a splendid career, and I'm pleased to meet a real fellow professional, especially one with such credentials. So your grandfather was with Admiral

Farragut at the Battle of Mobile Bay, and your father was Theodore Roosevelt's naval aide."

Bates stared, trying not to show any emotion.

"You know," the major continued, "we always admired that President Roosevelt. We patterned our own naval force after your Great White Fleet. But, of course, with your intelligence background you know all that, don't you, Captain Bates?"

He inquired after Bates's family, mentioned some of his Annapolis classmates by name and reported their present whereabouts—accurately, so far as Bates knew. Bates felt his stomach muscles tightening. For the first time in his life, he understood what it was to be trapped, totally, helplessly trapped. A rat in a cage, he thought, and they're toying with me. He said nothing as the major talked on. It was all pleasant and friendly. No effort was made to elicit information. After some twenty minutes of conversation, the major pushed back his chair.

"I have enjoyed meeting you, Captain Bates," he said, standing up. "I want to make sure you realize we know all about you and are going to need some little cooperation from you. I do hope you will be cooperative, Captain. Brother officers should never act foolishly. Do not force us to take unnecessary actions."

He started to leave, then turned around. "Captain, I'm going to give you some time to think over your response. I sincerely hope you choose the wise course."

An hour passed. Bates, tormented, wrestled with himself, weighing the price of bravery and the path of reality. Never had he been so alone. He craved to talk to his wife. He engaged in a long imaginary conversation, but one that seemed incredibly real to him, with his father and grandfather, both of whom were long dead. Finally he slumped back against the cinder-block wall, exhausted, even more so mentally than physically. It seemed he had just closed his eyes when his cell door again clanked open.

"Well, Captain Bates," the major said, speaking with military crispness now, "the time has come for decision. Will you cooperate with the few questions we have for you?"

Bates stood up and faced the major. "My name is Bates,

Taylor. United States Navy. File Number 7925." He spoke in a tired, but resigned, manner. "I am a prisoner of war, I was taken captive in uniform, and, as you well know, under the terms of the Geneva Convention I am not required to give you any more information than that."

They were silent for a long moment. The major shook his head. He appeared genuinely distressed. "I am truly sorry, Captain. Please reconsider your decision."

Bates said nothing.

"All right, Captain," the major said with a slight sigh. "I regret this, but you leave us no choice. This matter is out of my hands."

He turned briskly and left. Minutes later, the cell door swung open. Two young SS troopers this time. They marched Bates down a long corridor, through a doorway, down stone steps, through still another, heavier, door, and into a stone cavern of a room. The ceiling was arched, the two windows enclosed in bricks. In the center of the room were a table and three chairs. Standing before them, a few feet away, set in a wheel rim sunk in concrete, were two vertical two-by-fours. Leather straps were attached to the top and bottom of each wooden beam.

"Take off your clothes," one of the troopers ordered in English.

Bates hesitated.

The other soldier stepped forward while the first raised his submachine gun. Bates waved back the trooper and began to undress.

They strapped his left wrist to the top of the left pole and his ankle to the bottom. The trooper wheeled out the other pole to enable them to strap his right arm, the attaché case still attached, to its top and his ankle to the bottom. He was not so much spread-eagled as pinned like a moth on a cork block. Worse, he was standing upright, entirely naked. He felt horribly exposed, degraded, humiliated. He shouted once, "I am an American military officer, a prisoner of war, and I expect to be treated with all courtesies due my rank and status." But they paid no attention. Bates lapsed into silence. He was acutely aware of his exposed genitals. He never realized how mortifying, and crippling, it could be merely to be forced to stand naked in such a way before others.

His face turned crimson when the troopers stood before him, slowly examining him up and down. Then they left. He was alone.

The minutes ticked away. He heard movement in the corridor, then five people entered the room. The SS colonel who had first questioned him was accompanied by an enlisted man with stenographic equipment who took a seat at the table. Another enlisted man carried what appeared to be electrical equipment. He moved around and behind Bates. So did a man in a white smock. At least they have a doctor, Bates thought, as he noticed the caduceus—universal symbol of the medical profession, with its serpents and winged staff—on the smock as that man passed by him and out of sight. The colonel moved close to Bates. A junior SS officer stood a few paces behind and to his side.

Naked though he was, and cool and damp as it was in the vaulted stone room, Bates was sweating.

"Captain Bates," the colonel said, "you are making a very great mistake. You can end this situation by answering our questions. Then you will be transported to a prisoner-of-war camp and treated with all respect due your rank and professional background."

Bates said nothing.

"What were you carrying in your briefcase?" The colonel snapped out his question.

"Under the terms of the Geneva Convention, I am required to tell you only my name, rank, and file number," Bates said. "You have no right to treat an officer in this manner. I demand that you release me now."

The colonel ignored him. He spat out his questions: Where was your plane bound? What branch of intelligence are you assigned to? Who is your superior? Whom did you contact in London? They came rapidly. To each, Bates gave his same reply. Sweat poured down his body. He tensed, expecting at any moment a blow from the front or back. None came.

"This is your last chance, Captain," the colonel said in a deadly quiet tone. "Will you tell me what I need to know?"

Bates's reply this time was different, and barely audible. "No," he said simply.

The colonel took several steps back, still facing Bates,

folded his arms behind his back, and nodded his head. Suddenly Bates felt a pair of hands on the back of his neck. Then he felt fingers slowly moving down his spine as if counting each column. Somewhere just below his hip-bone wings, the fingers stopped. There was a pause. He felt the sharp prick of a needle pierce his back. Bates swung his head around to look; then a searing wave of excruciating pain shot through his lower back, all the way down the side of his body to his foot. That entire side of his body shook with a convulsive spasm. The pain stopped as suddenly as it began.

Bates had begun to experience the latest, and most effective, SS "interrogation" technique. Earlier, they punctured a prisoner's eardrum. The pain was intense, but they found they had no way to regulate or control it. Furthermore, unbelievably agonizing though it was, some prisoners still did not talk. The method they now used—an electrified needle inserted into one of the sacral nerves, with voltage applied in varying intensity—worked after some initial changes. At first, some captives suffered such severe muscle spasms that their backs were broken. Now the prisoners were strapped securely before questioning.

"Answers now, Captain."

He gave no reply. Another rush of pain, another spasm. And another. Now his head throbbed with a severe ache. It wouldn't go away. More questions, more pain, over and over. He lived only in the half-light of his pain. There were no other thoughts. On the second day, the technician turned up the voltage. The pain was even more severe. Bates's body buckled and lashed about uncontrollably, held in place only by the leather hand and leg harness. Desperately, he wished to pass out. Only once did he lose complete consciousness. When he revived, his sciatic nerve was seared again and again at fifteen-second intervals, the periods of torture interspersed always with the same questions. On the third day, he could hardly hear them. His mind recoiled from the pain even when there was none. His spasms came even when the machine was turned off. In his cell, where he was taken each night, the fear of recurring stabs of pain kept him awake. On the fourth day, in the morning, the SS colonel was called to his cell. He found Bates hunched forward in a fetal position on his cot. His face looked to be that of an old, old man in the final fading moments of life. He was whimpering. Saliva dribbled from the corner of his mouth. He long since had lost control of all bodily functions.

At first, the colonel thought he heard only gibberish coming from the wreckage of a man that was now Taylor Bates. But as he listened more carefully, he realized he was getting answers to his questions. They were not always intelligible, and far from lucid, but they were answers, with names and places and dates. Before he was judged demented and consigned to a concentration camp on June 10, 1942, his torn attaché case still attached to his body, Bates provided one last bit of crucial information—disclosure of the most sensitive and secret of American intelligence operations in Europe: that a key American operative, known by the code name Decatur, had succeeded in penetrating the heart of the Abwehr itself.

Canaris had one of his legendary tantrums. Never had his closest aides seen the Admiral so furious. He launched the most massive effort in Abwehr history, determined to discover the spy Decatur that jeopardized the security of his fabled organization and endangered its operations at this most critical of moments in the war.

14

Captain Richard Heinrich peered ahead into the pitch-black night and silently cursed. Nothing was going right. For the last 500 miles thick fog had greeted him every time they surfaced. They had been forced to travel underwater at very slow speed on the A machines and now, at best, visibility was only 200 feet. Their schedule was slipping badly. The North Carolina coast was still 15 miles away. To make it worse, only an hour ago, while submerged, he had received a radio message from another submarine. Shot to hell, it said. They couldn't blow the water out of their tanks and were sinking.

It wasn't fear Heinrich felt. He and his crew had experienced danger enough for a lifetime since their ship had been commissioned the winter before at the Krupp Works in Kiel. In crossing the Straits of Gibraltar they had been severely damaged by depth bombs and barely succeeded in limping back to L'Orient. And they knew what it was to prowl the North Atlantic from Iceland and Greenland and then down the American coast in search of merchant vessels. In the last six months they already had sent 46,000 tons of American cargo ships to the bottom. But this was different. To head toward Cape Hatteras they had to forgo the High Command's normal New Neutral Route. It meant they moved through enemy waters all the way. Twice they crash-dived to escape destroyers. Once they thought they had been spotted by a PBY overhead. Then they ran head-on into the weather, as foul as any they had encountered in nearly eight months at sea. Damned fool mission. Exposing them this way. And for what? Just to put two men ashore.

Captain Heinrich had only contempt for the superstitions of sailors, but this voyage had all the elements of a Jonah's trip.

A chill swept through him. He shivered in the clammy air. Damned weather. The muscles across his shoulders were bunched tightly together. His neck felt stiff with tension. He shook his head savagely, climbed down the ladder into his ship, and gave the order to submerge again and proceed, still on the A machines, at 2½ knots.

Inside, no one spoke; they barely breathed. It was eerily silent as they all rigidly performed their tasks. *U-204* moved slowly ahead until they felt a sharp bump. The submarine began to rock from side to side with the current.

They had reached the American shore.

Captain Heinrich ordered an additional air tank flooded so the ship would rest easier on the bottom. Then he walked to the cabin beyond the control room, knocked, and entered.

"We have arrived," he announced.

Willi and Gunther were bent over two wooden boxes on the deck.

47

"Thank you, Captain," Gunther said, rising. He turned back to his work.

The boxes were long and narrow. Inside, sheets of very thin tin had been attached to the sides and the lids to make the contents waterproof. Captain Heinrich glanced down and saw detonator caps, glass vials, fuses, wires, timing mechanisms, and several square black blocks that looked like lumps of coal but were, he knew, actually specially prepared TNT. He watched as they placed the lids back on the boxes and began to run strips of the same thin tin around the tops to seal them.

"I will give the order to surface in ten minutes, gentlemen," the captain said. "If you will check your watches, please. It is now exactly one-twenty A.M., the American Eastern War Time. Sunday morning has just begun. You will still be in time for church."

He left.

Willi and Gunther already had changed into their American dungarees, dark thick sweaters, sneakers, and woolen watch caps. They picked up the boxes, carried them to the lower bunk, and put them alongside their large sea duffel bags with the heavy rubberized lining and next to their green American Gladstone suitcases. Their civilian clothes, all purchased in the United States, were already packed inside. Willi lifted his suitcase and ran his hand one more time along the bottom, first inside, then out. Again, he was reassured. He still couldn't feel anything.

"Worried, Willi?" Gunther asked with a slight sneer. "They won't fall out."

Beneath the false bottom, eight packets, bound with thick rubber bands and wrapped in oilskin, had been placed side by side. They formed a perfectly even surface. Each packet contained $5,000 in American denominations of fifties, twenties and tens. In their wallets, packed inside their suitcases, they carried an additional $419 in cash.

Willi checked his tobacco pouch before placing it back in the suitcase. The white handkerchiefs carrying the names and addresses of crucial contacts, along with the specially treated safety matches enabling them to write additional secret messages, if necessary, were safely inside. He quickly examined the handkerchiefs a last time, holding them up to the overhead ceiling bulb in the cabin. Not a trace of writing visible. All they needed to bring out the writing, in vivid red letters, was a bottle of ammonia they could buy at any American drugstore.

"Five minutes, Willi," Gunther said sharply. "Now! It's time."

They put the suitcases and boxes inside their duffel bags and laced them shut. Willi lifted them, stepped across the cabin and out into the narrow compartmentway. He closed the door and stood before it.

Behind him, Gunther was kneeling by the bottom bunk and, reaching under it, pulled out a small stick of hard rubber.

15

On deck, they found themselves in the thickest of fog and darkest of nights. It hung around them like a living presence, leaving their hands and faces bathed in a cold clinging spray and their clothes sodden. The sudden change from the warmth and brightness of the ship into this total blackness and chilling dampness was startling and disorienting. Faintly, in the distance, they could hear the sound of the surf sighing and crashing on the beach.

"We are four hundred meters from the shore," Captain Heinrich whispered. "What do you think?"

"Christ," Gunther said, "this is perfect."

Gathered around them on the deck, shadowlike in the fog, were five sailors. Three crouched along the railing, their submachine guns pointed tensely over the sea. Two others bent over a rubber raft.

"Ready, sir," one of them said, barely breathing the words.

"Good luck, gentlemen," Captain Heinrich said.

"And you, Captain. A safe journey home," Gunther said.

He saluted, and moved quickly to the railing where the

sailors held the lines to the raft now bobbing alongside the submarine. Willi followed behind him.

They clambered over the railing into the raft and immediately began rowing away. Neither spoke. In a matter of seconds they no longer could see the outline of the submarine. It had disappeared in the fog. Through the night they heard a hum, muffled by the fog, as the A machines started up. The submarine began pulling away. Hanging over the water they smelled the heavy pungent odor of engine oil.

Steadily and silently they rowed away. The fog was so thick they couldn't see anything, even the ocean around them. The motion of the waves and their movement through the fog made them feel they were bouncing around in the air. Every few minutes they stopped and listened for the surf.

"Christ, we're going in a circle," Gunther snarled.

They struck out for the sound of the surf again.

The waves were rougher. Their raft heaved up and down. The spray lashed at them, stinging and cold. It was much worse than Quinzee Lake. Thank God we don't have those damned kayaks, Gunther thought. We'd never make it. There was nothing faint about the sound of the surf now; it roared in their ears, drowning out all other senses, even the feel of the waves rolling over and around them. That bastard! Gunther cursed. He put us out at high tide.

They were on a rollercoaster now. A wave smashed into their raft, and spun it wildly around. Two more crashed into them. They pitched from side to side and felt themselves sinking. The force of the last wave nearly tore Willi into the sea. He was numb with cold. He lost the feeling in his fingers. As he grimly reached toward his duffel bag to make sure it was still there, the oar slipped from his grasp. Another wave, even more vicious in its impact, engulfed him. Willi found it hard to breathe. He was choking on the taste of the salt water and soaked to the skin. God, it's cold. He felt himself slipping. The roaring in his ears increased. He was hurtling along, barely conscious, borne relentlessly by the tide toward the distant shore. Now he was underwater. Dimly, he felt the ocean currents tugging at his clothes, dragging him down into the sand. A heavy weight was forcing him down and down. He knew he was drowning. The force of the waves pitched him forward again. He was coughing up water in short, sharp, painful gasps. He reached out his left hand and felt wet sand. His right hand still clung fiercely to the duffel bag.

16

At 0245 the stick of hard rubber, soaked in gasoline, began to contract as the gasoline evaporated. As it did, the razor blade to which it was attached inside the small box fastened to the bottom of the bunk, snapped sharply out of its concave position. It made contact with the electrical wires running down to the detonator caps atop the six blocks of TNT. The explosion tore a jagged hole in the hull of *U-204* just back of the control room. She was still proceeding at half speed on the A machines and sank swiftly to the bottom as the ocean swept through her, quickly snuffing out the screams of her crew.

17

They huddled among the sea oats, on the ocean side of the dunes, as the first streaks of dawn broke the North Carolina sky. The beach was flat and smooth now, much wider than it had been when they were washed ashore and they could smell the stale heavy odor of the flats at low tide as a blood-red sun began to edge over the horizon.

"Ready, Willi?"

"Yes," he replied.

Their duffel bags, and the boxes, had been emptied and buried. One more time they glanced up the beach. Nothing. Still deserted. They stood up, brushed off their workmen's clothes, picked up their Gladstone suitcases, heavier with the additional weight they had just added to them from the contents of the boxes, and began walking away from the ocean. Gunther saw a flight of great blue herons skimming toward the sea. They reminded him of the gray herons at home. Within minutes the sound of the surf was being overcome by the humming of the cicadas. It was going to be hot. Already the sand flies were out. They could feel the humidity rising as they walked. Beads of perspiration collected around their necks and ran down their backs. Their shirts were beginning to feel damp.

They crossed a stretch of sand and struck out along a narrow path, winding among the marshes that ran along the oceanfront. After walking silently for nearly half an hour, they stopped. Ahead, they saw a small gray weather-beaten wooden shack. It looked abandoned. As they approached, a beagle puppy scampered out from inside. It raced toward them, barking sharply in loud staccato buglelike tones.

Willi held out his hands and gently called to the dog. He bent over, still calling soothingly as the puppy inched toward him. Then, suddenly, he kicked his right foot in soccer fashion at the dog's head. The puppy rose high in the air and fell back on the ground, its head crushed.

Gunther looked at Willi curiously, his eyes narrowing. The tension between them had become nearly unbearable. Neither said anything. Gunther circled the shed carefully, listening for any sound. He stepped inside. It was empty. When he returned, he saw Willi standing on a dune, his back to the sun, watching him closely. He instantly made a decision. "Look, Willi," he said, walking toward him, and shielding his eyes against the sun, "I've been thinking. We've made it this far, but it's crazy to stay together all the way to Washington. If something happens, at least one of us *has* to get there. So I say we travel separately until we meet there for our orders. What do you say?"

Willi was silent. His own suspicions about Gunther had intensified throughout their journey. He couldn't shake the idea that Gunther was something other than he seemed. "Yes," he said, after a brief hesitation. "That makes sense. Funny, I was thinking the same thing. One of us *must* get through. That's all that counts. So I agree. You're right. The only thing that matters is the mission. Let's get on with it."

They studied each other, momentarily lost in their own thoughts, then picked up their suitcases and continued walking. If they had landed anywhere near the area planned, they should reach Manteo in a few hours, and in Manteo they could get Greyhound buses and then transport north.

part

2

THE
CAPITAL

1

Amos Knight stepped out into the cluster of dirty gray tempos, hastily thrown together in a jumble on the Mall. Shades were drawn over the narrow windows. He walked toward the limousine parked on the circular driveway behind the faded whitewashed walls of the old Navy Building standing watch on Constitution Avenue. Stifling as it had been inside, it was worse outdoors. Heat still rose in shimmering waves from the pavement. The asphalt felt soft and sticky beneath his boots. Everywhere he looked a thick haze hung over the buildings and monuments. It blurred their shapes and softened the hard white marble glare that gave Washington so startling an appearance in broad daylight.

He drew a heavy breath and moved uncomfortably. Sweat dampened his uniform blouse. It formed around his collar and under his overseas cap. His eyes smarted. He wiped away moisture that began to run down the side of his face. Motherfucker, he thought. This never gonna be a good place to live.

As he neared the black Packard, gleaming from wax he had applied early that morning, he glanced at his watch. Seven o'clock. Two hours to blackout. He checked the headlights, saw that the black bicycle tape was securely in place across the top half of the glass, got in, and drove into the haze on Constitution Avenue. On Seventeenth Street, across from the buff-colored stone façade of the Mayflower Hotel, now wreathed in the heavy humid air, he pulled up before the Little Tavern. As usual, he parked in front and left the motor running.

"Okay, man," he said to the youth behind the counter, "sack me and Coke me."

He put fifteen cents on the counter, and walked out carrying a white paper sack with a hamburger, French fries and ketchup, and a Coke in its thick greenish-glass returnable bottle. Again he checked his watch. He got back in the Packard and headed down Connecticut Avenue, onto Seventeenth alongside the graceful old State and War Department with its towers and balconies hovering over the White House grounds. As he passed by, he glanced up at the heavy machine-gun emplacements across the top of the building, then looked across at the soldiers with fixed bayonets ringing the heavy black-iron White House fence beyond. It always surprised him how normal it seemed to see all the security. Only months before there had been none. Then he continued driving past the Washington Monument to West Potomac Park.

His customary spot by the cupola, shaded by a grove of massive Dutch elms and hemlocks standing a hundred yards from the Lincoln Memorial, was deserted. He put his food beside him on the same park bench overlooking the river that he used every evening during his break before returning to pick up the Old Man, checked his watch once more, idly noted a pair of ducks bobbing gently on the water, and began to eat.

Amos Knight, twenty-six years old, eleven months away from the cotton fields outside Gastonia, North Carolina, had just lifted his Coke to his lips when the world exploded. Two .38-caliber slugs slammed into the back of his head, tearing away part of his skull and shattering the Coke bottle. Brown syrup from the drink mixed with his blood and dribbled down his shirt as his body toppled to the ground.

He was the seventh colored man shot to death in the back of the head at dusk in the District of Columbia since the heat wave began three weeks ago.

2

Detective Lieutenant Kenneth G. Johnson turned to his sidekick, Detective Sergeant Will Stanton of the homicide squad, and said in his slow drawl, "How the hell does Thomas find out about these killings? He's almost always here before we are."

"Dunno, Lieutenant," Stanton said.

Johnson gazed silently through the window of their unmarked patrol car at the figure of a tall colored policeman who was standing impassively by the ambulance attendants who were kneeling over the body sprawled on the ground before them. The lieutenant shook his head in disgust, pushed open the door of his blue Studebaker, and huffed his way through the small crowd gathered around the ambulance and patrol cars.

In the department Johnson was known, behind his back, as "Waddleduck," a description that fit him physically but belied his personality. He was short and stocky, with rolls of fat that rippled beneath his uniform when he walked, and his plump pink face, with pale blue eyes and a fringe of sandy hair sticking out from his dark blue lieutenant's cap, gave him a soft, benign appearance. It was misleading, for Johnson, one of the more brutal members of the police force, was given to casual excesses of violence, especially against the colored in Washington. He was no more corrupt than anyone else in a department where numbers payoffs and cash contributions from businessmen, politicians, pimps, and bookies were everyday matters, understood by all and tacitly accepted as such by officials from the district commissioners and chief on down, and by every reporter assigned to both the District Building and Police Headquarters off Pennsylvania Avenue. Johnson was also typical of the D.C. metropolitan police force in other ways. He had come up from Augusta, Georgia, in the mid-1920s and now, some seventeen years later, he still retained a hatred for niggers, and none more so than for D.C. colored cops. It was bad enough they had any on the force; they could thank the bitch Eleanor, her New Dealers, and their Capitol Hill allies for that. But it was getting so the niggers were now pushing their way into real police work.

Johnson waddled his way into the small throng. He waved away Craig Bench, that dirty little prick from the *Times-Herald* who monitored all the police dispatcher radio calls, with a quick gesture and slow remark, "Colored, Bench, colored. Just another jigbo. Nothing here for you," and moved directly up to Detective Sergeant Leon Thomas.

"What you doin' here, Thomas?" Johnson drawled, looking straight up into Thomas's face. "No vice here. No clap, no con, no corn."

Thomas stood quietly, his big hands hanging loosely at his sides, his coal-black face, so ebony in color it had a burnished bluish sheen, showing no sign of emotion.

"I know that," he said, after a brief pause.

"You don't know enough to stay away from something that's none of your business, Thomas."

"No. I guess not, Lieutenant."

"No, sir. You say, no, sir, when you answer me. You hear?"

"Yes, *suh*," Thomas said, emphasizing the last word and drawing it out.

Waddleduck moved closer until he was almost brushing against the bigger man. His voice hardened. "Now you listen to me, Thomas, and you listen good. I'm gonna say this just once. This is homicide business. You get that? Not pussy patrol, Thomas. Homicide. And you never gonna have anything to do with that. Never. Now I'm gonna give you one little piece of advice. If I was you, Sergeant, I would just get. You read me? Get! Now!"

Thomas didn't respond. Then, casually, he stepped aside. "Yes, suh," he said softly, with the slightest hint of a bow of his broad shoulders. He began walking slowly toward the

Potomac Parkway to hail a cab. Not even a detective sergeant had a patrol car if he was colored in Washington in 1942.

3

Thomas stared out the window of the yellow cab as it jolted along the trolley tracks and cobblestones up Seventh Street from Pennsylvania Avenue past the dingy two-story brick buildings stretching uniformly ahead into the gathering night. His face betrayed none of the fury he felt, and his eyes barely moved as he mechanically noted the familiar activity around him.

Outside, in front of the credit clothing, Like Nu Furniture and Surplus stores, the Jewish merchants were locking the protective iron gratings around their small storefronts. Time for the Man to count his change, Thomas thought sardonically. Upstairs, he knew, behind the blinds, they were already counting the day's take from the bets placed at Laurel and Belmont and Santa Anita.

As the cab moved through the blackout past the shadows flitting in and out of the bars and gill joints of the Second Police Precinct, the radio boomed out the evening sermon from Elder Sweet Daddy Bolding's Radio Church of Jesus, with the call letters WJSU.

"Now hear what it say in the Book of Job," the deep voice called out. " 'My skin is black upon me, and my bones are burned with heat. My harp is turned to mourning, and my organ into the voice of them that weep.' Now sisters and brothers, why did Job say that? I'll tell you why. The Lord made some of us to suffer. He kind of put it that way to test us. Listen what the Book says: 'Naked came I out of my mother's womb, and naked shall I return thither.' That's the way we all is made. So the Lord he made Job suffer and Job did and the Lord give him twice as much as he had before. Praise ye the Lord."

Thomas shook his head and suppressed a flash of weary rage. Poor dumb niggers, he thought, they get taken every way. The Man takes 'em every morning and the preacher takes 'em every night. Then for five bucks, cash, they get doused in the crap floating in the Potomac and think they're saved.

What were those old lines that Sterling Brown talked about in his night course at Howard University? "Naught's a naught, figger's a figger, all fo' de white man, an' none fo' de nigger." Something like that. There was another one they discussed, from Douglass: "We raise de wheat, dey gib us de corn; we bake de bread, dey gib us de crust; we sif de meal, dey gib us de huss; we peel de meat, dey gib us de skin, and dat's de way dey take us in."

Thomas had taken his degree in history at Howard, and was thinking about night law-school courses there; but he had become fascinated by Negro verse, especially from slavery, and had started collecting all the books by early colored writers he could find. They moved him in a way he could not express out loud. He had come to love English poetry, too, especially the bawdy Elizabethan lines Brown had introduced him to. It was a side of himself he rarely showed; he didn't like to admit it even existed. What was the point anyway? None. So forget it, he said angrily to himself, as he shifted his gaze outside the window.

The cab crossed Florida Avenue, a block from the Howard Theater where the white folks came on Friday and Saturday nights to hear Duke Ellington play. It was near the District's largest gambling salon. Washington's leading white businessmen, dollar-a-year war executives, and political operatives gathered there each night around the roulette and card tables after the blackout began. Substantial old brick and stone row houses rose among the shadows of a darkened street as the cab drew to a stop near the corner. Thomas got out. He stretched to his full 6 feet 3 inches, shook out a slight cramp from the muscles bunched around his back, and strolled down the street toward an alleyway and Mama Nellie's.

In a city of false appearances, the alleyways of Washington were a world apart. And not by chance, Thomas knew. When the white folks planned their city, they laid out block after block and ringed them with imposing row houses. Out front were flower gardens, wrought-iron fences, and elegant stonemasonry. Hidden behind, among extraordinarily deep back lots, were hundreds of narrow twisting alleyways. They bore such names as Louse Alley and Slop Bucket Row and Pig Alley and Goat Alley. Ever since the Civil War thousands of colored people lived there in shacks and small frame structures invisible to passersby on the streets beyond. Every so often the reformers tried to do something about conditions in them. Just eight years before, in 1934, after prodding from Eleanor, Congress passed a law to clean up the alleyways. But it made no difference. The alleyways were still the center of an illegal world that existed for the convenience and profit of whites and colored alike.

Thomas had no sympathy with the reformers. If they had their way, the only people who suffered would be his, not the whites. Mama Nellie and hundreds like her would be out of business, but the whites would go on as usual. Instead of doing something about the real problems of a city as totally segregated as it had been during slavery, they made speeches and got headlines by trying to shut down the gill joints and dice games and cathouses in the alleyway. Fuck 'em all, he thought. His body tensed with anger as he pushed his way inside, squinting through the shadows cast by a single kerosene lamp on a small wooden platform halfway up the wall.

The first table was empty, two colored men sat at the second, and there, at the third, were Mama and Jim Yellow.

Thomas didn't say anything at first. No one else did either. Mama never could tell whether Thomas was on official business or relaxing. She was not even sure Thomas knew the difference. He was always distant. Strange cat, she thought. Can't tell nothin' about his head.

He crossed the room, thick with tobacco smoke and the pungent aroma of kerosene mixed in with the raw smell of alcohol, and pushed through a doorway from which a net of colored beads was hung. The beads swished softly, just loud enough to let the girls in the back room know someone was coming.

Beyond stood a cheap imitation of a Chinese screen. Thomas peered over the top. Odessa Williams was working away. Her bright red skirt was pulled up over her hips, exposing her dark loins, and her ankles were hooked around the slim young white boy's bare buttocks. He was fondling her large breasts through her open blouse as he quickly pumped away. His khakis lay in a pile on the floor where he had thrown them. Odessa rocked her hips under him and arched up and down to take him into her. The springs on the narrow old iron bed creaked rhythmically. As she caught Thomas's glance, she threw back her head, and said, "Oh, no!"

The soldier asked, "What'sa matter, honey, am I hurting you?"

Thomas smiled, turned quietly away, and walked back through the bead curtain to Mama's table. Sweet Odessa, he thought. Do these white bastards have any notion what she really feels?

"I need it, Mama," he said as he threw a quarter on the table and sat down.

Mama looked up quickly, trying, as always, to size him up, and, as usual, failing. Somethin' eatin' him, she thought. It was not like Thomas to admit to any need. She pushed back the chair, moved her bulk from the table, dropped Thomas's piece of silver into a cigar box, pulled out a gill—a quarter pint of corn whiskey, still called by the old British measure—from a nearby counter, and came back to the table.

"There you are, Mistuh Detective, your gill." She used the D.C. pronunciation, "jill," instead of the old English one.

He unscrewed the top, took a long drink, and shuddered visibly as the clear alcohol scarred his throat and burned his chest. The first drink always made him shiver. He would finish the gill without shivering again and, tonight, probably have a second.

"Mama," Thomas said, "you gonna have to be careful. There's gonna be more soldiers and sailors than you ever saw comin' to D.C. This town gonna be sinking from white boys.

You and your girls gonna be very, very busy. Nobody knows how long the war will last, but I think a long time. I hear it's going much worse than they let on, and that means we gonna have even more people coming our way. Now, you just take it slow. Don't go branchin' out. Stick to tricks. No dope, no hustle. And you tell your girls to watch themselves. There's something bad going on now. The colored is the target, and this war is gonna make it worse."

"I think it gonna be better," said Jim Yellow, a slight sallow man with light-colored skin, graying black hair, and a pencil-line mustache. "More work for us. We's busy around the clock at the railroad yard, and they's already hiring across the river for the new airport."

"That's right, Thomas," Mama said. "It gotta be better for us."

"Don't you go counting on it."

"Thomas, you gotta be kiddin'," Jim Yellow said. His quick brown eyes darted as he leaned forward toward the policeman. "It'll mean jobs and jobs mean money and money means the means to get on. And it's gonna mean more colored coming to town, too. They's already here. Up from the South. Take them there. I betcha they's new."

He turned and yelled across to the other table where the two colored men sat nursing beers. "Hey, man, this here's Dee-tective Thomas from the D.C. Po-lice De-partment. You tell 'em where you from."

The younger man, Ike, dressed in dirty tan slacks, a brown hunting cap, and a green short-sleeved sport shirt, glared sullenly for a moment. "What you want to know for?"

Thomas looked at him directly, then said softly but with quiet, unmistakable authority: "You tell me."

"I's from Grafton, South Carolina. Got in last week."

Thomas turned to the other man, shorter, heavyset, with a small scar over the bridge of his nose. He was wearing a nylon stocking over his head. "You?"

"Harlem, Georgia, Mistuh Po-liceman. Been here three months, and I been roughin' and toughin' it. Sometimes you just has to go along with the tough as well as the easy pickin'."

"Listen, niggers, why you all come up here?" Mama asked. "I mean it. Why?"

They were silent a moment; then, after Thomas nodded slightly toward them, Ike spoke. "Well, I tells ya. I thought jobs better here, but they ain't. I hates to say it, but it's the truth. I got family here, but they gives me no place to stay and no money. I guess I just come here 'cause I was all quivered up."

The man with the stocking cap shook his head in assent. "I'll tell you why I come. I just wants to travel. Anywhere in the world be better'n where I was. Had some friends here, so I started workin' up. Everybody wants to come to the capital. They wants to stay around where the President lives. They figger he eats, they eats."

Mama let out a loud burst of laughter. She slapped Thomas on the arm and said, "That's right, Thomas. You got to admit it. Mr. Franklin, he been good to us an' I think the war gonna be good for us."

She lit a Lucky Strike and let the smoke out slowly from both sides of her mouth so that it curled up to her eyes and made them tear.

"Shit, Mama," the detective said. "Roosevelt been good, all right, but the white folks still hate us and don't you ever forget it. The war's not gonna change that. You're right, too, Jim. More of our people's gonna get work with the war, but there's more of 'em here, and don't you forget that, either. I think things are gonna get much worse for us long, long before they ever get better. In some ways this war's gonna mean trouble between us and them. I can feel it already. I tell you, I can see it happening already."

He sat back and reached for his gill. Strange, Thomas thought, as he swallowed the liquor. Here's where I come to forget, and this earth mother and this sleeping-car porter from the Chessie who can't even speak my language always give me as much to think about as those conversations we have at Howard with Sterling Brown and Rayford Logan and Ralph Bunche and Thurgood Marshall and Frank Frazier. Thomas was about to ask Jim Yellow a question when a colored boy came rushing into Mama's. His shirt had been pulled out from his knickers. It was sopping with sweat and he was breathless.

"Mr. Thomas, Mr. Thomas," the boy shouted as he ran straight up to the detective's table. "Mr. Thomas!"

"Slow down, boy, slow down. Now easy. Tell me what you have to tell me."

"Dr. Luke, Mr. Thomas. Dr. Luke, he give me some money to fetch a cab and he say to tell you that a white man he never seen before from the Navy of the United States is messing with your body right now. He say hurry."

Thomas rose quickly from his chair. Without a word to anyone, he was out the door and into the alleyway, moving with surprising grace and speed for so large a man. As he reached Florida Avenue, he began running down the middle of the darkened street, searching for a cab.

4

Fog hung over the channel and the air was heavy and humid when the cab turned onto Maine Avenue along the waterfront. Out in the channel the harbor-police boat sounded a low warning blast from its horn at a passing oyster boat beating its way slowly back to Chesapeake Bay. Aside from the sound echoing off wharves where schooners and yachts were tied up for the night, the bustling Washington waterfront was still.

Thomas edged forward impatiently as the cab pulled up before the old white-framed church building. Its twin steeples were dimly outlined against the evening clouds. The stained-glass windows were invisible in the night. Carved over the doorway was the word MORGUE.

Standing in front, waiting, still wearing his thin white rubber surgical gloves and a white smock with white cap, was Dr. Luke. "He's still upstairs," said Dr. Luke, who was not a real doctor but the Negro who prepared the bodies for autopsies and burial. "Be careful, Thomas."

"Thanks, Dr. Luke," Thomas said, moving quickly up the steps, taking them two at a time, Dr. Luke following.

They passed through the dingy reception lobby, musty from years of use and falling plaster. The smells of an ancient coal stove intermingled with the unmistakable aroma from the grim work that had proceeded there around the clock, year after year, since the decade after the Civil War when the church was converted into the temporary D.C. morgue. Seventy years later it was still the temporary D.C. morgue. It remained so despite occasional newspaper stories about hopelessly crowded conditions and appalling heat and fumes that forced attendants to take decomposed bodies into the backyard to perform summer autopsies in the open air, attracting swarms of yellow jackets and flies and sending up a sickly sweet smell over the neighborhood of crowded row houses, restaurants, and waterfront market stalls. When it came to appropriating money for the District of Columbia, Congress had other priorities than the D.C. morgue, which was mainly used for colored anyway.

Dr. Luke and Thomas entered the creaking hand-operated elevator, an iron grating forming its cage, and took it slowly to the second floor. It was stifling as they got off the elevator. The large corridor fan swishing slowly overhead only served to stir the remnants from that day's 104-degree heat, most of which remained trapped upstairs. The slight stirring of the air carried with it an overpowering smell. Thomas felt, as always, a wave of nausea. Heavy piercing fumes of formaldehyde and decaying human flesh washed over him. God, I'll never get used to this, he thought. He instantly put it out of mind as he approached the autopsy room with its stone slabs, old-style "refrigeration boxes," and antiquated, worn surgical instruments lying where they had been casually placed.

In the corner, bending over a stone slab, he saw the back of a well-built man in a white linen suit and Panama hat with a red band.

"Don't move," Thomas said sharply. As the young man turned abruptly, Thomas drew his snub-nosed .32-caliber service revolver from a holster on the left side of his belt inside his suit coat.

Behind, Thomas saw the naked body of Amos Knight lying on the slab. The chest cavity already was cut open where Dr. Luke had been starting the prep work before the autopsy.

The young man looked calmly at Thomas for a long moment, a flicker of a smile playing about his lips.

"Very impressive. Really good," he said, slowly and sardonically, in a deep voice resonating with the unmistakable accents of Boston. "You must listen to the Lone Ranger every Sunday night. Where do you practice your fast"—he drew out the word, *faah-st*, in a tone of amused contempt—"draw?"

He cocked his head back slightly, and smiled openly. Then, slowly and deliberately, he extended his arms out widely to his sides, and turned his hands palm up toward Thomas. "Here's how I do mine, Kemo Sabe," he said in the same easy confident manner.

Still smiling, he casually drew aside his coat with his left hand, displaying a shoulder holster, and just as calmly reached inside with his right hand and slowly drew out his own weapon, a .38-caliber revolver.

"Okay, pardner," he said, pointing his revolver at the colored man's chest, "do we take ten paces and fire, or do you prefer the fluttering handkerchief trick?"

He's a damn cool cat all right, Thomas thought, studying the young man. Who the hell is he?

For all his fancy suit and fine white shirt and dark blue tie and white shoes, this one was no dude. He stared at the lean craggy swarthy face, with strong cleft chin, neatly trimmed curly brown hair, and dark eyes snapping out at him with an air both of mockery and hard, cold watchfulness from under thick dark eyebrows. This is no Waddleduck, Thomas thought. There was something about the way this one held himself that gave Thomas pause. He stood easily, almost indolently, with his chest slightly thrust forward, shoulders squared back, and feet planted apart as if he were on the deck of a ship. He conveyed a hint of suppressed yet restless energy. His manner was bold, cocky, and commanding. Looks like a damned young pirate, Thomas thought. *Who the hell is he?*

They stood silently, revolvers still aimed directly at each other.

Dr. Luke, transfixed in the doorway, broke the silence. "Now please, Thomas, and you young man, please, we don't want no more blood in this morgue. Talk, someone. Say something. Please don't go to shootin'."

"Okay, Tonto, you've had your fun," the young man said, his voice taking on a brisker, harder edge. "Who the hell are you?"

Thomas felt a flash of anger and quickly buried it. Not a hint of emotion showed on his impassive face as he spoke softly, choosing each word with deliberate slowness. "I am Detective Sergeant Leon Thomas of the District of Columbia police force. And I am in the business of asking the questions. So just who the hell are you, and what the hell do you think *you're* doing here?"

As he spoke, gravely and solemnly, he carefully shifted his revolver from right to left hand, reached inside his coat, and took out his wallet with his D.C. detective badge shield affixed to the front.

"That's who he is," Dr. Luke said quickly.

The young man glanced at the badge, looked across at Dr. Luke, smiled faintly, nodded his head and gave a half-chuckle. "Okay, Old Man, here's mine." He shifted his own revolver to his left hand and reached inside his suit-coat pocket. He pulled out a small black leather case, snapped it open, walked forward and handed it to Thomas. It identified him as Lieutenant Henry Wyatt Eaton of the Office of Naval Intelligence.

"How do I know you're who you say you are?" Thomas asked, after carefully studying the ID.

"Sergeant, you've seen my identification, and I've seen yours. Cut the grab ass. I've got better things to do than match my balls against yours."

He spoke sharply, as someone accustomed to being obeyed. The glint of rakish humor was gone. His eyes were black pools now, snapping with command.

Thomas felt another surge of anger, and again showed no sign of it.

There was a moment of uneasy silence. They could hear the fan swishing slowly away in the hallway. From outside, on the channel, came the mournful sound of an oyster-boat horn. Without a word, both men holstered their revolvers.

Thomas let out a sigh, then spoke. "I still want to know why you are here and what you want with Amos Knight's body." He stood deathly still, every muscle under tight control as he awaited Eaton's answer.

"I can't tell you that, Detective," the young man said, "and I wouldn't tell you even if you were the chief of police. All you need to know is I am here on official business of the government. It's top secret, which means it's none of your damned business."

Thomas drew in a deep breath, and let out a loud "hummph" of disapproval. He looked at Eaton and felt an overwhelming sense of weary frustration: it had been one hell of a day, and it wasn't over yet. The air in the morgue was more fetid than ever: it was thick with the sickly smell of formaldehyde. In the dank heavy humid night, the slight stirring of a breeze off the channel only made the inside of the autopsy room more discomforting. Their coats clung to their bodies, their shirts were sopping. They'll never get this smell out, Eaton was thinking. Scratch one new white linen suit. A crooked smile, ironic but engaging, creased his face. The amused glint was back in his eyes.

"Look," he said, stepping forward. "Time out. You might say we're in the same line of work, and this isn't doing us a fucking"—again, his accent drew out the expletive—"bit of good. Why don't we start again? Why are *you* here?"

"Why am *I* here?" Thomas repeated slowly. "Why am I here? I will tell you. I am here because you are here. I am here because *he* is here." He gestured toward Amos Knight's body. "I am here"—and he paused, pursed his lips, and continued, choosing each word with care, and speaking in a low, calm, but quietly moving, manner—"because seven colored men have been murdered. Seven colored men minding their own business and every one of them shot in the head. No one cares. The police don't care, my own department doesn't care. The papers don't care. The courts don't care. Just seven colored men, every poor son of a bitch of them shot in the head. No one cares. And there's no end to it."

In the doorway Dr. Luke shrank against the wall and raised his hands to his chest as if in prayer.

Eaton listened intently to that soft, deep voice echoing slightly through the old church turned morgue. He was no sentimentalist, far from it, but he found himself affected by the obvious depth of feeling and simple but effective way in which Thomas spoke. He never had been much impressed with policemen he'd met, especially the few colored ones he'd encountered. If he thought of them at all, his upbringing caused him to regard them as ranking below personal servants—although if anyone accused him of being a Boston Brahmin snob, he would have reacted with anger. He had nothing but contempt for those who acted in the grand *noblesse* manner common to many of his background. Pompous assholes, most of them. He thought of himself as having a reckless bawdy streak that set him apart from them. But this colored guy seems different from other policemen, he thought. This guy's an unusual sort of cop.

Thomas finished speaking. He stared again at the young white man standing so confidently before him. Suddenly, in a well of accumulated anger and frustration, he took a step toward Eaton. His voice rose: "No one, *no one* gives a shit. No one. Amos Knight there, he gave a shit and he's dead. And no one cares."

Eaton was stunned. Few persons had ever yelled at him, let alone a Negro.

"Look," he said, as he took a step forward, slightly holding out his hands. "Let's play this one over. I'm sorry, very sorry, about Amos Knight. But I didn't kill him. Or the others. I want to find out who *did* kill Knight. Whether you believe it or not, I want to find out just as much as you do. I wish I could tell you why, but I can't. It's a matter of high national security. That's all I can say."

Thomas was silent, but not appeased. They stared, awkwardly and warily, at each other. In the new stillness of the morgue, they were conscious again of the swishing sounds of the overhead fan.

Dr. Luke's soft voice broke the tension. "Would you want some coffee?" he asked gently.

"What?" Thomas, still angry, and startled at the intrusion,

snapped out the question, while still glaring at the young white man. "What did you say?"

"Coffee, Thomas, I said a cup of coffee." Dr. Luke turned toward Eaton. "And you, too, Mr. Navy. Wouldn't you like some coffee?"

Before either could answer, he slipped quickly through the doorway and disappeared. Thomas and Eaton shifted their positions. They said nothing. Jesus, Eaton thought, looking across at Thomas with studied casualness, you can feel the emotion pouring out of that guy, even if he's trying not to show it. At the same time he was struck again with the grave sense of dignity and strength that Thomas conveyed. He glanced toward the doorway as he heard footsteps in the hall.

Dr. Luke returned with two white porcelain cups, both cracked and chipped, some sugar in a small paper sack, a dingy-looking spoon, and a can of Pet condensed milk. He carried them all on a stained wooden slab. God only knows what else he uses it for, Eaton thought. He looked at Dr. Luke's improvised tray with a tinge both of disgust and grim humor. Jesus, what have I got myself into now? He watched, a faint smile playing at his lips, as Dr. Luke put the cups down on a nearby table, pushed aside a scalpel and an old surgical glove, drew up a canvas folding chair, and pulled forward an overturned barrel. He indicated for both to sit. They did.

Thomas waited for Eaton to doctor his coffee. He couldn't break the old habit, much as it annoyed him; he still instinctively waited for whites to take care of themselves first. Eaton, however, put nothing in his coffee. Thomas heaped in three teaspoons of sugar. Eaton was fascinated as he watched Thomas's big hand stir his coffee with the scalpel handle. He was more aware than before of the sweet sickening smell everywhere around them. It was like biology lab in prep school, but worse. The ridiculousness of the comparison made Eaton laugh out loud.

"Helluva way to meet, isn't it?" he said, chuckling, and gesturing around the morgue. He held out his hand across the table.

For the first time since they met, Thomas liked what he saw. At least he's got a sense of humor, he thought, warming briefly to the look of deprecating amusement in Eaton's dark eyes. He took Eaton's hand in a firm grasp. "Well, Lieutenant," he said, "in my line of work, you never know where you're going to wind up, or who you'll meet, and I guess the same goes for you." He shook his head slightly. Eaton noticed a look of deep fatigue and something more on Thomas's face: a sadness, incomprehensible and indescribable, but touching somehow. It seemed to well up from deep inside and light his face from within; then the fleeting expression was gone.

"Sorry about that back there," Thomas said simply.

"Sorry about what?"

"My shouting."

"Seems to me you're entitled."

"No, I was wrong," Thomas said. "I had no right. It was not professional. And I am a professional, Lieutenant."

He looked quickly at Eaton, sizing up his reaction. Except for a brief nod, there was none.

"You see, Lieutenant, it's not just Amos Knight over there." He waved his arm toward the cadaver on the slab. "There's something more going on here than just a bunch of random murders of Negroes. There's a pattern to all this. Every eyewitness we have so far to all seven of these poor bastards gives the same description of the murderer: a young white man, well dressed, wearing white shoes. And every single victim was shot with a .38-caliber revolver. Just like the one you're carrying."

They stared at each other.

Thomas spoke again, calmly and patiently. "The worst part of this is, Lieutenant, that these shootings are already having a tremendous impact in the Negro community—even if no one in the white community knows about them, or gives a good Goddamn."

His voice had risen slightly.

"Do you have any idea what it means in this city if colored people get the idea that white guys are going around out there deliberately shooting Negroes in the head and nobody gives a shit about it? Or nobody does anything about it? Can you possibly imagine what could happen if this sort of thing keeps going on this summer? Put that in your national security file, Lieutenant. Or maybe you don't think it's a big deal, either."

Eaton had been listening intently. His face was solemn.

"Listen, Detective—"

"They call me Thomas."

"Thomas. Okay, Thomas. They call me Henry—and sometimes a lot worse."

He smiled, reached across, and touched Thomas on the shoulder. "Look, Thomas, I'm not going to give you a lot of crap about what anybody else should be doing on these cases, especially on the D.C. government side. Christ, I've got enough problems with my own shop. But maybe we can help each other. *I* need all the help I can get. If you find out anything about the Amos Knight murder—and I mean anything—call me at this number." He scribbled his office number on a piece of paper and handed it to Thomas. "And I promise you I'll do the same for you."

Eaton picked up his cup and finished his coffee. Thomas drained his.

"All right, Lieutenant—"

"Henry."

"All right. That's a deal." Henry noted Thomas still didn't use his name. "You can get me at this number." He wrote down his own and passed it over.

They stood and shook hands. As he turned to leave, Henry realized that was the first time he'd sat at the same table with a Negro, or ever really talked to one.

5

Elias Robins opened the heavy double door with the two brass British lion doorknockers and nodded slightly at the young man standing before him in a white linen suit. "How do you do, Lieutenant," he said, reaching for Henry Eaton's hat. "It's good to see you again. Please come in. I know Mrs. Stith will be glad to see you."

"Thank you, Elias," Henry said. "How have you been?"

"Fine, sir, thank you." He gestured gravely at a chart, mounted on a corkboard standing on a polished cherry table and lighted by two tall candles on either side. "Your seating place is there."

Henry stepped farther into the foyer, dark and inviting against the summer sun outside. It smelled faintly of wax and perfume. He looked at the seating chart and found his name at Table 4. The name of one of the women next to his was familiar—a senator's wife, he was sure—but not the one on his other side. Elias handed him a small card with the number 4 on it, a reminder of his dinner table, and started walking slowly down the long Persian rug toward the curving stairway to the sunken dining room below.

"Please follow me, sir," Elias said softly. He led the way, a small courtly man with light, smooth skin who wore his tuxedo with such style that he seemed a model of good grooming.

They're from two different worlds, Henry thought, remembering the huge coal-black detective in the morgue with the anger and frustration pouring out of him last night.

He couldn't get that scene out of his mind. All day, while he studied Amos Knight's personnel file and rechecked the records of every person, officer as well as enlisted man, assigned to the admiral whom Knight had served as personal driver, he found himself recalling the unsettling encounter in the morgue. He could still hear the deep voice of Detective Thomas echoing throughout that terrible place. He felt a twinge of guilt at not being open with Thomas about the Knight case, but he knew the regs; and cop or no cop there was no way Naval Intelligence could share information about this one, especially this one, involving as it did an office charged with one of the most secret of American war efforts. Still, his inability to be of help gnawed at his conscience. He had no doubt that Thomas might be able to help him. Already he had helped, in fact, without knowing it: earlier that morning Henry had made a request, discreet of course but official, for all D.C. police records on those other Negro murders Thomas had described. Maybe the two of them could work something out. It was in their mutual interest, and Henry was a supreme pragmatist: he would take help wherever he could get it. It couldn't hurt, either, to have someone on the D.C. force you could deal with outside of regular channels. He wondered how capable Thomas was. Strong, obviously; good in a fight for sure; and intense despite the tight control he displayed. Probably tenacious, too—but could a Negro *really* handle a complicated case? The thought bothered Henry. He regarded himself as being open-minded, and certainly not a racist, but he suddenly realized he had never had to think, really think, about whether they were as capable as whites. He suspected they weren't. The idea made him uncomfortable; he didn't want to acknowledge it. It was contrary to his own sense of himself, who he thought he was, what his own family had stood for in the past. At least what they liked to think they stood for, even if, as Henry well knew, the reality was often otherwise.

He pushed aside the thoughts. What did he, or any of them, know about Negroes anyway? Then he followed Elias down the stairway, noting the Picasso, Matisse, and Cézanne on the walls.

Accustomed as he was to wealth and comfort, Henry was always astonished at the grandeur of Marjorie Stith's Georgetown home—and it, he knew, was only one of her estates. As a boy, when his father worked at Treasury under Andrew Mellon in Hoover's cabinet and he was attending St.

Albans on the Washington Cathedral grounds, they had been weekend guests at her thousand-acre farm in Pennsylvania, near Gettysburg. He had never seen her Fifth Avenue apartment overlooking the Metropolitan Museum and Central Park, but if it contained only a fraction of the treasures displayed in the old red brick mansion on O Street, extending half a block off 34th Street near the Georgetown University campus, it would be infinitely grander than even the world into which he had been born on Boston's Beacon Hill.

In the closed and sterile world of capital society, where even the colored classes rigorously avoided contact with the lessers of their race and counted themselves superior by the lightness of their skin and the white people for whom they worked, Marjorie Stith stood alone among the cave-dwellers of uppercrust old Washington. Though her father had been a British diplomat, knighted near the end of his service (Sir Hugh was a fatuous old goat with a string of young mistresses, Henry had heard from his father) who married one of the Astor girls in New York, it wasn't money alone or family credentials that made her so powerful a figure in the private world of Washington. Her family's investment holdings and social connections were important enough; but she also owned a huge block of RCA stock, as well as a string of radio stations and newspapers throughout New England and the Midwest. She underwrote the highly influential weekly opinion journal, *The Forum*, which, despite the miserably low scale of pay for articles, attracted such writers as Edmund Wilson, Dos Passos, Archibald MacLeish, Dorothy Thompson, Reinhold Niebuhr, and other intellectuals. In Washington, Marjorie was intimately involved in bringing together the small select circle of policymakers, diplomats, leading journalists, and national commentators. An invitation to her home was like a command, fervently sought, instantly accepted, and bestowing a special status on the honored person. Alice Longworth, Teddy Roosevelt's imperious and acid-tongued daughter, provided a more wicked salon, full of malicious gossip and character assassination of the mighty, but it was to Marjorie Stith's that the rich and famous and powerful came to meet, converse, relax from the tensions of the moment, and be entertained in the grand style. In some mysterious fashion, her dinner parties enabled the combatants of political Washington to put aside their daily armor, establish personal connections, and exchange views candidly in ways impossible during their demanding and all-too-public work days. Her home was a great hothouse of inside information. If any sort of consensus could be said to emerge from the competing factions of diplomatic, congressional, bureaucratic, executive branch Washington, they formed among the people who counted themselves privileged to gather at her two-hundred-year-old Georgetown mansion. All that Marjorie Stith cared about was that her guests be somebody, be connected to somebody, or be on the way to becoming somebody. All others did not exist. They were bores, and in Marjorie Stith's world to be thought a bore was the ultimate in rejection.

"Henry," she called out in a voice that always struck him as a caricature of upper-class tones, half exaggerated British nobility, half American boarding school. She sounded as if she had lockjaw and could not quite get out all the vowels and consonants. "How lovely to see you, darling. You are sooo good to come." He wondered if he sounded like that and didn't know it.

She swept toward him in a long silk evening dress, ice-gray in color, matching, he thought, her iron-gray hair. She brushed by Elias without a glance, looped her arm around his, and led him off into the crowded living room. Small knots of guests sipped drinks brought on silver trays by ubiquitous self-effacing colored butlers. All wore tuxedos, all had light skins. She hasn't changed at all, Henry noticed: she still had an ungainly horsey quality that Henry associated with finishing-school girls whose real experience and interest never got far beyond the high jump.

"Do come and meet some people, dear, we've had such a good turnout for my first Sunday-in-summer party, and how is your dear father?" She spoke with her head held back, as if looking down her nose, and with that same nasal accent he remembered so well from childhood.

Marjorie interrupted a group of five men, standing in a

circle. "I want you to meet Henry Eaton," she said. "He's Archie Eaton's oldest boy, and he's a dear. You remember Archie, of course. First Boston."

They nodded.

"Henry, this is Senator Bankhead of Alabama."

"How do you do, sir," the tall man with dark bushy eyebrows, lined, worn features, and solemn expression said slowly.

"This is Mr. Justice Frankfurter."

"I'm an old friend of your father's," answered the little man with the sharp eyes gleaming through a pince-nez, holding out his hand.

"This is Senator Truman of Missouri, who's been making all that trouble for the businessmen."

That's what I thought, Henry said to himself. It's his wife she's got me sitting by. The senator held out his hand stiffly and said hello in a flat, dull tone of voice. Henry thought he looked terribly uncomfortable and not at all like an important senator, as Bankhead did. I'll bet it's the first time he's been here and he feels out of place.

"And this is Admiral King. Ernie, I'm so glad you could get away for a little while."

The admiral, dour-looking despite his formal white dress uniform, nodded gruffly, and took another drink of Scotch. He recognized Henry's name immediately, and knew of his present secret and most sensitive intelligence assignment as the Attorney General's right-hand man, with authority to deal with all U.S. covert operations; but he acted as if he had never heard of Eaton.

"How do you do, sir," Henry said, feeling foolish and repressing the instinct to salute. Thank God I'm not in uniform, he thought, yet at the same time he felt certain the men were looking at him with contempt and wondering why he wasn't in uniform.

"Come on, dear," Marjorie called out, whisking him away to another group of guests.

"Harry, oh, Harry, I want you to meet Archie Eaton's boy."

She interrupted a sallow-faced cynical-looking man with pale unhealthy skin and deep circles under his eyes. His unpressed gray suit stood out in a room filled with fashionably dressed guests.

"This is Henry Eaton, a real dear. Henry, this is Harry Hopkins. We call him Horserace Harry, and some people call you other names than that, don't they, Harry?"

She drew out the *h*'s in elongated fashion and smiled serenely. Hopkins looked up sharply, smirked, casually tapped an ash from his Chesterfield, then watched some of it fall on the priceless Bokhara beneath their feet. The rest sprinkled his suit. He held out his hand.

"The banker's boy? How are you? Tell me, Mr. Eaton, I'm trying to persuade Krock and Lippmann here that Wallace was just right in his speech the other day. What do you think?" Hopkins had a mischievous smile, but his eyes also had hard-cutting quality as he watched Henry's reaction and waited for his answer.

He's a son of a bitch, all right, Henry thought, without showing a flicker of emotion.

"How do you do, Mr. Lippmann," Henry said politely, turning to the solemn-looking man in the blue pin-striped suit. "It's good to see you again."

"Hello, Henry," Lippmann said. "Do you know Arthur Krock?" He introduced the heavyset man beside him who was holding a Bourbon in a frozen silver cup.

Henry turned back to Hopkins. "I don't know, sir. I read the Vice President's speech, of course, but I'm not sure I understand what he really means by it."

Krock snorted. " 'Chosen of the Lord,' my ass, Harry," he said bitingly in a Southern drawl. " 'Divine mission to save the world,' with FDR as its instrument, I suppose. The New Deal as the New Islam. Now you tell me, how in the name of God can the President let Henry Wallace spout that stuff? You know damned well we're losing the war and here's that crazy Wallace talking about the beautiful world after the war. For God's sakes, Harry, tell him to start worrying about Rommel instead of the one-world crap."

Hopkins's eyes sparkled. He started to speak when Marjorie plucked Henry's arm and said, "Oh, Arthur, you're so incorrigible! Do let Henry Wallace have his fun. We've got little enough to laugh about as it is."

She swept away again, Henry in tow, moving from group to group, introducing them all, generals and ambassadors, cabinet officers and White House assistants, senators and congressmen, dollar-a-year war production men and Wall Street lawyers turned intelligence operatives. Often, she whispered deadly asides about them to Henry. ("Oh, there's old Harold Ickes. He's such a bore, but you should meet him." "That's Henry Morgenthau. He's the most constipated man I know." "Now there's someone I know your father knows well, dear, but I don't think you'll see him again. It's the first time I've even been able to drag Mr. Stimson out of his office for even a minute in the last seven months." "That's Barney Baruch. He's such a pompous old fraud." She delighted in pointing out a stout balding businessman in a somber three-piece suit talking with obvious self-importance to a slight British diplomat: *That*, she breathed delightedly, was one of the men whose name appeared in the black book seized last week after the FBI and D.C. vice squad raided the Harrison Institute in a luxurious Connecticut Avenue apartment building overlooking Rock Creek Park. The "institute" offered "medical therapy" only to blue-chip Washington clients. Police and agents arrested eleven young women there; they worked in what the papers were calling "the most notorious cathouse on the East Coast." "You should hear who else Edgar says is listed in the book," Marjorie chattered on in a throaty voice. "He tells me the girls even wrote down the sexual preferences of the customers and kept a code to identify them. Can you imagine that? Of course, everyone's *dying* to know who's in it, but Edgar won't tell. The little bastard." She laughed maliciously and continued her breathless description of her guests. "Over there is Oveta Culp Hobby." She nodded toward a severe cool-looking woman standing erect in the gabardine uniform she personally had designed for her Women's Army Auxiliary Corps. "You ought to say hello, but don't waste time on her. She's such a pain.")

Henry found himself whirling from group to group, smiling until his face hurt. Through the murmur of sound, low but steady and enveloping, he picked up snatches of conversation.

"You *did? How?* Tell me! I've been trying to get an X card

82

for weeks, but Walter says . . ." one stout dowager said to another about the new, and rare, VIP rationing cards that gave the possessor unlimited supplies of gasoline at any station.

"Yes! Can you believe it? That's what they wanted for *orchestra* seats. So I told Ruby, you call the manager at the National and tell them Mrs. Caldwell said . . ."

"You can by God bet that the CIO is never gonna let this administration control the rise of workingman's wages, and I'm tellin' you now . . ."

"It's a helluva note, Mr. Secretary, when the United States of America is in this kind of situation and a patriotic plastics company like ours with *real* know-how gets screwed on contracts because of cheap War Department political favoritism . . ."

"You just tell them over there that FDR better find another target for his anti-inflation program because American farmers are never going to tolerate lowering agricultural prices, and you tell them that Senator Nye says our farm bloc is never going to . . ."

Suddenly, Henry felt a wave of revulsion. My God, he thought, looking around at the comfortable, well-fed, self-satisfied crowd of men and women, if these are the people who are running the war, how do we have a chance?

A Negro butler held out a canapé on a silver tray. Henry's throat tightened. He swallowed hard and almost gagged as a sour mass of acid rose from his stomach. He remembered Amos Knight lying on that slab in the morgue last night, cut open and surrounded by that miserable sickening smell. Poor bastard. He was just doing his duty, and well as far as I can tell from my investigation so far. He never even had a chance. They'd have him working out in the kitchen here, I suppose, if they let him in the back door at all. His stomach churned. He looked around the room again in distaste, but this time his anger was directed as much at himself as at them. Once again, Henry felt deep doubts about his decision to come to Washington instead of going into combat as he had wanted, and as his younger brother already had succeeded in doing.

Henry was, as they said, well connected. When he entered Harvard College, he was the eighth generation of his family to do so. His father was a grave, proper sort of man. In his exquisitely cut gray three-piece pin-striped suits, ordered always from his tailor in London, with his Porcellian Club eighteen-carat gold chain always strung precisely in place across his vest, his gray mustache always neatly groomed and gray hair always combed straight back, and pale blue eyes that always appeared to be looking down on you, Archie Eaton seemingly was more comfortable in the club and the boardroom than in the cut and slash of the marketplace or the sweat and grime of the athletic field; but in the days of Santayana and William James at Harvard, he had been a legendary football hero, named to Walter Camp's All-Americans, and one whose exploits did not dim with the passing of years. His winning drop-kick field goal in The Game against Yale was still recalled and retold every fall when alumni gathered. There had been nothing soft about his business dealings, either. Like so many in his family line, Archie was capable of acting with utter ruthlessness when he deemed it necessary; and capable also of never troubling himself with moody introspection about the rightness or wrongness of his actions. Once he made up his mind, he simply entertained no doubts about whether he was right. That, of course, went without saying. He had the imperious manner of the divinely assured Yankee trader, whose descendant in fact he was. Henry had some of that, but in his looks and in his makeup he seemed, and thought of himself as being, far different from his father.

He had his mother's dark eyes and complexion, and from her he had inherited what he thought of as his "Mediterranean" side. It was French, really, but Henry always took relish in replying to some Boston windbag trying to make an ancient family connection by saying he didn't know much about genealogy. All he knew was that Mark Twain was probably right: Americans, even the greatest, didn't know who their grandfathers were, but then, the French, or so *they* said, didn't know who their fathers were. Since he was partly French, he therefore couldn't say much about who he really was. He always enjoyed watching the look of shock cross the grande dame's, or stuffed shirt's, face when he would say that, in mock humble style. In fact, Henry was interested in his family—or some of them—even though he habitually deprecated them in conversation. One of his ancestors had been Secretary of the Navy under Jefferson during the time of the Barbary pirates, and later the founder of a great clipper-ship fleet that paved the way to the Orient and the China trade. He had been, by all surviving accounts, a salty sort of a rogue, who left behind, or so Henry liked to tell his dates, more than a passel of blue-eyed bastards of differing colors around the world. Another that intrigued him, and whose shade he enjoyed evoking on certain stuffier than normal social occasions, was Old Ephraim Eaton, a Trustee of Harvard College in the early 1700s, who was found, at the age of seventy-eight, frozen to death in an outhouse behind his home in Quincy during a fierce January nor-easter—after, it was said, having serviced for the last time a West Indian housemaid in the pantry.

As much by rite of birth as Henry Adams, with whose line he was also collaterally related, and with as much ambiguity about the family connections as Adams in similar circumstances, Henry went to Harvard. He majored in Greek classics and philosophy, adding a *summa* to his degree in the process and lettering in track and field—being nearly good enough to qualify for the javelin-throw finals at the 1936 Olympics in Munich. He then took his law degree with the Class of '38 at Yale. For three and a half years, until Pearl Harbor, he worked for Sullivan & Cromwell on Wall Street. It was there, through the Dulles brothers, Allen and John Foster, and other partners from Yale, that he was persuaded to come to Washington, ostensibly with the Office of Naval Intelligence, the best intelligence operation the United States ever had, but actually as one of the select members of the supersecret Interdepartmental Security Committee. The committee had been formed four months earlier, in February of '42, under Roosevelt's direct orders. It operated clandestinely under the chairmanship of Attorney General Francis Biddle with most of its staff occupying a nondescript office in a tempo behind the Navy Department Building on Constitution Avenue and space kept near Biddle at Justice. There, behind an unmarked door, Henry helped coordinate its multiple activities. Already Biddle had come to think of

Henry as indispensable and relied heavily on his judgment. Henry proved himself to be highly intelligent, efficient, tough, and ruthless if necessary. He was singularly unawed, and unintimidated, Biddle was pleased to observe, by rank, no matter how high, or personal background, no matter how grand. These were invaluable assets for the job, which had a thankless but crucial mission. Biddle's committee was armed with a sweeping charter to facilitate the flow of intelligence information among all the jealous, warring, and mutually suspicious military branches and federal departments of government, and to coordinate efforts to eliminate security problems any of them faced. They had been given the highest authority to cut red tape, to assess, expand, or terminate if necessary, ongoing or planned intelligence operations. The group was so secret that few officials in Washington knew of its existence.

But here Henry was, disgusted, careening between stupid social parties and colored cops, and coming no closer to the real problems of the war or even the special new case to which he had just been assigned. He had been experiencing extraordinary pressure even before the Knight murder case. It came at a moment of heavy tension in his office. He knew what only a very few American officials knew: that the ONI agent Decatur had succeeded in leaving Europe bound on what was believed to be the most urgent of missions to Washington, one so secret and important that it already had created intense anxiety in his intelligence shop as they awaited word that Decatur had landed safely. So far they had heard nothing. Henry knew nothing else about Decatur, and didn't want to: he was privileged as it was, under the strictest security "need to know" tenets of his intelligence operation, even to have knowledge of Decatur's existence. That mere knowledge, though, added to his burden in checking other intelligence information filtering through the many military departments and civilian agencies cleared for high classified work. It was Henry's job to investigate potential leaks from any of them and thus safeguard the security of the highest level of operations being mounted or planned by the United States government. None had higher priority at the moment than Decatur. Under the best of conditions, it was an immense responsibility. Now, with the urgency of the Decatur mission gripping the highest officials, with so many other fateful and secret decisions about the war nearing final go/no-go stage, and with the spate of strange yet possibly connected colored murders in Washington, Henry felt even his immense self-confidence and always calm manner under pressure, all traits that made him the envy of his law-school classmates at Yale, affected by stress such as he had never experienced.

He drew in his breath, smiled again, and once more murmured his parting good-to-see-you as Marjorie plucked him away from yet another group. She led him into a small sitting room with French doors that overlooked a lovely landscaped garden in a courtyard shielded from the unwanted outside world by a high brick wall covered with ivy. Sitting on a bay window, framed by a huge magnolia tree and lilac bushes outside, was someone whose voice Henry instantly recognized as that of Alton Slater's. Beside him was a strikingly attractive young woman wearing a cool blue cocktail dress. He had never seen her before.

Since Elmer Davis gave up his radio broadcasts only weeks before to head the Office of War Information, Slater was far and away the best-known and most popular radio commentator in the country. Millions of Americans gathered around their sets at six o'clock every evening to hear his familiar crisp, stentorian, theatrical-sounding voice begin authoritatively, "This is Alton Slater with the news . . ." It was said he was a great favorite of the President's, and had been called to the White House the night of Pearl Harbor to hear Roosevelt unwind after news of the attack and magnitude of the losses to the fleet became apparent. For some reason, FDR seemed to enjoy having Slater around; the commentator was now counted among the small group of people Roosevelt liked to entertain in his White House living quarters, without Eleanor, naturally, when the President offered his personally mixed martinis before the colored steward brought in dinner on lap trays.

Slater was holding court about Tobruk. To a group gathered in a semicircle around him he recited, authoritatively, the alarming rate of merchant ships being sunk along the Atlantic. Henry was annoyed at the rapt way the young brunette, her legs crossed demurely, but still displaying a hint of exposed thigh and garter belt above her silk stockings, stared at Slater. From what he heard, people believed Marjorie was having an affair with Slater while her husband, Colonel Randolph Stith, was in the South Pacific with the Marines. It was probably true; Marjorie took men to bed, casually trying them out the way she would a new quarter horse, but without, Henry was certain, any kind of real feeling. I'll bet she's a cold lay, he thought. And Slater's probably nothing but another damned garter-snapper. He doesn't even look like that, Henry thought, examining Slater's supercilious manner and expensively tailored clothing more closely. He wondered vaguely why he was bothered by the girl's attention to an older, foppish-looking man like Slater.

"Alton, darling."

Marjorie again spoke in that voice no one could ignore. "Now just forget about the war for a minute. I want you to meet Henry Eaton, my friend Archie's boy. Henry, this is Alton Slater."

Slater held out his hand, ungraciously, Henry thought, brusquely, as if not wanting to be bothered. He wore rimless glasses, had pale gray eyes, short gray hair, a red face and bristling gray little mustache, square features, a turned-up nose. He wore a black-and-white polka-dot bow tie (probably a Sulka, Henry thought) and a white silk shirt under his double-breasted white dinner jacket. Henry disliked him instantly. A phony for sure.

Marjorie, oblivious, cried out again, in her nasal accent, "Now, Henry, I want you to say hello to Constance Aiken. She was Hazel's roommate at Smith, up from Charleston, and she's with us now here in Washington. I know you two will like each other."

"Oh, of course we will, Mrs. Stith." Constance drawled her reply in a soft liquid voice, and bowed her head slightly. She seemed to flutter her dark long eyelashes under disturbingly vivid greenish-blue eyes that betrayed a glint of amused mockery. She leaned forward slightly, extending her hand elaborately as if she expected it to be kissed, and showed more of her smooth pink breasts as she did. Henry had never liked Southern girls. This one especially seemed the Southern belle type, with classic features, perfect coloring, firm chin and jawline, and full lips set off by ruby-colored lipstick. Yet there was something unsettling about her. She seemed to be making fun of him, and exaggerating her Southernness as if to test his reaction and then make fun of it. It was confusing.

"And what do you do, Mr. Eaton?" Constance drawled again, making Henry suspect she was teasing him.

"I work for the government," he said stiffly.

"Oh, how interesting and unusual."

Damn you, Henry thought. Who needs this?

"Now, dear, you be sure and treat Henry well, won't you?" Marjorie said, and immediately pulled Alton Slater to his feet. She looped her hand and arm around Slater and marched him off, leaving Henry standing in front of Constance Aiken.

"Do you like the old geezer?" Henry asked.

"He's not an old geezer," Constance replied.

"Sure he is."

"How do you know?"

"I can tell."

"Can you now? How nice. Ummm, yes, now that you say it, I'm sure you *do* know about geezers—old *and* young ones of course."

"Why, Magnolia, I never thought you noticed."

"Well, Mr. Boston. 'Course I do, suh. I have had some acquaintance with the breed, you know, especially the Yankee version."

"Really."

"No, not really, Mr. Boston. We say truly. Truly I do know about them."

She ducked her head demurely, and fluttered her eyelashes exaggeratedly.

"And what, truly, can you tell about me?" she said softly, but with an even more pronounced accent.

"That you are a lousy judge of geezers. May I sit down, Magnolia? Or is it Scarlett?"

"No, it is neither. And I don't recognize you as Rhett,

either. But I certainly can't stop you from sitting. You do look tired, and we *do* need to be nice to our young men these days. That's what Marjorie says, anyway. You *are* a young man, aren't you, Mr. Eaton?"

She moved slightly to make room next to her on the window seat. Henry sat down. His attempt at conversation was having the opposite effect from what he intended. The more he teased, the thicker her Southern accent grew. And the more they talked, the more he realized he was being played with in return. He didn't have the upper hand. It was confusing, and somewhat frustrating, but intriguing.

"And what do you do, Magnolia?"

"I work."

"Congratulations. Where?"

"For the government."

Henry laughed. She was sharp, all right. She turned that one back on me.

"Look," he said, moving closer to her, and dropping his voice to a husky whisper, "why don't we continue this battle over a good drink afterward. I've got a cold bottle—"

But Constance had had enough of Henry's games. She turned to him, her face cold and eyes hard, and interrupted him in icy tones, no accent noticeable now: "Mr. Eaton, I was having a very nice time here until you came along. I was minding my own business, having a stimulating conversation with a really fascinating man, when you arrive talking through your nose with your superior Boston accent and all your 'funny' remarks about the South. No, I am not interested in continuing the conversation—or having one of the nice cold bottles you keep for little girls. As far as I'm concerned, you just go right off, drink it by yourself—and piss ice water! Which I'm sure you do quite well."

With that, Constance Aiken stood up briskly and began to stomp off. A few steps away, she stopped, turned, and said, "In case you didn't notice, Mr. Eaton, the South has risen."

Henry sat back, at first angry, then amused and admiring. Well, I'll be damned, he said to himself.

He was about to get up and follow her when Elias began ringing the little bell. "Dinner is served," he announced. Marjorie reappeared, breathless. "Come on, Henry, be my handsome escort to the dining room. Isn't Constance lovely? She's just so special. She was Hazel's very best friend, you know. And she's terribly smart, as I'm sure you noticed. I've got her next to a *most* attractive assistant secretary of state. I *do* hope they'll like each other."

He's probably a homo, Henry thought exasperatedly. He was surprised at his emotion.

They entered the long formal dining room, glowing with candles, set with ten circular tables with white linen cloth, each seating eight and each served by light-skinned colored women in blue uniforms who tended Marjorie's famous gold flatware and century-old Spode bone china. They were the best servants in Washington, self-effacing and as adept at serving the various dinner courses as they were at passing around the Upmann Cuban cigars and Calvados for the men after dinner.

"Now, dear, I've got you next to the wife of the Free French naval Attaché. I don't think her English is too good, but you do speak French, don't you? I know your languages are sooo good." Henry nodded and smiled again. "Oh, and I've also got you next to Senator Truman's wife. She's a bore, but I know you'll be nice to her, won't you, dear?"

6

They were hours late. The Southern lurched through the maze of tracks, twisted for twenty-five acres around the terminal and threaded into the long, narrow cement boarding platforms. It bumped and clanged to a slow shuddering halt with a loud hissing sound, backed suddenly, then jerked forward again, throwing the jam-packed passengers even closer together.

Gunther stretched as well as he could and lifted his Gladstone suitcase. Through the grimy windows, even more obscured by steam rising from the tracks, he could see masses of people, nearly all in uniform, departing from another train directly across from them. They inched along the platform in a slow continuous stream of Army khakis and Navy whites. He was stiff and cramped from having had to stand all the way from Rocky Mount, North Carolina, and he was feeling contemptuous.

They're so young and soft and naïve, he thought, glancing around at the soldiers and sailors pushing toward the rear of the car and the steep iron steps to the platform. God, and they're supposed to be the great American military. They sang their stupid songs—"Praise the Lord and Pass the Ammunition" and "Mairzey Doats"—and Gunther joined in for hour after hour, pretending to enjoy them, but taking secret pleasure in thinking they had no conception of what they would face. And if their trains were any indication, they would be helplessly inefficient in supplying and transporting their armed forces.

He smiled slightly, stepped down onto the platform, moved with the crowd up the steps to the upper level, then strode leisurely through the open doors into the main waiting room and great concourse. It was massive, one of the largest of its kind anywhere. Barrel-vaulted ceilings rose ninety-five feet above the white marble floors. The room was conceived in the Roman Imperial manner similar to the vast central hall in the Baths of Diocletian; the central pavilion was straight out of Constantine. Across the concourse, visible through five archways constructed of Vermont granite and the colonnaded portals beyond, he could see the immense pearl-white Capitol dome rising over the Hill a few blocks away. Everywhere, crowds of people congregated. They occupied each polished wooden bench. They spilled onto the floors. They sat among mounds of baggage. They stood and milled about, or slowly picked their way across the waiting room. The war had transformed this place into something more than a railroad station; now it, and the people who streamed through it, were part of an endless procession linked inextricably, somehow, to the great release of raw energy that had been set in motion across the American continent only months before with the attack on Pearl

Harbor. Since then 45,000 people poured into Union Station every day, day after day after day without pause or break or regard to time, whether morning or midnight. They were drawn to it, by personal choice or impersonal order. It was as if some gigantic magnet pulled them all toward the nation's capital, pulsing new nerve center of the war. Hour by hour the volume of new arrivals increased. On that sea of similar yet changing faces was stamped the same look of weary stupor.

Gunther maneuvered around the circular information desk to the baggage room, checked his suitcase with a colored porter, and bought a copy of the Sunday, June 21, *Washington Times-Herald* at the nearby newsstand. He scanned the headlines and front-page stories. In Washington, the White House announced Saturday night that Churchill was again in the capital, conferring with Roosevelt about what "will be very naturally the war, the conduct of the war, and the winning of the war." It was not announced how he had arrived, or exactly when or where. In Moscow, Foreign Commissar Molotov told the first wartime session of the Supreme Soviet that the second front was not far off. The Nazis could expect to feel U.S. blows before the end of 1942. In Cairo, dispatches from the front reported that Rommel's Africa Corps had split the British Eighth Army in two and had driven a wedge a hundred miles into Egypt. They were advancing at a rate of forty miles a day and once more threatening the garrison dug in at the Libyan port city of Tobruk. In Detroit, several thousand CIO union factory workers stopped work at the Naval Ordnance. They protested against the hiring there of eight Negroes to operate machines for the war.

Weak fools, Gunther thought. He crumpled the newspaper, threw it into a trash can, and walked through the archway, past the Ionic columns outside into the oppressive humidity of late afternoon in Washington. He had a few hours to kill before the rendezvous.

Nearly ten years had passed since he had been in Washington on that first mission for Röhm. He thought of Röhm again. Then, Röhm was closer than anyone to the Führer. Only he was granted the privilege of addressing Hitler with the familiar *du*. Even Göring, Goebbels, and

Hess were required to speak to him only and always as mein Führer. It was Röhm's Storm Troopers that put Hitler in power. They guaranteed his iron hold. But Röhm had outreached himself: he allowed himself to become careless and too comfortable. He indulged himself once too often.

It was a lesson Gunther would never forget, a mistake he was certain he would never make. He still vividly remembered how he first got the news, that June day when the phone lines were cut in Berlin and Himmler's men carried out their lightning bloody purge of Röhm, terminating him and his Storm Troopers. It was just a year after Gunther had been sent to the United States. His absence from Germany saved his life. That, and something else that only Gunther knew, now that Röhm and his aides were all dead: it was Gunther who took Röhm's personal copy of his famous *Lustknaben*, his list of "pleasure boys," with him when he was sent to the United States. As Gunther well knew when he stole it, that incriminating list would doom him if it fell into Himmler's hands. Its disappearance, too, saved his life. And he did his job well in America, as both Röhm's troopers and Himmler's Gestapo recognized.

Gunther had been hand-picked by Röhm to see that the "brown network" was firmly in place in the United States. Ostensibly, Gunther's role was to coordinate the network of Nazi agents—the diplomats, travel bureau personnel, museum directors, wine merchants, salesmen, journalists, machine shop operators, postal clerks, and others—being disgorged in the 1930s on American shores from virtually every ship sailing from Germany, and most commonly the *Bremen* and the *Europa*. His secret orders had been drafted at the Foreign Ministry in the Munich headquarters of the NSDAP, the National Sozialistische Deutsche Arbeiterpartei, or National Socialist Workers' Party, that directed the chain of command extending down from NSDAP's Foreign Organization Office at Hamburg and through the ranks of the American National Labor Party and various German-American organizations, leagues, and United German Societies then being established throughout the United States. But actually Gunther's role was to see that NSDAP's dreaded and ultra-secret

"Investigation and Adjustment Committee," or Uschla, that worked closely with the Gestapo to carry out the notorious secret tribunals that dispensed swift and ruthless punishment to anyone believed to be a traitor in the movement, was operative in America—and that every member of every Nazi cell was aware Uschla was at work, even though no one knew its members.

What he saw of the United States then as he traveled about New York, Chicago, Milwaukee, St. Louis, and finally Washington, convinced Gunther that Röhm was right in his characterizations of Americans: They seemed incapable of uniting to deal with crisis; their military was almost nonexistent and hopelessly weak; they showed no appreciation for what power could achieve for a country; and it was true what the Führer and Röhm always said—the Jews and Communists were seizing even more power. Franklin D. "Rosenfeld" was only their puppet.

Washington had changed since that time. The trolley tracks and wooden boarding platforms still ran down the center of Pennsylvania Avenue, as Gunther remembered them, but all the old structures that occupied the south side of the street since the Civil War—the saloons, gambling dens, and rooming houses like the one from which Whitman watched Lincoln's body borne to the Capitol in the long funeral procession—had been demolished during the New Deal. They were replaced with huge marble buildings housing the agencies of the greatly expanding federal government. Typically American, Gunther thought, as he walked down the avenue a few blocks away from Union Station. He noticed the grand structures on the south side and the same, small, old, dilapidated ones on the north he had seen before. Overstated and uncompleted. They have no sense of harmony or national planning.

He passed the National Archives and swung by the small storefronts on Seventh Street. His facial muscles moved when he saw a sign, COHEN'S DRY GOODS. Out front, on the sidewalk, a fat woman fanned herself and talked loudly to a small man standing beside her. His pace quickened.

From around the corner on a side street, he heard someone singing in a deep throaty voice, but with words he could not understand. It sounded hauntingly beautiful. He walked a few steps down the street, past a group of Negro youths playing catch, and saw an old colored man, a blind beggar with a tin cup, sitting on a stoop before an old storefront with windows painted blue. They were decorated with crosses, a picture of Jesus, and letters spelling out the words: THE TRUE CHURCH OF JESUS. A dirty gray felt hat was pulled down over his forehead to shield his face from the sun. Gunther could barely make out the beggar's features: mustard-colored skin, a broad flat nose, and a large mouth that showed gaps between the front teeth. But he was singing, mournfully and emotionally, in a way Gunther had never heard. The German stood transfixed. Then he noticed a young black girl standing and looking at him from the corner of an alleyway several feet away. She leaned against the wall of a red brick row house. Her body was half turned toward him. Her dress was short and her blouse opened so he could see her breasts. She stared a moment, then walked slowly toward him, moving her hips.

"Hey, you, blondie," she said in a low voice. "I been lookin' for you. I got a Sunday special today on sucks and fucks. Two bucks a blow, two bucks a throw. You just let Odessa take care of you, you hear? Come on, blondie, just come on."

She turned and strolled off slowly toward the alleyway, the movement of her hips tightening the fabric of her skirt around her buttocks.

Gunther watched, and then walked after her. The sound of the man singing followed him down the alleyway. He could still faintly hear the strains as he entered the small-frame two-story building in the alleyway and moved up the stairs to her room.

He had never had a black woman before and he was curious to see if they were different. Gunther seldom thought of women sexually. He didn't need them; they weren't that important to him. He used women casually, and usually brutally, from time to time, and enjoyed his feeling of total dominance and power over them. But he wasn't obsessed with them the way other men were. He regarded this as another sign of his strength and superiority. It was more complicated than he admitted to himself, though, and it went beyond his first furtive homosexual encounters with Father Schroeder when he was an altar boy, and long before his crisis in the seminary.

Even as a child Gunther was assailed by doubts and feelings of guilt about God. Once, when he was barely more than six, he dropped to his knees as if impelled by a great force. He prayed so intensely that tears came to his eyes. Over and over he said to himself, "If there is a God or if there is a heaven, give me some sign." None came—or none that he could be sure was *the* sign. The same emotions had overwhelmed him several times after.

Gunther was an only child, and he had worshiped his father, a quiet, distant, solemn sort of man who headed a small, financially failing music academy in Dresden. His father encouraged him in his early musical studies and made him believe he had the gift of genius. He had, at least, the gift of perfect pitch. Long before he began to speak, he could pick out on the piano any notes his father hummed or sang; and he could repeat entire chords and bars that he heard coming from their phonograph. God has blessed you, his father would say. He has a calling for you. On the terrible day of his father's funeral, when he watched his fat, emotional mother scream hysterically and try to throw herself on the coffin, beating on the sides and wailing awfully as they began to lower it into the grave, Gunther felt an immense sense of guilt. God was punishing him because he had failed his father and he failed God. He had lost the only secure thing in his life. He blamed his mother for that loss: if she had not incessantly nagged his father to be a better provider for them, pleading with him to give up the academy, telling him over and over in her whining but bullying tone that even a seat in the Dresden Orchestra paid better, he would not have driven himself to physical collapse and final fatal illness. Later, the priests took the place of his father. They, too, encouraged him in his music. Gunther continued to be assailed by doubts about God, complicated immensely by his guilt and his elation over his discovery of his new sexual prowess. Sex was not pleasure for Gunther. It was power. He learned he could control the young men and, finally, some of the older ones around him. He always was the stronger one.

Women did not excite him as much. They were not, in Gunther's mind, worthy of him. They were weak. He was fascinated, though, by this black woman's musky smell and the raw animal feeling she gave off. She was strong.

How dark her nipples were. They were coal black in contrast to her light color elsewhere. He squeezed her breasts so tightly that black-and-blue marks appeared on her cream-colored skin. Then he took her violently from behind on the bed.

She cried out loudly and Gunther grunted hoarsely. He had never experienced anything like it before with a woman. She rose with him, matching him thrust for thrust. She had the knack of contracting rhythmically on his penis in a way that held him, locked, deep inside her, deeper than he had ever been with a man, deeper than he believed it possible to be inside another human being. Gunther tightened his grip on her. He beat on her sides with his fists. She screamed again, but this time with fear as well as pain. Gunther lost himself in her. She was the Black Madonna. Not even Raphael could capture this rapture.

Always before, it was Gunther who coldly controlled the sex act, studying the reactions, priding himself in his power, preening himself for his force and strength, feeling superior to the weaker person he broke beneath him. He seldom had orgasms, and almost never with a woman. But now he let himself go in a way he had not before. For once it was Gunther who lost control. He dimly felt the pressure building powerfully, irrevocably, inside him, and then with a rush, he came. *"Ich komme! Ich komme!"* He shouted aloud. *"Ich komme!"*

Spent, he pulled back. Then he realized what he had done. What he had said.

Odessa was strong-willed and hard, but she had been terrorized. She turned her head around and stared at him in fear. "Who are you, mistuh? Where you from with that talk?"

She quickly bent down, pulled up her dress, and began to button it. Her back was turned toward him when Gunther slipped his watch and fob out of his pocket. The watch was at one end with the T bar for inserting through a button hole at the other. In the middle of the stainless-steel chain was a knot.

He noted the time. Five twenty-three. Then he quickly slipped the chain around Odessa's neck. He gripped the watch and T bar tightly and pulled sharply. The knot caught her Adam's apple.

Odessa tried to scream, but managed only a gurgle. Desperately, she clawed at the tightening strand cutting into her neck and stopping her breath. Her legs thrashed out. She kicked wildly backward. Gunther stood impassively, never loosening his grip on the chain. The gurgling stopped. Odessa's hands flopped to her sides. Her right leg snapped out involuntarily, twitched several times, then stopped. Gunther still held tightly to the chain. Slowly, he mentally counted off five minutes: one and two and three and four and five until he reached three hundred. Then he unwound the chain from Odessa's neck and let her body collapse on the floor. Her head struck the floor with a thump. He put the watch and fob back into his pocket, lifted Odessa onto her bed, noticed she was wearing no panties, and felt a sudden arousal and excitement again. He covered her with the thin torn sheet crumpled at the foot of the bed.

Gunther looked down at her. He experienced a flash of guilt and doubts such as he had not remembered since childhood. If there is a God, he thought, this is what He will punish me for. He braced himself, and quickly suppressed the thoughts. How ridiculous. There is no God. How can I let this get to me? Then, methodically, he wiped everything in sight with his handkerchief, opened the door, glanced into the hall, stepped out, left, and headed back to Union Station to get his bag.

7

"And I suppose you think I'm one of the ones *he* calls a parasite and wants to throw out of town?"

"No, sir, I don't," the general said quietly and coolly, looking straight into the eyes of the pink-faced rotund man in the dark three-piece pin-striped suit, standing with his back to the French doors. The rotund man angrily waved a long Upmann cigar with one hand and swirled his brandy glass in the other. "We can't win the war without you, but I do think the President has a point in asking labor *and* management for a ceiling on wages and a freeze on profits."

"Now let me tell you something, General," the executive said, still in an angry tone. "I didn't come down here to work for a dollar a year to be insulted by someone in uniform who never met a payroll. And I didn't come down here to help the king in the White House seize more power. I came down here to help win the war and save this country from state socialism, and I don't think—"

"Oh, excuse me," Henry said, as he bumped into the heavyset War Production Board executive. "Terribly sorry."

Henry pressed on, threading his way through the dark-paneled library full of men crowded in for their ritual after-dinner cognac and cigars. The polite dinner-conversation tone, set earlier while the women were still present, had vanished, as it always did. The masks were coming off.

He wondered whether it was the additional liquor or the absence of the women that made the difference. No, it was neither. It was the plain raw ambition of so many powerful people trying to impress each other with how important they were. The lack of women and the liquor just brought to the

surface what was already there. It was one of the things about
Washington that fascinated and repelled him. Boston and
New York had as many powerful people—many more, as he
well knew—but they didn't seem to take themselves so
seriously. They weren't as consumed by authority. The
Washington he remembered from his St. Albans days had
been a quiet, almost sleepy Southern town, where everyone
knew everyone else. The war changed that. Everyone, even
the clerks, seemed caught up in the surge of activity. Even the
way they walked was different. Washington had become a
city of swagger. Everyone was infected by an absurd sense of
self-importance. I wonder if it was like this in the Civil War?
Hell, it was probably just the same in Carthage and Rome.

Henry smiled to himself. I'm changing, too, he thought,
and I'm not even sure how.

He glanced around the room. Incredible. They act as though
we don't have a thing to worry about. And the war could
hardly be worse, as he, and nearly all of them, well knew.

They stood in small groups by the bookshelves and before
the thick draperies, drawn tightly now to prevent any strands
of light from escaping into the night outside. With the
Chinese porcelain lamps turned low, the thick cigar smoke
made the air look blue; but even in that dim setting, the faces
of many of the men were visibly flushed from their drinks
and their animated conversation.

Henry continued to circle slowly through the room.

In one corner he heard a farm bloc senator heatedly defend
his vote against repealing agricultural price supports.

"Sir," the senator said, "food will win this war, and it will
be the American farm belt that will have provided that
mighty weapon."

A columnist, openly contemptuous, couldn't resist
taking a dig at the way Congress had just voted itself Civil
Service pensions.

"I suppose, Senator, you also like the way Congress stands
for economy in all other nondefense spending, except of
course for pensions and farm supports."

He overheard a New Dealer talking earnestly about "the
Negro problem." A Labor Department official, equally
officious, said, "We really mean it. They'll lose their

contracts if they don't stop discriminating against Negroes, Jews, and Catholic workers."

There's the New Deal for you, Henry thought. What a pious fraud. It was all political. They didn't really care about the Negroes and Jews and Catholic workers.

A group of lawmakers and diplomats were talking about the President's new anti-inflation program. A slight, sandy-haired British diplomat asked if they thought the country would respond to the appeal for sacrifices.

"Do you really believe the American people will still back the President when he tells them their standard of living will have to be reduced?" he asked, in a faintly condescending tone.

"Yes," a pasty-faced undersecretary said. "Everyone's standard of living except those in the CIO and the AF of L."

"Well," someone replied, "you can't expect miracles, can you?"

"No, and I can't believe Sumner Welles has joined Wallace with that one-world horseshit, either. Even that Republican governor from Minnesota, Stassen, with his 'world legion' of international policemen makes more sense than that."

"At least Stassen's not an isolationist," the British diplomat said. "I gather he's someone to watch in two more years. Is that how you see it?"

Henry moved near them. He edged up to one of the small bars and heard a Commerce Department official denounce attempts to impose controls on all areas of the American economy, while a State Department aide turned to two Army officers in pinks and greens standing nearby.

"That's right," the State Department man said, "the Office of Facts and Figures says seventeen million Americans are against fighting the war all-out, and thirty percent of the population would be in favor of discussing peace terms with the German army if we got rid of Hitler!"

One of the officers said, "Why don't they send Eleanor? She's not on the Office of Civilian Defense anymore. She ought to be able to come to terms with Hitler easily."

Christ, Henry thought savagely as he reached the double library doors, why did I ever come? He quickly slipped through the doors and walked briskly toward the stairway leading upstairs, where the women gathered during the cigars-and-brandy period for the men.

"Elias," he said, turning to Marjorie's butler, "has Miss Aiken come down yet?"

"Why, yes, Mr. Henry, she surely has. She's already gone. That gentleman from the State Department escorted her home."

Henry was strangely upset. "Thank you, Elias, I'll be going now." He took the Panama hat Elias handed him and walked out into the night. It was still humid, still breathtakingly hot.

8

The station was as crowded as when he left. Gunther eased his way through the servicemen toward the baggage room, claim check in hand.

Now he was exultant; his brief moments of remorse and guilt back in the room where he left Odessa had passed. It was only temporary, and when it was over he felt confirmed in his contempt for the Americans. They were so weak. It was going to be so easy. Besides, Negroes needed to be eliminated anyway.

He glanced into the USO servicemen's lounge, a semicircular cavern of marble walls and columns and massive brass lighting fixtures once reserved as the President's reception room and now filled around the clock with young soldiers and sailors. They sat at card tables beside stout matronly hostesses in polka-dot dresses and finger-wave permanents and slumped on the leather couches beside the potted palms, idly turning pages of magazines and smoking one cigarette after another. Gunther smiled. They had no idea what they were facing.

The colored baggage clerk handed him his Gladstone suitcase. This one was black, he noted, the features more Negroid, not like Odessa with her light skin and smooth facial lines. The Americans really were a mongrelized race. You could see it in all of them.

He left the bright lights of the station with its constant droning of conversation, its pungent smells of stale smoke and bodies intermingled, and stepped out into darkened Washington of the wartime blackout.

The sounds of the streets were muffled, the lights in the buildings he passed along Massachusetts Avenue hidden from view by drawn blinds. People were out, but they were shadowy figures in the night, illuminated here and there by an occasional low-beam cast from faint car headlights. All of the headlights were masked with black rubberized tape. On every fourth block Gunther encountered an air-raid warden making his rounds. They had gas masks slung over their shoulders, armbands denoting their mission, and they all wore white steel pot helmets. Typical, Gunther thought. Even in the first war we never used those worthless things—and they paint them white!

Near the corner of Fifteenth Street, just beyond the towering steeples of an old church, he moved past the shuttered, but still guarded, German embassy high on a terrace behind the same low stone wall and narrow roadway that it had occupied since 1894. Not since 1917 had it been closed. Thirty-five years ago, Gunther thought. It won't stay closed long. Maybe they'll say we were the ones responsible for opening it this time. Whatever it is we are supposed to do.

We.

Willi.

Damn. He wondered again if he had been right in suggesting they separate. It made sense to go the last part alone by bus and train. Travel differently, arrive three days apart, then at least one of them would be able to function: that's what they had agreed. But what if something happened to Willi, what if one person wasn't enough? He'd never trusted Willi anyway. There had always been something unreliable about him. Willi could break. He's the kind that could talk. No, they should never have separated. The more he brooded about it, the angrier he became. Damn Willi anyway.

He continued walking briskly through the darkened

streets, turning off Massachusetts and past the broad thoroughfare of Connecticut Avenue toward the old brick row houses of Foggy Bottom near the Potomac grounds. Even in the darkness, the shape of the houses and the setting of the street were familiar: he had seen them often enough in the photos they had studied. In the middle of the block, without breaking stride, he walked confidently up the stone steps leading to the doorway of a three-story structure rising about him in the night. He knocked four times.

The door swung half open. Before him, dimly framed in the darkened hallway, was the face of a small, wizened man with a bulge on the left side of his forehead about the size and shape of an unshelled pecan.

"That which cannot be proved cannot be worth proving," Gunther said, in English, quoting Nietzsche.

"One must have a good memory to be able to keep the promises one makes," the small man replied, also reciting from Nietzsche.

The door opened fully and Gunther entered. Silently, methodically, he inspected each room. He opened all doors, checked every light fixture and the one telephone. Every step of the way he was followed by the small man.

"All right," Gunther finally said, speaking for the first time. "I have not eaten."

"Of course," the small man said. He led the way to the kitchen, opened the door of the Philco refrigerator, took out a bottle of milk, some cold cuts, and Nucoa oleomargarine and put them on the table.

"You like the radio, yes?" the small man said, gesturing to a portable G.E. on the counter. Gunther nodded.

The small man turned on the radio. The sound of a deep, resonant American voice echoed in and out over the airwaves, first faint and then loud: "This is London calling Columbia, New York."

Gunther listened intently as the newscaster reported on an RAF raid over Cologne. As he listened, he thumbed idly through the pages of a *Life* magazine lying on the table. Amazing. They really are incredibly soft. He looked at one ad and smiled. It showed a young woman in a low-cut satin nightgown sitting up in bed with curlers in her hair. "I'm patriotic!" the ad said. "Since rubber and metals are needed to win the war, I roll my curls in Kleenex tissues." Near that ad were others for elastic lace pantie girdles and Betty Lou velour powder puffs.

He turned the page and shook his head. The Americans were simply unbelievable. There, in a double-page layout, complete with artist's sketches, was an article about "the country's biggest school" being conducted by the United States Army. It described an Army facility "that teaches everything from house cleaning to aerodynamics of airships" for which the magazine had helped prepare a training manual—and here published them, sketches and all, for everyone to see! "The manual's official title is *Protective Measures, Individuals and Small Units,*" he read, "which actually means, in nonmilitary language, *How to Avoid Getting Killed in the War.*" He studied the sketches. They dealt with such things as how to guard against booby traps when entering a building, how to camouflage motor vehicles or guns, how to avoid being silhouetted when on patrol. Several of the sketches showed a farm before and after proper camouflage was used.

So, this is what they think a training camp is all about. Again, he shook his head silently in disbelief. Great God, what *naifs.*

The newscast was over. A stupid song began, with a cheery-sounding man singing: *"Have you tri-ed Wheat-ies, they're all wheat with all of the bran . . ."*

Suddenly the sharp sound of a whistle, followed by the tramping of feet and the rat-tat-tat of bursts of machine-gun fire blared out from the radio.

"And now, 'Gangbusters'!" an announcer's voice barked out. "Presenting the case of the heartless harborer who lived by shielding the guilty."

More machine-gun bursts. Again the announcer: " 'Gangbusters'! The only national program to bring you authentic police case histories based on official and federal law-enforcement files. 'Gangbusters'!"

More machine-gun bursts, and the whine of ricocheting bullets. "But first, a word from our sponsor." Bouncy music, then a male voice singing a jingle: *"Pepsi-Cola hits the spot, twelve full ounces that's a lot, twice as much for a nickel too. Pepsi-Cola is the drink for you."*

At first, Gunther was amused. Now his face darkened. "Enough, you fool," he hissed, turning toward the small man obsequiously hovering in the background. "You think I have nothing better to do than sit here listening to that decadent garbage."

"Certainly. Of course," the man said. He blanched and snapped off the radio.

Gunther wolfed his food in silence. Then he pushed back his chair and stood up. "Now. Is everything ready?"

"Of course," the small man repeated. "You will have complete privacy. No one but government girls are living upstairs, and they can enter only by the front. This way, please."

He led Gunther down a back stairway, into an alley, and through the darkness to the rear entrance of a basement apartment in another row house. It stood directly behind the one they had just left. The small man fumbled slightly with the key. Once it turned in the lock, he instantly and silently headed back across the alleyway.

Minutes later Gunther was in bed. As he began to doze, he wondered again about Willi.

part
3
THE
RENDEZVOUS

1

His room was spare and grimy. Its only saving
grace was the view of the James River and Belle Island and
the iron mill, where once there had been a Civil War prison.
Willi had never been in Richmond. All he knew about the
South was from books. American history had been one of
his favorite classes in Detroit, though, and he had been
fascinated by the Civil War. It was romantic: Lee and
Jackson and the great commanders fighting against
overwhelming odds, losing nobly for a real cause. He had
identified with all that, probably because of his father, but
now, like so much else he had seen and done that had
changed him, it seemed foolish, stupid even, worthless. War
was not romantic, dying was not glorious, killing was—well,
yes, he was a killer now. He wondered if his father had felt
the same way.

After all this, I still don't have the faintest idea what he was
really like or what he really felt, he thought bitterly. When he
was lying there in the mud on the western front, dying from a
bayonet wound in the stomach, did he think it had been
worth it? His mother tried to make him think so. She had
become hysterical when she got the news of his father's death
in 1917, and for sixteen days after had traumatized her
four-year-old daughter, Elsa. Even though he was only two at
the time, Willi never forgot the feeling of horror and guilt she
inspired in him then. From then on, and all during his
childhood, his mother incessantly, grimly, worked to keep
alive her husband's memory. She had his Iron Cross
mounted, framed, and hung alongside his picture over
Willi's bed. She read aloud imaginary letters from him to
Elsa and Willi. She invented stories about his mannerisms

111

and family background that in time she came to believe to be true. Even her nervous breakdown, in 1921, when Willi was six, didn't change her behavior; but it did lead to their leaving Germany, with its ravaged economy and desperate hunger and hardships.

His uncle Louie sent for them, so they came to Detroit to share his small attached house on Grant Avenue with his wife and three daughters. Willi loved Detroit. He became an honor student in public school, and a superb athlete who won varsity letters in football and baseball. It was a happy time, and apart from his mother, who remained as miserable as she made everyone else feel, he felt at home with his new family. Then disaster overtook them again. The small foundry that made cast-iron parts for automobiles closed in the depths of the Depression year of 1932, when Willi was seventeen. Uncle Louie lost his job. His mother lost hers as a housekeeper. Willi lost his as a grocery-store delivery boy. Out of that crisis came the decision for the family to separate: Willi's mother, who never adjusted to America and longed for Germany, and who despised Uncle Louie's wife as well, decided to return home, where, she kept insisting, everything was better. Late that year, against all his own wishes, Willi, as much out of guilt and a sense of loyalty to his dead father, accompanied his mother and returned to Germany. Elsa angrily refused, and stayed in Detroit.

So here he was again, he thought, a different person in a different world, heading for what?

He gazed down on the river. An early-morning haze hung over Richmond. Already waves of heat shimmered over the James. Those thick, stirring cloudbanks with odd changing formations on the horizon, tinged with the first faint streaks of pinks and yellows of dawn, had that heavy humid look. They promised another suffocating day. So this is the South, the capital of the Confederacy. There was nothing vaguely romantic about what he saw. If anything, it looked crumbling, sleepy, stagnant.

Willi couldn't shake off a deep sense of apprehension. It wasn't physical fatigue, although he was tired—the crowded trip from Raleigh, where he changed buses again after leaving Gunther in Rocky Mount, had been longer than scheduled and more wearying than he expected. But he arrived last night, as planned. So far so good. Only two days to kill before he rejoined Gunther. He felt, again, a slight tremor at the thought of Gunther and what lay before him. Once more he wondered how he would measure up, how good he really was.

I can't keep thinking this way, he said to himself. I've got to get a grip on myself. He bent and began a brisk round of calisthenics, letting, as always, his body drain away the strains of his mind and release his pent-up emotional tension as he rose up and down and twisted and then pumped off his push-ups from the floor. He finished, his heart beating strongly and regularly, his breath even, but even more restless than before. He stretched again, then strode out of the room, down the stairs, and into the city.

They said the worst thing we can do is sit in a room and wait, he remembered. It had been drummed into them: "Act normal. Behave naturally. Do just what you would do if you were visiting for a few weeks. Eat out. Go to movies. Be seen to enjoy yourselves. The moment you act unnaturally someone will notice and become suspicious. Do not—repeat—do not hide out. People who hide out are conspicuous. Anyone seeming to be hiding out always attracts attention, and that always leads to curiosity, and that leads to police. So always go out and do everything everyone else does."

All right, Willi thought. Besides, I need the exercise. I need more room to think.

He wandered easily through the downtown streets, tourist guidebook in hand, and found himself in Jackson Ward, a rundown area for Negroes. Everything about the South seemed heavy and slow, even the smells were somehow sweet and sickly. It must be the humidity: everything hangs in the air. How could they have ever fought in this weather? It wasn't at all like Detroit, with its fresh breezes always coming off the lake and its acrid odors from blast furnaces and industrial smokestacks constantly mingling with the sounds of the automobile factories on River Rouge.

Now he was moving back into the main area of the city. On East Broad, between North 24th and North 25th, he stopped before St. John's Episcopal Church, with its wooden white clapboard walls and its square steeple. Yes, this is the one, he thought, turning to his guidebook. It didn't seem like much, but then historic places seldom live up to the moments that made them memorable. With a smile, he pushed open the door, went in, and sat in the back pew. He sat a moment, alone in the church, trying to imagine what it was like when Patrick Henry spoke there about liberty or death; but he couldn't. It was just an old church, in a crumbling old Southern city.

He headed out toward East Broad to find his way to the capitol, Jefferson's capitol. Was he the first Virginian to be President? No, of course not. Washington. He remembered that of the, let's see, eight Virginia Presidents of the United States, the last, Wilson, was the one who promised lasting peace after the war. He permitted himself a bitter smile.

Inside the old capitol that Jefferson modeled after a Roman temple in France—Willi was amused at the thought—he joined a tourist group and listened as the middle-aged woman guide with the pinched, hawklike face and gray hair pulled back in a bun told them in a flat monotone of a Southern drawl that it was in this chamber that Aaron Burr had been tried for treason.

Willi wondered who would be thought the traitor and who the patriot this time.

2

In the days when carriages rattled through cobblestone streets from the Capitol to the mansions housing the powerful and the infamous public figures who made Washington their temporary or permanent home, the Grants, the Shermans, the Douglases, and the "Boss" Shepherds alike, the avenue leading to Mount Vernon

Square was a pleasant thoroughfare of handsome stone buildings and large red brick structures with wide porches overlooking terraced lawns and graceful old Dutch elms. The buildings and the trees remained, but the look had long since changed from gentility to the hard signs of poverty. Now the walls of the buildings were marked with chalk, the sidewalks bore the obscene scrawls that appeared overnight and became as permanent fixtures of the neighborhood as the black iron rails which stood rigidly in place before each house. The streets were filled with the sort of self-perpetuating debris and litter that no amount of sanitation-department effort could entirely sweep away for long, and the grandest of the structures, the place where white marble columns still stood solidly out front, had been transformed into the Second Precinct Headquarters of the District of Columbia Police Department.

The boundaries of the Second Precinct, branching out east and west of Seventh Street from the square, encompassed barely more than a mile; but within that geographical area lay what was, and long had been, the area of Washington that contained the highest rate of violent crimes. It also was the center for those crimes of chance and vice in which the only violence involved the expenditure of physical energy and passion along with the quick exchange of large sums of cash. The Second Precinct was entirely colored, but much of its clientele was white.

Detective Sergeant Leon Thomas moved slowly toward the large room with its rows of straight hard wooden benches for the early-morning ritual lineup.

It was a dingy place, as befit the role it now played in that area of Washington, but he paid it no attention. Everything about it had become second nature to him.

He picked his way through the crowd of Negroes waiting to be booked and then locked up in the cell block at the rear of the old building, barely noticing the familiar sights that varied hardly at all from morning to morning after the steady stream of police night work flowed to a trickle and the daily process began anew. In front of a partition where a desk sergeant entered names in a log, or blotter, one old man had passed out on the floor. Another urinated nearby. Off to the side, a young Negro was shouting "I got my rights," as he was dragged, by the shirt, and pulled back toward the cell block. Another, dressed in dirty tan slacks, Army combat boots, and a green sport shirt, was railing loudly, to no one and everyone, in a voice that boomed out over and yet intermingled with the constant chatter and sputter of the police radio broadcasting reports of crimes throughout the city: "Poor nigger, out there workin', tryin' to earn a living. Police go out, shoot 'em down. Bam! Justi-fiable homicide. Nigger! Put yo' hands up on the wall. Turn round. Shoot 'em in the back. Bam! Justi-fiable homicide."

Thomas brushed past wearily and moved into the lineup room, its air stale as always with the smell of tobacco and urine, its once gleaming white walls faded into nondescript drab gray, and took his place in the third row reserved for colored policemen. The whites always occupied the first two rows. Talk about rights, he thought, that poor dumb nigger doesn't even know how bad it really is.

As soon as the roll call was completed, he eased his way up from the bench, with his deceptively slow manner, and moved without apparent intent toward the rear of the big room. He approached a small white man with heavy eyelids, a flat nose, thin sandy hair no longer yellow and not quite fully gray, who wore the same sort of blue coat-sweater as the cops. He slouched in the corner by the wall.

"Mr. Nelson," Thomas said softly. "Mr. Nelson, can we take a walk?"

Nelson looked pained.

"Whattabout," he grumped, looking sullenly up at Thomas. "What's on your mind?"

"It'll only take a minute," Thomas said. He began to reach gently for Nelson's elbow to nudge him along, thought better of it, and withdrew his hand. Nelson hadn't noticed.

"A good story, Mr. Nelson, a real good story. That's what it's about. That's why I called you, and just you. A damn good story. Maybe even a front-page story."

Nelson cocked his head, and rose up slightly from his habitual slouch. He was intrigued, but did not want to show it. After thirty years of being the police reporter for the *Washington Post*, he had assumed the jaundiced manner and

even the appearance of the cops he covered. He even thinks
more like the white cops than the white cops themselves,
Thomas believed.

"Look, Thomas," he said, in an openly condescending
tone while studying the detective through his pale blue
washed-out eyes. "My time's valuable. I've got a million
things to do, and I can't crap about with maybes. If you got
something, it better be Goddamned good. You get me?"

Thomas was respectful and patient. He nodded solemnly.
"Oh, I understand, Mr. Nelson. I understand, indeed. I
would not waste your time, believe me. Just hear me out.
Hear me out."

He was speaking so softly Nelson had to lean forward to
pick up his words. As he spoke, he sidled along the wall
farther away from the other policemen. Nelson followed.
Thomas turned to face him. Nelson instantly adopted his
usual all-right-but-make-it-quick attitude.

"You read the blotter, Mr. Nelson," Thomas said slowly,
"you hear the talk. You know about these colored deaths.
Seven now, all shot in the head."

Nelson interrupted him. "Shit, Thomas. So what? Is that
your great story? You got me over here for this? Jeesus
Kee-rist! I couldn't get that on Page B-19. What's the matter
with you, don't you know better than that? We get colored
homicides every day in this fucking city. So what makes this
any different?"

"I realize all that, Mr. Nelson," Thomas said, still speaking
in the same slow, respectful, understanding manner,
although it was becoming more difficult to stay calm. "The
difference is Seventh Street. Go out on Seventh Street
tonight. You'll see what I mean."

Nelson was confused, and then angry. "I don't know what
the hell you're talkin' about," he said sharply.

"What I mean, Mr. Nelson, is there's no one on the streets
at night anymore. And I'm not talking about the blackout,
either. This is summer, Mr. Nelson. It's hotter than the blue
blazes of hell, so hot you die if you stay indoors, and yet no
one's on the streets now. And it's all been since this business
began. The colored folks are scared to death, Mr. Nelson.
That's why they're not on the streets."

Thomas noticed Nelson had stopped fidgeting. He bent down, lowered his voice even more, and said, "You remember the summer of 1919, don't you, Mr. Nelson? I believe you were here then."

Nelson nodded, all attention now. That had been the one night he would never want to repeat, a night of terror without parallel in Washington's history, when thousands of whites and Negroes fought a pitched battle with guns, knives, and clubs, when blood flowed through the streets, when mobs of whites ran down and attacked every Negro in sight with cries of "There he goes!" when colored men and women were pulled from the backs of trolley cars and left beaten into bloody pulps on the ground in sight of the White House and Capitol buildings, when Negroes retaliated in kind by firing point-blank into the mobs from rooftops and shuttered windows and swept the streets of any whites they encountered, when hospital staffs desperately worked until dawn treating wounded patients, when even the military forces Wilson ordered into action failed to stop the constant clanging of ambulance gongs and the rattle of shots in the hot summer night. Oh, yes, he remembered. Even now, nearly a quarter of a century later, it had been the worst story he ever covered.

"You remember what happened then? And you remember how it started, and where? I'm telling you, Mr. Nelson . . ." He paused and shook his head gravely. "I'm telling you, it's building up for another explosion. I have never seen these people more tense and more afraid. There's a lot of talk going around, a lot of talk about the white people deliberately murdering innocent colored folk—and you know what that can lead to. You saw it before."

He was almost whispering now.

"All I'm saying, Mr. Nelson, is go out tonight on Seventh Street and see for yourself. See if you don't think *that's* a story. No one has even written a line about these murders yet, and what they're doing to the people. You would be the first. It's all yours, Mr. Nelson."

Nelson backed away, looking scornful as usual.

"Look, Thomas," he said with a small, deprecating wave of his hand. "Maybe it's a story, maybe not. Maybe I'm

118

interested, maybe not. Maybe I even go to Seventh Street tonight to see what the hell you're talkin' about, and maybe I don't. But I want you to know a couple of things. First, my desk doesn't give two shits for these colored shootings. They're looking for news, and news ain't about nobodies, it's about somebodies. Second, those people don't read our paper, so why *should* my desk give two shits?"

He drew up himself to his full 5 feet 6 inches, and said, "Finally, Thomas, there's a war going on, and my desk is a helluva lot more interested in that than any of this other chickenshit Mickey Mouse. But, like I said, maybe I'll look into it."

With that, Nelson turned and walked away.

Thomas stood by the wall, his face still outwardly calm, drew in a deep breath, and held it as he so often did to maintain his composure.

"Hey, Thomas, telephone!" Patrolman Lewis stuck his head inside the doorway and shouted at the detective in the back.

Thomas sighed inaudibly, then strolled toward his cubicle. Lewis had put the receiver down on his desk. He picked up the receiver and spoke quietly and directly into the mouthpiece, holding both in one huge hand: "Thomas here."

It was an upset, near hysterical, Mama Nellie calling about Odessa.

"She in trouble?" Thomas asked.

"She dead," Mama answered.

Thomas listened carefully, displaying no tonal emotion, although a small tic began to twitch in his upper right eyelid. He put a finger of his free hand on the tic to try to stop the flutter, but without success, all the while continuing to murmur into the receiver, "Yes ... Quiet, now ... Be calm ... Just tell me what you know ... Yes ... no ... Don't touch anything ... Don't move until I get there." Then silence. Again, he spoke softly, "Hmmm. Remember. Don't touch anything and don't say anything to anyone. That's right. Yes. I'll be right there. Of course. Right away."

He hung up, reached for his straw hat, the one with the blue band, and told the desk sergeant he would return shortly. Outside the precinct he walked to the cab station.

Before the white driver could tell him not to, he got in the back seat.

"Howard Theater," he said, as, to avoid trouble, he flashed his police badge. "Let's go!"

The taxicab pulled away.

Thomas was too numb with emotional fatigue built up over the past weeks to experience anger. Sweet Jesus, when's it gonna stop? he thought, as the cab sped back into the colored section. He directed the driver to turn on the side street and stop before a storefront church alongside an alleyway. He got out of the cab, moved quickly down the narrow alleyway to the two-story frame building, and climbed the stairs to Odessa's apartment.

Mama Nellie stood by the door, tears glistening on her dark face.

"Oh my, oh my," she moaned, rocking back and forth on her feet, clasping and unclasping her hands, as she saw Thomas. "Oh, my!" she called out. She began to sob loudly.

Thomas reached out, wrapped his arms around her, and held her tightly and silently for a moment. He gently moved her toward the open door and eased her into the dingy room.

He pulled back the sheet and stared down at Odessa's face, puffy now, with a bluish tint showing through the smooth, light brown skin. An expression of terror was locked forever into place.

Mama began to sob again, softly at first, then louder, as she pressed her hands against her face. She looked away from the bed. "Oh, my! Oh, my! Oh, Jesus, Lord!"

Thomas pulled the sheet down the entire length of her body and let it fall to the floor at the end of the bed. He scanned Odessa. There was no wound visible. No gunshot, no knife puncture, not even any blood, nothing but black-and-blue marks on her breasts and sides. Gently, he lifted the deadweight body and turned it over. An arm flopped onto the side of the bed, the fingers touching the floor. Still no wound, no sign of blood. He returned the body faceup, and placed the dangling arm back over her chest.

It was only when he knelt beside the body to sniff at the open mouth for poison that Thomas noticed the necklace of coagulated red beads rashed around her neck.

Thomas got back up with a barely audible sigh. He covered Odessa and turned to Mama Nellie.

"Mama," he said very slowly, very softly. "Now listen to me, Mama. Listen to me carefully. Pay attention. I want to ask you some questions."

He drew his small green spiral notebook from his pocket, took out a pencil, and began his police catechism:

"Why did you come here?"

"Was the door locked or open?"

"Was the light on or off?"

"Where was Odessa?"

"Was she in the same spot?"

"Did she look the same?"

"Did you touch anything?"

"Did you speak to anyone else?"

Mama Nellie answered all his questions. Odessa hadn't shown up for their regular morning coffee and conversation at the gill joint. She thought she might be sick. She tried to call her, but there was no answer. She tried several times and then walked over. No, she came alone. The door was locked. She knocked and knocked, and then opened it herself. She had a key. The light was off. She turned it on. Odessa looked just the same, just the way she looks now, just lying there. Her voice broke, and she started to sob. No, she hadn't touched anything, she hadn't talked to anyone else. She called him immediately.

"Thomas, aren't you going to call the police?" she said suddenly and angrily. Then, when she realized what she had said, she began to giggle hysterically.

"All right, now, Mama. All right."

Thomas again reached out and took her in his arms. "Listen, now. I want you to put out the word. Can you put out the word, Mama?"

"Poor baby," Mama cried, "poor baby."

"Can you put out the word, Mama? It's important. I want anybody—you understand?—anybody who saw her come in here yesterday, anybody who saw anything. You understand?"

Mama nodded slightly.

"All right now, Mama. Here ..." He stepped back and

scribbled some numbers in his notebook, tore out a page, and handed it to her. "You call me if you hear anything." He turned aside and started to pick up the phone on the small nightstand by the bed, then cursed sharply and kicked the leg of the table violently.

"What's the matter?" Mama, startled and frightened, asked.

"Nothing," Thomas said shortly.

Thomas had lied. Much was the matter. Once again, he felt a flash of uncontrollable rage as he cursed to himself at the unfairness of the system in which he was forced to work.

There would be no fingerprint dusting here, no forensic analysis, nothing. The District of Columbia Police Department, as the orphan of the federal government, had to rely on the FBI for all its crime-laboratory work; and the D.C. Police Department never bothered the FBI with colored murders unless the victim was a prominent white killed by a Negro. They certainly never bothered themselves with the murders of colored prostitutes off Seventh Street.

3

Johann Brink reached to pull the thin cord signaling the trolley conductor that he wanted off at the next stop, stood up among the white passengers filling the front of the streetcar, and headed toward the door.

Washington's racial segregation amused Brink. Back home, in Pretoria, where the British were always striking poses about humanitarianism, Negroes were treated far less well than here. But Brink didn't hate the Negroes. He hated the British.

As he stepped down from the trolley onto the wooden platform in the center of Pennsylvania Avenue, he casually but carefully scanned the roadway as if to avoid passing cars.

The same blue Plymouth with two passengers that had been parked a block away from his house near the legation had eased to a stop on the curb lane down the street. He smiled to himself, then jauntily sauntered across the avenue, and began to stroll purposefully among the procession of thick lines of pedestrians, most of them in uniform, and most of them young, that filled the sidewalks of downtown Washington in a steady stream. It was already too damned hot and too damned humid, more like Durban than Pretoria, and it's only ten o'clock in the morning, he thought. What in hell is it going to be like in July and August? No wonder they made Washington a hardship post for diplomats; it felt more like a swamp than a civilized capital.

Brink hadn't known what to expect when he was assigned to Washington, but his posting six months ago came at a perfect time: there were now 200,000 of his countrymen in uniform, the majority English-speaking, but a fair number spoke only Afrikaans, which was why he was chosen for his job at the Legation of the Union of South Africa in the American capital.

He turned down F Street, and moved with the crowds past the small stores that formed the center of the city's premium shopping area. All were located within a few blocks of the White House and surrounded by the massive white marble government buildings that overflowed with tens of thousands of new personnel because of the war. When he came to Harris & Ewing, with its carved inscription over the door, THE PHOTOGRAPHERS OF THE PRESIDENTS, he stopped and glanced in the window. There, mounted on easels, were a Brady portrait of a brooding Lincoln alongside one of a solemn and cold-looking Wilson and a jaunty one of Roosevelt. The three war Presidents, all photographed at Harris & Ewing. Brink studied the portraits briefly: Lincoln's, by far, was the most interesting, all lean long lines and mournful dark eyes staring out of the pockmarked, bearded face. Wilson looked gray and prissy, more like a dour minister than a President, and Roosevelt's picture gave off a feeling of avuncular softness.

None of them looks like a military commander, Brink reflected. Then he turned and walked inside.

"May I help you?" asked the store manager from behind a glass counter of photographic equipment.

"Why, yes," Brink answered as he handed over a roll of 120 film. "I'd like these developed. And two prints of each, please."

"Any particular size?"

"Five by seven."

"Yes, sir. They should be ready on Wednesday."

"Thank you so much," Brink said, sounding to the manager as if he were British, but somehow not quite.

He pocketed the receipt for his film, strolled to the door, opened it, glanced easily around while mopping his forehead with a handkerchief, stepped out into the crowds, and walked away.

Diagonally across the street, standing in another doorway and looking at merchandise displayed in the window, was one of the two men in the Plymouth that had followed Brink from his rooming house. He waited a minute until Brink was out of sight in the crowd, then crossed the street and went inside Harris & Ewing.

"Yes, sir, what can I do for you?" the manager asked.

"This is official business," the man said crisply. He displayed credentials that identified him as James E. Morrison of the Federal Bureau of Investigation. "That customer who just came in here, the thin man in the light brown suit and tan straw hat."

"Yes?"

"We want duplicates of whatever photographs you're going to print for him. Without him knowing, of course." Morrison spoke pleasantly but in a businesslike tone. "We also want to know if he comes in here again with more films or negatives. Call at this number." He handed over his card containing office and home phone numbers.

"Can I ask what—"

"No," Morrison interrupted, politely but firmly. "This is a government matter, and it must be kept confidential."

"Of course," the manager said, slightly flustered. "I told him his photos—he wanted us to make five-by-sevens—would be ready Wednesday. Do you—"

"Fine," Morrison interrupted again. "Do that, but have

ours by this time tomorrow. And call us before that to let us know they're ready."

He turned away from the counter. "Thanks for your cooperation," he said, and left.

The manager immediately called his darkroom assistant to tend the counter while he, without explanation, rushed off to begin developing and printing the roll of 120s.

He put on his rubber apron, souped the first sheet, and watched the black-and-white images grow and harden. It was a photo of men and women seated around a table. Looks like a party, he thought. He developed another. It was the same party. So was the next, and the next. He dried them all and took them out into the natural light at the rear of the store, away from the front windows, and examined them carefully. Just men and women at tables, and obviously all at the same place, but nothing that seemed at all unusual. He held them up again to the light and studied them more closely. Nothing. He took up a magnifying glass from a desk in the back and bent over the pictures, gazing at them intently one by one. He tried to make out a sign or symbol in the background, even a matchbook on a table, to see if he could tell where the people were when the pictures had been taken. Still, nothing but what he had seen before: men and women at tables, well dressed, with drinks, at a party.

Damned if I get it, he thought. Who are they? Draft-dodgers, spies, what?

He returned to the darkroom and began printing copies. He made four sets of five-by-seven glossy photographs—two for the customer, one for the FBI, and one for himself.

4

Henry walked down the fifth-floor corridor toward the Pennsylvania Avenue side, his heels clicking rhythmically on the terrazzo, the sound echoing off the Mankato stone walls. He glanced at the slip of paper in his hand, and noted each of the aluminum-framed blue signs that identified which official occupied what office. As he approached 5633, the displays mounted in the glass cases along the walls became larger and more assertive: Dillinger's revolver. Pretty Boy Floyd's tommy gun. A huge blow-up of Bruno Hauptmann's fingerprints next to a photo of a blindfolded Hauptmann in the electric chair. An entire exhibit of page-one newspaper headlines and pictures chronicling Lepke's surrender. All with the Director, of course. He doesn't hide *his* under a bushel, Henry thought maliciously. What a difference a few hundred yards makes. On his side of the fifth floor, along Constitution Avenue and the black-walnut suites surrounding the Attorney General's wide, bright corner office, it was all WPA art deco murals: The Great Codifiers of Law. Man, Woman, Child, and Justice. Frescoes about tenements and sweatshops and achieving justice in the slums. Mounted plaques celebrating public service. Over here, it was as if you stepped into Pharaoh's Land. Everything glorifies the Director and his successes in bringing to justice the nation's most wanted criminals. Well, that fits. The Justice Department hasn't even been housed in this great mausoleum for eight years yet, and already he's swallowing it up. His Bureau is beginning to run the whole department. What an operation. He's actually got people believing *he's* the one who's saving the country.

When he came to an office near the Director's huge reception room, which contained even more grandiose wall displays of the Bureau at work, he stopped by the closed door. The sign identified it: THE OFFICE OF THE DEPUTY ASSISTANT TO THE DIRECTOR. Without knocking, he turned the aluminum doorknob and entered.

Two women at adjoining desks looked up from their Remingtons.

"Hullo, Magnolia," Henry said in his clipped, breezy manner. His dark eyes sparkled. "I know the South has risen, but does the government still stand? Or is that Top Secret around here, too?"

The younger woman, her dark hair swept back and curled at the ends, her eyebrows freshly plucked into two slim black curving lines that accentuated her high forehead and angular cheekbones, was standing before four stacks of correspondence arranged in neat piles at the end of her desk, as she peered at him over her steno pad.

"Well, if it isn't Boston," she said, with a slight, slow nod of recognition. A faint flush briefly colored her face. She looked solemn, but the smile in her greenish-blue eyes gave her away. They really are extraordinary, Henry thought, looking at her: they change color as she speaks. "Why you know, Lieutenant, we government girls wouldn't know anything about secrets, would we, Thelma?" She turned toward the older woman at the other desk, and struck a pose as everybody's helpless female office worker. "We leave all that to you brave boys, just the way we expect you, especially you Yankees"—she drew out the word, in an exaggerated drawl—"to win the war for us. Isn't that right, Thelma?

"Oh, Thelma, this is Lieutenant Henry Eaton from Boston. He knows everybody. Lieutenant, Thelma Ryan. She's from Boston, too, aren't you? But do the Eatons speak to the Ryans, Lieutenant, or aren't you allowed to say? I've always wondered, just what is proper in that kind of situation? What *do* they teach you all up there?"

Henry laughed. He was delighted.

"How do you do, Miss Ryan," he said.

"Pleased to meet you," she replied in a broad Back Bay accent.

"You see, Miss Aiken, we actually know how to speak to

each other in Boston—and we can even understand each other, too."

He laughed again, the fine lines around his eyes crinkling into a web. His smile gave his mouth a crooked, yet somehow battered look. He stepped forward lightly, moving, as Constance noticed, with easy assurance and just the trace of a swagger. When he smiled, as he was now, his whole face was wreathed in criss-crossing lines and his dark eyes had a little boy's mischievous glint. He wasn't really handsome, certainly not in the Arrow-Collar-Man kind of look, Constance thought. Just as well. Her taste ran more to charming bastard Humphrey Bogart types than to Tyrone Power ones.

"And what, may I ask, do we owe the honor of your presence—or did you just get lost and stumble in? We are good at giving directions, aren't we, Thelma?"

Constance tried to maintain a cool and quizzical expression, and almost succeeded. Her heart beat faster, though, and she felt a catch in her throat. She didn't think he could tell.

"Tell you the truth, Miss Aiken, I did get lost. Lost last night at dinner, that is. I've been trying to find my way ever since. Now that I've finally tracked you down, I thought you might help me. Now. Over lunch. Real impromptu, spur-of-the-moment stuff, you know. And since we both work for the government, and both work in the same building, at least let me try to convince you that all Yankees aren't as bad as you think. Will you let me plead my poor personal case? And, besides, Scarlett"—and Henry bowed gravely—"this time we're on the same side so it's really all right for us to be seen together. Even *he* won't mind." He gestured toward an adjoining office.

Constance was amused, and she was more interested—intrigued, really—about Henry than he possibly could have suspected. She'd thought about him after the party, and again this morning while rushing to catch the 7:15 Federal Triangle bus from the Meridian Hill Apartments to her office at FBI headquarters in the Justice Department. I suppose I was too hard on him, she thought, even if he did have it coming to him. He's certainly far more interesting than the men she'd met recently. And there was something about him that was, well, just *different*. She wanted to know more.

When she got to the office, she checked the Bureau files. What she discovered heightened her curiosity. Lieutenant Henry Wyatt Eaton was assigned to the Office of Naval Intelligence. She was also fascinated to learn that Lieutenant Eaton was much more than a Naval Intelligence aide; it seemed he was Attorney General Biddle's fair-haired boy and his ONI job was a cover for something so sensitive and secret that even *they* didn't have all the information about it, a fact that incensed the Director, as his repeated handwritten marginal notes in the files clearly indicated. "What do we know about this? Who authorized? Who in WH? Chief? Pursue," read one of the Director's first marginal comments in the files. It was written in that familiar, precise, almost prissy, school-masterish hand that carried such power, if not terror, throughout the Bureau. Other comments became increasingly sharp and frustrated as he inked in his terse commands. "I am not pleased with performance on this," he wrote, on one classified file. "Report progress immediately." Still, he was obviously dissatisfied as succeeding reports came over his desk. "I am amazed at ineptitude this matter. This involves highest national security priority. Repeat. Highest! Report personally immediately."

Constance reflected none of this knowledge. "Do other men in Boston try to act like Clark Gable, Thelma?" she asked, as if suddenly concerned. She stood up from her desk, began sweeping the papers into the top drawer, and without giving the older woman a chance to respond, continued speaking. "Why, yes, Lieutenant," she said while locking the drawer and then stepping around the desk, "they still do let us eat lunch here. Sometimes, anyway."

Her eyes became a more vivid shade of green as she smiled. "I'll be ready in a jiffy," she said.

Constance was unusually conscious of how she looked as she disappeared out the door and walked to the ladies' room. Damn, I wish I'd had a chance to put on something nice, she thought. She looked at herself in the mirror, put on fresh lipstick, smoothed her dress, bent down and looked back to see that the seams in her stockings were straight. Satisfied, she went back to her office.

"All right, Rhett, carry me off," she said, beckoning grandly to Henry. She looked at Thelma, said "Thanks," and turned toward the door, leaving Henry to follow.

"Have fun," Thelma called.

"Let's walk," Henry said as he caught up to her.

They moved down the corridor, past the elevator toward the stairway. As they passed the reception room next door, Constance whispered, "The Director."

"I know," Henry said dryly.

He knew all too much about John Edgar Hoover and his Federal Bureau of Investigation, and the more he knew, the more he disliked. Henry had been an exceptionally good young lawyer at Sullivan & Cromwell, even if he found the work boring. For all his distaste for convention and proper form he had an innate sense of the rightness of certain things. He was anything but a self-promoter by nature, instinctively wary of anything that smacked of self-aggrandizement. His natural inclination was just the opposite: he took pleasure in deflating pomposity and playing down his own achievements. Besides, too much authority offended him; and Hoover and his FBI had elevated self-promotion and authority to an art. In the eighteen years since Coolidge had appointed him Director at the age of twenty-nine, Hoover had fashioned the greatest propaganda machine in the history of the United States. Every child was indoctrinated into the glories of the G-man, in peace and war. They sent away for their little Junior G-man badges and practiced taking fingerprints with white flour, studying them with their magnifying glasses after listening to "Gangbusters" on the radio. They thrilled to the exploits of the G-men and the Director in the movies, on the comic pages in the popular strip *War on Crime*, in the breathless articles that poured out year after year in the papers and magazines. Every paper, and just about every congressman, had become part of the national FBI cheering squad. Even before Pearl Harbor, Hoover was regarded as a little god. He was the tireless, ever-vigilant, incorruptible chief Gangbuster, the arch foe of the gangsters, a name whose very mention supposedly sent ripples of terror through the ranks of the criminals, great or small. With the coming of the war and the support of his growing army of public admirers, his Bureau had assumed the status of Protector of the American Dream and Safeguarder of the American Security. It was far more popular, and in many respects far more powerful, than the American armed forces, which still were thought of as being a last refuge for people who couldn't make it elsewhere. And everyone understood there was no real career, and no future, in the military.

Henry knew that much of the Bureau's reputation, for all its genuine successes, was undeserved. He also knew how, and at what price, some of its successes had been achieved. He knew all about Hoover's famous files, his network of paid informers, and what uses, especially in Congress and throughout the government, he made of the fruits of electronic surveillance. He remembered the famous *Harvard Law Review* article Brandeis had written back in the nineties on "The Right to Privacy." It dealt with Brandeis's concerns about excesses of the press intruding into people's private lives. And Henry recalled how Hoover had written in the same Harvard law journal, a year or so ago, that while wiretapping "may not be illegal, I think it is unethical"—and he knew what a fraud that was. Hoover and his agents had been vigorously tapping phones and electronically bugging offices and personal quarters since the Germans invaded Poland in September of 1939. Henry knew that in May of 1940, the same year Hoover publicly proclaimed wiretapping "unethical," the President had secretly given Hoover virtual carte blanche authority "in such cases as you may approve" to use wiretaps to combat "fifth column" activities. "It is too late to do anything about it after sabotage, assassination and 'fifth column' activities are completed," the President had written—and Henry knew firsthand from his own intelligence work how aggressively Hoover had acted on that mandate "to authorize the necessary investigating agents that they are at liberty to secure information by listening devices directed to the conversations or other communications of persons suspected of subversive activities against the Government of the United States, including suspected spies." He also knew that Hoover was bugging and tapping many more Americans than those suspected of being spies. He had personally heard his own boss, Attorney General Biddle, tell of the time Hoover had been called on the carpet in the Oval Office before the President and the Attorney General. Hoover's agents had been caught installing a tap on the West Coast longshore union leader, Harry Bridges. Biddle, with faint but clear disapproval, told Henry how delighted the President had been as he listened to Hoover's admission; and then, flashing that famous big grin, had exploded, "By God, Ed-gar, that's the first time you've been caught with your pants down!" As the FBI Director left their private White House session, he received a sound, vigorous, hearty, good-fellow presidential slap on the back.

Well, Henry thought, you can't say he doesn't have the highest support. He wondered if the President would back *them* as fully and aggressively as he did Hoover and his Bureau. He wondered, too, what Brandeis—or Holmes for that matter—both of whom he had come to hold in uncharacteristic reverence, would think about the rights of privacy if they were around to see how this government agency was performing. But aren't I doing some of the same things? he suddenly thought, and not for the first time. And are we really different from Hoover? What was it Lincoln had said in the Civil War? Oh, yeah, "Must a government of necessity be too strong for the liberties of its people, or too weak to maintain its own existence?" Well, that's still the dilemma, and we *are* at war—and if that's not a "clear and present danger," as Holmes said in the last war, then what the hell is?

Christ, maybe Hoover's right. If *we're* justified, then why isn't *he?* It was Goddamned confusing, and he wanted to put the thoughts out of mind.

"How does Hoover like Southern girls, or don't you deal with him directly?" Henry asked Constance lightly, in a teasing fashion. They were moving quickly down the Justice Department steps to the first-floor exit.

"I deal mostly with his deputy," Constance said. "And *he* appreciates Southern women, or so I've heard." She laughed.

I'll bet, Henry thought.

"Okay, Scarlett, here we are."

They walked across the circular lobby with its bas-relief panels representing the history of law and through the heavy, large solid-aluminum doors with black surface designs of lions and heads of wheat. "Tell me," Henry said, as he glanced at the grillwork on the doors, "I understand what the lions stand for—real strong lords of the jungle. Aawaah!"—he struck his chest Tarzan-style—"but for Christ's sake, Lady Jane, what's the wheat got to do with it?"

Constance glided out into the sunshine and humidity and without turning her head or missing a beat said, in half-pitying tone, "Why, fertility, of course. Or is that word banned in Boston, too?"

Henry roared. He knew then that he liked her. As she walked ahead of him, her hips swaying faintly but enough to send the linen rippling softly across her rear, he stared as the bright sunshine shone through the dress. It highlighted the lines of her figure. She looked even softer and more appealing than before. Good legs and one helluva arse, he thought, smiling to himself. He imagined what she looked like without the dress, and again smiled at the thought.

They hailed a cab. "Harvey's," Henry said, as they got inside.

The taxi moved into the heavy traffic running alongside the clanging, sputtering trolley cars on the Pennsylvania Avenue tracks. It headed toward the Treasury Department and White House shimmering in the haze and heat of noonday Washington. The sidewalks were thick with pedestrians. Henry noticed that even the heavy air of the heat wave, that made you gasp the moment you stepped outdoors, failed to slow down those surging lines of people. He felt reassured when he looked at the young servicemen and women, and their Washington government-worker counterparts, moving along so aggressively. There's strength and energy there, all right, he thought, with a surge of pride. Maybe we're not as bad off as I think.

Aloud, he said, "God, this heat must be the Germans' secret weapon. How in the hell can people keep going in this weather? Oh, but your side knows about fighting in the heat, I suppose."

"A little," Constance said. "At least they thought they did."

She smiled, more rueful now, but still dazzling. "What a waste that was. You have to give us credit, Mr. Eaton of Boston. When it comes to conceit and one-hundred-proof arrogant stupidity, no one can top a Southerner. And ah speak from experience, suh." She was mocking herself again, and him at the same time. "After all, ah'm from Charleston, and we fired the first shots, you know."

Their cab stopped for a light at Thirteenth Street. "Have you seen that yet?" Constance asked, pointing to the Warner Theater marquee spelling out the title of the new film that had just opened, YANKEE DOODLE DANDY STARRING JIMMY CAGNEY. A sign in front of the theater announced that part of the proceeds were going for war bonds.

"No," Henry said, "but I did see *This Gun for Hire* when it opened at Loew's a couple of weeks ago. That Veronica Lake's terrific."

Constance ducked her head to her side, shook it until her hair hung down by her shoulder, pursed her lips and looked pouty, then lisped, in low throaty tones, in imitation of the actress, "I knew you'd like blondes who can't see 'cause their hair keeps covering their eyes." She straightened. "I hear *he's* terrific," she said, referring to the new star, Alan Ladd. "Those blue-eyed blond American males are just my type, honey."

They laughed, then fell silent as the taxi swung around the White House fence facing the Ellipse. As always now it was ringed with soldiers, and as always the sight made the war seem real when so often it seemed so far away.

"Do you know Washington well?" Henry asked a moment later.

"Yes," she said, more seriously now, turning to look straight at him, dropping the sarcastic thrusts and flippant tone they both had indulged in. "I used to visit here often before college. My uncle and my grandfather were senators. I come from one of those dreadful Southern families where everyone, it seems, at one time or another served in Washington for generation after generation."

She paused, her tone lightened, and she picked up the

Southern burlesque again. "Befo' de wah, naturally, that is, and ah don't mean the World War, suh."

Their taxi pulled up to Harvey's, adjoining the Mayflower.

"Okay, Constance Aiken, the order here is Harvey's Original Crab Imperial," Henry said, briskly taking her arm as they entered the century-old restaurant. "Best in town."

George nodded in recognition. "This way, Lieutenant Eaton," he said, conducting them to a choice table in the corner.

Across the room, thick with smoke and the hum of voices and the clatter of dishes, Constance spotted Alton Slater. He was deep in conversation with a French diplomat she'd also met last night at Marjorie Stith's. She nudged Henry, puffed out her lips, held her breath until her face began to turn red, and then softly mimicked the radio announcer: "This is Al-ton Sl-ater, with the news!" They both laughed.

"Christ, we can't escape him," Henry said. "Oh, oh," he suddenly whispered, "get ready for geezer attack."

Constance looked up. Slater had recognized her and was heading toward their table.

"Good afternoon, my dear," he said with a courtly bow. "You look even more lovely in the daylight." He reached over, took her hand, and kissed it. She noticed a faint trace of men's cologne. He looked as though he had just come from the barber shop: his mustache was freshly trimmed and she could detect the smell of talcum powder. He was even more nattily dressed than last night, with a white silk shirt, polka-dot bow tie, red this time, and matching red silk handkerchief jauntily peeking up out of his double-breasted suit jacket. "I'm *delighted* to see you're learning the good places to eat," he said, still bowing slightly over her hand. "The Dover sole is superb here. Just the right lemon sauce. John is the absolute best chef in town." He had ignored Henry entirely.

"Oh, thank you, Alton." Constance was flustered. "You, uh, you remember meeting—"

"Eaton, Henry Eaton." Henry was brisk. He nodded up at Slater.

"Yes, of course." Slater paid no further attention to Henry. "Now, my dear," he said, leaning over Constance, to Henry's fury, *"do* enjoy your day. Oh, and by the way, there's a

135

spectacular exhibit of Oriental art at the Corcoran. You must come see it with me. The Ming Dynasty vases are just magnificent, truly magnificent. I'll call you later."

He bowed again and left. They were silent. Both felt last night's tension returning. Constance was awkward and embarrassed. She glanced idly around the restaurant, thinking how to recapture their lost mood. "Oh, my God!" she said suddenly. She let out her breath and her face paled. "The Director!"

She looked directly at a round corner table in the back of Harvey's. There, seated in his usual chair, in the very corner against the wall, was a squat, pasty-faced little man in a dark double-breasted pin-striped suit. A maroon handkerchief, arranged in two small triangles, rose from his breast pocket. His dark hair was combed straight back and parted three-quarters of the way across his head. He had a serious, no-nonsense look, emphasized by strong thick dark eyebrows, a small nose, more a pug nose really, that, with the slight sag of jowls hanging from his jaw, made him look like a bulldog.

He was reading the *Evening Star* sports page. Seated next to him was a big, heavyset, graying man of florid complexion whose iron-gray hair was cropped short in almost military fashion: the sports editor of the *Star* who was also the paper's racing handicapper, and frequent luncheon companion of the Director at Harvey's. He's probably giving tips on the daily double at Belmont, Henry thought cynically. I wonder if it's fixed, and I wonder if *he* knows it's fixed. I'll bet he's got a straight line with the bookies from Lindy's or the Stork Club, and he probably checks it all out with Winchell before he bets.

Henry was struck by Constance's tone and look. She sounded both in awe and afraid—and neither seemed characteristic of her. He looked across at Hoover. Well, from what I know, you could have reason to be afraid. He runs his damned Bureau like a secret army, and he acts as if he's a law unto himself. Henry had heard, of course, some rumors about what the Bureau was doing, and he knew firsthand about many of their operations. It was hard to believe even Hoover would dare go as far as some of the whispers about him indicated—especially about the Vice President and Mrs. Roosevelt. But, as Henry was learning, you never really knew about anything—and what you thought you knew for sure, you'd better damned well not count on being so. In Washington in the war, nothing, and no one, was what they seemed; they all wore masks. And, Henry suspected, after it was over Washington would never be the same. Neither would anybody who had been in it. Any way you looked at it, this was a remarkable man. Yet he looked absolutely unremarkable, no more interesting than a two-buck tout at the track. But he's a high roller, all right. That much I know.

He was a higher roller than even Henry guessed. J. Edgar Hoover at that point had been Director of the FBI since 1924, and now, all those years later, he was still only forty-six years old. The Bureau's manpower and money had grown with the bootleg era and Prohibition. It expanded into a force that now, in wartime, spanned the country and vastly extended its reach into distant corners of American life. Hoover, in fact, as Henry heard whispered, had ordered the Vice President shadowed, his mail opened, his phone tapped, his friends followed, his supporters trailed and observed by agents and informers alike. Henry Wallace was, after all, dangerously naïve and, quite likely, a genuine security risk.

Mrs. Roosevelt was something else. Hoover had to be careful there, but she and some of her closest friends were being watched, too. He'd even gone so far as bugging hotel rooms in which she stayed when away from the White House, then listening, at whatever hour, to the tapes received. He had never liked Eleanor; but in the last year, ever since he got that personal letter from her, his feelings had turned into outright hatred.

Eleven months before Pearl Harbor she wrote him, on White House stationery, an indignant, stinging letter of protest. She learned that a female friend of long standing, then attached to the White House, whose father and husband had been admirals in the Navy, had been investigated by the FBI. Mrs. Roosevelt was also outraged to learn that agents were making inquiries about another friend, the columnist and writer Dorothy Thompson. They were also watching Miss Thompson's apartment house. They recorded her comings and goings, how much company she had, who they were. In words that struck Hoover like a brand, Mrs. Roosevelt wrote: "This type of investigation seems to me to smack too much of the Gestapo methods. . . . I cannot help but resent deeply the action in these two cases and if you have this type of investigation of other people, I do not wonder that we are beginning to get an extremely jittery population."

Hoover immediately wrote back a long, two-page, single-spaced letter marked *Personal and Confidential by Special Messenger*. The FBI chief rushed it to her at the White House. He abjectly apologized for "the resentment which this incident has caused you," sought to put at rest the notion his Bureau was in any way "indulging in any activities which might be construed as improper or un-American methods in the conduct of investigations," and explained that he was acting under higher authority: "In connection with the necessary expansion of Governmental agencies incident to the National Emergency, the policy has been established of sending to the Federal Bureau of Investigation the names of persons working for these governmental agencies, in order that inquiry might be made as to their background, integrity and loyalty. I want to point out that this work was not sought by the Federal Bureau of Investigation, but was assigned to it."

But the old bag had coldly rejected his reply, responding only, "My Dear Mr. Hoover: Thank you very much for [your] letter of January 27 in answer to mine. It was very good of you to write in detail." Since then, among his most intimate aides, he had taken to describing her as "the old hoot owl and her claque"—and he ordered some of her friends tailed and their hotel rooms bugged. He also ordered the tapes brought immediately to him. He even ordered his agents to follow and shadow Mrs. Roosevelt when she left in her own limousine. It was risky, but he knew enough about the President's relationship with his wife to feel reasonably secure—and the President's own views about security emboldened him. In his own mind, Hoover was certain Mrs.

Roosevelt associated with known security risks. He suspected, though he was not yet entirely convinced, that she herself was a security risk. "I often wonder," he scrawled on one document in the rapidly growing file he was keeping on her, "whether she is as naïve as she professes or whether it is just a blind to lull the unsuspecting."

Henry found himself staring at Hoover, deep in thought.

"You don't like him, do you?" asked Constance, studying his expression.

"Well, at least we're on the same side, and in the same business—or we ought to be." An edge of bitterness had crept into his voice.

"But you don't like him."

"I don't know him personally. But, yes, I don't like what I know about him."

"Why?" Constance persisted.

Henry paused, and shook away his grim look. "Let's just say that I have a certain basic reservation about the mentality of the career bureaucrat—and he's the all-time champion, the Babe Ruth of bureaucrats. I suppose," and he smiled slightly, "he comes by it naturally. His father was a bureaucrat, you know. So he grew up in it, right here in Washington. It's all he's ever known. I've also wondered why the Great G-man spends so much time with Winchell and that Broadway bunch of gamblers."

"Oh, come on," Constance said sharply, "surely you don't believe he's doing anything *against* the law. That's the most ridiculous thing I ever heard."

"I didn't say that." Henry was annoyed. "I do know he's doing some things that are, to put it mildly, outside the pale—and if the public ever finds out about them there'll be hell to pay."

Constance grew defensive. Her strong sense of loyalty was offended. "Like what?" she said in a disbelieving tone.

"Like having Mrs. Roosevelt followed, and the Vice President, too."

Constance was shocked. "I don't believe you," she said. "You can't be serious. How dare you say such a thing." She looked sternly at him. He sat back and looked thoughtful. "You asked and I told you." He shrugged and waved his hand.

"Maybe you're right. Maybe it's just another rumor—and you know how rumors are in Washington now."

She watched his expression carefully, and was confused. He seemed serious, but now he seems to be making a joke of it, as if he's afraid I *will* believe him.

Henry slipped back into the banter again. "Maybe it's just my fixation about his mother that's the problem, Mrs. Freud."

"What do you mean?"

"Don't you know about her? A real Fundamentalist. Hard-shelled as they come. Mencken would have a great time with her. I thought everyone in the Bureau knew about her, or is that a secret, too?"

"No, I didn't know. Are you serious?"

"Check it out. See if I ever tell the truth."

They smiled at each other. "Here," Henry said, "have you tried these?" He handed over a red box with a white top, red monogram, and red letters that spelled out REGENT CIGARETTES, KING SIZE over a red monogram in the center. "They're new. I like them." Constance took one from the box and waited for Henry to light it. He did, then took one himself. They inhaled the smoke deeply, and, as if reading each other's mind, exhaled in slow mock sultry style.

"Do I look like Marlene?" Constance drawled.

"About as much as I look like Bogie," Henry said.

Their waiter came. "The crab imperial?" Henry asked Constance. He was fascinated by the way her coloring, not just her eyes, seemed to change with her moods, soft and white, then suddenly touched with flashes of red and high in her cheeks. She was glowing now, and relaxed. "Sure, I'll test your taste." Henry also ordered a bottle of Meursault, 1939. "There's not going to be much of this left, you know. So what the hell, let's do it right. We can even toast the Director."

Constance paled, but then smiled.

"Do you like Mr. Slater?" she asked.

"I don't know him either."

"Henry . . ." It was the first time she had called him by his first name. She was surprised how natural it seemed and how comfortable she felt being with him. "Don't be so Boston," she said quickly, an amused look crossing her face. "Say what you feel, for Christ's sake. I won't tell."

He shrugged, and held up his hands in a mark of surrender.

"Okay, Charleston. Yeah, I listen to his broadcasts. He's informed, and obviously well connected. But kind of a stuffed shirt, don't you think? He puts on a helluva lot of airs. And, let me tell you, when it comes to knowing stuffed shirts, I'm an expert. They were all around me in Boston."

"Well, I like him."

"I didn't say I didn't." But his raised eyebrows said otherwise.

Their appetizers came. The wine steward opened their bottle, and poured a little in Henry's glass. He tasted, and nodded. He never said anything to the steward and never thanked the waiter. It wasn't done.

They ate in silence for a minute. Constance glanced at Hoover. He was still engrossed in the sports pages.

In the middle of their crab imperial, they began, tentatively, talking about themselves. Henry confessed, ruefully, that he had intended to be a novelist when he was a Harvard undergraduate. "I devoured the *Partisan Review*, couldn't get enough of it. One month I cut all my classes, locked myself in my room in Eliot House, and read thirty novels from the Modern Library series. One a day." He shook his head, and put on his little boy's look. "It was the toughest time I had at college, unless you count games against Yale, or with girls." He smiled in such a way that Constance knew he was teasing—and testing—her. "Instead, God help me, I became a Wall Street lawyer."

Constance laughed in the husky but soft sort of way that Henry was beginning to associate with her. His tastes had never run to Southern girls. They struck him as phony. The ones he had known always seemed determined to try to be like Scarlett O'Hara, a superficial, shallow, empty-headed, flirtatious type that was, he thought, a ridiculous model. Constance had the drawl, but there was nothing fake about it: it was soft and melodious, but not a honey-mouth mush, and not at all indolent-sounding. She was quick and bright and sharp. He liked her laugh, and he liked the way her voice matched her changing moods.

"Well," she said softly, as she gave a small "hummph" of

pleasure, "I guess we have something in common after all. When I was at Smith, I wanted to be the next Edna St. Vincent Millay—even if it's heresy for a Smith girl to worship a Vassar girl."

She laughed again, and shook her head slightly, her curls jiggling softly as she did. "God, how I loved her—and I don't mean just that 'my candle burns at both ends' business." She shook her head again, and smiled regretfully. For a moment, she thought she'd tell him about New York, but decided that was too personal, too complicated.

"Now the only poetry I write are memorandums for my boss, who isn't very literary, I'll tell you, and the Director."

Henry smiled. "I'll show you my unpublished novel if you'll show me your unpublished poetry."

"I'll show you my unpublished poetry if you'll show me your unpublished novel," Constance said, and quickly added, "God, it sounds like we're playing doctor, or didn't you ever indulge in those medical arts with your girlfriends when you were small, Lieutenant?"

They both burst out laughing.

An elderly couple at the next table looked at them disapprovingly. Henry and Constance caught the looks and smiled again.

"Why'd you become a lawyer then?"

"Laziness, lack of talent, family, the thing to do: we're supposed to be bankers, lawyers, doctors, ministers, government officials. Proper people, you know. Nobody breathes about the real old bastards and blackguards that are lurking back in our shadows. And you?"

"If it hadn't been for the war, I suppose I would have gone home, met a Southern novelist—unpublished, of course, much more romantic." She arched her eyebrows dramatically and looked soulful, in the Greta Garbo style. "And married."

"Hubba hubba," Henry said.

She laughed again, and so did Henry. The elderly couple stared at them as hard as they could and muttered to each other.

"No," Constance said after they stopped laughing, "seriously, I guess I would have wound up marrying a lawyer, and hating it but never showing it—ah come from long-suffering stock, I'll have you know, Lieutenant Eaton—and then scribbled away in my upstairs garret while my sons went to Princeton and my girls went to Smith, because that's the way *we* always do it."

They were quiet a bit, but felt comfortable looking at each other.

"You sure gave me a hard time when we met at Marjorie's," Constance finally said. "Trying to score points, I guess."

"Wait a minute," Henry said. "I wasn't trying to score points. I was trying to score." They both laughed.

"Well," she said, turning serious, "you asked where I work and I told you the government, and you found me. But what do you do? I mean what do you *really* do in the government; what are you doing now, for instance?"

She looked at him curiously and watched for his reaction. Other than frowning and twirling his fork on his all-but-empty plate, he had none. He stared down at the table a moment, then lifted his eyes. He looked at her thoughtfully and seemed, somehow, to be measuring her.

"I'm a cop of sorts. I handle a lot of different kinds of investigations for ONI. The Office of Naval Intelligence. Right now I'm looking into the murder of an admiral's Negro driver." Funny, Henry reflected as he spoke, I have no hesitation telling that simple fact to her when I wouldn't say the same thing to the Negro detective. "Most of my work's pretty routine. Not the murder, I mean, and not routine for a Wall Street lawyer either, which I was, but the sort of things they assign a young naval officer in intelligence." He decided to leave it at that. There was no point in really telling her what he did.

"Who murdered him? Do you have any idea? And why should ONI care?"

"The answers are no, no, and I can't say. But there is a curious thing."

She leaned forward, staring intently at Henry.

"Just before I met you, I met the damndest Negro I've ever encountered."

"What do you mean? How so?"

"He's a D.C. cop, a detective, to be more precise, and he's working on the same case and six more like it."

143

"Six more Navy drivers?"

"No, no. Six more Negroes. All murdered. All shot in the head."

"But they were all in the service, you mean?"

"No, the rest were all civilians."

"Then why would that involve you? I thought you . . ."

He grimaced, and leaned closer toward her.

"That's what I was starting to tell you about this Negro cop. Thomas is his name. I met him at night in the morgue. It's a horrible place. I hope you never have to see anything like that. You know, I don't want to spoil your lunch, but when I was in law school I had a close friend in medical school. I was still thinking about becoming a writer someday—and I had the typical thoughts that we all think are so terribly important, so unique, but of course aren't: about the meaning of death, the reality of it, what it's like to experience it, how you describe it? I'm sure you've had those sorts of thoughts many times. You think, only *I've* ever felt quite so intensely before, only *I've* got the power to make others understand what *I've* been feeling and thinking. It's very naïve and very arrogant, and very young. Do you know what I mean?" He looked over at her, as if for reassurance.

Constance shook her head slightly in agreement. She knew exactly how he felt, and was pleased to hear him open up. He *is* sensitive, she thought. He's much more than a charming bastard. She was touched.

"Anyway, I got my friend to take me into the autopsy room at Yale one night. Not supposed to, but he did. I was just—well—just curious about what it was like, how I'd react. Do you understand?"

She nodded, her expression silently encouraging him to continue.

"Well, I put on the smock and the rubber gloves and he showed me the cadavers they were working on in these aluminum boxes. I had no reaction at all. Nothing. They were just like pieces of clay. I kept trying to tell myself that these were people who felt and thought and hated and loved, but I couldn't. That's not how I felt in the morgue here the other night. That was entirely different. Maybe it's because I knew this poor guy had just been killed. Maybe it's because you can't help identifying with the war and all the killing. How senseless this seemed. What a waste it was. I don't know. But it got to me. And so that's where I met this Negro cop. Extraordinary guy. Very big, strong, quiet—but you could feel his emotion. He made *me* feel how *he* felt. I suppose it doesn't make sense. In a way it's odd how it affected me. But it did. It had quite an impact. Not long after that I met you. And made an ass of myself."

He stopped, then suddenly spoke up.

"Oh, the point of the whole thing is that these Negro killings are really spooking the colored community. This detective says there's going to be real trouble unless someone comes up with an answer. The rumor among the colored people is that whites are out to kill the blacks. That's all we need now—a race war here at home."

Constance sighed. "There's so much violence," she said. "It makes me sick to think of all the people dying in the war. Then this sort of thing. Has the world gone mad? Do you sometimes worry that we'll all just get hardened to it, that we'll take it for granted, that we won't be able to feel anything at all? What a terrible time!"

The waiter brought their coffee. They welcomed the interruption. It was too depressing. They felt much closer, but they both wanted to recapture their earlier, lighter, mood. Henry spoke first.

"Hey, Constance"—Henry realized he was using her first name for the first time—"do you like baseball? The Senators are playing the Red Sox at Griffith Stadium tomorrow afternoon. It's in the Negro section, and you have to be careful up there, but I'll provide the protective services of the United States Navy, all at your command. Besides, it may be the last chance to see Ted Williams."

"Henry, you really don't know much about Southerners, do you? About the only thing worthwhile we seem to have produced in this century are Southern writers and Southern ballplayers. We take our baseball seriously in the South. Sure, I like baseball. But I'm not a Red Sox fan."

"The Senators?" Henry was incredulous.

"No, not the Senators, stupid. The Yankees! I just love Joe DiMaggio. Now there's a secret passion."

"The Yankees! Christ almighty, Constance. The Yankees! I hate the Yankees!" Henry was indignant. "The Yankees? *You* like the Yankees?"

"I love the Yankees," she said. "I love them because they have Joe DiMaggio, I love them because they win, I love them because they're in first place again, I love them because they beat the Red Sox. But what makes you think I can get off to go to a ball game? There is a war on, you know, Lieutenant."

"I've heard," Henry said tersely. "You just tell 'em over there at the Bureau you're following the orders of the President. You read what he just said in the paper, didn't you? 'It's best for the country to keep baseball going. There will be fewer people unemployed and everybody will work longer hours and harder than ever before.' So, as our President says, 'it's thoroughly worthwhile'—and it's in the national interest. And I'll promise you this, once you see Ted Williams hit you'll forget all about Joe DiMaggio."

He grimaced, drew his fists together, struck an imaginary left-handed batting stance, and said, "Bam! There she goes! Come on, Constance, you owe it to yourself. Tell you what, you tell that Miss Ryan from Boston that you have a chance to see Ted Williams play. See if she won't cover for you for a couple of hours. After all, it's as patriotic as having a Victory Garden, according to the President, and who are we to argue with *him?*"

"We–ll . . ." Constance began. Then, glancing at her watch and looking panicked, she said, "Oh my gosh. I've got to get back."

She stole a glance toward the Director, felt reassured to see him still sitting at the table, talking to the gray-haired sports editor, and quickly got up. As she started to move away from the table, she had a sudden, nasty thought: I wonder if he picked this place because he knew the Director would be here and wanted to check my reaction to him? That's just the sort of thing a charming bastard would do.

They hurried out of the restaurant, hailed a cab, and headed back toward the Justice Department.

over the burner. He crossed the room again, took off
[ne]w James Atwood tropical worsted suit jacket, hung it
[on a h]anger behind the door, put on a butcher's apron, drew
[in] deeply on his cigarette, walked back to the cluttered
[work b]ench, sat down on a work stool, snapped on a table
[lamp], took another puff, and glanced around the room
[befor]e beginning to work.

[Th]e room was cluttered with wire, old telephones, tools,
[solde]ring irons, and diagrams.

[Ho]lston picked up one of the two telephones Tony Russo
[had] just sold him. He unscrewed the mouthpiece from the
[black] receiver, took out the small microphone, about the size
[of a] half-dollar, and threw the rest of the receiver into a trash
[can] by the bench. He carefully examined, and then tested,
[the] microphone. It was a workable one. Then he plugged in
[a] soldering iron, took some wire from a spool next to his
[e]lbow, and proceeded to solder two strands of wire to the
[back] of the microphone. After unwinding twenty feet of the
[stran]ds, he cut the wires. He got off his stool and walked
[acros]s the room to a locked file cabinet. From behind several
[jars o]f nuts and bolts on a bookcase shelf he took some keys
[and] unlocked the file cabinet.

[In]side was a black bag. It was the same kind a doctor uses
[when] visiting patients.

[Ho]lston took the black bag from the file and put the
[micro]phone and wires into it. He returned to his workbench
[and] methodically repeated the same steps with the second
[teleph]one. When he finished, he also put this assembly into
[the b]lack bag. He snapped the bag shut, checking to make
[sure i]t was closed securely, reached down and put it into the
[burla]p sack.

[He] stubbed out his cigarette, lit another one, poured his
[last] cup of black coffee, finished both, exhaled more
[smoke] into a room already blue and stale from it, got up,
[turn]ed off the table lamp, relocked the cabinet, placed the
[keys b]ack behind the jars on the shelf, hung up his apron, put
[on his] suit coat, walked to the window, and raised the shade.

[He, G]rover Holston, paper bag in hand, stepped outside,
[shut] the door that said KEEP OUT, and walked away down the
[outdo]or corridor.

5

Business was very good for Antonio Russo,
especially his scrap-metal and scrap-paper business, or
scrapple, as he called it.

Before Pearl Harbor, he sold most of the scrap metal he
bought to the big agents for the Japanese steel-makers. Now,
as the war consumed all materials and rationing created
shortages in everything from sugar to gasoline (Jesus, he
thought, who would've believed you'd even have to turn in an
empty tube of toothpaste before they'd sell you a new one?),
more and more people were turning up at his junkyard with
scrap to sell. Each day grammar-school kids in their corduroy
knickers brought wagons loaded with newspapers. He'd give
them forty cents for a hundred pounds, and no questions
asked about how they got it. And no lectures, either, when
they brought him aluminum foil from cigarette packages that
they rolled into balls and were supposed to take to school and
donate for the war.

Tony was patriotic, and he figured they were, too—but he
also believed in free enterprise. That's what we're fighting
for, he would say to himself, and you gotta make a living,
don't you? Besides, Tony knew it all went back to the war
machine, or most of it did. So no big deal. And he was
providing a service, wasn't he? Otherwise how come his
business kept on booming, and he kept on getting more and
more new regular customers? Jesus, he'd even had to buy a
German shepherd to roam the place at night and he put a
double strand of that fancy new barbed wire on top of the
high chain-link fence that surrounded his junkyard grounds.
And still more and more people kept making their way across
the Anacostia River, out Kenilworth Avenue, to Russo's

Salvage Company high above the flatlands marking that corner of the District of Columbia boundary near the National Arboretum grounds.

"I got some more for you, Mr. Holston," he said now to one of his best, and classiest, new customers.

Behind him, on the wall facing the door of his corrugated tin shack, Tony had hung a new poster, the same one they were putting in the factories. It showed the huge, solemn but determined face of the President superimposed against the broad red, white, and blue stripes of the American flag with just a few stars gleaming over the head and the bold black letters below spelling out the words:

SPEED! will save lives!
SPEED! will save this nation!
SPEED! will save our freedom!
Let's Go, Everybody—Keep 'Em Firing!

"How do you like that one, Mr. Holston?" Tony said proudly, gesturing to the poster. "Just got it."

Tony liked posters; they made him feel he was doing his part, and he pasted them up, everything from the Minuteman BUY UNITED STATES DEFENSE BONDS STAMPS to the BE PROUD, AMERICA P-38 ones, all around the shack. Another new one, from the Office of Civilian Defense, was on when and how to use your flashlight in a blackout. He pasted that one so that it stood near the big Eveready flashlight he kept standing, lens down, like a sentinel on his desk. He even kept the double thickness of newspaper tied around the lens with a string, in the officially prescribed blackout manner. For added measure, Tony had cut two discs of paper and inserted them under the lens. He never went out in the blackout himself, and so had had no occasion to use the flashlight, but he liked to point it out to his customers. *That's how you do it*, he'd say, knowingly. It was another sign that Tony was doing his part. Alongside the blackout poster was Tony's favorite, the see-no-evil, hear-no-evil one with Hitler, Tojo, and Mussolini as the three monkeys, but with ratlike faces, and a stern Uncle Sam towering over them in the background admonishing Americans, Idle Talk Costs Lives!

"Attaboy, Tony," Grover Holston said. You've got 'em ready?"

"You betcha, Mr. Holston. Right here.

Tony liked to deal with Grover Holston. He always dressed nice, with cuff links a clasp and his shoes shined, and he sm Probably that new Seaforth shaving lotio and Vaseline Tonic for sure. And Mr. Hol top dollar, too.

Funny thing was, he didn't want no scra wanted only one thing. Old telephones. Just j Tony had no idea what Mr. Holston did with never asked, naturally, and Mr. Holston nev just collected all the phones he could get, Holston bought 'em all.

"Thanks, Tony," Mr. Holston said as he paper grocery bag Tony handed him and turne payment. "See you later."

He turned, went out the door that Tony ha another huge poster—the War Production Boar HOW SCRAP IRON AND STEEL GO TO WAR and ending, SCRAP INTO THE FIGHT!—walked past the moun metal, got into his green two-door DeSoto, a Fluid Drive that he had bought for $965 helluva price, but he figured it might be his l time, and Holston liked cars), and drove bridge over the Anacostia and headed dow

After he parked in the employee lot, he er Department through the corner door c Avenue, took the elevator to the fifth floor, long corridor, paper sack in hand, and stop marked KEEP OUT. Holston put a key into th door, walked through, turned, and bol crossed the room, pulled down the windo flipped on the light switch. Next, he reach pocket, took out a silver cigarette case, op a Wings, the cheapest cigarette available, long drag, exhaled, and then touched the to the Bunsen burner on a bench. Th slightly as Holston picked up a coffeep

6

Gunther studied the papers carefully. He had awakened early, as usual, and walked up to Pennsylvania Avenue to buy three morning papers—the *Times-Herald* and the *Post* of Washington and the *New York Times*—from a newspaper vendor and strolled back to his "safe house" in Foggy Bottom. Upstairs, he could hear the sound of the girls getting ready for work. So they start early, too. They'd better. He smiled, flicked on the radio, and sat at the small dining-room table, reading.

The news was good, very good: Rommel had taken Tobruk in North Africa in an unmitigated disaster for the Allies, captured 33,000 British troops and vast quantities of supplies, including 10,000 cubic meters of petrol, and was poised to enter Egypt. On the eastern front, Kharkov already had fallen. In the Crimea, the great Black Sea naval base of Sevastopol, the key to the crucial Caucasian oil fields as well as the vital American supply-line link to the Soviet Union, was besieged by ten Wehrmacht divisions comprising Manstein's Eleventh Army assisted by two Rumanian divisions in the war's bloodiest battlefield. It seemed certain to be taken despite desperate hand-to-hand, house-to-house resistance by the Russians. The papers reported the Russians were fighting a last-ditch battle amid the scent of acacia and stench of rotting corpses; but it was clear the battle was almost over, leaving the way to Stalingrad open. On the American West Coast, the first war dead and battle casualties from Alaska were arriving in Seattle harbor after the Aleutian Islands of Attu and Kiska had fallen last week with stunning ease to the Japanese. On the Atlantic Coast, the

Navy announced that German submarines had sunk fifteen merchant ships in a period of only days with a loss of all hands aboard, marking ever-rising tanker sinkings and immense tonnage losses in the Battle of the Atlantic. Already residents of coastal towns from Florida to New England were becoming accustomed to hearing the nightly sounds of battle offshore and witnessing the flames rising into the inky night from burning, sinking ships. They awakened to find their beaches fouled with naval debris and their tides carrying slimy smears and washing up gobs of thick oil deposits onto the blackening sands.

These Americans are extraordinary, Gunther thought. Only they would publicly report such devastatingly demoralizing bad news, in such detail—and yet it doesn't seem to sink in to them. They seem far more concerned about their personal comfort than anything else.

He was fascinated with the ads in the papers, especially the ones for women. All they seem to care about is how they smell, or how to keep themselves from smelling. Every page has a new deodorant ad: "Yodora, a dab a day keeps P.O. away" . . . "Odorono Cream, to guard against underarm odor and dampness" . . . "Etiquet stops underarm perspiration odor 1 to 3 days." He wondered if that black woman had used any of it, but didn't think so. At least she hadn't been ashamed of how her body smelled. Or maybe she was. No matter now. He smiled slightly. Even the ads that dealt with the war were unbelievably naïve. They have to be told what foods are good to eat. He read one put out by the government's Office of Defense Health and Welfare Services. "Government authorities have set down in simple easy-to-follow rules the scientific findings of modern nutrition experts," it began. So what is it their great science tells them? "Eggs—because eggs are one of the best productive foods, everyone should eat at least one egg a day."

Gunther grinned and shook his head. The Americans were obsessed with the way they smelled—even the men, he thought, looking at an ad showing soldiers in bayonet practice and a line that read "In This Man's Army Lifebuoy Really Fights B.O."—and with food, not even real food. He was struck by how many ads there were for canned meat—Mor, Prem, Spam, Treet. And they think they are able to fight us?

The best they can do is fight each other.

He read every word of the stories about black-market rings operating openly in the highest circles of Washington, about new protests over rationing, and about members of Congress grumbling because of problems caused them by the blackouts. And the government itself was fighting with American industry! The government had accused manufacturers of plastic glass used in military aircraft of forming a cartel with German firms and the Imperial Chemical Industries to restrict the supply of that glass. They were charging the owners of certain patents with holding up construction of Flying Fortresses.

That wasn't entirely true, Gunther knew, but at least some of his work from a few years ago was paying off. God knows they had spent enough money for bribes of congressmen and payoffs to industry through the America First Committee. So it wasn't all a waste. Already, they are crumbling within, even faster than we could have expected.

He listened as another stupid jingle ended "With men who know tobacco best, it's Luckies 2 to 1" and then heard the radio announcer introduce Irving Berlin's new hit song, "I Left My Heart at the Stage Door Canteen." A soft, moony male voice almost weeping into the microphone sang something about a soldier leaving his heart with a girl named Eileen. Gunther listened intently as the singer crooned on that the soldier was doomed even before any battles began. Then, thrusting the papers aside, he stood up and sneered. No wonder. The Jews even write their songs.

He was immensely restless. What he read made him all the more convinced in the ultimate success of his mission and strongly reinforced his already overpowering sense of personal and national superiority. How could anyone fail against these people? He wondered how Roosevelt and Churchill were reacting to the bitter war news during their meetings inside the White House. If they were smart, they would give up now and let the Germanization proceed to unify the Aryan West and eliminate the Communists and Jews and the mongrel races.

Well, he said to himself, stretching and flexing his big hands, they said we shouldn't stay cooped inside. So let me see this Washington that thinks it's at war. He opened his Gladstone suitcase and rummaged among the civilian clothing he brought with him, all made in America, all with American labels, until he took out a Norwegian Army officer's uniform. It had been his idea, and they had approved it, to have it so he could blend in with other men his age in uniform but not have to answer to American military orders and units. He liked it for another reason: Gunther served in Norway, both in the early blitzkrieg and occupation, and, with his great gift for languages, had become fluent in Norwegian.

He dressed, checked to make sure everything was in order in the apartment in case anyone entered while he was gone, and strolled outside, for all the world as if he were a foreign officer on leave seeing the sights in America's capital. Well, he was, Gunther thought, with a flash of pleasure. That's just what I am. A broad smile creased his face and his pale blue eyes sparkled with his secret joke.

Gunther felt supremely confident as he moved easily through the swarms of people on the streets. He wandered past George Washington University toward the Corcoran Gallery, a ponderous mass of white Georgia marble. It resembled more an ancient sarcophagus than a stylish modern repository for great art. Diagonally across the street was the State, War and Navy Building and only a few hundred feet farther, the White House.

As he walked up the broad steps flanked by a colossal set of bronze lions, he thought of Willi. How different we really are. He has no appreciation for fine art or classical music and probably never read a decent book. He knew nothing of Heidegger or Kant or Nietzsche. The few times Gunther had tried to engage Willi in intellectual conversation, he quickly changed the subject. It seemed to make him nervous. He withdrew. Willi was always withdrawing, Gunther mused. All the more reason—and he fingered his watch chain, an act that by now had become almost reflexive.

He had heard, in Germany, or read in some of those American publications they studied daily (he couldn't recall which now) that the Kress Collection of Italian Art was especially worth seeing in Washington. But that was at the National Gallery, the new one opened just a year, he was told, when he inquired at the information booth inside the marbled and colonnaded hall. He thanked the little woman behind the desk, and went outside. This one, it seemed, had nothing but American art; Gunther had nothing but contempt for it. He walked down Seventeenth Street, to Constitution Avenue, wondering again how Americans endured this miserable heat and humidity, strolled past the old gray Navy Building surrounded by its cluster of tempos on the Mall, walked several blocks past the Smithsonian Institution structures, and approached the new gallery. It was immense and graceful, a soft pink palace of hand-picked marble quarried in Tennessee.

When he reached the Mall entrance, he climbed the steps, paused, and turned to look across the reddish-brown sandstone turrets of the Gothic old original Smithsonian "Castle" Building; then he gazed up at the new gallery and recalled lines from his seminary education: "This is not a building; too big; not a monument; too alive. It has to be an edifice." At that time in his life, when he had experienced so much personal rejection and torment, use of that term had sounded awkward and unmanly. Now, *edifice* seemed exactly right for such an enormous marble tomb for art.

He pushed through the high bronze doors and picked up a bulletin at the information desk that listed the artworks in the collection. One of the brochures noted the new building was built to last a "thousand years." As long as the Third Reich, he thought. Maybe I can become its director someday. They will owe me something when I finish here.

Gunther walked to the rotunda with its fountain gurgling beneath the feet of a sixteenth-century sculpture of *Mercury*. He looked left and right down the two corridors leading away from *Mercury* and his fountain, and judged each to be over a hundred meters long. He decided to try the west corridor and wing first. As he walked slowly down the corridor, he paused to examine two sculptures by Jacopo Tatti: *Venus Anadyomen* and *Bacchus and Young Faun*. Lovely, he thought, just lovely.

From his brochure, he noted, too, that the sculptures had been booty that Napoleon stole from Italy to endow Paris. He enjoyed the thought. Now we're looting Paris to endow Berlin. I wonder who will loot Berlin in a thousand years. He smiled, and almost laughed out loud.

"Look, Emily, how nice that that young man has such an appreciation for art," one stout matron in a long rayon dress decorated with flowers and wearing "sensible" shoes whispered to her companion, a slight woman in her sixties peering at a tour book. "I wish some of our young men had as much good taste."

Gunther wandered over to the Kress Collection, but it was Raphael in which he lost himself. He plunked down on a sofa and was transported by the *Alba Madonna*. Only the passage of a guard in the corner of the small gallery room broke his spell. He looked at his watch and was startled to see he had been examining this exquisite painting (he thought it Raphael's best) for nearly half an hour. The beauty of the Madonna and the commanding innocence of the child gripping his simple wooden cross left him in rapture. Again, he thought of his seminary days.

He vowed, as much to the Madonna as to himself, that when it was all over he would come back to share more fully in this scene. Then he left to continue his tour of Washington.

It was approaching noon when he stepped into the Pennsylvania Avenue traffic. The heat was as great, if not greater, than when he had walked along the other side of the avenue from Union Station just yesterday, but the difference in the crowds was striking. The Americans must be bringing everybody to Washington, he thought. Nothing about this resembles the sleepy, quiet, slow Washington I remember from just a few years ago. The pace of the people moving along the sidewalks was brisk; everyone, men and women alike, seemed to walk with a spring of a purpose. If you didn't know better, you'd think they believed they were winning the war. Fools!

He found himself swept along by the tide of people. Despite the heat and the sweat that began to dampen his shirt and wilt his collar and seep through to his uniform blouse, he started walking more briskly, too. When he passed the old

Willard Hotel, he turned up Fifteenth Street along the Treasury Department and walked to the landscaped grounds of Lafayette Park across the street from the White House. Gunther cut across the avenue and strolled leisurely through the park. He crossed back and moved directly up to the iron fence running across the front of the executive mansion. Like the rest of the tourists, he stood and stared through the fence at the simple, clean, balanced lines of the building with its colonial portico and four columns just a few feet beyond. He noted the added security: anti-aircraft guns on the White House roof, heavy chains over the iron entrance gates, artillery, machine guns, and more anti-aircraft guns emplaced behind false terraces on the lawn before the mansion. Posted every few feet on the sidewalk before the fence were American soldiers. He thought they looked young, inexperienced, and nervous.

So Churchill and Roosevelt were inside right now: in all the world, only the Americans would put them so together and so open to the public at such a time. Could they really be so stupid, or was this a fake?

He started to walk away, when someone tapped him from behind on his left shoulder.

"*Hej,*" (Hello) a man's voice rang out.

Turning easily, and without missing a beat or showing a flicker of concern, Gunther quickly replied, "*Hej, så flott att möta en landsmann.*" (Hello, and good to see you, my countryman. I salute you.) He smiled and seemed delighted as he saluted. Then he held out his hand to the tall slim young man standing before him in the uniform of a Norwegian naval officer.

"And I you," the officer said. "Olaf Gilchrist, naval attaché at the embassy. I was not aware we have new officers in Washington."

"Eric Haarfager," Gunther said, introducing himself, "from Hornelen."

"Ah, islander," Gilchrist said. "You come by the name naturally." He looked at Gunther's hair.

"Yes, fair hair, that is me." Gunther appeared excited at meeting Gilchrist, and spoke animatedly, with delighted smiles.

"So, tell me, you came—"

Gunther started to speak, stopped, laughed, moved forward, put his arm around Gilchrist in a gesture of good-fellowship, and said, still in Norwegian, and with a teasing, joyous smile, glancing around at the crowds and the soldiers standing stiffly before them, "I think we better speak English. No? Otherwise, the Americans will think we're Nazi spies." He slapped the attaché on the back and laughed again.

"Of course," Gilchrist said, slipping easily into English as they began walking away together. "But tell me, what are you doing here, when did you arrive? I don't think I got a message about you."

"No?" Gunther said. "How strange." He glanced at Gilchrist more closely, and regarded him with faint but unmistakable suspicion. "No? How strange," he repeated. "I just got in today, by the train from New York. Before that—but surely you know. We docked Saturday night on a British destroyer from London. Good berth, too. Right next to that French ship, the *Normandie*. I've been assigned to a mission at our consulate there. But surely they informed you. I've got a three-day pass and always wanted to see Washington. So here I am, the happy tourist." He smiled again, and waved his arms exuberantly. "I've gone to the galleries, died in the heat, seen the White House, and now I want to go to the very top of the Washington Monument." They were walking toward the monument looming a block away on the Ellipse, its perimeter of flags hanging limply in the heat. "But come, come, please be my guide, then we must have a drink and a good talk at the embassy."

Gunther beckoned Gilchrist to keep up with him as he walked toward the sloping grounds leading to the monument entrance.

The attaché hesitated briefly; then, as if delighted to escort a fellow countryman, quickly moved along with him. He was, in fact, more and more doubtful Gunther was what he claimed to be. His story was, well, credible, the Norwegian excellent, but ... He gave no outward sign of any doubts though, and fell in with Gunther as they waited in line with a group of tourists, then shuffled into the elevator and, packed in with the tourists, fell silent as the elevator slowly rose to the top of the 555-foot marble shaft.

Gunther seemed genuinely excited as they stood together looking out the small windows cut into each wall of the masonry structure. As they moved from window to window, he babbled about the capital panorama below. Just as the tour group was about to enter the elevator for the ride down, Gunther's manner suddenly changed. He had something to pass on urgently, he whispered to the attaché.

With a gesture to his lips, he turned back to the window and waited until the elevator left and they were alone. Then, beckoning the attaché closer, he reached down to check his watch, took out the watch and chain and said, in a worried tone, "Can this be right?" As the attaché leaned forward and down to look, Gunther slipped behind him. In an effortless movement, he had the chain cutting tightly around Gilchrist's neck. With one violent twist, he strangled him. Not a sound came from the attaché as he slumped forward, dead.

Gunther easily caught Gilchrist before he fell. He lifted the body as if it weighed nothing and quickly propped it up in the viewing aperture. His pose was so lifelike that his face appeared to be looking out over Washington. Calmly, Gunther waited to descend in the elevator. My own little artwork for Washington, he thought, his face flushing. My own little Madonna for the Mall. On the ground, he disappeared into the crowds of summer tourists who were mopping their brows and fanning themselves in the humid air.

7

Eugene Parks, a real M.D. from the Howard University Medical School, one of the hopelessly few Negro doctors who tried to cope with the rising rate of colored disease and death in Washington, the worst in the nation, took off his bloodstained apron and handed it to Dr. Luke. He sat down on a stool near the cadaver cases in the second-floor autopsy room of the D.C. morgue. Thomas, standing nearby, waited silently. Parks lighted a cigarette and blew out a billow of smoke. He was exhausted, and showed it. He had been tending an emergency case, a stabbing, late that afternoon in one of the segregated wards at a hospital on Capitol Hill when Thomas called from the morgue with another one. As always, Parks came immediately. He would do anything for Thomas. When his cigarette smoke cleared he said, wearily: "She was very young, and very beautiful."

"I know, Gene," Thomas said shortly. "And now she's dead. Another one. Man, how many do we have to take?"

Parks gave his friend a concerned look. He had never seen Thomas so tense. In fact, he'd never seen him show any strain until these past few days. He nodded, and cleared his throat. "Death was by strangulation."

"How?" Thomas asked.

"A metal chain or a knobbed wire. It couldn't have been a rope. No burns. Only small, regularly spaced contusions almost completely around her neck. She couldn't have been dead more than twenty-four hours." He looked at his watch. "You found her this morning? I'd say it was sometime late in the afternoon yesterday. Whoever killed her, totally surprised her. And it was someone very strong. Very strong.

160

Probably took her from behind. She had just had sex before she was killed. There were a few blond hairs in her pubic area, bruises about the body but otherwise no marks, nothing except the throat. She was beaten, but she certainly wasn't choked with bare hands." He stood up and sighed. "That's the best I can do, Leon."

"Thanks, Gene. Can I buy you a cup of coffee?"

"I'd like that. I'd also like to know what you think this is all about, if you can talk about it."

"I can talk. But I don't know much."

They took the creaking old elevator to the first floor, walked through the reception lobby, and had just stepped outside onto the Maine Avenue waterfront, when Dr. Luke called, urgently, after them. "Thomas, phone for you. It's Mama Nellie. She says she's got to talk to you now."

Thomas sprang back up the steps and followed Luke to the phone in a small room off the lobby. "She's real excited, Thomas," he said, as he handed over the phone.

"Yes, Mama."

She was breathless and kept repeating, "Thomas, Thomas."

"Easy, Mama, now just slow down. Take your time and talk to me."

"Two people, Thomas. T-two people!" She almost shouted the words. "Two people who saw Odessa with a big white boy. I got two of them. And you can describe him, can't you, boy? Can't you?" She was speaking away from the phone now, but Thomas could hear her clearly. "Can't you!" He heard a mumbled, "Yes, Mama." It was the boy Dr. Luke sent to fetch Thomas to the morgue after Amos Knight was murdered and who always followed Odessa and waited to run errands for her.

"All right, Mama. That's great. Just great. Now you keep him there, hear me? Hold him right there. Who was the other one?" Thomas snapped angrily.

Mama still paused, then said softly, regretfully, "First, I gotta ask you somethin'."

"What is it?" Thomas said sharply.

"You gotta promise me not to do anything. You promise?"

"Promise what, Mama?"

"Promise, Thomas. You gotta promise."

Thomas thought a moment, drew in his breath, sighed, and said calmly, "All right, Mama, I promise. Now who is it?"

"It was the blind man who sings, the one who sings in front of Daddy Bonner's church. He saw 'em good. But, Thomas, you ain't gonna let on he ain't blind? Now, you promised. Remember, you promised."

Thomas chuckled. He'd known all about that one ever since he took up panhandling years ago as a singing cripple in front of Daddy Bonner's. Thomas couldn't care less. It was a good corner for hustling. The pimps and the prostitutes were charitable, much more so than the churchgoers who passed him by without dropping a nickel in his cup. In return, the "blind" man sang a song to warn them if the cops were around. By now, Thomas could sing that song himself.

"No, Mama, I won't let on. I promised. But Mama—" his voice became harder—"you keep them right there. You understand? And I mean right there. You tell them I'm on the way. Now, don't you let them out of your sight. Okay? I'm coming now."

He hung up, thought a moment, then picked up the phone again, dialed the Second Precinct, and asked for Sergeant Russell Walker. Of all the white policemen in the precinct, Walker was the one Thomas felt a certain closeness to. They weren't friends, but they respected and trusted each other. He had come to Washington from Birmingham, Alabama, eight years ago in 1934, and, like Thomas, talked about taking night law courses; but unlike Thomas, who still talked about it but had become more involved in his literature and philosophy courses at Howard, Walker actually enrolled at Columbian College. And he was doing well. Like so many other white policemen, so many of them Southerners, who took night law courses there, Walker's ambition was to become a Special Agent for the FBI after being admitted to the bar. He and Thomas worked together easily in the past. Thomas helped Walker when asked; Walker was helpful to him on occasion. And he had developed, as Thomas well knew, close connections at the FBI.

"Sergeant Walker, excuse me, Thomas here," he said when Walker came on the line.

"Yes, Thomas, what can I do for you?" Walker said, speaking in a slow, warm, and friendly Southern accent.

"I need help."

He explained the situation in detail, told him about the two eyewitnesses, and asked if Walker could see if an FBI sketch artist would meet him and the witnesses at Mama Nellie's. Russell, as always, said he would get right on it.

"Gene," Thomas said, turning to the doctor standing nearby and listening intently, "I need a lift. Can you drive me to Mama's now?"

"Of course," Parks said.

They left immediately.

Mama had closed the gill joint. She was pacing around the boy and the beggar, who were seated at a table underneath the kerosene lamp when Thomas arrived. "Oh, Thomas," she said, running to him. He hugged her, patted her, and went directly to the table.

The boy was frightened, but he told Thomas what he had seen. He was a tough little one, as Thomas knew, full of street smarts and observant. The "blind" man was just as helpful. They both liked Odessa. She had been nice to each of them. She treated the boy like a little brother, always giving him money to buy Baby Ruths; and she always put money in the blind man's cup whether he sang a warning song or not. They just liked her.

A beefy white man with a pink fleshy face, bright blue eyes, and curly red hair showing from underneath his Panama hat stuck his head in the doorway of Mama Nellie's and shouted, "Is there a Detective Thomas here?"

"That's me," Thomas answered, rising from the table.

"Walker called. I'm O'Malley of the FBI."

"Oh, great," Thomas sputtered as he went to the door, stuck out his hand and said: "Please come in, Mr. O'Malley. I appreciate your doing this."

O'Malley was carrying a portable drawing board and box of artist's pencils. With grave courtesy, Thomas introduced him to Mama Nellie, the boy, and the beggar. "Is this light all right?" he asked as he pulled up a chair for O'Malley at the table.

"Not great," O'Malley replied.

163

Thomas said, "Wait a minute, I'll be right back." He started to leave, then turned back. "Mr. O'Malley, would you like some gin, or anything else?" O'Malley shook his head. He was uncomfortable enough as it was. He'd heard about gill joints, but he'd never been in one, and he'd never been back in the Negro alleys before, either. He looked around the place, his quick eyes taking in everything at once. Boy, I'll have something to tell Becky later, he thought. He sat uneasily at the table, fiddling with his pencils and sketch pad. No one spoke. What the hell am I doing here? O'Malley wondered.

Several minutes passed. Still, no one had spoken or moved much. It was miserably hot inside. The air smelled of alcohol, cigarettes, and kerosene. Shadows from the kerosene lamp were flickering across the wall. O'Malley became visibly nervous. He was just about to get up and leave, when Thomas rushed back through the door. They could all go across the alley and around the corner to Daddy Bonner's church, he announced, and quickly ushered them outdoors. Walking them over to the church, he opened the door and led them inside.

In the center of the church, under a single bare but bright bulb that hung from the ceiling, they all sat together on a crude wooden bench that served as one of the pews. O'Malley, sketch pad in hand, briskly went to work. With the help of Thomas's questions to the boy and the beggar, Sean O'Malley, Cooper Union graduate and FBI technician, sketched an amazingly accurate portrait of Gunther, curling scar, bent nose, firm jawline, flaxen hair, and all.

"That's him," the boy whispered, in awe, "that's him." The beggar nodded. Neither had ever seen an artist work. The process seemed unbelievable to them. It frightened them a bit, too.

Thomas took out his green notebook, where he had meticulously recorded Mama's responses to his questions about Odessa early that morning, the autopsy results by Gene Parks just an hour or so ago, and the brand-new descriptions of the killer. In his own hand, he carefully copied O'Malley's sketch in the notebook, closed it, rolled the sketch O'Malley had given him, thanked O'Malley again and said he'd walk with him to get a taxi. He gestured the others out of the church, turned off the light, and locked the door behind him.

To Mama Nellie, as he was leaving, he said, "I'll see you tomorrow, Mama. And thank you."

"Thomas," she called after him in a stern voice. "You get him. Hear?"

8

When she was a child, she thought of Washington as a city sleeping in the summer sun, a place of wide and empty avenues offering glimpses of marble monuments surrounded by dark stands of trees and greensward. It was bigger and far more imposing than home, but colder somehow, more distant and remote, despite the same sort of sultry heat and scents of magnolia and flowering trees and accents with which she had been familiar all her life.

They would come up from Charleston on *The Champion*, arrive at Union Station, be met by two of her grandfather's aides, and then were immediately escorted, bags and all, in a limousine to his Senate office only three blocks away on the Hill across from the Capitol. Even as a young girl she thought that foolish; why couldn't they walk and let them bring the bags? But it wasn't done. They had to be chauffeured. It was a ritual, one that he insisted upon each year after school was out and before Congress went into its long recess for the summer. Constance learned to dread it, and to dislike Washington. It was a stuffy, slow, predictable place, and she hated the constant political talk.

Nothing but politics, don't they *ever* talk about anything else, she used to say to herself. She couldn't imagine living in

Washington, or wanting to, for that matter. But it was different now.

She had been stunned at the change when she first came down from New York—could it have only been six months ago; it seemed like six years at least?—to take the job at the Bureau. It had been a hard decision, for it meant leaving *The New Yorker*, where she had been working as a checker/researcher ever since she got out of Smith and returned from that final trip to Europe three summers ago. She loved *The New Yorker*, with its shabby wonderful warren of old cluttered offices on Forty-third Street and its stable of writers (she couldn't believe she was actually working around E. B. White, Wolcott Gibbs, St. Clair McKelway, and the rest of that group). Even though many of her personal illusions about them were shattered, just being there still made her feel in awe. So what if some of them turned out to be charming bastards, and garter-snappers, too. And why shouldn't they be, Constance had thought, as she threw herself into her work and into her first real affair. It was an intense, passionate, stormy in-love-with-being-in-love one with a slender, pale, dark-haired young reporter for the *Herald-Tribune*. He had an apartment in the Village on Eleventh Street, where they made love with an energy and vigor more athletic than tender. His first and only novel already had been turned down by six publishing houses. He took the rejection, or pretended to, not as a mark of his failure but of their stupidity for failing to recognize his real worth and talent. How those bastards would crawl later, he would say. Now he was a private under a general named Patton, training for an amphibious operation somewhere, and she was in Washington working for Hoover.

It hadn't made her decision to leave New York easier to know the Bureau job had been arranged through her family's, and Marjorie Stith's, connections with Hoover's top aide, who was from South Carolina himself. That was another thing she had hated about Washington before. Washington—as she used to tell anyone at Smith who asked what the capital was like, after they found out about her family's political prominence—was *bogus*. Everything was based on who you were and who you knew. Connections, much more than talent, counted.

That, as she quickly discovered, was the old Washington, although, of course, who you were and who you knew still counted. But much of that old Washington had vanished with the war, just as the Old South had disappeared eighty years ago (and for the better Constance thought, despite all the romantic Confederate nonsense instilled by her family during her childhood).

There was nothing sleepy about Washington now. It was incredibly, excitingly, alive. Yet she also thought it was a bit frightening to see how quickly everything was changing. New office and apartment buildings were rising everywhere. New roads, new little bandboxes of houses were springing up along the previously wooded hills of Arlington overlooking the city. Every hotel was booked solid months in advance. It seemed you couldn't get a room without a bribe or the highest official orders. The palm-decked lobby of the Carlton, the marbled and favored hotel of the business lobbyists three blocks from the White House, was jammed with bigtime lawyers and corporate executives. They set down their bags, opened their briefcases, and prepared for Supreme Court cases or agency sessions while sprawled on sofas or standing around tables. The management had actually opened a "club room" in the basement, where middle-aged executives in dark double-breasted pin-striped suits could shave, shower, change shirts, even put their belongings in a locker until, and if, a room opened—and they conducted business in the "club room," too. In government buildings, whether tempos or new, in old auditoriums pressed into new service by the war, in garage lofts, mansions, and even in theaters, the surge of new workers spread, octopus-fashion, into every corner of every room in Washington. The War Department people alone were occupying twenty-one different buildings until the massive new Pentagon Building, the world's largest, opened that April. And still, space was so short even lieutenant commanders were huddled together in makeshift offices where four officers were assigned to work around three desks pushed together; and still the mass oath takings of new defense clerks, hundreds a week, continued, day in and out; and still, the housing shortage grew so intense, with prices rising so high at rooming houses (as much as four dollars a week for a single) that even Congressmen were forced to double up in narrow rooms with their aides.

Constance often wondered what her grandfather would think of Washington now if he were still alive. He probably wouldn't like it. Certainly, he wouldn't understand it.

Not long after she arrived, she was struck by an interview with Sherwood Anderson in *The Washington Post*. "A great novel is going begging for the writing here in Washington," the famous writer told the reporter. "The heroine came to Washington from some inland American small town with high hopes, got engulfed among the growing wave of similar girls, and . . ."

He's right, Constance realized. You can see it all around you. And it's different from the New Deal, which in just seven years, from June 1933 to June 1940, had caused the number of federal employees in Washington to double from half a million to a million, or so she had read in an article recently. Even before Pearl Harbor, the defense buildup—starting in 1940 and accelerating rapidly in geometric fashion throughout 1941—had turned Washington into the biggest boom city in the nation. The per capita rate of spendings and earnings (and drinking and telephoning and going to restaurants) suddenly had become the greatest in the nation, and thus the world. In 1941, 75,000 new employees arrived each month from around the country. After the attack on the Hawaiian Islands, there was no way to keep track of the monthly figures. The tide of new arrivals became too great.

Now I'm one of the government girls myself, Constance thought. I do my stockings with Lux in my room at night; I show my pass to get into the office every morning; I go to Hall's in Southwest on Saturday-night dates for crabs from the Chesapeake Bay; I go to the cocktail lounge at the Mayflower Saturday afternoons, when I can get away, and stand on line for tables and a chance to dance the Lindy Hop; I go to the free Sunset Symphonies on that shell the WPA built by water's edge and sit on those steps beneath the

Lincoln Memorial and listen to the National Symphony raise my morale; I eat lunch at the Bureau cafeteria at Justice (unless someone like Henry shows up) and have the usual cheese sandwich and glass of milk for a nickel apiece. And I'm just about as broke on my salary as the rest of them, though I do better than most. Where most of the government girls started out as Grade 2 stenographers at $1,440 a year and then advanced to a top of Grade 3 at $1,620 or $31.15 a week, Constance as a confidential secretary with a high-security clearance to a man holding one of the government's most sensitive positions, was not hired under Civil Service regulations. She began at $40 a week. Good as that was, and it was much more than most got, as she well knew, she still had to watch her pennies. Even with wage and price controls, everything still seemed to get higher and higher. She was shocked when she went to the Safeway the other day to see that half a pint of whipping cream was selling for 23 cents. A pound of butter was up to 43 cents. But she could make do, and she'd die before she'd ask her family for anything.

When she had first moved to Washington, she stayed for a month in Georgetown with Marjorie Stith. Through Marjorie's help (connections again, damn them, she thought, but sometimes you *do* need them), she moved into the "Taft House."

It was a lovely old pile of a red brick town house with high windows and ornate stonework five stories high. Once it had been the adjoining homes of William Howard Taft, the corpulent President who weighed a good 300 pounds naked when he stepped into his custom-made bathtub, and Admiral George Dewey, the hero of Manila Bay, in Teddy's war. Now, in a different war, it had been made into a rooming house for thirty-four girls and twenty-two men. They each paid $40 a month for room (and roommate), breakfast, and dinner.

Constance loved it. She and the other roomers ate together under Admiral Dewey's old high chandelier, and often, after dinner, sang, depending on their moods, "White Cliffs of Dover" (sentimental, but *really* nice, Constance thought), "Coming in on a Wing and a Prayer," and "Praise the Lord

169

and Pass the Ammunition" (corny lyrics, she knew, but they all liked them nonetheless) or "They're Either Too Young or Too Old" (the girls enjoyed seeing the men squirm when they sang that—and it was *so* true!). Someone always had on a radio. Often they listened to programs together. Constance's favorite was Fred Allen; she especially liked Senator Claghorn ("Ah say there, ah say . . ."), and didn't at all mind being teased about her own Southern accent: "You should hear some of the politicians where I grew up," she'd say, with a quick laugh. Sometimes they'd put on records and dance to Tommy Dorsey or Harry James. Constance loved jazz. She brought some of her favorites from New York—Jack Teagarden and Turk Murphy and Pee Wee Hunt. When she really wanted to get in the mood, in her room with only her roommate, or, better yet, alone, she would play some of her blues records. Bessie Smith's rumbling, moaning voice, soft and tender, dipping and gliding, suddenly belting out her feelings in a torrent of emotions, tore at her heart; she could never hear her without being deeply stirred and saddened. If it was true, as they said, that they wouldn't let her into a hospital because she was colored after the car accident that killed her a few years ago, it was something that outraged her as an American. As a Southerner, she was mortified and ashamed for everyone who lived there. It was one of the reasons why she felt she could never go back to live in the South. The only white woman who even came close to Bessie Smith's haunting sounds was Libby Holman. Constance kept *Blues Till Dawn*, her Decca album by Holman, next to her bed. If she was feeling low herself, those throaty, mournful, almost whispering sounds of Holman's "House of the Risin' Sun," with that young Negro accompanist, Josh White, on the guitar, really set her off. Next to Bessie herself, they moved her in a way hardly anything ever had. And although she'd never let on to him, and didn't want to admit to herself, they touched her more deeply by far than all the lovemaking thrashing about that she and her young man had experienced, sometimes three and four times a night (well, at first, anyway), and then lied to each other about how wonderful it had been.

She missed the Taft House terribly. Although she

suspected, she never knew exactly why they wanted her to move. They never said. Five weeks after she began working for him, her boss told her, nicely enough, but firmly, that "they" thought she'd like it much better at the Meridian Hill Apartments. Physically it was a swell place, all right. All the "nice" government girls lived there if they could get in; but it just wasn't the same as the Taft House. She had a single room. Everyone seemed to stick to themselves. And there was no singing or dancing at the Meridian Hill. It was probably the hardest place to get in, and she knew there was a waiting list of months, maybe years, but they had found her one. She had no choice but to move. Despite its elegance, she was lonely there. Well, I'm even more like the real government girls now in that, too, Constance thought.

At first, both because she wanted to and because she felt so alone, Constance started keeping a diary. She had the idea of using it as a basis for something she would write about Washington later, probably after the war. Maybe she'd be the one to write that Anderson book. In the beginning she had been diligent in recording her impressions, most private of thoughts, even composing some verses, when she felt moved; but as her job became more and more demanding, she put it aside. It wasn't just fatigue. The more involved she became in her office, the more disturbed she began to feel; the more she knew about some of the things that were happening, the more troubled she became. It was confusing and upsetting all at the same time. She wanted to talk to someone, and didn't think she could, or should. Or even what she would say if she had the chance.

She was thinking about this, and wondering about Henry Eaton, as she walked through the lobby toward the front door and across the street to the public garden that Constance thought had the greatest pretense and yet the most delicate beauty of any in the District of Columbia.

Constance loved the park. Its twelve acres were entirely surrounded by a yellowish-brown concrete wall that extended from the base of the hill back up to the top, flanking Sixteenth Street. Often at dusk she would stroll the promenades and grand terrace, designed in the formal Italian style, all enfolded in lush shrubbery and shaded by huge elm branches, and feel a wonderful sense of peace and calm after the tensions and pressures of her day at the Bureau. Everywhere there was the soothing sound of water: from fountains, from falls, from pools, all rushing downhill toward the center of Washington spread out below. Someday they'll have concerts here, she had heard. How perfect. Music and water and the best view in Washington: a panoramic look over the entire city, with the White House and towering Washington Monument directly below, soft dark lines of the gently rolling hills of Virginia faintly visible across the Potomac beyond. She wondered if you'd also be able to see the new memorial to Jefferson they were building now at the Tidal Basin just behind the monument.

She was always amused at the bronze equestrian statue of Joan of Arc, a copy of the original which stood before the Cathedral at Rheims. She wondered what Joan would have done to get this war over with in a hurry so everyone, Constance included, could go back to their normal lives, though she suspected that "normal" would seem boring to many people after this experience. Nothing would ever be the same after this war.

"So the hell with you, Joan," she said lightly, chin up defiantly, as she stepped out the main door and glanced over at the park.

"What'd you say," Henry said, looking up at her from the curb where he stood beside his parked car. "Something the matter?"

Constance flushed. "No, no, nothing. I was thinking of something else."

Henry had a '41 Nash, blue, with white sidewalls. Like everyone he knew, he'd bought a new car at the end of last year. It was supposed to have great economy, over 500 miles on a tankful of gas, the dealer had said, though he'd never checked the mileage—and the fourth-speed forward worked all right; but it wasn't nearly as much fun as the little Ford coupe with the rumble seat he'd driven after college. But, what the hell, the Nash was practical, and this was a time for everyone to be practical. There was no telling when you'd be able to buy a new car now. With the war, probably not for years.

He held open the door next to the driver's side for Constance. At the same time he reached over and smoothed a corner of the new small black sticker with a big white A in the center attached to the windshield in front of the passenger seat. "This won't get us far," he said, patting the gasoline ration sticker, "but I guarantee it'll get us to Griffith Stadium."

"Henry," Constance said, quite naturally now, she realized, as she said his first name, "I don't know why you even bother. I checked the paper this morning. The Red Sox are already nine and a half games behind the Yankees, and the Senators are in next-to-last place."

"Well, that's better than being in last place where they always are," Henry said, laughing. "Come on, get in. Wait till you see Ted Williams—and they have the best DiMaggio, little Dom—and Doerr and Pesky, and Joe Cronin's still over .300. Tex Hughson's the best pitcher in baseball, too. Great team! Besides, the Senators aren't that bad. Case is leading the league in stolen bases, and he and Spence are in the top five in batting averages. Of course, Ted's ahead in everything, home runs, RBIs, batting average, the works."

He glanced away from the wheel and looked at her. "I'm glad you could get away. Did you have trouble?"

"No, I just told Miss Ryan of Boston to cover for me. It's her team, too. You people do stick together."

That was true about Thelma. What Constance didn't say was her boss *wanted* her to go. She had told him, as required, she had been asked out by Lieutenant Henry Eaton of ONI, now attached to that special intelligence branch operating directly under the Attorney General, and, maybe, under even higher authority. ("We can't really have any personal life anymore, Miss Aiken," he explained to her, in a fatherly sort of way, shortly after she joined the office. "Not here anyway, and especially not now. It's just another sacrifice we have to make. You do understand?" She did, of course, but not entirely.)

They drove down Sixteenth Street alongside the park, turned left on Florida, and proceeded east through the traffic toward the stadium on Seventh Street behind Howard University.

"It's not a helluva good neighborhood," Henry said.

He gestured out of the car as they passed rows of old red brick attached houses, storefront churches, and funeral parlors. Old women walked slowly down the streets, shielding their heads from the sun with open umbrellas. Stray dogs crawled under metal front steps and curled, asleep, their heads sheltered under their paws, in the alleyways. On corner after corner, young colored men stood idly together, lounging against the buildings and seeking whatever shade was available. If he hadn't put on the uniform, Amos Knight could have been passing time like them without a care, Henry thought. Or maybe his race had nothing to do with his murder. Again, Henry began replaying in his mind everything he knew—but most of all what he didn't know, and had yet to learn, about that case. He had become consumed by it, and was trying not to show his concern. Damn. Too many things were happening too fast, and I don't have time to handle anything. He felt a flash of frustration and tension. Maybe I shouldn't have done this. He stole a side glance at Constance. He liked her, really liked her, but that wasn't the reason he was here now; she could help him, if she would. He wondered, again, how to ask her.

"And Griffith Stadium's not so hot, either," he said, in the same holiday-tone spirit he had been using with her. "But it's my kind of ballpark. It's old and small and looks kind of shabby. Not like Yankee Stadium. But it's got character, Constance, character. Just like Fenway. Seats about the same, too, I think. Around thirty-three thousand."

They parked on a side street a block away from the stadium and filed inside. It *is* old, Constance thought. She had to admit he was right: it has character, and with that high right-field wall way way back from the home-plate grandstand nobody's going to get an easy home run here.

"I don't think your Ted Williams will do so well here," Constance said, teasing, as they took their seats behind third base just over the Red Sox dugout. The Red Sox were about to finish batting practice. "Why, he's just a kid," she said after Henry pointed out Williams. "He looks like an unshelled stringbean in baggy pants with a child's face." She was genuinely surprised.

"Just wait till you see that kid hit. He'll make you forget all about Joe DiMaggio."

"Henry, even if I did, that still wouldn't make any difference to the rest of the country. Didn't you see the Gallup Poll the other day? Next to the President and General MacArthur, Joe DiMaggio is the most admired man in America. Your Ted Williams wasn't even on the list."

Henry snorted, then ordered two hot dogs, two bags of peanuts, and two Senate beers, the one brewed in D.C. She bit delicately on her hot dog, careful not to let the mustard remain on her lips, and watched as Henry mashed his into his mouth. When the mustard oozed onto his lips, he simply wiped it away with his tongue. Obviously he couldn't care less about what anyone thought of his manners or lack of fastidiousness. Constance smiled. If a less sophisticated man behaved that way it would be boorish, but with Henry it was stylish. He does have a flair, she thought. He seems to relish acting outrageously. Yet it becomes him. He has a way of letting you know he's not going to act the way you think he's supposed to, and he doesn't give a damn who knows it.

He looked at her rather impishly. She felt, and not for the first time, a stir of emotions. What was it that old garter-snapper in New York had said? Oh, yes—and she smiled widely at the recollection. "Nothing like a good rush of blood to the loins to get you going, my dear." I do believe I've had a rush of blood to the loins. I wonder what you'd think of that, Mr. Henry Eaton of Boston, or do you think that couldn't happen to nice Southern girls? She was delighted with her thoughts, and tossed her head in pleasure.

Constance had begun to feel something about him that was a little frightening. She didn't want to fall in love. Everything was too uncertain these days for that, whatever *that* was. You couldn't count on anyone being there long, or even surviving, so why let yourself get all involved emotionally only to be hurt or devastated in the end? she often told herself. Besides, the only thing that really mattered was winning the war. That was infinitely more important than what happened to any one person—and Constance wanted to make a difference. It was why she came to Washington in the first place. And she wasn't looking for another affair. That could get painful and messy, too, she knew. But already she found herself thinking about Henry constantly. After lunch yesterday she had a hard time concentrating on her work. It wasn't like her; she was always efficient and crisp. Never before had she let her emotions intrude on her job. Yet she couldn't help wondering how he was, what he was doing right then, what he was thinking right now. She worried about him, too. He was so deeply involved in that murder case, and obviously with other very secret things, too. It had to be dangerous. When he phoned her at home last night, after working so late, she had been childishly excited to hear his voice and had to restrain herself from reacting emotionally. He sounded so tired. She wished she could share his burdens, or least make it easier for him.

"Henry," she said, turning toward him, "have you had any luck on your case?"

He looked at her quickly. His eyes seemed to have shadowed. "No, nothing," he said shortly, "but I'm still at it. There's been no letup on anything."

Constance was hurt. He obviously didn't want to discuss it with her.

The crowd fell silent as "The Star-Spangled Banner" was played. Constance felt goosebumps rise on her arms and the back of her neck tingled. There was something about the way everyone responded to the National Anthem now that was deeply personal and moving. It was almost eerie. Not a sound in the entire stadium, absolutely still, and yet you felt an incredible closeness to everyone there, to everyone in the country even. The war really has changed the way you feel.

She stole a glance at Henry and noticed he had lost all his jovial manner and teasing looks. He was standing straight at attention, his shoulders back and his chest out in a gesture of almost fierce grim pride as he stared, intently, with deadly seriousness at the flag stirring limply in the hot air from the pole in center field. I'd like to be able to read your mind, Mr. Henry Eaton, she said to herself. There's a lot more going on in there than you let anyone know.

For a second, after the music stopped, an even deeper kind of silence hung over the ball field. It was as if the entire place, players and fans and vendors and groundskeepers alike, had taken one last deep breath and held it in a moment that everyone instinctively savored. Then, just as swiftly, they let it out, and the familiar roar of the crowd filled the ballpark.

She was wrong about one thing. In the very first inning, on the very first pitch, with a swing so smooth it seemed effortless, slow really, Ted Williams, that stringbean of a kid, hit the ball far over the distant right-field wall and entirely out of the ballpark. It disappeared into the Negro homes beyond.

Henry jumped up and down and yelled and whistled. He reached over and grabbed her. "Well, Miss Aiken, what about that?" She smiled back at him. "Not bad, Mr. Eaton, not bad."

He kept his arm around her shoulder and squeezed her. Then he turned, and, growing serious, looked straight at her in an expression both soft and yet somehow concerned. "You know, I like you a lot, Constance," he said, his voice low and strangely hesitant. She felt a catch in her throat, and looked directly back into his eyes as if almost afraid of what she would find there, or wouldn't. He wasn't teasing now. He paused a moment and, for the first time since she had known him, looked immensely troubled. "I really do. I like you, and I want to be around you—and I need your help."

9

Thomas put down his pencil, rubbed his eyes, and leaned back from the table. He was tired, bone-tired, but for the first time in days he felt better. At least they had something to go on now. He looked at the pile of drawings he had sketched out carefully, one by one, hour after hour, on small sheets of white paper for most of the night. Now Mama and the rest could pass them around. It was a long shot, but they did have a description and they could circulate the drawings he had just made.

"Leon, are you ever going to sleep anymore?"

Saundra Thomas, slim and tall with smooth chocolate-colored skin and an almond-eyed look that made her seem almost Oriental, stood in the entranceway to their dining room and looked at her husband seated at the table, now covered with scraps of paper, pencils, and erasers. In the center, its corners weighted down with ashtrays, was a large scroll containing a sketch of the face of a white man with a slightly hooked nose, pale cold eyes, and a faint curl of a scar running from behind his left ear. She stared at it, but said nothing. They seldom talked about his police work. Saundra despised what Leon had to do, and he did not like to discuss anything about his job. Lately, he had become obsessed by something but was even more reticent in talking about what he was doing. She had never known him to be so withdrawn—and to look so grim and run-down, too.

"I've got to go to school now," she said, leaning over and giving him a hug, "but I do wish you'd get some rest. I'm worried about you."

"Now, baby, don't you go worrying about this old man," Thomas said, pulling her closer to him with his right arm.

He looked up at her and noticed how worn she seemed. She's doing too much, he thought, and again felt a sense of helpless frustration, and guilt, at not being able to provide better. For years she had been holding down two jobs, teaching at the Negro grammar school in Deanwood near their small rented home in Northeast Washington and working weekends, as well as many week nights these days, as a maid in Georgetown. For several years after he joined the force, Thomas had had a part-time job, too, as a cab driver; but when he became a detective, he gave it up. Truth was, he resented feeling he had to have the other job. Besides, he was determined to show them what a Negro could do on the force. He devoted full-time to his police work. Still, it wasn't good enough, he knew, and when he looked at her now he wondered again if he shouldn't be doing something else. As always, he let none of this show. He pushed back his chair, stood up, and, smiling widely, drew her closer to him. Then he took a step back to look at her.

"How do you do it?" he asked. "What's your secret, *mia, mia*. You haven't changed a bit. You're still the best-looking woman in Washington!"

"All right, now, Sergeant," she said, pleased, but trying not to show it, "you're not going to change the subject with that talk. Seriously, Leon, you're overdoing it even more than usual. It *can't* be worth it, whatever it is." Or whoever, she thought, as she glanced at the big drawing of the white man and all the small sketches of the same face on the table.

"Yes, it is. Just take my word for it. It is."

He had lost his smile, and sounded unusually short. They were both silent as they looked carefully, and uncomfortably, at each other. Finally, with a shrug of resignation as she let out the breath she had been unconsciously holding, Saundra broke the momentary tension. "All right, Leon. I'm not going to lecture you. I've said all I'm going to say."

She paused, and grew more serious. "But don't forget, you promised to take James to the ball game and talk to him. I've tried to tell you that I'm really worried about him. He's becoming, he's—he's becoming terribly bitter and I just can't talk to him. I hope you can."

Thomas nodded, and reached out to pat her arm gently. "Don't worry. I'll take care of everything."

"All right, I've really got to go." She kissed him and left.

Thomas gathered up all the sketches he had made, rolled the large drawing, straightened out the clutter on the table, went into the living room and picked up the phone on the small table beside the couch. He dialed *The Washington Post*.

"Mr. Nelson, please," he said, putting on his crisp professional voice.

"Ah'll ring," the female operator's voice drawled.

Thomas drummed his fingers on the table as the phone rang and rang. Finally, it clicked stop.

"Nelson," said the voice.

"Mr. Nelson, this is Detective Thomas. I—" But before he could finish, Nelson interrupted.

"Listen, Thomas," he said, sounding exasperated, "I told

you I might look into it, and I might not—and that I'd let you know if I did. You hear?"

"Yes, of course, Mr. Nelson, I do appreciate that," Thomas said slowly and respectfully. "I just thought—"

Again, Nelson cut him off. "Look, do yourself a favor and don't think. Okay?"

No sound from either end. Thomas checked himself before starting to speak, but it was Nelson who spoke up first, and in a different tone of voice.

"Oh, and Thomas, you're right. There's no one on Seventh Street at night."

Thomas looked at the receiver, listened to the hum of a dead line, and broke into a grin. He hung up and, still smiling broadly, punched his right fist into the open palm of his big left hand. "S-weet Jesus!" he said aloud. He slammed his fist into his palm again. "S-weet Jesus!" Then he moved lightly across the living room to the stairs leading to their upstairs bedrooms. "James," he called out. "Come on down, son, we'd better get going. It's gonna take us an hour and a half to get there, so if we want to see Josh Gibson take batting practice, we gotta hustle."

He stood at the banister, looking up the stairs. A door upstairs slammed and a young man's voice called out, "All right, I'm coming." Thomas heard quick steps then saw his son starting to bound down the stairs.

At sixteen, James Douglass Thomas was not as tall as his father, and not nearly as big-framed, but he was tall enough, almost 6 feet 2 now, and moved with a wiry, supple, quick athlete's grace. James had more of his mother's looks: far lighter skin than Thomas's burnished bluish-black color, and the same sort of black almond eyes that, in his young, unlined, pale and intense face, gave him a smoldering appearance. Thomas watched as James took the steps down two at a time. It was going to be awkward, he knew, and from what his mother had said James was in no mood to listen.

Ever since James was born, and later with his sister, Harriet, too, Thomas consciously refrained from talking to them about race relations. He spoke little either about his own experience growing up in the South before coming to

Washington or his police work since. It wasn't fear or shame or lack of concern that motivated him. He just didn't want to inflict his own real bitterness and emotions on them, especially on his son. What was the point? he had said to himself many times. All it will do is make it harder for him. Thomas had seen too many Negroes become crippled by their feelings of inferiority and their suppressed hatred of whites. Those kinds of attitudes would only hurt his son's chances. As it was, it would be hard enough for James without starting out that way. At the same time, he would not pretend everything was wonderful. Thomas was not a "Tom"; he would never want his children to think of him that way. He was a believer himself in following the far more militant course set by a W. E. B. Du Bois than in being a Booker T. Washington kind of white man's nigger. But when it came to his own son, it was hard to know how to handle it. Consequently, and deliberately, he said little. Lately, that was becoming more difficult.

It wasn't just the war, though that was a big part of it, but new currents were flowing, and it was hard to see how they would come out. In every Negro community, no matter how impoverished or crime-ridden, something deep and elemental was being stirred. The years just before the war had brought the rise of Joe Louis to national fame along with a host of Negro entertainers—Satchmo, Bessie, Bojangles Robinson—whose songs and sounds and dance steps had become popular across the country. The Depression and the New Deal had contributed, too, in generating new feelings of promise and hope. At the same time, as Thomas knew too well, an even stronger white reaction was building. And now all these murders of Negroes here.

The war was making everything more complicated. They wanted more Negroes in the armed forces and in the factories, but the more colored people that enlisted or signed up to work, the greater the tensions and disturbances. In the factories there were sit-downs and work stoppages and strikes from white union members. They refused to work in the same plants with Negroes. In the Army camps and in the towns around them there were incidents of assaults, whether involving individuals or large groups, between white soldiers and Negro servicemen. Every Negro newspaper recounted tales of more race riots. Every Negro in every city knew what had happened in Alexandria, Louisiana, earlier in the year. Twenty-nine colored soldiers were injured, and one was killed, after white military policemen and white civilian police members fired on them. And it was only a few days ago, this same month of June, when the Navy and Marine Corps finally relented, under pressure, and dropped their ban on accepting Negro recruits for combat duty (until then, they were accepted only to serve as mess attendants). The combat units would still be, of course, segregated, and still led by white officers.

Maybe it was all happening too fast, Thomas thought. He didn't like to concede that, but above all he was a realist. It was changing damned fast.

"Ready?" he said quickly, pushing the thought aside, as James stood beside him. The boy nodded. "Let's go. If we hurry we'll get that next bus."

They stepped out into the heat and walked briskly toward the bus stop for the line that would take them, after a series of transfers, across the Potomac and down to Alexandria, Virginia. There, they would walk a few blocks to the George Mason field and see the Washington Elite Giants of the National Negro League play the Homestead Grays. For Negroes in the Washington area, the great rivalry was when Washington's Elite Giants played the New York Black Yankees. But nothing, not even Satchel Paige or Judy Johnson or Cool Papa Bell or Slim Jones, drew out the colored fans as much as when the great Josh Gibson came to town. He was their Babe Ruth, and, everyone believed, better than the Babe himself had been. Of course, there were still some who whispered that the Babe had Negro blood; and the white ballplayers of Ruth's time, the Southerners like Ty Cobb and the rest, had taunted him with jeers of "niggerlips" when he came to bat. The epithets made Negroes, and the players in the Negro Leagues, admire the Babe. They thought of him as a secret brother whose family at one point had fooled the white people and successfully crossed the color line.

The bus lumbered to a stop. Thomas and James got in and

took their seats in the back. They both stared out the windows as the bus started slowly forward.

"Your mother tells me you been saying some things about the war and how you feel about the white people," Thomas finally said. He looked closely at James. "You wanna talk to me about it?"

James shifted uneasily. He stared at his father and then blurted out, "Well, yeah, Poppa. I guess I do." Bit by bit, in halting fashion, as the bus rocked along, James began to express himself. "I mean, well, I've been thinking, and, well, what has this war got to do with us? Why should we fight for *them?* What are we gonna get out of it? Do you really think it's gonna make things any better for us? *Really,* Poppa, do you *really* think so? What do we owe them? Why should we die for them? I mean, do you *really* see any difference between them and the Germans?"

Thomas was surprised, and disturbed, to find that his son was far angrier than he had been at the same age.

10

Inside it was cool and dark against the glare of the midday sun. Ahead, the alabaster rail and gleaming white altar and flickering candles were soft lights standing out of a sea of darkness.

Gunther felt a tremor as he walked down the aisle, enveloped by the darkness and the familiar sound of tinkling bells and chimes and the heavy sweet scent of incense in the air. He was surprised how quickly it came rushing back, and, even more, how he felt a pang of something, an ache, a need, a physical hurt inside. Not a spiritual need, he was sure; he was purged of that, but still a need. He thought he was past that forever. Yet from the moment he walked inside the bronze portals of St. Matthew's Cathedral, with its great green copper dome rising above the massive red brick and stone walls and dominating the center of downtown Washington around the corner from the Mayflower Hotel, memories of his boyhood and the seminary had come flooding back. It was a weakness, but only momentary. Still, as much by instinct as by deliberate design, he genuflected and crossed himself when he reached the sixteenth row and then sat in the pew on the right side of the aisle.

"Shrivel," the wizened little man who was his primary contact, had silently passed him the message, scrawled on a scrap of paper that he quickly destroyed. "Matthew 16: 2–3." So here he was at St. Matthew's, row sixteen, right side as on "the right hand of God," facing the altar and waiting. It was precisely two o'clock.

He knelt and bent over the wooden back of the pew before him as if deep in prayer, conscious of the sounds of others stirring around him but paying them no attention. He appeared locked in his own thoughts.

The cathedral was crowded these wartime days, especially in the luncheon hours. Even those who long since had lost their Catholicism, or thought they had, slipped in regularly, alone, and offered prayers for loved ones now far away. It was very private, and something you didn't tell anyone else about; but it couldn't hurt and might just really make the difference. They came and went, swiftly and silently, so many passing shadows in the cathedral, day after working day.

Gunther was aware that someone was sliding into the pew behind him and settling there. He felt the presence of someone kneeling forward, just behind his right shoulder, but continued to seem deep in his own thoughts. Then he heard a man's soft voice in a whisper so low he had to strain to hear it, "When it is evening, you say, 'It will be fair weather; for the sky is red.' " In the same low sibilant tone, barely audible out of the corner of his mouth, Gunther whispered back, "And in the morning, 'It will be stormy today, for the sky is red and threatening.' "

The whisper came again, longer this time, lasting some sixteen seconds in all, and stopped.

Gunther heard the stir of movement behind him, then

knew he was alone again. He remained kneeling, repeating slowly word for word everything he had just heard. Carefully, he repeated the mental process two more times. Then he counted to sixty, crossed himself, slid out of the pew, knelt again, once more crossed himself, turned, and began walking, head down, as if in deep contemplation, back up the aisle. When he neared the vaulted ornate ceiling a few feet from the bronze doors, he appeared to notice the confessional boxes alongside the Italian marble walls. They stood beyond the aisles and huge structural piers of the cathedral. He moved toward them, then, barely glancing around, slipped through the side curtains and inside one.

A full two minutes earlier, Johann Brink had paused a moment before stepping out through the doors and onto the broad flight of steps leading down to the sidewalk running along Rhode Island Avenue. The sunlight blinded him. He seemed to shield his eyes from the glare with his hand as he put on his tan straw hat and then moved down the steps into the lunchtime crowds below.

From his perch across the street, where he stood looking into a store window half a block away, Jeremiah Delaney caught a glimpse of Brink as he reached the bottom of the cathedral steps. Then, casually, Delaney swung around and began following him toward Connecticut Avenue.

Brink turned right on the avenue, where the crowds were even thicker. At the corner, he stopped briefly, bent over, rammed a piece of paper down deep into a D.C. Department of Sanitation trash can, and continued walking. Delaney quickened his pace. He pressed forward more aggressively through the pedestrians. Ahead, Brink counted to fifteen slowly. He stopped a moment, glanced back, saw Delaney rummaging through the trash and stuffing pieces of paper in his pockets. Brink smiled and resumed walking. By the time Delaney finished going through the trash, Brink was on a trolley heading north around Dupont Circle. He looked out over the white marble fountain and bronze statue of old Admiral Dupont standing in the center of the circle and smiled again. Trashing always stops them, he thought. He wondered what they would make of that invitation to last week's garden party at the Cuban embassy.

Inside St. Matthew's, Gunther sat quietly in darkness peering out through the latticed opening of the wooden confessional box. At the front of the cathedral, near the doors, he noticed a man looking toward the confessionals. He watched carefully as the man glanced around the church, then turned and went outside. Gunther remained sitting, patiently scanning the cathedral over and over.

The minutes ticked slowly by. Gunther was in no hurry. As his eyes roamed the pews from front to back, systematically and methodically, he felt at peace in the stillness and darkness of the cathedral. Once, a young sailor knelt before the latticework and began to offer his confession. Gunther even felt a touch of pity for him as he whispered, "No, no, my son, not here now. I am offering a special novena before accepting confession." The sailor, flustered and embarrassed, mumbled, "Oh, excuse me, father, forgive me, I didn't know," got up and moved across to another confessional.

Gunther smiled. He remembered how tortured with guilt he used to feel when he went to confession. How much he had changed, and yet, in some ways, how little. He imagined kneeling outside the confessional before him, seeking penance from St. Matthew himself. Yes, he was guilty of all three sins of apostasy, impurity, and bloodshed. He was a fornicator, he was guilty of the sins of the flesh, he was guilty of usurping a power that belonged to God alone, and of course St. Matthew would forgive him his sins and grant him absolution. That was the beauty and simplicity of Catholicism: you were forgiven if you confessed. The odd thing was, you did feel better. Even now, after so long and so much that had happened to him, he felt himself cleansed.

He kept up his constant scanning of the cathedral; but he saw nothing out of the ordinary now, no one who resembled the man he had seen briefly in the vestibule. Whoever that had been, Gunther was certain he had not seen his face. After an hour had passed, he slipped out of the confessional, ambled toward the aisle, and left with a group of worshipers.

Outside, he turned right on Rhode Island then immediately made a quick right again alongside the cathedral onto St. Matthew's Court, which housed a few garages and several old residences that had been converted into studio apartments. It was a narrow alley with a fancy name, but its width and turns permitted Gunther to stop every few feet and look back to satisfy himself that no one was following. No one was. He followed the alley out to N Street, made a quick left turn, and sauntered toward Connecticut Avenue, confident he was alone.

Behind him, on the other side of the street, three-quarters of a block away, still gulping air after racing around Rhode Island to N Street and trying not to show the sudden exertion, was James E. Morrison. He hadn't "made" Gunther yet. All he had seen was the back of his head in church and now the back of his head and broad frame moving ahead of him on N.

Morrison's impatience got the better of him. He crossed the street, strolled quickly ahead until he passed Gunther without so much as a glance, and entered a clothing store on the corner of Connecticut. As Gunther passed the store, Morrison got a look at him. Then he turned away to examine shirts in a glass case, waited a few moments, and left to pick him up again on Connecticut. But he couldn't. Gunther was gone.

Jim Morrison had no idea who he was or what, if any, connection he might have to Johann Brink of the South African legation. But by that evening, the Special Agent in charge of the Washington Office of the Federal Bureau of Investigation had a detailed description of a white blond heavyset male, aged mid-thirties, observed sitting in a pew at St. Matthew's Cathedral in close proximity to subject Brink, last seen at 3:13 P.M., Tuesday, June 23, 1942, proceeding south on Connecticut Avenue.

11

Damn, Constance thought. She picked up the phone and dialed Henry's extension. He wasn't there. The pleasant-sounding man with the easy, confident Midwestern accent on the other end of the line didn't know when he would be back.

"Would you please leave him a message? Tell him that Miss Aiken—A-i-k-e-n, that's right, Aiken—won't be able to meet him for dinner tonight. Yes, thanks so much."

It was always this way. Just when things were getting interesting personally, something always came up to change them. She had returned to the office after the baseball game, glowing, and looking forward to the evening. Now this. What a difference a few minutes make. Sounds like a song, she thought, and smiled, her good humor briefly restored. She was bothered, though, and also anxious and tense about tonight. All he had told her when she got back was they had a operation tonight. She was supposed to be back here in headquarters by nine o'clock.

Constance got up, walked over to Thelma Ryan's desk, and sat down in the chair next to her. She liked Thelma, though she didn't feel *really* close to her. They were just—well, different. Still, she trusted Thelma and, up to a point, confided in her.

"Did I do right in saying yes?" she asked.

Thelma, who had a habit of licking her lips before talking, did so now, and answered, "Absolutely. Look, Connie . . ."

She always called her that. While Constance didn't really mind, after all, her closest friends did, too, and to a very few at Smith she had been called Con, still it annoyed her a little.

Something in my Southern background must have stuck after all, she thought.

". . . first of all, it isn't done for anyone to say no to anyone higher up. I mean, it just isn't done. In my ten years here, the only person I know who said no isn't here anymore. Besides, it can be fun."

"Fun? How's that?"

"Well, for one thing," Thelma said, licking her lips again, and looking over at Constance with a twinkle in her blue eyes, "you meet nice young agents, and who knows? Know what I mean?"

Constance smiled and nodded.

"Then, too," Thelma went on, fiddling with a pile of paper clips on her desk, "every once and a while something goes wrong and all hell, pardon my French, breaks out. That's fun."

"Is it dangerous?"

"Oh, yes."

"How?"

"Well, all those young men carry guns. I always presume they'll use them if they have to."

"I see," Constance said, still not reassured. "Thanks, Thelma. You're terrific. I really appreciate it."

She looked at her watch. Well, she'd just have time to finish up, see that the files were in order and locked up, go home, have a sandwich, clean up, change, and then be back here. I wonder what he means by, "All you have to do is accompany an agent on a stroll." Well, I'll find out soon enough.

"Thanks again, Thelma," she said, as she got up and returned to her desk.

She was arranging the correspondence to file away in the locked security section when a courier came into the office. He handed her a folder marked SECRET. Constance signed for it and peeked inside. Everytime she did, she felt as if she were prying or, worse, reading someone else's mail. She knew that was probably foolish—after all, she *was* cleared to handle the most sensitive material, and she was working for the government—but she just couldn't get over the feeling.

Enclosed was a memorandum about a Johann Brink, attaché at the South African legation, and copies of glossy photographs. All of the pictures seemed to be of men and women at a party.

She immediately carried the material into her boss's office directly behind her and handed it all over to him. He nodded silently, and immediately began reading the memo, glancing at the pictures as he did. Constance, as usual, stood before his desk waiting to see what he wanted done. Finally he looked up at her.

"Vanity, Miss Aiken, vanity," he said, continuing to sift through the pictures. "It's always their most serious weakness and worst enemy."

"I beg your pardon, sir?" Constance said, puzzled. "I don't understand."

He gazed at her through those cold gray eyes with that look that always made Constance feel foolish, or stupid.

It wasn't that he was unpleasant or discourteous. He was never that. His manners were proper, if distant. Everything about him gave off a sense of reserve: he always wore a dark blue suit, no matter what the season or weather, with heavily starched white shirts and a somber tie, and he never took off his suit coat in the office, and he always kept that new Breezewood pipe, the one made from burls in the Great Smokies, either in hand or in mouth, and he always seemed immaculately put together. His thinning sandy hair curled in waves, almost ringlets Constance sometimes thought. Not a strand was out of place (he must put on pomade). His blond eyebrows were so neat and faint above those disturbing cold eyes that Constance wondered if he didn't pluck them. He had a thin long nose, a physical trait that, along with his light coloring and strong firm chin, she somehow associated with Southerners; but he seldom smiled and he never really let you know what he was thinking, which wasn't at all like the people down home she knew. Whatever else you said about them, they were much more gregarious and outgoing.

He just makes you feel you aren't too bright, she thought. He makes you think he always disapproves of what you do. She realized, not for the first time, and protective family connections notwithstanding, that she was a little afraid of him. She didn't exactly know why.

"It's not *that* complicated," he said dryly, in that little remnant of a drawl he had not entirely succeeded overcoming. "See here." He pointed to Brink in one of the photographs. "We suspect he's a spy, or about as close as you can get to being a spy. German sympathizer, for sure. What we now know from these photos is who he associates with. It's very simple: we try to identify these others and then tail them a bit to see where it leads. Sometimes to zero. Other times, Bingo! Big Casino! Grand Slam!"

"I see," said Constance doubtfully. She wondered how many people the Bureau had to employ just to follow other people. She knew about all the informers they dealt with every day, but this means there must be hundreds more, maybe thousands. "But—"

She stopped and didn't know what to say. The one thing she didn't want was to appear even more naïve than he must think.

"Oh," he said, still looking directly at her. "Yes, the vanity. Well, I don't know why, Miss Aiken, but they keep taking pictures of each other and passing them around among themselves. They all seem to want them. All of them do. The Communists are the worst. They're *always* having their pictures taken. But the Germans and their allies aren't far behind. Like our friend Brink here." He tapped the pictures. "He has the deadly disease of vanity, too."

He looked down and put the pictures aside. Then, after asking her to get him the Special Agent in charge of the D.C. Field Office, he abruptly dismissed her.

"John," she heard him say, after the agent came on the line, "I've seen the Brink party photos. They may help. How has the tap gone? Oh? Still tonight, then? Okay, I'll be there. Thanks."

Constance checked her watch again. She'd better hurry if she was going to get home and be back here on time. Again, she turned to her files.

At that moment, five blocks away, a telephone company truck backed out of a garage onto Ninth Street Northwest.

The driver wheeled it expertly along the street to New York Avenue, where he turned left and pulled alongside a parked black Ford sedan and stopped. He kept the engine running. At the wheel of the sedan was Jerry Delaney. Beside him was

Jim Morrison. They both looked over at the driver of the telephone truck. Grover Holston, sitting behind the wheel, tipped his phone company hat to them. The small man next to him simply looked straight ahead. The FBI agents smiled and gave a small wave in reply. As Holston began to pull away, Delaney turned the ignition to start the Ford and followed.

Holston was out of sorts. He was happy only when everything worked according to Hoyle and Holston—and this operation was doing neither. All they'd got from the tap on the South African was a lot of small talk.

It had been a month since Holston climbed the telephone pole with his lineman's tester, using a wrench to short every telephone in the box for less than a second until he located Johann Brink's phone. He called the number and asked if this were the Acme Grocery. By the time an irritated Brink responded, Holston had the tap on the correct lugs.

Since then, for day and night without stop, relays of FBI agents had listened to all of Brink's phone conversations. Nothing. Oh, as always, they learned about his love life. Depending on the particular agent listening, their secret knowledge of the suspect left them feeling amused or jealous. Anyway, this guy was getting plenty. Those legation guys had it made, they thought. These horny gals around now will let almost any of those diplomats, especially the ones with their fancy talk from British Commonwealth countries, get in their pants.

But their tap revealed nothing to back up their belief that Brink was a spy. No evidence, no hints, nothing. The tap gave them nothing more to go on. Now they would take the next step and bug Brink's house. At least the tap let them know when he'd be out for the evening and where. In their business, that was all they needed for a B&E, or breaking and entering. Of course it helped to have a friendly embassy issue him the dinner invitation for this night. That way you even knew how long the dinner party was planned to be, and how long they'd have to work in his house.

The key to a black-bag operation was surveillance, constant surveillance, and, at the same time, always the appearance of normality.

In this, the women were essential. Too many men on the streets would arouse suspicions. It would blow the operation for sure. So they used their women, drawn from the ranks of top-level confidential secretaries from the key offices in the Bureau, to make it seem more natural. And of course it did: what could be more natural than young couples casually strolling down a street, seemingly interested only in themselves?

All Constance knew was that she was supposed to act just as if she were being escorted home from a date. Don't worry about anything else, they told her. Just enjoy yourself. They'd take care of everything. By now, after all the operations of the last two years before and after Pearl Harbor, the B&Es had become routine in Washington.

No sooner had Brink driven away from his house than the twenty-four-hour observation post, mounted and manned in the building across the street since Holston put on the tap a month ago, flashed the all-clear signal. The operation began.

A young couple strolled around the corner. They were eating ice cream cones and chatting. A telephone company truck drove past and stopped. Two men got out. Other men came up the street. Two of them joined the men from the phone company. The others split, one walking north, the other south. Two more couples strolled around the corner. Across from Brink's house, the young pair eating ice cream cones stopped. One of them, the tall brunette, spilled chocolate on her pink blouse. "Damn," Constance said. Her companion took out his white handkerchief and reached over to wipe off the ice cream. Then he realized he would be wiping her breast. He blushed and handed her the handkerchief. She thanked him. Another car appeared. It pulled up to the curb a few feet beyond Brink's place. An older man in a dark blue suit and a gray fedora got out. So even *he* came, Constance thought, looking over at her boss.

On the front porch of Brink's modest white clapboard rented house, Holston and four other men stood together. "Okay, it's yours," Holston said to the dour-looking little man who had ridden with him in the phone company truck.

The dour man nodded, opened his black bag, and took out

a pick kit. He had checked it out of the Bureau's property room earlier that afternoon. With a tension bar, he quickly began to apply pressure on the lock. He dropped the bar back in the bag then applied a rake, turning it until the fingers fit the ledges of the lock and opened it. The door gave way. All five men entered. They all wore those thin rubber gloves that surgeons use.

Holston immediately opened his own black bag. He took out the bug he had prepared from the junk telephone. This was the part he liked best, his final display of craftsmanship. He wasn't interested in proving something to anyone, or showing off; Holston was just a perfectionist who gloried in how well he could fix things from car engines to the most intricate wiring jobs.

He held up the bug and quickly looked it over. This microphone was ideal. It was suited to voice frequencies and would suppress other sounds, such as room electric fans that often were a big problem. Once he planted it behind a curtain and ran the wires out a window, the agents at the other end would be able to hear everything that went on—from Brink's screwing to his opening of dresser drawers.

It was boring work for them, Holston appreciated, and they always maintained two listening shifts: from nine o'clock in the morning to midnight, and midnight to nine. They all preferred the "screwing shift," as they called it. There was usually nothing during the day, other than the slam of doors or opening of drawers. At least on the screwing shift they could compare notes on Brink's performance and technique.

While Holston was working with his customary efficiency, the two "technical" members of the team briskly went about their job. They were experts at "interrogating a house," as they termed it among themselves. They knew what to look for. They could get what they wanted without disturbing anything.

With them, always, was a fifth man. The Director insisted that a senior agent accompany every break-in team; and one had gone along on all their black-bag jobs. Of them all, Holston was the most at ease. He loved installing his bugs and then hiding them in such a way that they were almost impossible to detect. Holston understood that the others were less comfortable. Certainly, they showed more tension. It wasn't a matter of doubt, but of the consequences of getting caught. They had no doubts, the younger men especially. They were, as Holston often reflected, mainly poor Irish-American kids who had gone to Fordham or New York University Law School. When they hadn't been able to get jobs during the Depression, they had joined the FBI.

Holston knew, too, that they burned, particularly the younger ones, with the certain belief they were on the side of the angels. The war made it easier to justify their actions, if they entertained any doubts about what they were doing. Few did. What didn't make it any easier, Holston thought cynically, was the absolute knowledge that if any one of them were caught on any of these operations, the Director would disavow them and denounce them publicly. He would throw them to the wolves.

In a way, they were far more afraid of the Director than of any suspected spies or subversives they were assigned to bug and watch. And, God, they had to shadow a helluva lot of them these days—and not just foreign nationals, either.

Actually, Washington was a good city for all their surveillance operations, especially for tailing suspects by car, and the agents liked it. The key was to know where your "mark" was at all times. If you lost him, the entire show had to be called off—and in a hurry. But they had their operations worked down to a tee now; they ought to, they did enough of them.

You ran your dark or maroon Ford sedans on streets parallel to the car being tailed. That way the mark would never see the same car. Of course, a lot of the foreign agents had their favorite tricks. They would slow when they saw a traffic light about to change. Then, just as it did, they'd break the light and leave the Bureau agents stuck behind. But that wasn't much of a problem usually. The agents would simply radio the car ahead to pick up the tail.

When Brink left the party at the British embassy, they were all set. He drove off earlier than expected, but that was no problem. Immediately, Brink was picked up by the tailing Bureau car. Then, on Massachusetts Avenue, he suddenly made a U-turn. It was the classic device to shake a possible tail: the following car cannot similarly respond without giving itself away.

Special Agent Burke Carmody, sitting on the passenger side of the car, grabbed for the two-way G.E. radio fastened below the dashboard. It was dead. "Shit!" he shouted. He pounded the radio with his fist, drew up his right leg, crouched back on the seat, and kicked out. It remained dead. "Fucking mother of God! Goddamned battery."

Carmody's car sped away to an all-night drugstore. The vehicle was still moving when Carmody jumped from it and ran inside to a pay phone. He fumbled in his pocket and discovered he didn't have a nickel to dial headquarters. "Jesus God, Murphy's Law," he hissed. Frantically, he turned to a customer, an old woman, standing nearby and tried to borrow a nickel. She shrank away from him, terrified. As he came closer, she started to scream. Behind the counter, the druggist reached for a baseball bat he kept hidden there. He picked it up and started for Carmody.

By the time Carmody produced his FBI identification and calmed both the old woman and the druggist, it was too late. Brink was pulling into his driveway.

Inside, Holston and the team snapped off their flashlights and plastered themselves to the walls of the hall and living room. Only seconds before, as Brink's car moved onto the street, agents outside flashed them a warning signal.

Brink got out and moved rapidly toward his door. He put his key in the lock, opened it, and walked into the foyer. Just as he reached for the hall light, he was slugged from behind and knocked unconscious.

Outside, still directly across the street, transfixed and horrified, Constance heard a sickening crunch—*th-waap!* it sounded like—then a *thummp*. Through the half-opened door, framed against the darkness inside, she saw Brink's shadowy figure falling to the floor. Then, swiftly, she saw her boss. He had raced to the door the moment Brink entered. Now she could see him kneeling over the body, rifling the pockets.

"Come on, we've got to move." The young agent beside Constance whispered urgently and took her elbow. "God, I can't believe this," he said. "They must have lost him. Come on!" He pulled her after him.

Inside, her boss took Brink's watch, ring, and wallet. The other agents quickly moved through the house. They opened drawers, strewed clothes, emptied closets, and took more valuables. As they left, Holston picked up the phone and called the police. He reported a burglary.

Constance and the other couples scurried around the corner to their cars. Another couple was already in back. When she climbed in, they drove off. The agents were tight-lipped, grim, and tense. There was little conversation. Constance was shaken. She felt sick at her stomach.

At the Justice Department, where they let her out, she went immediately to her fifth-floor office in the Bureau. Her boss was already there. She barely got to her desk when the buzzer on her phone rang. "Yes, sir," she said. She grabbed her steno pad and two sharpened pencils and hurried into the assistant director's office.

"Miss Aiken." His eyes were colder than usual. Otherwise he seemed the same.

"Yes, sir."

"Please sit down."

She pulled up the chair in front of his desk.

"I want to dictate a report about tonight. Make it to the Director, 'Secret,' and mark it 'Personal and Confidential.' " He paused and pressed his fingers to his temples. Then: "On June Twenty-third, 1942, at approximately eleven-nineteen P.M., Special Agents of the Federal Bureau of Investigation ascertained that one Johann Brink, attaché at the Legation of South Africa, a British subject, is in the employ of a foreign government hostile to the inimical interests of the United States of America . . ."

Constance couldn't believe what she was taking down. If tonight was a success, she thought, I wonder what a failure would be like? But it wasn't just what happened tonight that bothered her. She had been troubled ever since that conversation with Henry (God, that seems like a hundred years ago) at lunch when he talked about the Bureau's operations against the Vice President and Mrs. Roosevelt. She hadn't believed him, and thought it terrible of him to say something like that, even if he were only joking, which was how he left it. But when she got to her office, she thought about it and discreetly checked the files. She was shocked—and that wasn't the right word—to learn Henry was right. The Vice President and Mrs. Roosevelt, too! She was appalled, and deeply disillusioned. Now this. She felt a sudden need to talk to Henry about it.

Her boss had stopped talking. He leaned back in thought, frowning. Then he picked up his phone and dialed an extension.

"John," he said sharply. "Do we have anything? What? You're sure? The whole police thing is working? They buy the burglary?"

He began to laugh, a high, thin laugh not at all attractive in an executive. It was, well, nasty, cruel-sounding, Constance thought on the rare times she heard it.

"Okay. Keep me informed. With anything." He hung up, looked visibly relieved, and resumed his dictation.

"Thank you, Miss Aiken," he said, when he finished. "Make sure the Director gets this first thing in the morning, with copies in the Espionage File."

Constance went to work immediately. She put carbons inside three sheets of 8½-by-11 white stationery bearing an Old English letterhead reading *Federal Bureau of Investigation, United States Department of Justice, Washington, D.C.*, rolled them in her Remington, then swiftly typed the words *Office Memorandum*, and began transcribing. When she finished, she stamped it SECRET at top and bottom, added the stamp numbers for the recording and indexing files. On the top and side she affixed the stamp bearing the names of the top Bureau officials besides the Director who would receive copies. An open line beside each name gave space for them personally to check off their receipt of it. She made the proper distributions then carried copies to the locked Espionage File cabinets in an adjoining room.

It was bulging, and from far more than just Bureau material. Here were copies culled (and intercepted) from throughout the entire United States government: from the War Department's Classified Message Center, Incoming and

Outgoing, and from its MID; from the Office of the Chief of
Naval Operations and the Office of Naval Intelligence; from
a host of other agencies, including classified documents from
foreign embassies, friendly or neutral.

As Constance started to place the new copy in the file, she
noticed the extraordinary one from the Director, dated
yesterday, she had filed just that morning. She placed the new
one in the file, hesitated, then slipped the other one out and
took it with her.

12

Every twilight, except on the coldest winter days,
he emerged from the heating plant on the campus, unfolded
his chair with torn canvas cover and rusting legs, one of
which had lost its dirty white rubber foot, and tipped it back
until it perched delicately against the wall by the side of the
building. He had it down to a science, this balancing act. It
gave him pleasure to end the long work day this way. Only
when he was comfortably positioned, feet raised up, head
back, ready to watch the day pass into night, did he begin his
final daily ritual. He carefully filled his corncob pipe from a
can of Prince Albert tobacco, scratched into flame a kitchen
match with his fingernail, lighted his pipe, and began to puff
away in contentment. He noticed the young couple strolling
hand in hand among the trees on the green some twenty yards
away. He half turned his head to watch them when,
simultaneously, the deafening sound of an explosion broke
the still, hot summer air and the sight of a bright flash caught
his peripheral vision.

The young students didn't hear the sound, but they saw the
sudden flash. They whirled sharply. The chair and the
colored man in it were falling to the ground. In the same
quick glance they observed a white man running away from

the building and across the campus green toward the woods beyond. They raced toward the building and the man on the ground. When they got closer they both stopped in horror. The young woman looked down at the spreading dark flow of blood coming from the man's head. She covered her mouth with her hands and started to scream. The muscles in her neck bulged and tears streamed down her cheeks. Her companion stood, frozen, over the body and the smoldering tobacco strewn on and about the body. He started to shout, too. The only sounds that came from either of them were hard, croaking guttural noises.

13

"Thomas, Nelson of the *Post* here."

"Yes, Mr. Nelson."

"About that latest colored one, last night."

"Yes."

"Well, I—well, I'm gonna do a story on it, and I wanna hit that Negro angle I came up with. You know, all colored, everybody afraid, like 1919. Tie 'em all together. You follow me?"

"I follow."

"Well, look, Thomas, I wanna make sure it's the same as the others. Get what I mean?"

"Another sniper. Shot in the head, .38. Same story, Mr. Nelson."

"Okay. Great, terrific. Now, Thomas."

"Yes, Mr. Nelson."

"You haven't talked to anyone else about this, have you? You haven't talked to Crown of the *Star* or Burch of the *News* or Byrnes of the *Times-Herald?* I mean, I already told my desk about the colored angle I came up with on this, and I told 'em I got this exclusive. Now I don't wanna get screwed on this."

"I haven't talked to anyone else, Mr. Nelson. Just you. It's all yours."

"Okay. I'm counting on that, Thomas. Understand? An exclusive."

"Absolutely, Mr. Nelson."

"Great. Now I got my desk all ready for this, and here's what I want you to do. I'm comin' over to the precinct in about half an hour and I want you to pull all those homicide sheets. You know, times, places, dates, names. The whole thing, the way it all ties together."

"I'll have them for you."

"Swell. And just me, right? Just me."

"Just you, Mr. Nelson."

"Helluva story, Thomas. Like I told my desk, I knew there was somethin' goin' on. I knew I'd put this one together."

"You have put it all together, Mr. Nelson."

"Okay. Now, Thomas, have those sheets ready. And just me, right?"

"They'll be ready, Mr. Nelson. Just for you."

"Okay."

The phone clicked and then hummed. Thomas felt nothing. No anger, no exultation, no emotion of any kind. He was drained, numb, exhausted. He stared blankly ahead of his cubicle wall, tuning out the sounds of the precinct. Then he remembered some lines from a Dunbar poem:

> *We wear the mask that grins and lies,*
> *It hides our cheek and shades our eyes—*

To wear the mask, he thought, you had to want to cover up the real face underneath, but I don't even know anymore what my real face looks like or how anyone would describe it if they saw it. He started gathering the Negro homicide material for Nelson. It wasn't hard. He kept a complete file, all up to date as of this morning, in his top desk drawer.

When he finished, he sat back, deep in thought. Then he fished around his vest pocket until he found the slip of paper with that young naval officer's number on it. He picked up the phone and dialed.

"Lieutenant Eaton?"

"Yes, this is Lieutenant Eaton. Who is this?"

"This is Detective Sergeant Thomas, Leon Thomas of the District Police Department. We met—"

"Of course," said Henry, interrupting. "What can I do for you, Thomas?"

"I'm not sure, but there's been another murder."

Henry felt his pulse quicken. He gripped the receiver tighter.

"It happened last night, around twilight," Thomas continued, then paused. "It was another Negro. Shot in the head, same way."

"Where?"

"At the Columbia Institution for the Deaf out Florida Avenue. It's a school for the deaf and dumb. Three schools, actually. One of them's a college called Gallaudet. The dead man was a janitor at Gallaudet. Guy named Robertson, Frank Robertson. About fifty-five or fifty-six years old. Apparently minding his own business, as he did every night, when he was shot. Unless you know something I don't, there are no secrets at Gallaudet."

Henry sensed the sarcasm, or was it disapproval for his refusal to tell Thomas more about the background of Amos Knight? Whatever, he ignored it. "Any witnesses?" he asked.

Thomas sighed. "Two kids," he said wearily. "Gallaudet students. We had the damndest time trying to talk to them. Communicate with them, I mean; we couldn't talk to them. Had to get somebody from the school who knew sign language. It was frustrating. In the end, I had them write it all down."

"Why did you call me? How can I help you?"

"Well, I'm not sure if you can help or not, but I thought you'd want to know because of the Amos Knight business. By the way, you don't have anything on that, do you?"

Henry paused. "No, I'm afraid not."

"Sure, well, I know you'll let me know."

They were both silent. Thomas spoke again. "Thing is, Lieutenant, as my father used to say on the farm when the rains were late coming, I'm getting powerfully worried. Powerfully worried. I'm afraid the storm's about to hit."

"What do you mean?"

"What I told you before. I'm worried about a race riot."

For a long moment neither said a word.

"Thomas, I think we ought to meet again." Henry kept his tone even and chose his words with care. "We ought to talk all this over. Privately, that is."

"That would be fine, Lieutenant. I think it's a good idea. Where do you suggest we meet?"

Nothing in Thomas's voice betrayed the mixture of emotions, irony and anger both, that he felt. He thought of the conversation with his son, James, and wondered if James would be disappointed in him for not expressing his anger. There were damned few places a Negro could meet with a white man, even if they wore the same uniform or were in the same line of work.

Henry caught something, though. He suddenly realized they couldn't just have lunch or a drink somewhere. He hadn't thought about it before.

"Well, not at the morgue anyway. They have lousy coffee there. What do you suggest?"

"How about Chinatown?" Thomas said.

"Sure," Henry said crisply, secretly relieved to have the problem solved for him. "You pick it and I'll be there."

They set the time and place. After he hung up, Henry looked down at his memo pad. He saw that he had written the words *race riot* several times.

14

It was a good thing he got there early. The line at the Greyhound station already was longer than the bus, which reminded him of a gray-blue duckbill. The trip north was going to be crowded, and long. The man at the ticket counter said it was a local that stopped all the way between Richmond and Washington. It would take four or five hours.

Willi found a window seat. Good. He could pretend to

doze or stare out the window instead of being forced into a conversation with anyone. A large man in blue overalls and a gray fedora with a large black band sat down beside him. "Crowded, huh?" he said as he settled into the seat, occupying more than half of it. He had pudgy fingers, pink skin, and gray hairs hanging from each nostril. Willi nodded, and turned his face to the window. He was almost certain the man was not an FBI agent.

The engine coughed once and the bus lurched forward, throwing the standees in the aisle backward into each other. Some laughed. Others cursed. Then the bus slowly began to snake its way through the streets of downtown Richmond toward the route north along U.S. 1, the old King's Highway, for the 110-mile journey to the Greyhound station in Washington.

Willi continued to stare out the window. The sun was such that he caught his own image reflected in the glass. He was surprised to see that he was frowning. He raised and lowered his eyebrows to erase the frown. After all his tension while waiting in Richmond, he now felt relieved. He was glad to be on his way. It would soon be over. Again, he thought of Gunther. His body twitched in spite of himself. The pudgy man beside him turned toward him. Willi saw his curious look reflected in the window. He said nothing. Willi tensed then relaxed. The man turned away.

A gleam of sunlight danced off a piece of chrome on a passing truck. It reminded him of the glint of a bayonet in the sunlight. For the longest time, Willi had been convinced he would die as his father had, with a bayonet in his stomach ripping his life from him. He used to dream about it. In basic infantry training, during bayonet practice, he had summoned all his resources not to show his fear. It had taken enormous psychological strength to overcome his dread, but in the end he had conquered it. He had mastered the art of making his mind a blank. Odd he'd think about that now. But it seemed as if it were all only yesterday. He could see everything so clearly: he remembered how he used to think that somewhere at that very moment, in another training camp in England or France or Russia, other recruits were being trained to parry and thrust their bayonets into the stomachs of people like Willi, and all were being trained to shout aloud as they did so. He wondered if it would be the same with some American? A shout at death's time. What did it feel like? I wonder what your last thoughts are? He tried to picture his father, but instead Gunther filled his mind's eye.

Gunther. He knew he might have to kill Gunther someday. The thought didn't trouble him. What bothered him was Gunther's suggestion that they separate. He wondered again if he had been right in agreeing to split up on their way to Washington. There were risks in being apart, great risks. And why had Gunther suggested it? At the time, Willi welcomed their separation. He needed time to be alone, time to think, time to be away from Gunther's prying eyes. Now he wasn't so sure he had been right. What was Gunther up to?

The bus hissed to a stop beside a country store along the highway. No one got off. Four more young soldiers carrying duffel bags boarded. The aisle was packed even more tightly. Willi stretched his arms and glanced around the bus, idly looking at the passengers. Satisfied, he turned back to the window when the bus pulled out again. His mind was back on the mission. He wondered how specific the next and crucial set of instructions would be—and wondered if then, at last, they would receive their final orders and target. He thought of the contacts he and Gunther were supposed to make. Who were they really, how do they operate? Do they lead normal lives? Are they married? Probably. It was better cover. Do their wives know? Were they Americans, Germans, or German-Americans? Were they Bund members? No, unlikely. They would be the most obvious targets for surveillance. The Admiral probably planted them in America years ago.

Beside him, the heavyset man started to snore. Willi stole a look at him. He seemed to be really asleep. Their bus was picking up speed now and rocking from side to side. The passengers seated were dozing off. Those standing had grown more silent.

Willi kept staring, lost in his reverie, then slowly gave up the window ghost. He adjusted his focus so that he was really looking out of the window instead of at it. For the first time since they left Richmond, he was conscious of Virginia's rolling hills and lush countryside. He took in the cows and horses, the small, neat, trim white farmhouses, the fields filled with rising stalks of young corn, the hawks and crows circling slowly over stretches of woodland. Suddenly, he felt an overpowering yearning. It was all so beautiful, all so peaceful. He hungered to be outside, to be finished, finally to be free. God, I've missed so much. He wondered, after all he'd been through, if he'd ever be able to have a normal life again.

Their bus lumbered to a stop again. Willi looked up and saw a sign pointing to the town of Quantico. A number of young Marines got off. He watched as they headed toward the guarded gate of the Marine Corps base. If I had stayed in Detroit, I'd probably have enlisted in the Marines, Willi thought mordantly. The bus started up again. They were only thirty miles outside of Washington now. Willi forced his mind to become a blank again.

15

The sound of three buzzers echoed softly in the corridors, alerting agents throughout the building. He was moving again.

Swinging away from his desk made of timbers from the "Resolute" and out of his Oval Study, directly above his Oval Office, and two floors above the new Map Room he had ordered installed to resemble Churchill's in London, his strong hands swiftly propelling the wheels of his lightweight steel wheelchair with surprising speed, was Franklin Delano Roosevelt.

Two Secret Service agents preceded him. They led the way down the long, wide central corridor, now filled with streams of late-afternoon sun shining through the huge west-wing window that covered the entire second story of the White House. Two more agents moved briskly behind him. They kept themselves an equal distance behind and apart so that he was, at all times, bracketed by his guards. Smoke from his cigarette holder, clamped firmly in his teeth and extending out at a jaunty angle, curled back down the hallway and around two men in uniform walking just beyond the trailing agents. He cocked back his head over his right shoulder, in his habitual movement, and called out, in America's most instantly recognizable voice, a quick question to Admiral Ernest J. King, Chief of U.S. Naval Operations, and Lieutenant General H. H. Arnold, Chief of U.S. Air Forces.

It was a familiar scene, repeated these days almost around the clock. The difference now was in the size of the procession: until a few minutes ago British as well as American officers would have accompanied the President as their round of conferences moved from room to room. But Winston Spencer Leonard Churchill and his aides Major General Sir Hastings Ismay, Chief of Staff to the Minister of Defense, Sir Alan Brooke, Chief of the Imperial General Staff, and Field Marshal Sir John Dill had left shortly before with General George C. Marshall, Chief of Staff of the U.S. Army, to take a special train from Union Station that would carry them overnight to Fort Jackson, South Carolina. There, in the final official act of Churchill's short fateful visit, he and his aides would inspect the American troops being trained for combat. (For Churchill and the British command, the inspection would reinforce their worst fears. It "would be murder" to put those troops into combat against the Germans in a cross-channel invasion later that fall of 1942, as the American military command was then urging, Ismay told the Prime Minister. Churchill made the point more delicately in private, stating his belief to the Americans that "it takes two years or more to make a soldier.")

Since the German invasion of Poland that initiated the Second World War nearly three years before, there had been no darker moment for Britain, and now as well for its new American partner in arms. Churchill's trip itself reflected the extraordinary circumstances confronting the allies. For the British War Cabinet to decide he should leave England at such a climactic moment in the war was an unspoken but powerful testament to the gravity of the situation.

He knew, too, how dangerous this trip was—his second now to Washington in the six months that had passed since America entered the war—and had taken the most unusual step of officially informing the King, in writing, just before setting out one week ago today that "in case of my death on this journey I am about to undertake" the monarch should entrust the formation of a new government to Anthony Eden, his young Secretary of State for Foreign Affairs.

But, for Churchill, there had been no choice but to make the exhausting and long twenty-seven-hour flight, with additional hours for stops and luncheons. His flight took him across moonlit glistening seas. For hours he sat in the co-pilot's seat, admiring the soft peaceful scene below; but it made him reflect even more soberly on the reality of the war being fought there and around the globe. Finally, at dusk on Thursday, the eighteenth of June, his seaplane dipped down over the American capital and the Potomac River. It descended on a line and at an elevation that headed it directly toward the Washington Monument. Their course of approach caused Churchill to caution his pilot wryly that "it would be peculiarly unfortunate if we brought our story to an end by hitting this of all other objects in the world."

The war news could not be worse. For month after month following Pearl Harbor the Japanese forces, so underrated by American and British military strategists, spread out across the Pacific like a rapidly opening fan. Their reach extended thousands of miles east from Tokyo into the small island bases of the mid-Pacific, south all the way to the shores of Australia, and west in a sweep that threatened to penetrate the coast of India and lay open the subcontinent of Asia. In the map rooms of London and Washington the pins marking new and daily Japanese conquests were being moved rapidly about on the great charts recording the progress of the war. Still, the movement of pins on the maps failed to keep pace with the dramatic Japanese advances. They offered mute but vivid testimony to rapidly changing, and always worsening, battle conditions on land and sea.

Churchill's gloomiest fears, dismissed as unduly

pessimistic by the Americans only a few months before, were perilously close to realization: that the Germans, after crashing through Russian defenses at Sevastopol and marching relentlessly east across the Don toward Stalingrad and the Caucasus, would then slice through the Middle East for the final victorious linkup with Japanese troops who were racing west toward them through India. In the Atlantic, German submarines roamed at will. Losses of vital war materiel from daily sinking of American merchant vessels were far worse than the public of either the United States or Great Britain was remotely aware. Neither American coast was secure. After the fall of Corregidor and surrender of the remaining American garrison on the Philippines just six weeks before, the American mainland lay open to attack. Only two days ago, on Monday, June 22, a Japanese submarine surfaced and shelled Fort Stevens, Oregon. It was the first attack on a United States continental military base since the War of 1812. Officials were certain this shelling presaged coordinated air attacks on the major cities along both Atlantic and Pacific shores. Despite that situation the Americans, under desperate daily prodding from the Russians, went ahead drafting plans to open a second front by launching an invasion of Europe only a few months away. Churchill was certain an invasion then would end in disaster. It would turn the English Channel into a river of blood. German successes in arms made them so confident of victory they made no attempt to hide the ruthlessness and barbarism with which they crushed their foes. Now they openly boasted of committing atrocities. Just days earlier they announced publicly, for all the world to ponder, that they had "extinguished" an entire Czech village called Lidice. They executed all its men, put all its women in concentration camps, sent all its children to "appropriate educational institutions" in Germany, then leveled the town. Not a trace of its previous existence could be found.

Beyond all these alarums, Churchill had a greater and compelling reason to make such a journey at such a time—the reaching of a joint decision with the Americans on the "Tube Alloys" project, which the Americans called by the code name of "S-one."

Churchill brought with him all the secret papers on Tube Alloys. He was prepared to share them with Roosevelt and the President's constant companion and most intimate adviser, the shadowy, consumptive, pale Harry Hopkins.

Even more than the grim battle reports, the implications of Tube Alloys filled Churchill with a sense of the gravest urgency, and a feeling of dread. Creeping into the British secret documents were more and more highly sensitive but reliable intelligence reports about the efforts the Germans were making to obtain supplies of "heavy water." These repeated reports made Churchill think of that term as being sinister, eerie, unnatural. Yet he and the Americans could not ignore it.

His own scientists assured him, just before he left, that they were making great progress on Tube Alloys. They were convinced they would be successful before the war was over. But so could the Germans! The Americans were progressing, also. Just eight months ago at the end of October, four and a half weeks before Pearl Harbor, the President wrote Churchill and suggested the two nations pool their best scientific minds to conduct their secret research jointly. Instantly, Churchill agreed. He clandestinely dispatched a number of top British scientists to the United States. Now, with the coming of summer, their months of shared efforts had convinced them the project was practical; but a decision had to be made urgently. They must decide whether or not to go forward with large-scale production plants at vast cost. And, if approved, where should the plants be located? England, with the Blitz, was out. Canada was a possibility. But the United States by far provided the best location.

Churchill was driven by a nightmare: that his scientists were right in predicting success, but that the Germans would win the race to produce a bomb that, incredible though it seemed, when detonated would release unbelievable and devastating amounts of deadly energy by atomic fission.

He knew the President felt something of the same urgency; but he still wasn't sure about the true measure of this man with whom he was in such close contact and on whose shoulders now rested such great responsibility. Not only the fortunes of the United States, but also those of the British

Empire, were largely dependent on the actions and leadership of the American President. Fate had conspired to place the outcome of the war in his hands. Churchill knew this and was troubled by it.

There was a side to the President—was it an innate frivolousness, shallowness, or a bravado born of his infirmity?—that Churchill, with all his dour introspection, his bouts of "black dog" spells of depression, and his highly developed sense of his own historic destiny, could not penetrate.

And from the very beginning of this whirlwind meeting between them, he had been confounded again by Franklin Roosevelt.

No sooner had Churchill's plane bounced down at the small airport near Hyde Park (where he flew from Washington to meet the President), and in the worst landing the British leader had ever experienced, than the waiting Roosevelt insisted on driving the two of them off in a hair-raising demonstration of recklessness. Roosevelt's specially designed open touring car had an ingenious arrangement of controls that permitted him to handle all the functions of braking, accelerating, and steering entirely by the use of hands and arms that Churchill found to be amazingly strong and muscular.

Whether the President was testing him, Churchill could not be sure. That he wanted to demonstrate both his strength and skill, he knew: the President even asked him, in that jocular but proud manner, to feel his biceps.

When Churchill did, the President, delighted, boasted that a famous prizefighter had envied his muscular development. Then he set off, with Churchill by his side, in a motor tour of the grounds of his estate and the surrounding Hudson River countryside. The Prime Minister tried not to show his alarm as the President wheeled and turned and poised above precipices, their car overhanging the river far below, all the while conducting the most serious of conversations about the war.

Roosevelt was intensely attentive and serious, though, all that Friday and throughout Saturday as they discussed the Tube Alloys project, Hopkins always by their side. Churchill saw another side of this complex character when, after hours of intense discussion, the President would lose himself in his stamp collection and cast aside all cares of state.

With his historian's eye at work, Churchill silently watched as the President's personal military aide, General "Pa" Watson, brought him large albums and a number of envelopes filled with stamps he had long wanted. Deep in thought, the President carefully drew out the stamps one by one and placed them in their proper places in the album. It was a moment that made Churchill wonder what else there was about Roosevelt he didn't know. Then they resumed their discussions. Before they boarded the special train that carried them from Hyde Park back to Washington that night, Churchill was relieved to hear the President say he thought the United States should begin the production of the atomic-fission weapon. And so the decision was reached. They jointly agreed to press the Tube Alloys/S-one effort. Ramifications of the decision were immediate. Not the least of them was the even greater sense of urgency over security that swept Attorney General Biddle's secret intelligence coordinating committee whose responsibilities included keeping closest watch on the S-one project then headed by an admiral operating clandestinely out of one of the nondescript tempos on the Washington Mall, and whose Negro driver had just been murdered.

Once back in the White House, Churchill again occupied the upstairs Lincoln Room, with its high four-poster bed and old rocker and small bath. Most important to him physically, its air-conditioning system permitted him to enjoy thirty-degree-cooler temperatures than most of the rest of the mansion. It was blessedly more pleasant than the appalling and uninhabitable Washington heat outside. Churchill was pleased to be staying once more directly across from the room where Hopkins was living and down the hallway from the President's Oval Study. Again, Churchill found the President to be a sensitive and effective partner as they worked hour after hour.

He especially appreciated the considerate way the President acted after breakfast Monday morning. Without a word, Roosevelt handed him a telegram with dreadful news. Tobruk had fallen and its entire garrison had surrendered.

Not the slightest hint of national gloating or scapegoating was exhibited by the President and his circle of military advisers. Churchill would have understood had such been shown. He believed this latest disaster sorely affected the reputation of British arms. It quite possibly could lead to his own leadership being challenged with a vote of no confidence in Parliament when he returned. And he could appreciate why. Twice now, in only the space of three months, vastly superior numbers of British troops had laid down their arms to the enemy. First had come Singapore, where 100,000 capitulated to far fewer Japanese troops. Churchill thought that defeat ranked as one of the most disastrous in British history. Now Tobruk, where 33,000 seasoned soldiers had surrendered to half their opposing number of Germans!

The President only asked Churchill what he could do to help. When told he could give the British as many Sherman tanks as possible and ship them at once to the Middle East, the President instantly summoned General Marshall. They discussed the request, and the President immediately gave the order even though the tanks were only then coming into production and the Americans themselves desperately needed them. After lunch, when Churchill returned to the Lincoln Room, the President sent two young American Army officers to meet him. Churchill knew nothing about either. Hopkins passed the word that Roosevelt believed Churchill should meet them: both the President and Marshall thought highly of them.

He was impressed with the young major generals, by the names of Eisenhower and Clark. They spent the next hour together discussing the prospects for the proposed cross-channel invasion, which the Americans termed by the code name ROUNDUP.

For the remainder of that day, on through Tuesday and for most of Wednesday, the twenty-fourth, until he left with Marshall for South Carolina, Churchill and the Americans continued their discussions about ROUNDUP and BOLERO, which encompassed overall plans for an invasion of France, and GYMNAST, the operational status of a prospective landing in French North Africa, possibly around Casablanca. As he headed off with Marshall, Churchill was certain these last few days in the White House quite likely would determine the fate of the war.

The President thought so, too; but as he wheeled rapidly out of his Oval Study and moved down the hallway, he had more on his mind than Tube Alloys/S-one and the European and Mediterranean operations.

His time for decision also had arrived on whether to approve an amphibious assault on an island named Guadalcanal, in the southern Solomons across from Port Moresby in New Guinea. A land victory in the Pacific was desperately needed to check the Japanese tide, and in a few hours the President had to decide on giving the final signal for that invasion in the Solomons.

He called out another question about the invasion plans to Admiral King and General Arnold as they kept pace behind him, to the right of the agents, and continued vigorously rolling himself down the corridor. At its end he swung left into his bedroom, wheeled to a sharp stop before an overstuffed leather chair, and lifted himself easily and without assistance into it. He slipped off his suit coat with the black silk armband on the left sleeve he had been wearing each day since Pearl Harbor and quickly began loosening his bow tie and unbuttoning his shirt.

"Ready as ever, George the Fox," he called out in a melodious, high-pitched voice that carried within it both a clear tone of banter and also the exaggerated accents of Old Harvard and Old Wealth.

Although the presidential greeting was a familiar one, the agents, now stationed quietly around the room, smiled. They never tired of his breezy, school-boy camp manner, and his delight in calling intimates, whether servants or officials with whom he dealt daily, by lighthearted improvised nicknames. He was entirely impartial in it, delivering his sobriquets to those who were secretly offended by his teasing manner and those who loved it: Harry the Hop, for Hopkins; Harold the Ick, for Ickes; Hackie for Louise Hackmeister, his chief White House phone operator (also, on occasion, called the Empress Josephine), while his taciturn, grave private secretary, William D. Hassett, was Cardinal Richelieu.

For the more solemn among the President's advisers, this

was maddening. It was a sign he was not a serious person. To the agents, it was one of the traits about The Boss, as they called him, that endeared him to them. It made them even more protective of him. While no one really knew him, he was not a stuffed shirt and he took special pleasure in deflating the pompous. They enjoyed, too, though always tried not to show it, how he invariably made little of, without actually belittling, royalty. After Queen Wilhelmina of the Netherlands, whom he liked, came by the other day for a visit, he referred to her as Minnie and "the old girl." And now it was time for "George the Fox," George Fox, his masseur.

Fox stepped forward and lifted the President from his chair. Roosevelt's legs flopped loosely as he did so. Then, gently, Fox deposited the President, on his back, on the rubdown table. It stood next to the newly installed telephone lines, including the one that connected Roosevelt directly with Churchill's living quarters in London.

As Fox started to finish undressing the President, Roosevelt called out one more quick query to King and Arnold, standing just inside the doorway; then, with a wave, he dismissed the admiral and the general. Only the agents, and Fox, were witnesses to this daily late-afternoon ritual.

Fox pulled down the President's trousers and handed them to an agent, who silently hung them up. Roosevelt was left wearing only his striped boxer undershorts, although he kept his rimless pince-nez perched archly over the bridge of his patrician nose. His withered legs lay limp and immobile on the table.

The sight of those legs, in startling contrast to his powerfully muscled upper torso, had shocked the agents when they first saw him undressed. Now it was routine for them. But no matter how often they observed this sight, the agents were struck forcefully by just how helpless this seemingly indestructible and indispensable man really was. They stood silently, staring straight ahead as if instinctively not wanting to stare and thus embarrass, but always taking in the scene before them. They noted every movement as Fox carefully turned the President over. The legs flopped about again as he did. They watched carefully as he began the rubdown. His strong supple hands moved first along the neck and down into the back muscles. Expertly they massaged the lower back and then the fleshy soft buttocks and hips.

Watching silently off to the side, intently as always, was Mike Reilly, chief of the President's personal Secret Service detail.

In some respects, Reilly was closer to FDR than anyone alive, and he was easily the most protective, feeling often more like a father to a child than anything else. Certainly, he was more aware even than Eleanor of the many secrets in the private life led by this most secretive and private of American Presidents, who paradoxically was thought to be the most public and open of politicians. Reilly knew what the American people did not: that this supposedly inseparable couple, these cousins with seemingly such common backgrounds and family threads and roots, these extraordinary partners in public and, it was believed, private life, hardly ever dined together, never slept together, and usually met only for formal morning sessions at which she briefed him on political matters. Occasionally they met in the late afternoon where they spoke stiffly to each other of their children and other family matters.

Reilly didn't know whether they had always been this way, or if something had happened to change them. He didn't know, either, just what was involved with Mrs. Rutherfurd, the tall, slender, beautiful but somehow sad-looking woman from South Carolina the President had begun seeing secretly in these months since the war began; and he didn't care, either. All he knew was that she was important to the President, and Roosevelt needed her. He always returned exhilarated after Reilly arranged for them to meet in separate cars on a road beyond Georgetown. They would drive off together, alone, Reilly and his agents following at a discreet distance, and return a couple of hours later.

To Reilly, whatever eased the President's burdens was a wonder, and he would do anything to help him escape momentarily from his horrible pressures. These last few days had been especially bad. Reilly hated it when Churchill came. It was bad enough that the second-story family quarters of the White House became the headquarters of the British Empire, and bad enough to see their admirals and field marshals and aides racing about officiously through the hallways, carrying their old red leather dispatch cases with their war plans and secrets stowed inside; but when Churchill was there, too, *all* the living habits changed.

The President liked to go to bed early; Churchill never seemed to sleep. His habits shocked the staid, self-effacing White House staff. They still hadn't recovered from the time when the Prime Minister padded, naked, down the hallway of the living quarters. And he would drink brandy at night and talk endlessly, not only about the war, but about the sweep of world history. Roosevelt was fascinated by him. He didn't want to miss any of Winston's rambling performances in which he would quote poetry, reminisce about World War I, range back through British history, and at times invoke the great personages and grandeur of Imperial Rome. Reilly grew more concerned, and privately more annoyed, as he saw new signs of fatigue around the President's eyes and new weariness affect the timbre of his voice.

But Churchill wasn't Reilly's concern now. For hours he had been waiting for this moment when he would be more or less alone with the President. He was seething inside as he stepped forward toward the rubdown table. Held tightly in his hand was a sheaf of papers. Each bore the letterhead of the Treasury Department, United States Secret Service, and the date of this June 24, 1942. Stamped boldly at the top and bottom of each sheet was the word SECRET.

"Mr. President," Reilly said, a tone of unusual urgency breaking through his normally phlegmatic manner, as he waved the papers vigorously before Roosevelt's eyes, "I've been handed a report from the head of our New York office. They've just learned that the FBI believes that ten or eleven days ago Germans were landed from a submarine on a Long Island beach. They found boxes buried in the sand, German uniforms, a cache of U.S. money—and listen to this—" His voice rose sharply. "They found a whole bunch of explosive devices that they believe are, quote, Apparently for a specific purpose and not a mere sabotage job, unquote."

Reilly paused, took a breath to control himself, and stepped even closer. "Now our source—a New York cop who inspected this stuff and who interviewed the Coast

Guardsman who first found it and called the FBI—says the FBI has all this material sitting right here in its lab in Washington. And he thinks we ought to know what the hell's going on."

He hesitated, then said angrily, "Mr. President, I think we ought to know what the hell's going on, too. And we ought to know why Hoover is keeping this from us."

Roosevelt, still lying on his stomach while Fox continued his massage, cocked up his head, smiled mischievously, and said, in exaggerated tones of delight, "Why, Mike, you don't think Ed-gar the Hoo"—he drew out the word—"would keep anything from us, do you?" Then he grew serious. "Let me see those, Mike." He pushed himself up effortlessly from the table by rising up at the waist and thrusting back with his powerful arms, swung around so his legs dangled limply over the side, took the papers Reilly handed him, and glanced at them intently. His face colored. "Get me the Attorney General," he snapped.

16

She was nervous about seeing him and wasn't sure how she would react. All day she had been upset. As the time came for him to pick her up at the Meridian, she grew even more troubled and uncertain. While she did her nails in her room, getting ready, she kept up the same imaginary conversation with herself: back and forth, she mentally wrestled over whether she had done right in taking the Director's secret memo from their intelligence files. Or what *right* was, for that matter. Everything was so confused now.

Finished, she held up her hands and studied her nails. They were fine. Constance got up from her dressing table, dabbed on a touch of Chanel No. 5, put on her best silk Minikins ("brief as a breeze" panties), garter belt, and Mojud nylons. She picked out a simple sleeveless white linen dress that she bought from Tailored Woman on her last trip to New York. She added a single strand of pearls. It contrasted with the thin old gold bracelet her mother bought her on Via Condotti in Rome three years ago after her graduation, before they took in the opening of the World's Fair in New York. Then she topped it off with the white cloche hat and jaunty small red feather that she also bought in New York, at Bendel's.

All right, Miss Aiken, she said to herself, you might as well wear them all now because they won't last forever. By fall, they say, you won't even be able to get nylons on the black market and all the clothing materials will be restricted by the new regulations. Even box-pleat skirts, like everything else, will disappear "for the duration."

She was suddenly ashamed at herself. How can I be so frivolous, she thought, with so many terrible things happening? She was feeling apprehensive again as she went downstairs to meet Henry. But as soon as they were together she felt at peace with herself, and with him.

They rode through the warm night air toward Crisfield's beyond Walter Reed just over the District line into Maryland, talking all the way ("Wait till you have the soft-shells," Henry said, "the ones from the bay are the best you can get anywhere").

It wasn't hard to express herself. In the restaurant, amid the shouts of the waitresses calling out orders to men in rubber aprons who were shucking oysters and clams behind the copper raw bar, she blurted out the confusion and fear and disgust she felt during last night's break-in at the South African's house. After she described what happened, he told her of the latest Negro murder at Gallaudet, of his own growing tension over the slayings, and his uncertainty over whether they had any connection with critically important intelligence operations. That's why, he said, he needed her help. He didn't beg, he didn't plead, he didn't make excuses. He understood how difficult it was for her to help him, and appreciated how divided her loyalties would be. He simply laid out, in general, as much as he could and explained why he needed—why *they* needed—to know anything that was being kept from them that could help. It was more important than any one of them, or any of the people they worked with or for; but he wasn't cheap and he didn't wave the flag about that, either.

She believed him, and she had never been an entirely trusting person.

After dinner, they drove to his apartment on Capitol Hill. It was charming. It was on the first floor of a nineteenth-century town house just behind the Supreme Court. Big bay windows overlooked the Library of Congress. Before the blackouts began, Henry said, he had the best view of the Capitol dome in all of Washington. Now every time he came home at night he felt strange, and guilty, too, to see the great massive dome looming in the darkness, silhouetted against the evening sky like some huge toadstool towering up out of the shadows while around it the buildings of government lay dark and still. On a clear night you could see the stars, which you hardly ever could in peacetime; but it only brought home more sharply to him how the war had changed Washington and the country. It made Henry want all the more to be overseas and away from Washington. He envied his younger brother, Quincy, who had just taken part as a Navy pilot in the Battle of Midway. It wasn't right that Henry was safely here and Quint was there; it should be the other way around, he said to her. She liked that in him, too.

The apartment was what she would have expected: old comfortable chairs, worn but lovely Persian rugs, two Boston rockers, one entire wall filled with books from floor to ceiling, and wonderful prints of naval scenes—clipper ships and whalers and renderings of British, French, Spanish, Dutch, and, of course, American military engagements. Some went as far back as the early 1700s. He also had marvelous prints of the Drury Lane Theater in London, done in 1804, and one of a boxer, in tights, from about the same time. They all seemed, somehow, to reflect Henry. She felt at home there. On the coffee table she noticed copies of *The New Republic* and *The Saturday Review of Literature*.

"Now *there's* a combination," she said, picking up one of two books from the same table. "What's this, Henry? Is this required reading for Naval Intelligence officers these days? And is *that* your escape?" She pointed to the second book.

She held up a thick book. Inlaid on its front binding was a black cameo portrait of the profile of a thin-faced, hawk-nosed man with a curling pipe in his mouth. The cameo was set against what looked to be a brown wallpaper design. The portrait of the man with the pipe was bracketed by jagged white pockmarks that formed the letters *V.R.* "Really! Sherlock Holmes! And Bulfinch's *Mythology*. You are something."

Henry laughed. He took the Holmes book from her. "I'm addicted," he said. "Not to cocaine, like Holmes, I mean, but addicted to the real Holmes stories. They're wonderful. Thank God I read them before Hollywood got into the act. Look at this. Isn't this superb?" He ran his hand over the binding with the cameo-and-paper design. "That, Miss Aiken, is a reproduction of the wall over the mantel in Mrs. Hudson's chambers at 221B Baker Street. And those"—he fingered the *V.R.*s—"are 'bullet-pocks.' They spell out the initials of Victoria Regina. Are you familiar with the story?"

She shook her head no.

"It's from *The Musgrave Ritual*. Here"—he thumbed through the pages—"let me read it to you. Yes, here it is. This is Dr. Watson speaking: *'I have always held that pistol practice should distinctly be an open-air pastime; and when Holmes in one of his queer humors would sit in an arm-chair, with his hair-trigger and a hundred Boxer cartridges, and proceed to adorn the opposite wall with a patriotic V.R. done in bullet-pocks, I felt strongly that neither the atmosphere nor the appearance of our room was improved by it.'*"

"I see," Constance said. "And I suppose you get out your old trusty hair-trigger pistol and bullet-pock your walls with a patriotic U.S.A.? And where, may I ask, Lieutenant, does the Bulfinch's come in?"

Henry laughed again. "When I was a child, I loved those stories. Later, when I studied Greek at Harvard, I was fascinated to see how the mythological legends influenced the way people acted out the myths down through the ages. The Germans are the same as the Greeks. Anyway"—his voice lowered and his face looked tense and grim—"lately

221

they've been great escape for me. I've been feeling a helluva strain." He hesitated. "I know you have, too," he said softly.

They looked silently at each other. She reached out to him first.

There was no struggle, no pawing and no games. She liked that in him, in *them*, and smiled to herself. They didn't need to play; they were better than that. He didn't press her, and she was ready. *Ready!* I was like a swamp down there, she thought, pleased, just after. And we didn't have to say any of those awful little things that people say, or play any little games of deceit, the way so many of them thought they had to. She liked that in them, too. They were honest with each other. And he really does like me. He likes my body. He likes women's bodies, *really* likes them, appreciates them, I could tell. He was gentle and passionate, and considerate, not like the make-out boys. She *hated* that. He wasn't that way at all. And he did make me feel. She shivered at the memory. I felt I could take him all the way to my chest. It was like being cut in two. I loved his hands, too. She had been struck by them from the beginning. They were short and broad and stubby, not at all as you would expect from someone with his background. But strong. Peasant's hands, really, but they were gentle and soft and I loved the way he ran them over me. I wonder if he was surprised at me. She smiled again to herself. If so, he didn't show it, and I know I pleased him.

He *had* wondered. She gave herself with an abandon and ardor that completely surprised him. It wasn't so much her passion, but her lack of any female artifice that he had become accustomed to in other women. She didn't try to pretend. That was it. She was totally open in expressing what she wanted and liked—*Now! Here!*—and let him know it with an urgency and yet at the same time an ease and assurance that made him know she was no stranger to men; and obviously she couldn't care less if he did know. The way she tucked her right leg under her left and held up her hips, and the way she thrust herself at him, and the way she talked: God, she was extraordinary. No little clinging or shrinking Southern-girl type. But then, he realized, maybe there are no types. Certainly not with Constance. She was even more beautiful than he had imagined. He loved the way she felt, and the way she took pleasure in wanting him to explore her. She even enjoyed pointing out what she called, laughingly, her little imperfections. "This little nipple never quite came all the way out, as you can see, Mr. Eaton," she said, holding out her left breast. "I guess I'll always be just a Sub-Deb." She shook her head sorrowfully. "And you see here the perils of inheriting a weak appendix." She traced the thin, slightly raised and faded scar running up from her thick mass of curly black hair below. "Now you know why I'll have to be careful about these new two-piece bathing suits they're bringing out this summer," she said with an air of mock solemnity. And, after, when she knelt on the bed, Constance realized she was exposing herself to him, then laughed, and said, without a hint of embarrassment, her eyes crinkling as she looked back over her bare right shoulder at him, "I can see I'll have to watch that pose next time, Mr. Eaton." There was not an ounce of girlish coquetry in her, and none of the kind of flattery that always annoyed Henry. She was absolutely natural.

They both felt they could talk to each other, *really* talk to each other. That was the best thing. It was, they realized, rare. Their bond went far beyond the physical. Our souls have touched, Constance thought, in wonder. Oh, she knew there were things about him she would never know and never truly fathom. But that was true of everything and everyone. It was also true of her.

She didn't hesitate turning over the memo to him. "I think this is something you'll be interested in," she said after she got out of bed and had retrieved her purse. After all her anxiety about it, now it seemed the right thing to do. And it *did* deal exactly with what he had talked about. So they can hang me or denounce me for a fool, she thought, stubbornly, as she got back into bed beside him and silently handed him the memo. I don't see how it can hurt and maybe, as he says, it will help.

He looked curiously at her, then began to read. She watched him closely. "My God, Constance," he said, "this is just incredible!" He sounded angry.

"I thought you would be interested," she said, a trace of concern in her voice.

"That's the understatement of the year," he said. His voice was tight. He read it over again, and let out a whistle. "Jesus! Oh, and thanks. I can't tell you how much."

He felt, strangely, no sense of triumph. For most of his life, Henry had used people. It was a gift he had. He could get them to do things, often things they didn't want to do. It was just the way he was born. He could charm them or tease them or dare them into giving him, or doing for him, what he wanted and asked for.

It wasn't something in which he took special pride. In fact, sometimes, if he thought about it at all, it bothered him. He was not as good at giving as he was at receiving. And he did, he had to admit, often make people believe he felt something for them when he didn't. He also dropped them quickly. He supposed he'd hurt a number of people who trusted and believed in him. It was more a careless than a calculating trait. Or so he liked to tell himself.

That wasn't the way he felt about Constance, though. She was different. There was a certain—what?—a braveness, a stubbornness, an almost recklessly honest pride about her that commanded immense respect. She almost dared you to let her down. She made you think she understood exactly how you felt and thought, really thought. Of course, no one knew that.

Henry often wondered what other people were thinking, especially women. How did they feel when they made love or you touched them here and *there?* Is it the way I feel? Is their heartbeat different from mine? He remembered one who said her knees became weak and she felt something moving all the way up her legs from her toes after he began kissing and stroking her. Was that true? Then why didn't he feel that way? Yet he didn't wonder that way about Constance. He wanted her to wonder about him, and was curious if she did.

He suddenly thought: *I'm* the one who could be let down this time. The thought gave him a certain wry amusement, but it also bothered him.

"Come here, Magnolia," he said, reaching out to her. "Life's too short, especially these days. I just want to hold you."

He drew her to him, reached over, and turned out the light.

"How did you know I always did fancy bears, Mr. Eaton,"

she said, nuzzling into the mat of hair on his chest. Then, playfully, she stroked his chest, and sharply pulled out several strands of hair.

"Ouch! Damn it, Constance," he said, hurt but laughing. "You're too much."

"I do hope so, and I'm glad you think so, Mr. Eaton."

They had started to make love again when the phone rang. "Damn," Henry said, at first trying to ignore it. The ringing persisted. "Oh, for Christ's sake," Henry muttered as he sat up, snapped on the light, and reached for the receiver. Constance looked up at him and smiled, then felt a chill as she saw Henry's dark complexion turn ashen. "Oh, no!" he said heavily. Her heart skipped. She felt something stir uneasily in her stomach. Henry listened intently and slumped back against the pillows, a look of shock and hurt on his face. "When?" He listened acutely again. "I see." He had regained control of himself; his tone was harder, more businesslike. "Yes, of course, and thank you." He hung up and stared straight ahead, numbly.

"Henry, what—"

Constance was afraid to say anything else. He looked so terrible.

He turned to her.

"It's Quint, my brother. He was killed, shot down in the Pacific."

He sighed and shook his head. He was a study in dejection. His eyes were dull. Somehow, he looked older. She noticed lines in his face that weren't there before. He seemed unaware of anything else.

Her hands flew to her face. "Oh, Henry, I'm so sorry." She was heartbroken for him. She wanted to fold him into her and comfort him, but felt so helpless. She reached out and took him in her arms and pulled his head down to her breasts. "Oh, darling," she said, "I wish there was something I could do for you."

17

A uniformed chief petty officer, with a .45-caliber pistol holstered on his hip, stopped before Henry's desk, snapped to attention, saluted, and presented a copy of an EYES ONLY TOP SECRET folder he had been ordered by the Secret Service to deliver immediately from the White House. Henry returned the salute, showed his identification, signed the receipt, and thanked the non-com, who saluted again and left. He cut the seal and drew out an eleven-page document. His face darkened with rising anger as he read a document from the District No. 2 Secret Service office at the Church Street Annex in New York. It was the same one that Mike Reilly had given the President late yesterday afternoon.

"Damn!" he said in a low voice.

"What's the matter?"

Lieutenant Commander Arnold Thorson looked up from his desk across from Henry. He had never heard Henry sound, or look, so angry. Thorson was worried about Henry. Since the news about his brother last night, he had seemed driven and taut and held together by wires. He refused to take any time off. "No, thanks, but there's no point in that now," Henry said after Thorson suggested he go to Boston and see his parents. "I've talked to them. Besides, I figure I can honor Quint more by doing what I'm doing here. This is no time for any of us to take leave."

Thorson repeated his question to Henry. "What's the matter?"

"It's that damn Hoover again."

Thorson put his fingers to his lips and smiled. "Shhhh," he

said. "Mr. Hoover has big ears, a long memory, and a short fuse. You mustn't insult him, Henry. Now what's he done?"

Henry liked Arnie Thorson. He appreciated his kindness about Quint and his attempt to ease Henry's grief. But, he thought, he just doesn't understand how I feel. Henry wasn't sure he understood that himself, but he knew he was obsessed by a cold, murderous fury. Henry, for all his charm, was a hater.

Arnie was, Henry often thought, the kind of person that really ran Washington: unspectacular, anonymous, even undistinguished—at least by Harvard, Yale, and Wall Street standards—but competent, hardworking, decent, utterly loyal, and trustworthy. Thorson liked Henry, too, though on the surface they had little in common. At forty-eight, with a twenty-year medal from the Metropolitan Life Insurance Company where he had worked as an insurance agent in his hometown of Omaha, Nebraska, Thorson's career was over at the time of Pearl Harbor while Henry's was heading toward levels Thorson never dared dream. Like so many others, with the exception of the year he spent aboard a destroyer in World War I after graduating from the University of Nebraska, Thorson's life till then had been void of any excitement; and he didn't see action in that war, either. As the years passed, though, his stories about World War I grew grander in the telling. In all the time since his discharge as a lieutenant j.g. in 1919, Arnie never grossed more than $4,800 in any year. But he had survived the Depression, made friends, kept selling those nickel-and-dime policies to small businessmen, farmers, and laborers, joined every fraternal order in Omaha, and went, it seemed, to every wedding and funeral. Still, until the Japanese attacked Pearl Harbor, Arnie felt his life was over: he was balding, bored, childless, and getting paunchy. That very December 7, he quit his job, rushed back into the Navy, and wangled a lieutenant commander's commission. All those weddings and funerals helped, as did his friendship with his congressman and senators. He kissed his wife good-bye, and was immediately posted to Washington. Now he was assigned keeper of the gates and the person in charge of the flow of paper in Mr. Biddle's top secret shop. Arnie had never been happier in his life. He was, at last, doing something really important, and doing it well. Though he didn't talk about it, he knew he could never return to Omaha. Not after this.

"You're cleared for 'Eyes Only,' aren't you, Arnie?" Henry asked, his face still dark and his figure tense.

"You bet," Arnie said, with a wink. "Eyes only for you and pretty girls. You know no paper passes by me that I don't see, Lieutenant."

"Well, I've got something else to show the general now."

Henry checked his watch, and stood up. "Wait till you see this after I get back," he said, waving the new Secret Service document at Arnie. "Hoover's gone too far this time."

He put the document in a folder beside the memo Constance had given him last night, along with another marked PRIORITY TOP SECRET from the Record Section Message Center bearing the notation at the bottom, *The making of an exact copy of this message is forbidden.* He opened the door to their office, and walked down the long marble corridor to the double-paneled doors of the Office of the Attorney General, Francis Biddle, his immediate superior.

Minutes later he was ushered into Biddle's large corner office overlooking Constitution Avenue and the National History Building of the Smithsonian Institution, the one everyone called "the National Museum."

"Good morning, sir, how are you?"

"How are *you?*" Biddle said. "I'm terribly sorry to hear about your brother. I've spoken to your father this morning. Is there anything I can do for you?"

"No, thank you, sir, but I appreciate it. I really do."

"I expect you to let me know if there is."

Henry murmured his thanks, and accepting the Attorney General's gesture, took a seat before the large oak desk.

"I have something very disturbing, sir," he started to say as he looked across at the well-groomed, slight, graying man in the oxford gray pin-striped suit sporting a small neatly trimmed mustache.

Everything about Francis Biddle bespoke perfect grooming and quiet self-assurance. He was a withdrawn man, rather shy, really, Henry suspected, but immensely proud. Henry admired him. In his mind, Biddle represented the best of the New Deal: a truly distinguished person who was honestly dedicated to public service. So far as Henry could detect, he was without the slightest sense of personal ambition. His actions were motivated by principle, not politics. Unlike many in Washington, he had no awe of rank or public station. He held the ubiquitous publicity-seekers and self-promoters of the capital in icy contempt.

Part of this stemmed from his background. He was a Philadelphia Biddle. His public career had been marked by quiet dedication and competence as he served as Roosevelt's chairman of the National Labor Relations Board, then on a federal circuit court of appeals bench, then as United States Solicitor General, then finally last year he accepted the President's nomination as Attorney General. But Biddle was also a Randolph of Virginia, a direct descendant of the original William of Turkey Island and, through him, in direct line of Sir John of Tazewell Hall, said to have been the best-educated man in Virginia and greatest lawyer of his day; down from John, the Loyalist; Edmund, the Secretary of State; Peyton, the Governor; and all the Jeffersons, Lees, and other Randolph cousins who forged American history by deed and lightning. Like them all, he was immensely proud of that background and record but, in keeping with the clan, congenitally given never to boast nor even to refer to his illustrious ancestors.

He had, Henry knew, a firm and old-fashioned devotion to civil rights and civil liberties and the rule of law. The realities of the war, and the essential extra-legal operations to which the old rules of law no longer applied, created conflicts for him personally. For him, and for Henry and many others as well, the war made them face daily personal struggles of kinds for which they were unprepared rationally or emotionally. They found themselves forced to balance their normal beliefs and standards against sanctioning actions that embraced the very essence of an end-justifies-the-means mentality which, they appreciated, contained the seeds of the very forms of vast abuses of power and assaults on freedoms they were now combating. There were no easy precedents. Few historic guidelines seemed applicable.

Henry was aware that Biddle was troubled by some of these actions, especially the latest painful episode he had just concluded days before. After much anguishing, he gave the order to "relocate" 110,000 Japanese-Americans and place them in internment camps for the duration.

Typically, Biddle was more troubled than he let anyone know. He confided his concerns only to the diary that he, and so many others in Washington, now maintained. He, like the rest, knew they were passing through a momentous period that promised to change forever the old America they had known. And he felt compelled by a sense of history to record his most private thoughts and impressions about this passage. On numerous occasions he argued with the President about the question of civil rights in wartime. Biddle had been opposed to the internment of the Japanese-Americans; but he found himself almost alone.

The President baffled him. With his teasing, bantering manner, his cavalier dismissal of the objections Biddle raised, his constant allusion to how Lincoln had acted in similar circumstances during the Civil War by suspending *habeas corpus*, his authorizing drum-head court-martials and imposing martial law, his casual assumption of powers not granted to him and his pragmatic method of doing whatever necessary to achieve his ends, his secretiveness and deviousness, Franklin Roosevelt was different from anyone Biddle had known, and infinitely more complex.

Not that Biddle was soft. In his own right, he felt as ruthless as Roosevelt about the prosecution of the war—and, most of all, about the very real internal security threat the United States now faced, especially in these days when the nation was so weak and vulnerable. Biddle took those responsibilities with deadly seriousness, and was proud to have been able to recruit such talented and devoted people as Henry to his service.

"Yes, Henry," he said, in a fatherly sort of way, "what's the matter? I can see something's really bothering you."

Henry fumbled with the folder, opened it, and took out the memo Constance had given him. "Sir, last night I came into possession of this document. It was written three days ago by Mr. Hoover. I have no doubt of its authenticity."

"Where did it come from, Henry?"

"Well, sir, I—ah—I received it personally from a source who is friendly and entirely discreet and trustworthy. And I . . ."

Biddle nodded gravely. "Yes. And?"

"Well, listen to this. This is from the Director himself and it's restricted for internal Bureau distribution. It's marked 'Secret.' "

Henry began to read: " 'The Federal Bureau of Investigation has definitely established that two groups of trained saboteurs have been landed on the shores of the United States from German submarines since June thirteenth, 1942. One group landed on Long Island near Amagansett and the second group landed in Florida near Jacksonville.' "

Henry looked up, his face solemn, and said, "And listen to this, sir. It goes on to say: 'Data have been developed that on approximately June thirteenth a third submarine landed naval officers somewhere in the vicinity of Cape Hatteras.' "

He paused. The huge room was eerily silent. "Cape Hatteras, sir. *Cape Hatteras!* How could he know about *that?* Is Hoover bugging us, too?"

Biddle was grave. "I don't know, Henry. Let me see that."

Henry gave him Hoover's memo. The Attorney General immediately began to read it.

"And this morning, sir, just a few minutes ago, I received this from Mike Reilly at the White House. It's from their New York office. It says the Bureau's got incendiary devices, boxes, uniforms, and American currency with serial numbers that all date from 1928 to 1934. They believe all of it came from the German sub. They've got it right here in their crime lab."

He handed over the other document. Henry was disturbed at the Attorney General's lack of reaction to this last bit of news.

"If I may say so, sir, I believe this ought to be taken directly to the President." Henry stopped again, and then blurted out, "For God's sake, sir, which side is Hoover on?"

Biddle looked sternly at him, an unspoken look of rebuke on his face. He fell silent a moment; then he pushed a button on his desk and lifted one of his three phones.

"Esther," he said, "please tell Thorson and Mowbrey and Hornblower to come in. And ask Joseph to bring coffee for five. Yes. Thank you, Esther."

18

There was a knock on the basement door. Gunther froze. He checked his watch. Eight o'clock, Eastern War Time, an hour to blackout. Through the drawn windows, shafts of sunlight still beat at the curtains. They kept the apartment locked in a mass of sultry air. Behind him, only the low sound of the radio broke the stillness. He slipped backward silently into the kitchen, picked up the bread knife, and carefully placed it inside his sock alongside his right ankle bone, covered by his trouser. Another knock, sharper this time. Gunther moved toward the door, patted the .38 caliber with a silencer inside his belt, planted his feet apart, dropped into a half-crouch, reached for the handle, turned it, and opened the door. Facing him in the half-shadows of the English basement stairwell were the wizened man and Willi. For a moment no one spoke. They stared at each other, then Gunther backed up silently into the foyer as Willi rose out of his own half-crouch to his full height. He picked up his Gladstone suitcase, and quickly walked inside. "So," Gunther said, "the family is reunited at last."

part

4

**THE
STAMPS**

1

Henry was already there. The Chinese proprietor wouldn't seat him alone, despite his annoyance, so he sat, perched on a wooden chair near the cloakroom, next to a man waiting to take out an order of chow mein.

He was restless and tense. There wasn't enough time. Nothing fit together. He felt as if he had grabbed a loose piece of wool at the end of a sweater and watched it unravel faster than he could roll it into a ball. Roll it? he thought, as he shifted uncomfortably in his chair. Hell, I can't even see where the wool threads connect.

Thomas felt the same frustrations. Like Henry, he wasn't looking forward to this meeting. He was certain it was going to be a waste of time—and time was something he couldn't afford to lose, especially now.

As he approached the restaurant on H Street in Washington's small Chinatown, he passed the old Surratt boardinghouse. It stood near the District of Columbia Library, a grand marble structure built long ago when the area was fashionable. Now the library was surrounded by the dilapidated Negro homes of the Second Police Precinct. There was nothing to identify the old boardinghouse, but Thomas knew all about Mary Eugenia Surratt's boardinghouse. He doubted many others did.

It was one of the things about Washington that fascinated and angered him: the places that really shaped Washington's history often were unmarked and unknown, while the marble palaces that rose around them took no note of events Americans ought to commemorate. Everyone knew that the National Archives Building a few blocks away on Pennsylvania Avenue, which had opened several years ago in

235

the President's first term, proudly displayed the Declaration of Independence and the Constitution inside; but there was nothing to indicate that this was the site of the old Center Market where the daily scene of chained slaves being auctioned in sight of the Capitol ignited the early bitter debates that presaged the coming of the Civil War. Everyone knew about Ford's Theater, too, also only a few blocks away; but few were aware of Mary Surratt's boardinghouse. It was there that John Wilkes Booth and the other conspirators met to rehearse their plot to assassinate Lincoln.

Whenever he came to Chinatown to eat, or strolled its streets to try to see who was dealing in opium and heroin, Thomas thought about Mary Surratt. He had studied the case and couldn't decide if she was guilty or innocent. Once, he went to Mount Olivet Cemetery, way out on the Bladensburg Road which the British had used for their march on Washington in 1814 when they burned the White House and Capitol and much of the city. He wandered around the old burial grounds, inspecting the tombs and mausoleums scattered about the high hill overlooking the city, until he found a small stone. It was nearly obscured by shrubbery. Only the words MRS. SURRATT were on it. Again he wondered whether she had been hanged legally or lynched. Not far away he came upon the tomb of Henry Wirz. He was also hanged after being convicted for acts that took the lives of thousands of Union soldiers at the Confederate prison of Andersonville, in Georgia, where Wirz was commandant. Thomas noted, with clinical anger, that among the old war heroes and notables buried in that cemetery no Negroes were interred. But then none was buried next to whites anywhere in the city.

He thought once more of Mary Surratt, and wondered, too, as he often did, about Booth and Lincoln. Suppose they had been able to find out about their meetings here at Surratt's. How different would history have been? He reached the restaurant several doors away from the old boardinghouse and pushed open the door.

The proprietor, a small man in rolled shirtsleeves, dark pants, and bedroom slippers, shuffled forward. He greeted Thomas with great respect, affection, and a small bow.

236

"Mr. Thomas."

"Ching Hsiao," Thomas said, pronouncing the name with the correct accent.

He saw Henry stand up, and pointed to him. "This is Lieutenant Eaton."

"Very pleased to meet you," said Hsiao, bowing.

Henry nodded at Hsiao, and, more stiffly, at Thomas. He stepped forward and held out his hand. Thomas was even bigger than he remembered. At their last tense encounter at the morgue Saturday night (God, could that have been only five days ago? he suddenly thought, shocked at how much had happened since), Thomas had seemed enormous. His grip lived up to his looks. It was strong and hard. The two men stood apart awkwardly, without speaking. They started forward as Hsiao beckoned to them.

"Please."

They followed as Hsiao picked up two fly-specked red menu cards from a counter and led them toward a distant wooden booth.

The table had not been cleaned. Hsiao removed the dishes as Thomas and Henry stood by.

"I'm glad you could come," Henry said, turning toward Thomas. "I've been wanting to talk to you."

"Glad to," Thomas answered.

They became silent again. Each felt acutely aware of what was left unspoken and of their mutual doubts and suspicions.

Thomas was startled by Henry's appearance. He was drawn. His eyes had lost their sparkle. They were shadowed by dark circles. If Thomas didn't know better, he'd swear this guy had aged dramatically. He exhibited none of the brittle cocky banter of before. Now he seemed visibly weary, and troubled. "Looks like you've been working hard," Thomas said, a trace of concern in his voice. "I recognize the signs. You okay?"

"I had some bad news. My brother was killed in the Pacific. It's hard to accept." He swallowed hard and stared ahead but gave no other sign of emotion.

"I'm sorry," Thomas said, lowering his voice. "The worst thing is, there's nothing anyone can say or do that makes you feel better. I know." He paused. "I lost a brother, too."

Henry looked at him in surprise. "In the war?"

"No, a long time ago, Lieutenant. Before I came to Washington. He was lynched."

He said the words in a matter-of-fact tone. Henry, shocked, searched Thomas's face. He detected no sign of anger, or even bitterness, but he could feel, somehow, suppressed sorrow and other hidden, deeper feelings. "Oh," he said, "I, I'm sorry. I didn't know. I—"

"Thank you, Lieutenant. It was all so long ago. But I think I know how you must feel. It *is* hard to accept. And you can't get it out of your mind, even if you try to. I don't mean you should try to forget. I just think you won't. I am sorry for you. It's a terrible thing to lose a brother. I do have some idea what you're going through."

Henry glanced at him and looked away. He remembered his conversation with Arnie Thorson earlier that morning and was ashamed. He had expressed his frustrations to Thorson about being unable to stitch together all the loose threads, then, after telling Arnie he was meeting that Negro detective, Arnie replied, with a rueful smile, "And you think the Negro is a sweater knitter?" Henry didn't know what to think about Thomas, or if Thomas knew anything that might help. Probably not. But he was much more than a sweater knitter.

They watched as Hsiao spilled a bit of leftover tea from the remaining cup on the table and washed down the dining surface between the booth benches. Hsiao set out dishes and silver for two.

"You chopsticks?" he asked.

Henry nodded and was surprised that Thomas did, too. He wouldn't have thought he knew how. Hsiao left briefly, and returned with two sets of chopsticks. He handed them the menus, bowed slightly to Thomas, and disappeared toward the front of the restaurant.

Neither spoke. They studied the menus in silence. Then Henry said, "Saw that page-one piece in the *Post* this morning about all the murders you talked about. Quite a story. I see they had the latest one at Gallaudet and mentioned the Amos Knight shooting, too."

"Yes."

He's not going to make it easy, Henry thought, as another moment of silence settled around them.

"Got anything new on that Amos Knight case?"

"No."

"You?"

"No," Henry said, shaking his head.

Hsiao returned. They ordered and fell back into a stiff period of quiet. Thomas took out a package of Beech-Nut cigarettes. He offered Henry one. "No thanks," he said. Thomas lit one and as he exhaled the smoke, watched Henry. Their orders came—mooshu pork and orange beef, with egg rolls—and they began to eat, occasionally making small talk, but mainly eating lunch in silence. Hsiao took away their dishes and brought fortune cookies. Henry broke open his first, and read aloud: "Your career is about to leap forward. 78435." Thomas cracked the thin yellow shell with his long fingers, drew out a slender white sheet, chuckled, and read, also aloud: "Be wary of any new acquaintances. 80076." They laughed. For the first time they felt the tension ease.

Thomas suggested they play 076 in the numbers game tomorrow. They began to warm to each other. Henry ordered another pot of tea.

"Look, Detective Thomas," he said, pouring tea into Thomas's cup, "let me tell what I can about the Knight business and see if there's anything you have that might be of use. Of course, this conversation between us never took place, right?"

He smiled conspiratorially. Thomas nodded but didn't smile back. "Of course."

"Well," Henry said, "as I told you the other night when we met—and that *was* a helluva way to meet, wasn't it?—this case is very damned sensitive to the government. So damned sensitive I shouldn't even be saying anything about it."

He took a sip of tea and leaned closer to Thomas across the table. "Knight was the personal driver for an admiral whose name you would know immediately, but I can't even mention it now. Anyway, this admiral is charged with a top secret project that is absolutely urgent. Absolutely! Believe me when I say it's the most sensitive in the war effort. It's that big."

He took another sip.

"Well, the people who work with me are naturally concerned about anything that touches that project. Or seems to. We tend to be suspicious by nature, and lately we've had reason to believe that extraordinary efforts are being made to penetrate our highest security and our defenses. Some have even suggested Knight might have been in the employ of enemy agents and was shot to keep him quiet. I don't know that, but it's my job to check everything I can about him. So you can see why I need help."

Thomas had listened intently. He shook his head slightly, as if genuinely sorry about what he had to say.

"Lieutenant Eaton," he said slowly, choosing his words carefully. "I'm afraid there's not much I can do to help you. I do not know what, if anything, Amos Knight's murder has to do with the government, or with the war. As far as I know, it has nothing to do with either. All I know is Knight was assassinated by a person, or persons, who have systematically, and without apparent reason, been killing Negroes throughout this city. The same as the janitor at Gallaudet. I do not know whether there is a government connection with any of them. They all appear to be random, although I am convinced there is some connection. As you read this morning, and that doesn't begin to tell the story, as I've already indicated to you, it is having enormous impact in the colored areas of Washington. So I don't know. But I'll check through all the cases to see if there is any possible government link that I have missed. And I will let you know. Aside from that, I have nothing now that would seem helpful to you." He held out his hands in a gesture of mute frustration. "I'm sorry. I really am."

Henry leaned back and let out a sigh. It's what I expected, he thought. Nothing. They were both silent again.

"Detective Thomas—" Henry began. Then, on impulse, added, "May I call you Leon?"

Thomas nodded gravely, pleased, although he didn't show it.

"Look, Leon—and please, as I said to you before, it's Henry—about these, uh, Negro murders. Ummm, they've all been recently, is that right?"

"That's right. Since the heat wave began."

"And they've all had the same MO? Right?"

"Not all."

Thomas paused.

"Oh?" Henry asked. "I thought—"

"The ones in the story were all the same as Amos Knight and the Gallaudet case, but there's another one the reporter didn't have. It was different. A woman, a young prostitute. Also Negro. She was strangled sometime Sunday night by a suspect I believe to be a white male."

"Strangled." Disappointed, Henry was tuning out. Another false hope: just a weekend sex case. Well, there's enough of those.

"Yes, but very premeditated and calculating. Somehow, I don't think it had to do only with sex. From the marks on the throat, she was strangled by some sort of thin but very strong chain."

"What did you say?" Henry's voice rose, and he leaned forward sharply. "A chain? What kind of marks?"

Thomas stared at him, startled by his sudden intense reaction. "Well, it left small, regularly spaced contusions almost completely around her neck. Sort of like a string of red bead marks around her neck. The coroner thinks it was from a metal chain or knobbed wire. From the way it cut into the neck, it was used by someone with great strength."

"I'll be Goddamned!" Henry was visibly excited. "The same MO."

"What are you talking about? What do you mean the same?"

Thomas's voice had risen, too. Heads turned in the restaurant.

Henry looked at him quietly, thinking quickly. He'd have to trust him. And obviously he needed him.

"Look, Detective—I mean, Leon," he said, his voice low. "I'm going to violate security and take you into my complete confidence."

He paused. "All right. A few days ago I was assigned to investigate the murder of a Norwegian military attaché. His body was found propped up at the top of the Washington Monument."

"How's that?" Thomas said sharply. "I didn't see any homicide reports about a Washington Monument murder."

"No, you didn't. We felt we had to keep that one on ice. We put a freeze on it. A total lid. Don't ask me how. You know there are times now when we have to take certain national-security steps. Anyway, there were no papers, and no reports, even to your department."

Thomas looked angry.

"We had to," Henry said half-apologetically. "We couldn't take a chance on any publicity. The attaché was helping us in that matter involving the admiral I mentioned earlier. That's just one indication of how sensitive it is."

He could see Thomas was still upset. "Anyway, Leon, here's the thing: the attaché was strangled by what our naval coroner said was some kind of metal chain that left a ring, or necklace marks, around his throat."

They stared at each other.

"The same MO, the same fucking MO," Henry whispered.

Now it was Thomas who seemed stunned. He sank his chin into his left hand, and rubbed his cheek with his fingers, back and forth, round and round in circles. "I'll be damned," he finally said.

"Leon, what else have you got on this woman? You say you believe the suspect was a white man. How do you know? What makes you think that?"

Now Thomas was the one withdrawn. He looked over at Henry and, again, mentally sized him up.

"Okay," he said after a long silence. "I have not reported this to my superiors, but I have eyewitnesses who say they can identify the suspect. A big man, white, with blond hair and blue eyes. And . . ." He hesitated slightly. ". . . I've also been able to come up with an artist's sketch."

Henry's dark eyes turned almost black. The same cocky sort of smile Thomas noticed when they first met back in the morgue returned.

"Leon, I'd give my left one to see that. And these, ummm, witnesses, I'd be interested as all hell to have a chance to talk to them. Do you think that could be arranged? Of course, anything I can do for you, you just ask. I'll cut any red tape and bend any rules for you. You've got my word on it."

Thomas measured him with cool eyes. "I think that might be arranged, Henry," he said cautiously. "But it, uh, will take a while to set it up, and"—he looked appraisingly over at Henry again—"it will have to be on my turf."

He's a crafty sort of guy, Henry thought. There's a lot more going on there than you would think at first. You can't tell what he's really thinking. He's a lot deeper and a lot shrewder than he seems.

"Sure. Of course. You bet," he said aloud. "Wherever you say, whenever you name it. Just call me. I'll be there." He pulled out a notebook and wrote down two phone numbers. "You can usually always get me at that first number I gave you before," he said, tearing out a page and handing it over to Thomas. "But if that doesn't work, and it's really urgent, you can always get a message to me by using these numbers. The last one is my private line at home. I'll get back to you as soon as I possibly can."

Thomas slipped the piece of paper into his suit-coat pocket. "I'll see what I can do," he said.

2

It was a grim museum, Gunther thought. He peered into a glass showcase and read the card that identified a vertebra of John Wilkes Booth placed next to a few tufts of hair removed from the area of Abraham Lincoln's death wound. Nearby, in other cases, Indian scalps, helmets, armor, and weapons used in the last World War were displayed along with another vertebra taken from the British General Braddock after he was slain while leading his redcoats and American colonials during the French and Indian War. Odd how the Americans highlighted their failures for everyone to see. They even had the field case, sword, and uniform from the surgeon who fell along with the rest of General Custer's annihilated command. It was set apart in a special display in the corridor.

Gunther continued taking careful notes on the displays in an 8½ by 11 notebook as if he were one of the many scholars who joined with the throng of daily tourists to visit the Army Medical Museum, the largest such in the United States.

He wondered if Brink chose the museum because it was safe or because he has a sick sense of humor. Maybe both. It was immensely popular though, particularly since the war began. In a perverse sort of way, he could see why: it housed the most remarkable collection of displays of gunshot injuries, along with surgical and medical specimens that ranged from Indian crania and poisonous insects to skulls of the dugong and fangs of a rattlesnake. Its human anatomical models and extensive dental and ophthalmological exhibits encompassed all branches of pathology. The first specimens, he noted with genuine interest, had been shipped to Washington from the Civil War battlefields in barrels of whiskey and mounted dry or in alcohol.

So, he thought, Brink wants to give me a lesson about war.

He joined the crush of lunchtime tourists, government workers, young servicemen, WAACS and WAVES, filing into the old building that had been standing on the Mall just east of the National Museum of the Smithsonian since the 1880s. Slowly and methodically he inspected case after case, floor by floor. Before each, he jotted down careful notes in his book. He was dressed in an inexpensive, and rumpled, brown gabardine suit, with white shirt and dark tie, neither expensive nor tasteful. His head was covered by an old gray felt fedora.

To anyone who observed him, he appeared engrossed in his efforts. He inspected specimens from various angles, bent over and at times knelt before cases, muttering to himself as if in surprise or delight at what he saw. Then he took more notes, and moved on.

He worked his way to the east end of the corridor housing the Lincoln-Booth case and stopped to view an illustrated exhibit of venereal disease. It made him wonder if that colored woman had the clap or syphilis. He should have brought a prophylactic kit from Germany; but, no, of course, it would have been forbidden. He glanced at the large wall clock. Almost four o'clock, half an hour before closing. It was time.

Slowly, still holding his open notebook in his left hand, occasionally pausing to add another careful entry, he made his way back downstairs to the main floor. He strolled down the corridor, past the periodical room of the medical library, and headed for the main entrance.

As he approached the cloakroom, where a line was forming, he stumbled alongside a tall receptacle topped with sand for putting out cigarettes. His fountain pen slipped from his hand. He bent toward the floor, mumbling to himself, and reached down to retrieve the pen. As he did, he imperceptibly jostled the cigarette urn. Deftly, he removed a small cloakroom check beneath it. He rose, clumsily, pen in hand, muttered again half aloud, and slipped the check inside his notebook as he closed it and put his pen in his pocket. Then he inched forward on the line and presented his claim check to an old man with a white mustache behind the wooden counter of the cloakroom.

The man returned with a large sealed manila envelope. Gunther took it, thanked him, started to wander absentmindedly back into the museum, turned, and walked outside, the envelope firmly in hand.

Outside, he stopped to buy the *Evening Star* from a paperboy hawking the Night Final red-streak edition. With a mere glance at the headlines, he folded the paper, put the manila envelope inside, and wandered slowly off through the perspiring crowds back down Independence Avenue. It took all his considerable willpower not to open the envelope. He forced himself not even to think about what might be inside, and studiedly took his time, even stopping to rest on a park bench near the Washington Monument grounds to wipe his brow and fan himself with the paper, as he made his way back to the apartment in Foggy Bottom.

Willi was not there. Good. It was better. He wanted to be alone for this.

He quickly withdrew to his bedroom and closed the door. Eagerly but carefully he slit open the envelope with a knife. Another envelope was inside. He cut this open. Then he drew out a sheet of paper. It contained coded though obviously lengthy and detailed instructions. Other items were enclosed. He held up several glossy photographs, looked at them, reacted strongly, studied them intently, and put them down.

There were also two packets of postage stamps. They were encased in cellophane envelopes. He looked at them, curiously, and placed them beside the photos. Then, with rising emotion and anticipation, he began decoding the instructions. At one point he audibly drew in his breath and looked astonished. He stopped, hurriedly reached for the photos and stamps again. This time he examined them more closely. He put them down and bent to his work, his face flushing a bright red as he did.

3

The line for the 1:00 show at the Palace was surprisingly long. From the numbers of civilians waiting to buy tickets, along with the inevitable gathering of young soldiers and sailors, Willi guessed that many government workers were stealing time on their lunch periods to get away from the increasing pressures of their jobs. They ought to, he thought. It's certain to get worse. Besides, Spencer Tracy and Hedy Lamarr are a draw anytime. He didn't know about this other featured actor, John Garfield, but Tracy had been one of his favorites and he had loved Steinbeck's *Tortilla Flat*.

Willi had a strong streak of romanticism, or used to, he thought gloomily. He read Steinbeck's book the only other time he was in Washington. Then, he was swept up in the story of California *paisanos*, dispossessed but free men proceeding toward their fates like knights-errant in an Arthurian legend. That was in June, too, only four years ago in chronological time but four centuries in the reality of his experience since then. He'd always been attracted to tales of heroes, especially doomed heroes. In recent years, he often wondered why. Maybe it was his father; but no, it was more than that: he had thrilled to read of the exploits of Custer, once fancied himself a figure like Kit Carson, and, of course, back in Detroit worshiped Hank Greenberg. When he read Steinbeck's tale of how Danny had died in one last glorious helpless assault on the gods, it struck him forcefully, almost mystically. Maybe it's a good omen to find it playing in Washington now, he thought, as the line began moving forward. In any event, it's an escape for now. He had the afternoon to kill before meeting Gunther back at the apartment.

As always with them, they said little to each other. Part of it, despite Gunther's daily sweep of the apartment for listening devices, was their habitual wariness at saying anything that could be interpreted as being suspicious in any way. Part of it was just them: there had always been that tension and distrust between them. Now it was palpably greater. Their long silences after his arrival last night had been charged with an undercurrent of heavy, unspoken emotion. They both felt it: it left them profoundly uneasy and restless. They had made it this far. They still didn't know why they were here or what they were supposed to do.

The man standing in front of Willi took his ticket and turned toward the theater doorway. As Willi stepped forward to the cashier, he heard a voice directly behind him whisper, "Any news from home? Chaucer wants to know."

Without turning or making any other movement, and barely moving his lips, Willi softly replied, "No."

"What did you say?" asked the woman cashier in the glass booth before him.

"One, please."

She punched the ticket. He took it and walked into the theater.

Inside, the frigid air was a startling contrast to the glare and the midday heat. He took a seat at the back of the theater. The lights dimmed, then it was dark. It *is* an escape, he thought. My God, it's the first time I've been in a movie theater in, what, three, four years?

Across the screen, to the accompaniment of a burst of sound and then the staccato dramatic tones of an announcer, flashed a montage of black-and-white pictures. Willi had forgotten what the RKO Pathé News was like. As a boy in

Detroit, he loved the RKO Pathé News. He especially looked forward to seeing *The March of Time*. It filled part of his longing for adventure and action. Every Saturday morning he went to the early show. He sat with his friends in his corduroy knickers in the back of the theater and felt transported to all corners of the globe, to sights of distant lands and sounds of wars in Manchuria and Abyssinia and Spain.

He remembered those moments with pleasure when suddenly he felt a jolt to the pit of his stomach. It was as hard and real as if someone struck him violently. Rumbling across the screen were German tanks, diving from the skies were German *Stukas*. The newsreel footage shifted rapidly from the North African desert to the Russian steppes east of the Caucasus. Then, five feet tall, filling the entire screen, was the figure of the Führer. He shook his fist furiously, his face contorted with emotion, and he elicited thunderous applause as he addressed a rally. They were celebrating Rommel's victory at Tobruk. Willi's entire body tingled. A cascade of boos and hisses resonated throughout the darkened theater. Next to him, a middle-aged woman stopped eating a Milky Way. She shouted angrily at the celluloid figure on the screen. Willi joined in the boos.

The movie wasn't nearly as good as the book. They never are, he thought, as he stepped back into the blast of stifling air. It was so hot it took your breath and left you feeling drained.

He wandered with the crowds onto G Street. Willi experienced a strange mixture of emotions, anticipation and apprehension, loneliness and assurance. He was a part of the crowds, and yet not with them. I've been alone too much, living inside myself too long, he thought. I wonder if it shows. He passed a Kresge's and realized he was starved. He went inside.

It was crowded. All the little tables were taken. At the lunch counter, the hum of conversation and clatter of dishes and shouted orders to the cooks were oddly reassuring. He felt comforted by all the anonymous people around him. Overhead, four large fans stirred the air with slow, soothing, rhythmic swishing sounds. It was all so normal. For a moment, he felt at peace. It was even possible to forget who he was. He glanced around the room and relaxed. Everyone looked so healthy. There were so many different types all around him. In Germany, nearly everyone seemed stamped out of the same ethnic strains. Here, it really was a melting pot. In the faces of the people in this little luncheonette could be seen much of the history of America.

He slipped onto the first empty stool at the counter and sat next to a tall slender young woman. She was reading the menu. Willi picked up his and studied it. The luncheon special was soup or tomato juice, chicken-fried steak with two vegetables, rolls, dessert, and beverage for fifty cents. He ordered it and glanced back at the woman beside him. She was extraordinarily pretty. Not like Rita Hayworth or Betty Grable, but better, really, more wholesome and genuine. She wore a white silk blouse (and white cotton bra underneath, he noticed), and a plaid skirt that made her long strawberry-blond hair, with waves of curls, stand out. Her eyes were deep blue. They reminded Willi of Kathleen Brophy, the girl he had dated all through high school in Detroit. He still felt a pang when he thought of her. He wondered where she was now. His lunch order came but, without meaning to, he kept staring at the young woman beside him. He couldn't keep his eyes off her.

Finally, she couldn't stand it any longer.

"Do you always stare?" she said, turning to Willi.

"What?"

"Do you always stare?"

"I'm sorry," he said, flustered and feeling foolish.

He looked down at his lunch and put a fork into his soup bowl. She laughed, not unkindly. Willi turned and smiled. She smiled back.

"I really am sorry," he said. "It's just that, well—"

"Yes?"

Willi glanced around to see if the waitress were listening. "It's just that I think you're very pretty and—"

"Thank you."

"I mean it. Really. I didn't mean to—"

"I didn't doubt you."

"Do you live here?"

"In Kresge's?"

"You're making fun of me."

"No I wasn't." She smiled again. "Now *I'm* sorry."

"Look, will you have a cup of coffee with me?"

She looked at him, her eyes twinkling. "What do you think we're having now?"

"No, I, I didn't mean here. I mean somewhere else, somewhere with chairs and a table. Somewhere where we can talk. I just want to sit across from you and talk."

She looked at him seriously now. He had a good face, quite handsome even, and he seemed incredibly fit; but there was something about him that both touched and at the same time vaguely disturbed her. He seemed so—so troubled. There was a sadness, a hint of melancholy, about him. His dark brown eyes were strangely old and worn for someone so young and obviously energetic.

"I don't know you. For all I know, you could be all kinds of things. And what do you think I am?" Her voice took on a slightly bitter tone. "Do you think I'm another one of the 'Willing Women of Washington' just waiting to serve the right man in the war?"

He looked at her even more seriously and hesitated a second. Then he shook his head. "No, I don't think that," he said slowly. "I really just want to talk. I'd like to spend a little more time together. Only a cup of coffee somewhere. Please?"

She studied him again, then smiled. "All right," she said, reaching in her purse to put down two quarters and a nickel tip for her lunch. "Just a cup of coffee."

Willi put his change on the counter, too, and they left.

As they set off down G Street, she stole another look at him, trying to measure him even more. He was attractive; but many of them were, and she was instinctively cautious.

She had been in Washington for five months now, part of the great procession of people, especially young women like herself, who flocked to the capital with the war, lured by adventure and a sense of duty. In Oklahoma City, after graduating from the university at Norman, she had been a legal secretary. In Washington, while waiting for her application to be processed for Officers' Candidate School in the WAACS, she had taken a temporary job as a saleswoman at Garfinckel's, the Saks Fifth Avenue of the capital.

At home, in Alva, Oklahoma, her mother was worried about her. Reports about how women in Washington were acting particularly alarmed her. Every time she wrote home—and that was several times a week—she tried to reassure her mother that her worries about men and "demon rum" and easy women in Washington had no foundation. Her mother remained skeptical.

She hated the climate. Hot as Oklahoma was, it was nothing like the miserable steamy swamplike weather of Washington in the summer. For the first time in her life, she was taking salt tablets daily; but this summer, in this heat, so was everyone else. Yet she found the East and Washington indescribably lovely at times. In the spring, and even now in the summer, she liked to cross the Potomac bridges to Arlington at sunset and look on the blue hills and see how the grass seemed to turn golden, like great dunes of threshed wheat, in the last rays of sunlight. She had never seen anything so beautiful. There was a freshness and lushness in the East unlike anything she had known in the flat barren brown fields of the Southwest. There, the trees were gnarled and stunted and the prairie winds constantly threw up clouds of dust as they whistled and sighed over the land. She was fascinated, too, with the sense of the greater world beyond that was everywhere so apparent in Washington.

On Tuesdays and Thursdays, during the noon luncheon period, she worked as a volunteer hostess at the Pepsi-Cola Center for Service Men and Women a block away at Thirteeth and G streets. Garfinckel's encouraged them to do volunteer work at the USO or other service centers. It was patriotic and good for business, and she enjoyed it. Today, before stopping at Kresge's for her own lunch, as she always did, she talked to Canadian WACs, a Scottish soldier. She'd have to write her mother—or maybe she'd better not—about the Free French soldier, complete with cane and limp (*très distingué*, she thought) she met there.

There were other things about Washington she found entrancing, and some not so.

Monday night, a man she met who worked for Donald Nelson at the War Production Board took her to dinner at Hogate's. It was an old seafood restaurant. For decades it had stood at the edge of the Potomac. Inside, the walls were paneled in dark wood. There was a great mahogany bar. A huge painting of a reclining nude hung behind it. Candles on the tables made everything seem soft. It was very romantic. Best of all were the windows that overlooked the boats anchored at the piers. Sailboats and side-wheelers plied lazily up and down the water at dusk. It was beautiful. She was thrilled just to be there. Later, after a movie, her date took her to the Occidental on Pennsylvania Avenue. They had coffee and sandwiches served by old Negro waiters in black mohair coats. They tried, unsuccessfully, to identify all the framed pictures of Presidents and other Washington notables from the nineteenth century that filled the walls. She liked it, and thought she liked him; but afterward, it was the same thing. Back at her small basement one-room apartment on Nineteenth Street he tore her stockings and almost ripped her panties as they wrestled on the daybed.

It wasn't that she was a Puritan or a prude. She could give herself to the right man—she'd already had one unhappy love affair; but she believed it should be love, and in Washington love, real love, even real tenderness and caring, was increasingly hard to find.

She understood how hard it was for everyone now, especially for the men. They were constantly moving, and they never knew if they'd come back. You couldn't blame them. No one could make plans; you couldn't count on tomorrow. So people took what they could. If someone got hurt, well, that was too bad. It was even worse for the women. Competition for men was so great that she noticed many of her friends becoming hardened. They talked among themselves about going "wolfing" to meet their next "pin-up boy." After work they haunted the La Salle du Bois where extra-large cocktails were served for forty cents during the five-to-seven-o'clock cocktail hour. Later, they'd go to the Lotus and the Copacabana for the "hottest rhumba band in town." In time, they got to know all the other downtown places where the single—and married—men congregated after work. Some of the young women she knew even started carrying packages of Trojans, the rubber condoms, in their purses. If the men weren't prepared, they were prepared for them. She couldn't do that. It was so cold-blooded and impersonal. As the months passed, she grew increasingly lonely and distrustful.

She wondered if she were being foolish again as she walked off with this young man. They didn't speak as they moved along, but she felt good with him.

Someone had told her about the strawberry pie at Reeves Bakery and Restaurant, around the corner on F Street, but she'd never been there. Well, there can't be any problem in going there, she thought, as she led them to it. They passed up the counters and took one of the small tables. She sat across from Willi.

"Well," she said, smiling easily at him, and, she was pleased to feel, naturally, "you said coffee. I believe they can provide you with that. They do say the strawberry pie is special. I shouldn't, but I will if you will."

They ordered coffee and strawberry pie.

"I can only stay fifteen more minutes," she said, "then I have to get back to work. I'm late as it is."

She was touched by the look of dismay, or disappointment, on Willi's face. He really looks upset, she thought. He seems, I don't know, lost, hurt.

Willi was feeling more at ease than he had in years. It was almost magical. He wanted to hold on to this moment and savor it. It had been so long since he had done anything remotely normal. He leaned across to her intently, looking earnest.

"Look, I know what you said before. I know we don't know each other. I don't even know how much time I have, how much time we have. But I—I—well, look, I've always believed you can live a lifetime in just a few hours if you take the chance. Do you? I want to see you again. Now. Tonight. For dinner. Somewhere we can *really* talk. Anywhere you want. You name it. Just say yes. Yes?"

She sat back and stared at Willi, hard and searching. For a long moment she was silent. She took another sip of her coffee, and looked back at him. "Yes, I'd like that." She pushed back her chair and got up. "I really must go now."

Elated, he picked up the check and followed her to the cash register.

Outside, on F Street, she surprised herself when she turned to him and said, "Why don't you come to my place? I'll fix something. Do you like spaghetti? The soft-shell crabs are just in from the Chesapeake. Do you like them? I can get some."

"Anything. Whatever you want will be wonderful." He sounded childishly grateful. "I'll bring wine. You drink wine?" She nodded and smiled.

He walked with her down the street to Garfinckel's. She told him her address. "Why don't you come by at seven-thirty." Then she turned and walked inside the store.

Willi stood watching until she disappeared among the first-floor crowd of shoppers. He checked his watch, glanced around, crossed the street, and went into the liquor store on the ground level of the National Press Club Building. He bought two bottles of wine, one red and one white. At a florist, next door, he asked if they had fresh-cut red roses. They did, at four cents apiece. He bought a baker's dozen for forty-nine cents. Outside, on the corner, he stood for a moment. He couldn't bring the roses and the wine back to the apartment and answer Gunther's questions. When the traffic light turned green, he again crossed Fourteenth Street and went inside the old Willard Hotel, directly across from Garfinckel's and the Press Building. He walked up to the bell captain's stand in the lobby, passed over a five-dollar bill, and asked the young man in a bell captain's uniform to keep the flowers and wine for him. He'd pick them up about two hours from now, say at 6:45 that evening.

"Okay, Mac, but just remember I go off duty at eight o'clock. I'm not gonna be responsible for them after that."

Willi nodded. He told the bell captain he'd have another fin for him when he picked up his packages, and he left through the Pennsylvania Avenue entrance. The afternoon sun was shining directly down Fourteenth Street from across the Potomac, turning the skies a deep crimson. The city seemed bathed in a soft warm light. Even all the white marble buildings had taken on hues of pink. It was lovely. Willi couldn't remember when he felt so at peace. If I live a thousand years, I'll never feel better than this. A thousand years. He laughed at the thought. He stretched to limber his muscles, and began slowly walking back, around the White House grounds, past the Corcoran Gallery, toward the Foggy Bottom row house.

4

Marjorie was surprised at her own restraint. Normally, she couldn't bear to have fewer than a dozen people for dinner. But here she was with only Alton, Constance, and Henry, and it even had been her own idea. Well, it was Constance's idea to try to cheer Henry up, Marjorie thought, but I decided on having a quiet, elegant evening just for the four of us. She was pleased to do something for them. Constance is so lovely, and Henry, the poor dear, he must feel terrible. It's so sad about Quint. It just breaks my heart to think about it.

Constance looked radiant. At first, Marjorie thought it was her new hairstyle, then the new dress. Then she realized it was her new freshness. Yes, that was it, a new freshness. She attributed that to Henry. She was so glad she had introduced them.

Henry looked different, too. He was wearing his uniform and looked very handsome in it, although, Marjorie thought, the jacket was a "bit too tailored" and seemed a "bit tight." He was tired, though, and seemed withdrawn. Well, of course he would be. But she wasn't going to mention *that*. The whole idea was to be light and entertaining. She counted on Alton for that.

Alton was going to be in rare form, Marjorie could tell. By this time in their relationship, she could read Alton as well as a blind person could read braille; only, in her case, she didn't have to run her fingers over him. With Alton, you just had to listen. Marjorie liked him because he was so entertaining, and, of course, he was so famous. People were just fascinated to listen to him. To Marjorie, he was important because he was somebody. He was an adornment. You could always count on him to impress people at dinner parties and at the theater.

Henry and Alton stood in the drawing room while the women sat. Elias served cocktails. Constance and Marjorie each took a Dry Sack sherry. Alton had a Rob Roy. Henry took a French aperitif, a Lillet. Indecorously, much to Elias's secret amusement, he spooned a few ice cubes into it and then stirred his drink with his right forefinger. He hadn't wanted to come, and wouldn't have if it hadn't been for Constance, but he understood, without saying so, what she and Marjorie were trying to do. He appreciated it. And it was going to be an early evening, Constance promised, with cocktails at 6:45, an early supper, then home.

Alton was being Alton. He finished his second Rob Roy and continued pontificating about the differences between Roosevelt's burdens as a wartime President and Lincoln's. He had a captive audience, and warmed to his monologue. What a bore, Henry thought. Slater, as usual, was dressed elaborately. This time, he sported a pink-and-blue polka-dot bow tie, with matching silk handkerchief sprouting from his breast pocket. His famous voice sounded even more pretentiously theatrical. He reminds me of a soft, plump toad croaking away, Henry thought unpleasantly, and I hate it when he keeps calling me "dear boy." Thank God that conversation's over, he said to himself as Elias called them to dinner. He decided, as much for self-protection as any sense of competition, to enter more into the conversation.

At the table, Henry brought up the subject of contemporary American novelists, and singled out John Steinbeck. He had been in awe, he told them, when he saw the Broadway version *Of Mice and Men* five years ago. "You know," he said, "until I got in the service, I didn't believe there were people like Lenny. I thought Steinbeck invented him. In the Navy I've met many of the Lennys of this world. It's funny. I had the same feeling when I read his *Grapes of Wrath* last year before the war began. I mean, I was pretty much unaware of the Depression. Oh—"

He noticed Constance's look of surprise, and maybe of disappointment, and addressed his words directly to her.

"—I read the headlines, and I passed the apple stands and saw the bread lines, and I knew people were hurting and all that. But I mean our lives didn't change. We have the summer place on the Cape and our big house in town. My father lost a lot in the market, but he still did well. We still had our cars and the chauffeur and the maids and the cook. We just took it for granted, I guess."

No one said anything. Henry continued. "I never thought about the Okies either until I read Steinbeck."

"And do you think about them now?" Constance asked.

"No, not really. But I do think of Steinbeck. He's a helluva social writer. I think he represents the same kind of values and conscience to this generation of Americans that Dickens did to his in England. In an earlier day, I guess we would have labeled Steinbeck a 'muckraker.' "

"I haven't read him," Marjorie said. She sounded bored.

"He's not worth reading." Slater pronounced his judgment with imperious disdain. "Don't you agree, my dear?" He turned toward Constance.

Constance flushed. She didn't like to disagree with people in a social setting, especially among friends, but she spoke up anyway.

"No, I really don't agree. I'm sorry to say I haven't read *The Grapes of Wrath*, but I was terribly moved by the film. There was one scene in particular that I keep thinking about. It was the one where the children are in the store and Henry Fonda's paying for some purchases. The children are staring forlornly at the candy, then the owner gives them some. It made me cry. And I loved *Of Mice and Men*."

"That's just the point, my dear," Slater said condescendingly. "It's maudlin. It's what we used to call a 'bleeding-heart story' when I was a young reporter on the *Indianapolis Star*."

"Is that what a sob sister wrote?" asked Marjorie.

"Yes," Slater said. "I was no sob sister, you understand. But I wrote my fill of tearjerkers."

"I didn't know you were a newspaperman," Constance said. "I thought you always worked in radio."

"No, no, no." He seemed annoyed. "I came up as a reporter. I started as a cub on the weekly newspaper in my county. After a year, I got a job as a sportswriter on the *Star*. Then I went to cityside, and covered everything there. That's when I knew it was time to leave. And that's when I went to Europe. I got a job on the *Paris Herald*. God provided me with a rich voice and the right opportunity: radio was just coming into its own, and I came into mine."

"Alton never went to college," Marjorie interjected. Both Constance and Henry looked at him in amazement.

"Never went to college?" Constance sounded as if she had learned some absolutely unbelievable fact.

Slater sat back in his chair and looked at them with a bored and pitying expression. "That's right, my dear. Like Mencken, I did not go to college. However poorly, I am self-educated. I now count the lack of a formal education as a blessing. It made me work all the harder to understand and appreciate superior cultures and civilizations."

There was more silence as Constance and Henry tried to absorb Slater's revelation. Marjorie, sensing a difficult moment, and Constance's embarrassment, discreetly signaled to Elias who immediately began offering second helpings of their main course, prime ribs.

Henry spoke first. "If you had gone to college," he said to Slater, "what would you have studied? I mean, what did you think you wanted to be?"

Slater gave him another condescending look. He pushed his plate away and said, "That's easy, dear boy. An archaeologist."

It was Marjorie's turn to be surprised. "An archaeologist?" she said incredulously.

"Why does that surprise you?"

"Well," Marjorie answered him, "I can't picture you in those short little pants and pith helmet, digging away with a shovel and a pickaxe. I mean, *really*, Alton!"

"Why, Alton?" Constance asked.

"Why what?"

"Why an archaeologist?"

The table had been cleared. As Elias quietly brought dessert—fresh strawberries, heavy cream, and freshly baked cookies—Slater began to explain.

"It begins with Heinrich Schliemann—"

"He discovered Troy," Constance blurted out.

Hers was the last interruption for the next twenty minutes as Slater, seemingly himself entranced, mesmerized them with an assessment of Schliemann's legacy to civilization by leading the great German expeditions that set new standards of scholarship and spurred worldwide interest in archaeological collections.

Slater leaned back and his eyes brightened and his famous voice became even more stentorian as he spoke. "He was a great genius. A great genius. His work and his life were Homeric. He invented Greek prehistory. I have been fascinated by him ever since I was a child. He grew up in a tiny village in the Mecklenburg-Schwerin province. Not unlike where I grew up in Indiana. His father was a poor Protestant minister, and my father was something of a preacher, too—an itinerant one who married late and settled down to farming. But he never filled my head with tales of grandeur and glory the way Schliemann's father did his." Slater sounded resentful somehow. "Schliemann's father was always telling his son stories about ancient times and ancient towns and the wonders of mythology—"

Constance glanced at Henry. *I wonder if that's how he became interested in Bulfinch's mythology,* she thought. *I'd like to know more about his father; he really hasn't said much about him.* She noticed that Henry was listening intently. *Good, that will take his mind off other things.*

"—and when Heinrich was only seven years old his father gave him a book for Christmas. It was *Universal History*, written by a Dr. Georg Ludwig Jerrer. In that book was an engraving of Troy in flames. Heinrich was consumed by the picture. He began to insist to his father that the Troy of Homer's *Iliad* was real, that it was buried somewhere, that it could be found, that *he* would find it. Absolutely remarkable. No one at that time believed Troy ever existed. But that boy did. Somehow, he *knew* it. Think of it! A small boy in an obscure village, who grows up consumed by an idea. All along the way he is ridiculed by the experts"—his voice became scornful—"and the scholars from the great universities. But he never wavered. He persisted. It's another of his marvelous attributes that I admire. Of course in the end he triumphed. He not only discovered Troy, my dear young lady, but he also excavated Mycenae and Tiryns with all their treasures. And then they honored him, oh, yes, all those great learned scholars who had scorned him. They couldn't praise him enough. And he was just one of the great German archaeologists. Dörpfeld and Schuchardt and Furtwängler, and there are great ones today. As a jealous American archaeologist friend of mine says, 'There are thousands of them.' They are methodical, precise, persistent, industrious—just like Schliemann! That's the tragedy of this war. The Germans have so many of the qualities that make great scientists and technicians, doctors and scholars. But their archaeologists—ah.'' He sighed heavily. "They are magnificent. I've read almost everything they've written, in German. I've visited their museums. I even planned to accompany one of their expeditions to the Aegean, but the war ruined that, too.''

I'll be a sonofabitch, Henry thought. He remembered the intelligence analysis that crossed his desk a few weeks ago about German archaeologists. Many of them, it said, were ardent Nazis who, under the guise of scientific endeavors, had charted every submarine base and pen for the German U-boat fleet in the Aegean during 1938 and 1939. He started to put Slater down with a sarcastic remark about how great the German archaeologists really were, but thought better of it. What was the point? It's just another indication of what an ass Slater is.

No one spoke. Finally, Marjorie said, "Well, Alton, I must say, I *still* can't see you wearing your little shorts and your pith helmet.'' She looked at her watch and got up from the table. "Well, dears, I promised Henry it would be an early evening, and it's still daylight, so I kept my word.'' They said their good-byes, and left.

5

He was about to turn the key in the lock when the door opened. Willi tensed and stepped back, ready. It was Gunther. He had a beatific smile. Willi didn't know what to make of it, but it made him uncomfortable. Something was wrong. He started to speak, but Gunther swiftly shook his head, put his finger to his lips, motioned for silence.

"We have a letter from home, Willi," he said softly.

He beckoned Willi to follow, again gesturing for silence. They walked down the alleyway silently.

"We have heard from the Admiral," Gunther said urgently, in a tight low voice. "I cannot say anything until we are completely alone and secure."

Gunther put his right arm around Willi's shoulder. "So, come, let us be tourists together in Washington," he said expansively, and led them off, making small talk as they walked.

They wandered through Foggy Bottom and then moved on to Constitution Avenue. Though they smiled and chatted, each felt an inner tension that grew with every step they took. It was hard to keep their facial expressions normal. They walked on until they were almost at the Lincoln Memorial, which rose above the river.

Gunther led them around the circular walkway where they mingled with the thick lines of summer tourists, many of them in uniform. The wide flight of marble steps leading up to the massive brooding statue inside the Greek temple was filled with people. They moved up and down in endless procession as they made their pilgrimage to the shrine. Beneath them, mirrored in the long reflecting pool shaded by a stand of huge English elms, were the shimmering images of the white marble Doric columns of the memorial intermingled with the long wavy lines of the Washington Monument almost blocking the view of the Capitol far beyond. Willi glanced at his watch. It was nearly 6:30. He thought of the girl. No, he couldn't think of that now; but he was uneasy, off stride. His brain was not working. He berated himself, and forced his mind to be blank. He looked around, taking in the scene, and appeared to be enjoying himself. They moved slowly around the memorial, following a throng of passersby crossing the long Memorial Bridge over the Potomac to the slopes of the Arlington National Cemetery directly ahead.

Willi noted the sculptured words marking the entrance to the bridge. *Valor. Sacrifice. Peace.* Every country celebrated the same things. He was struck, too, by the huge figures of eagles, some eight feet high, cut from solid blocks of granite that decorated the bridge entranceway. They reminded him of Berlin and Nuremberg. Ever since the Romans, and possibly before them, everyone had made emblems of eagles. He didn't understand why those carrion birds had become such symbols for nations down through the ages.

A DC-3 passenger plane, its silver wings sparkling in the late-afternoon sunshine, roared low overhead on its path to the new National Airport a mile or so downriver. People stopped, shielded their eyes, and stared up. Willi and Gunther joined them. Then they moved across the wide white bridge with its graceful arches forming perfect circles in the waters below and on toward the high semicircular wall that marked the entrance to the cemetery. Another plane flew over. Again people stopped to stare, then continued walking toward America's most hallowed burial grounds.

The cemetery closed at seven these summer months. It was fifteen minutes before that hour when they walked onto the grounds through the massive iron gates, surmounted with more eagles and medallion seals of the United States and its Army, Navy, Marines, and Coast Guard. The western skies had turned into a deep crimson. Strong rays from the sun played over rows of small white marble grave markers and cast shadows among the giant oaks. It was still inside. The cemetery grounds were steeped in the perpetual hush that always affected those who entered. Even small children felt it, and were silent. The hot air was still, too. Somewhere above they could hear the soft chirping of birds. Off to the right, in a grove of trees, a whippoorwill added its distinctive sharp sound to the day's end.

They moved away from the small clusters of tourists and wandered along the winding black asphalt driveway until they reached the crest of the hill. Below them, and beyond the river, lay all of Washington. They found themselves in a grove of Scotch pines surrounding a huge memorial to the Civil War dead. They were alone.

Gunther stopped. He turned around and looked at Willi. That same beatific smile creased his face. He looked slightly flushed. Willi didn't like it. He waited silently before Gunther. No extraneous thoughts now; he was alert to every sound, and filled with a sense of the greatest alarm. Once again, he felt that droning buzzing sound in his ears. He began to slip into that state of dreamlike unreality where all his responses were instantaneous and without thought. He watched, calmly and coldly, as Gunther stepped toward him, looked around to be sure they were entirely alone, and began to speak. In German now.

"We have our orders, Willi," he said. "The Admiral sends them to us personally from the Führer." He smiled again, even more widely. "We are to be part of history, Willi." He was standing directly before Willi now. "You'll never believe what our mission is." He sounded almost taunting. "We, Willi, you and I, are to eliminate the President. In a single stroke it will all be over."

He paused. Willi said nothing. "What do you think of that, Willi? How does *that* make you feel?"

Gunther was silent for a long moment. Willi still said nothing. He was acutely aware of every sound and movement. Gunther moved beside him. He looked excited, exultant.

"And, Willi," he said, lowering his head while at the same time reaching out to put his arm around Willi, "the Admiral also has relayed the most extraordinary information."

His voice became barely audible. He leaned closer and started to whisper in Willi's ear. "He knows, Willi." He eased back slightly, and spoke again. "He knows all about you."

Gunther had his watch chain in his hands now, and swiftly tried to loop it around Willi's neck.

Willi's reaction was swifter. He lunged to his left, ducking under Gunther's hands, feinted with his left leg, and delivered a sharp brutal chopping blow from the flat side of his left hand with all his force against Gunther's neck. Gunther, staggered, fell back, grasping his throat. Willi was deadly calm, and quick. He moved forward rapidly, feinted again, and struck two more fast blows, a vicious smash, with his right hand this time, to Gunther's right collarbone, and a short left hook to the ribs. Gunther grunted heavily. He was awash in pain. His collarbone felt broken and his windpipe was torn. He heard himself rasping. He staggered backward, and began to stumble away across the ridge. Willi, relentless, pursued. He was moving with deliberate, icy calm. His face was set and his only thought was to destroy Gunther, totally and swiftly.

Gunther drew a second breath and moved more rapidly around the tombstones and monuments. A hundred yards away, a startled guard walking his measured post before the Tomb of the Unknown Soldier froze at the sight of the two figures battling along the ridge. He was torn between leaving his post to investigate and remaining on duty. Then he lost sight of them as they disappeared amid the carefully tended shrubbery and 200-year-old oaks blending now in the lengthening shadows.

Willi caught up with Gunther on a knoll beside a mound of freshly turned earth and an opened grave prepared for burial ceremonies at dawn the next day.

They faced each other in the gathering shadows, each in the half-crouch that was second nature to them. Willi circled slowly around and forward, drawing closer and closer with each move. He danced from side to side lightly, watching Gunther's responses, feinted once, twice, and once more, made a sudden half-move with his right arm, watched Gunther turn to block him, and then with lightning swiftness shifted his weight and left his feet in a dive that smashed with the full force of his body and strength into Gunther's left knee and thigh. Gunther cried out in pain and dropped to the ground. A tight, hard smile crossed Willi's face. He moved forward for the kill as Gunther writhed on the ground, apparently lost in the grip of waves of agony.

As Willi reached over him, Gunther suddenly turned his

body and kicked out with his right leg. He struck Willi short, hard, and directly on the left ankle, breaking it. Desperately Willi tried to recover his balance, but fell. Gunther summoned every last reservoir of strength. He pounced on Willi, planted his right knee in the small of the back, and with watch chain drawn tightly about the neck, broke his back.

He sank over the body, gasping for breath. His pain was excruciating. He was certain his left knee was broken, his left leg was swelling alarmingly, and the blood vessels felt as if they had burst. His neck throbbed violently from the blow that nearly ended the battle. He was afraid his right shoulder might be separated.

Behind him, he heard shouts. He stumbled to his feet, kicked Willi's body into the opened grave, quickly tossed down dirt to cover him, and limped away into the darkness.

The bell captain looked at the lobby clock. It was almost fifteen minutes after eight o'clock. He looked at his own watch to check the time. He waited five more minutes, then waved good night to the night captain. He picked up his newspapers, the bottles of wine, and the flowers and left the Willard. He threw the flowers into a trash bin on the corner across from Garfinckel's and went home.

She waited with rising anger and began to pace back and forth in the small kitchenette, checking the clock with increasing frequency and frustration. Once, she went outside and looked up and down the street. She hurried back. He might be trying to call. Then she realized, with a flash of disgust, more at herself than at him, that she didn't know his name. They hadn't even introduced themselves. What a fool she was. She fixed a drink of Scotch, then threw it out. At 9:30, after checking the clock one last time, she dumped the crabs and the asparagus and the salad into the garbage pail. She felt a flash of violent, unreasoning bitterness. She was furious. She hated all men. Then she began to cry.

6

He knew something was amiss the moment he walked in the office. The usual banter was missing. Everyone was whispering. There was a heaviness in the air. Arnie Thorson's cherubic face was pale and thin. He looked as if he had lost weight overnight.

"Arnie, what the hell's going on?" Henry said anxiously, leaning over Thorson's desk.

Thorson looked up, stricken.

"Decatur is dead." His voice sounded flat, weary, drained of any emotion.

"What!"

"He was found in an open grave at Arlington Cemetery."

"Arlington Cemetery! For Christ's sake, Arnie, what was he doing in Arlington Cemetery? How was he killed? Who found him? What do we know?"

Henry was nearly shouting his questions. For once, his supreme self-confidence was badly shaken. He had lost his poise and with it what he had always believed to be his ability to remain calm, detached, and coldly analytical under the greatest stress.

Arnie wearily waved his hands. "That's not all that happened last night, Henry. Somebody tried to kill Churchill just before he took off."

Henry was staggered. Now his face was drained, and he sat down heavily in a chair next to Arnie's desk. "All right," he finally said, collecting himself, "let's take this one by one. What do you mean someone tried to kill Churchill?"

Arnie sighed, fumbled among the papers on his desk, picked up a single sheet, and quickly glanced over it.

"There's not much at this point, Henry. Just that it happened. As you know, Churchill left the President at the

White House last night and was taken to his seaplane, which was waiting in the Baltimore harbor. Harry Hopkins and Averell Harriman were there to see him off. Well"—he glanced down at the sheet of paper again—"he was just about to board down that narrow, closed-in gangway they had set up across the water to the plane, when the MPs caught some guy fingering a pistol. Great deal of excitement, everybody running around. They got him before any shots were fired, but it was one hell of a scene. It's all on the highest QT, of course. No stories, naturally. They're still questioning him. They don't know if he's just a nut or someone else. But he was there at just the right time and just the right place—which ain't supposed to happen, Lieutenant—and he had a gun!"

Henry drew in his breath. He couldn't remember feeling so tired.

"And Decatur?" he said quietly, looking at Thorson.

"We don't know much about that, either. A guard at the Tomb of the Unknown Soldier saw two men running through the cemetery at dusk, fighting each other."

"Why the hell didn't he do something?" Henry said bitterly.

"Good question. He didn't. Never leave your post, or something, I suppose. Later, they found the body in an open grave. Anyway, the Old Man is distraught, absolutely distraught. He was the best we had, the very best. Indispensable, really. We don't know anything else. *That's* the most disturbing thing of all. Especially now. All we've got are questions, lots of questions. And no answers."

"Is that all you can say?" Henry sounded impatient.

"Yes."

They were silent.

Henry was deep in thought. "How was he killed?" he finally said.

"I don't know exactly, Henry. You'll have to talk to the medical people. They should be finishing up the autopsy at Bethesda now. We had him taken there to maintain absolute secrecy. But the preliminary report says his back was broken and he was strangled."

"Strangled! Did you say strangled?"

Thorson looked at Henry curiously. He'd never seen him so worked up. The pressure was getting to him.

"That's what I said, or that's what they say. You'd better check it with them. But why does that get you going?"

"I'm not sure, Arnie. I just wonder if it's the same as with that Norwegian."

"Check them, Henry."

They looked at each other in silence again.

"Arnie, I need to know more about Decatur. I need to know everything we've got."

Need to know! Damn it, he thought, that was part of the problem. Sometimes they were too protective by half for their own good. They got caught in their own webs of secrecy. Maybe if he had known more, Decatur would still be alive. All he had known—*all he had needed to know,* supposedly—was that Decatur existed, that he had landed, that he was on the way, that he had arrived. Nothing else. He wondered if anyone really knew it all. The President knew; at least he assumed he knew, but he couldn't even be sure of that. The Old Man knew. But what, exactly, did he know? And who the hell was Decatur, anyway? The FBI knew. That seemed certain now. They had to be bugging ONI. Henry was upset and angry and confused all at once.

"Arnie," he said again, after Thorson didn't reply, "I need to know *now.*"

Thorson drained the dregs in his mug and took a deep, long drag on his Chesterfield. He was fond of Henry. More important, he had come to have great respect for him. Henry was superb, and he knew the Old Man held him in special regard, too.

"All right, Henry," he said quietly, and reassuringly. "Yes, of course. The Old Man has the folder on his desk. I'll get it for you. You understand, naturally, about the conditions: Read only, no notes, and you never—*never*—refer to this in any way at any time. Never. Check?"

Henry nodded.

Arnie got up from his desk and went to retrieve the file. When he returned, he led Henry down the corridor to a small windowless room they used for special interrogations and interviews. He considered, and dismissed, posting an armed guard outside the door as they had done earlier that morning at the Bethesda Naval Hospital. That wasn't necessary with Henry. He put the folder on top of the single desk, bare but for a telephone, ashtray, and reading lamp, looked hard at Henry, nodded, and walked out, locking the door as he left.

Henry settled into the wooden chair, turned on the lamp, and picked up the dossier. It was about half an inch thick and marked with the highest security classification of the nation. Inside, arranged in strict chronological order over a four-year period, were an assortment of memos, decoded messages and cables, and official reports. He started reading.

On top was a "Memo for the Record," badly typed, with misspellings, corrections, and words x-ed out from a Lieutenant Commander Taylor Bates, ONI. Fleetingly, Henry wondered where Bates was today. He'd heard his name before but wasn't sure where. He didn't really have that much contact with the ONI people even though ostensibly he was a part of their operation. He's probably in the Pacific where I ought to be, Henry thought sourly. Then he became engrossed in the memo.

It was dated "17 June 1938," under the letterhead of "The Department of the Navy, Washington, Security (Intelligence) Section," and began, in simple narrative style: "At 1531 hours today Chief Bosun's Mate Ted Maliszewski knocked on my door and when ordered to come in reported that . . ."

Bates then described in minute, almost encyclopedic, detail his extraordinary encounter with a man who identified himself as William (Wilhelm) Gehrman, age twenty-three, an *Oberleutnant* in the German infantry who arrived aboard the S.S. *Berengaria* in New York ten days ago on leave to visit relatives in Detroit, Michigan, and was scheduled to sail back to Germany on 19 June 1938. Subject Gehrman presented himself voluntarily and said he had concluded, after much anguish and emotional turmoil, that he could not support the aims of the Third Reich under Führer Hitler after what he had personally witnessed upon returning to Germany with his mother from the United States six years before. He claimed to be particularly outraged by German treatment of the Jews. Subject Gehrman said he had shared his feelings with his former high-school teacher and priest on his trip to Detroit. They had urged him not to return to Germany but to stay permanently in the United States. He had inquired about the process of becoming an American citizen and seeking an American military commission and had been referred to this office after interviews with—and there were three names, one in Detroit and two in Washington.

The record in the memo was amazingly complete. Bates must have taken shorthand notes, Henry thought, as he noted the time the interview concluded. It had ended at 1854, after lasting nearly three and a half hours, and everything was recorded. He was impressed, too, with Bates's skill as an interrogator. It was obvious he had great experience. He seemed to have asked all the right questions and to have maintained a proper degree of skepticism without scaring off Gehrman. He would make a helluva trial lawyer, Henry thought.

By the time he finished reading the voluminous memo, Henry thought he knew Gehrman. He even had a picture of him in his head—and then he remembered Mr. Lippmann's warning about not letting yourself get trapped by the pictures in your head. Henry prided himself on his memory, virtually a photographic one: he could scan a page and then recite it verbatim. How had Mr. Lippmann put it? "There was a moment when the picture of Europe on which men were conducting their business as usual, did not in any way correspond to the Europe which was about to make a jumble of their lives. There was a time for each man when he was still adjusted to an environment that no longer existed. All over the world as late as June 25 men were making goods that they would not be able to ship, buying goods that they would not be able to import, careers were being planned, enterprises contemplated, hopes and expectations entertained, all in belief that the world as known was the world as it was. Men were writing books describing that world. They trusted the pictures in their heads." That was 1914 he was talking about; it was no different now.

He then picked up an 8-by-10 OFFICIAL NAVY PHOTOGRAPH. It was taken that day of William (Wilhelm) Gehrman.

Henry examined it and was startled. The picture in his head, formed by Bates's careful description, was entirely different from this Gehrman frozen in time by the studio camera.

Bates's Gehrman was earnest, open, sincere, obviously intelligent, and painfully candid about his conflicts: between his feelings about the land of his birth, Germany, and the land he said he felt to be home, America; between his feelings for his mother and the illusory, probably false, image of his father; between his oath of duty as a soldier and his disgust at what missions German soldiers were being trained to perform, including eventually destroying the United States. The camera's Gehrman was stiff, unfriendly, hard, suspicious, withdrawn. The brown eyes, for example, were as vacant as the barrels of a shotgun. The mouth was set in a straight grim line as if afraid to betray any hints of emotion that lay hidden within.

Henry had liked, and felt empathy and respect for, Bates's Gehrman. He didn't like this Gehrman he held in his hands. He wondered if Bates had noticed the difference. He held the photograph up more closely and studied it intently. He wouldn't want to meet this Gehrman in that proverbial dark alley—or in Arlington Cemetery either, he suddenly thought. He put the picture down and pushed his chair back from the desk. The room was oppressive; but that wasn't what was bothering him. He stretched and shook himself and then paced back and forth. God, there's something monstrous and unclean about everything that's happening. What is this war doing to us?

He returned to the desk and sat down. He'd only read the first memo. There was much more.

Bates had appended a second lengthy memo late that evening after Gehrman left. You had quite a day, Commander, Henry thought. This contained what Henry now regarded as Bates's customarily detailed account of his actions and recommendations about Gehrman. Gehrman agreed to provide ONI with intelligence information upon his return to Germany. Bates gave him instructions on how to do so. This would put Gehrman at the low rung of the ONI ladder in Germany that led, step by step, to the naval attaché at the United States embassy in Berlin on 39 Bendler Strasse. He recommended that ONI, itself, check out Gehrman in

Detroit and that the ONI net in Berlin make inquiries about him in Germany. If Bates had any doubts about Gehrman, he didn't record them.

One thing struck Henry as extraordinary, especially for that time. Bates specifically requested that ONI—not the FBI—check out Gehrman in the United States. Henry smiled faintly. I'd like to meet you someday, Commander, he thought.

The rest of the file grew piece by piece until the cumulative portrait was overwhelming. Initially, Gehrman provided elementary military statistics, of no real value, nor were they sought as such. But they proved to be entirely accurate. Slowly, almost tentatively at first, Gehrman interspersed political judgments into his fragmentary military reports. These, too, proved correct. Then, step by step, month by month, the file reflected the changing nature of the relationship. Gehrman was assigned a "keeper," a senior Navy officer in Berlin who in reality was the top ONI officer for Western Europe. They met only once. From that time forward, Gehrman's reports were treated with highest priority and dispatched immediately to Washington. For months at a time, after the invasion of Poland, when Gehrman was in combat, there were no reports. Then they resumed.

Henry was astonished. Decatur, or Gehrman—he still couldn't think of him that way—was everything he had been led to believe. He was ONI's best agent. He read a brief, but riveting, account of his recruitment by Canaris's Abwehr and of his being trained to kill and commit sabotage at a special camp. It was laconic in style, with no other details. It had been filed from France with the information their submarine was to land near Cape Hatteras, in North Carolina. There was no indication in the file of how the report was made.

He turned the pages, absorbing everything. The next to last report was a telephone log of a call Decatur made from Richmond, Virginia, last Sunday night, the twenty-first. Henry experienced a jolt at what he read. Gehrman described his companion, who went by the name of Gunther Haupt, real name unknown, as a heavyset man, blond, blue eyes, with slightly bent front nose, and faint scar from left ear to line of jaw. He should now have arrived in Washington. Under no—the word was repeated—circumstances was he to be followed. He almost certainly would detect any tag, and anything that aroused his suspicions could blow the mission. Decatur didn't know their mission. They had been led to believe—by Canaris himself! Henry read incredulously—it was the most sensitive of the war. They had been trained to kill and commit sabotage. Other attacks were to be made, on Jews and Negroes and various civilian and defense installations. That was all he knew. They would get their final orders somehow in Washington.

There was one sheet left. It was dated yesterday and bore a single notation from an ONI field agent. "1307 hours. Contact made Palace movie theater. No report."

Henry sat holding that sheet in his hands for a full minute. He was exhausted. Nothing he had experienced before prepared him for this. He felt as if he had entered some awful dank cave and couldn't get out. Jesus, he said to himself. Now I know everything, and nothing. His hands were trembling and he was short of breath. He took a few deep breaths, put down the last sheet, leaned back in his chair, and rubbed his eyes. He knotted the tie he had loosened, what, hours ago, picked up the phone, and dialed Thorson. He came a few minutes later, quickly studying Henry's expression. Neither spoke. They exchanged signatures on the receipt for the folder, and started to leave. As they walked into the corridor, Henry asked if Thorson could arrange for him to go to Bethesda and speak to the Navy doctor who performed the autopsy on Decatur.

"Sure," Arnie said. "Want me to come?"

"I don't think so," Henry said.

Arnie looked at him sharply. "What's eating you, Henry?" he said. "What's on your mind?"

"Nothing, Arnie, nothing."

Mentally, Henry kept turning over and over the same set of questions: Why were two Nazi agents like that sent to Washington now? What were they supposed to do? Blow up something? What? Congress? The White House? The new Pentagon? Kill someone? Who? Marshall? Churchill? Roosevelt? And how? It was impossible. Then why was

Decatur killed? What went wrong? He was still lost in thought when Thorson told him a driver was waiting outside to take him to Bethesda.

7

"What's the matter?" she said, staring at him.

He was sitting inside his Nash. He didn't even get out, she thought, annoyed, as she walked toward him from the Meridian. He was staring ahead, his head slightly bowed, and he seemed unaware of anything outside. Her annoyance disappeared when she saw his face. He looked hard and grim. She had a wave of concern and doubt. For a moment, she didn't recognize this Henry. It was frightening to see how angry, even vicious, he seemed. She wondered if she really knew him after all.

"Come on, get in," he said impatiently. He reached over and opened the door from the inside. "Let's go." His voice had a bitter tone, one unlike she'd ever heard him use.

She slid onto the seat beside him. Henry turned the ignition key. The engine had just coughed into life when its sound was obliterated by the sudden sharp piercing wail of a siren. It rose up and down in volume, echoing off the buildings over the hill and the park. Then, in precise intervals, another siren—and another—and another—and another—sounded from distant points scattered across the city. They blared out and merged together until all of Washington was filled with one long loud wailing sound.

Everywhere, people stopped and looked to the skies. Then they started heading indoors.

Constance and Henry sat motionless in the car. Those air-raid sirens are the most terrible sound, Constance thought. They sound alive; they physically tear at you. In the park, near her favorite fountain, she saw a small boy, he couldn't be more than five, in short pants and cotton shirt with red stripes, drop to the ground and curl himself into a little ball. His hands were clamped tightly over his ears, as if desperately trying to shut out the sound that surrounded him. The Negro nurse, or maid, who had been taking him for a walk before supper, reached down and tried to get him up. He burrowed even tighter into himself. Constance wondered if you ever got used to it. In London, did they think of it as just another familiar sound like a fire engine now? Did they really take it all in stride now as people were saying they did? And what if this were real, what if every time you heard the sirens you knew the bombs were about to fall? How did you take that in stride? She shivered. We've really been lucky so far. Then it stopped. The air-raid test was over. They looked at each other but said nothing. They didn't need to. Each could sense the other's thoughts.

"Do you want to talk about it?" she finally said.

He shrugged. "Not right now. Maybe a little later."

Henry drove down the hill toward the center of the city, and then headed out through Georgetown on the road running north alongside the C&O Canal. Constance tried to think of something to say.

For several blocks he drove in silence, then said, more to himself than to her, "I never wanted to be a doctor. Now I've gone to my second autopsy in a week. I didn't want to be a detective, either. Now I've got two unsolved murder cases on my hands. And these aren't just little murder cases. They're as important as anything I'll ever have to deal with in my life. More important than you or me or anyone we know. I *know* they're connected, but I'm not getting anywhere. I don't have the Goddamndest idea of what to do next. And time is running out."

He told her, briefly, about the death of Decatur. "I just had to get away for a little bit and clear my head." He fell silent again. Constance stared silently out the window.

They drove out of the city, past the locks fashioned from huge timbers the riverboat men had employed in the days when the canal was a commercial enterprise instead of a featured tourist expedition. At least it's a little cooler here, Constance thought. They could hear the hum of crickets in the trees and the soft sounds of the Potomac flowing lazily beyond the canal. The river was screened from view by a short stretch of woods a hundred or so yards away. Normally, it was relaxing. Henry often came this way for a moment of escape and release. It was one place in Washington where, briefly, you could forget the cares of the capital. That and Great Falls, where he was heading. But it wasn't working today; he felt knotted inside, tense, angry, and impotent all at once.

The road curled away from the canal. They passed Glen Echo, where the servicemen took their dates on the amusement-park rides. As usual these long summer days, it was jammed.

Constance saw a young blond Navy pilot in white dress uniform. He was holding hands with a pretty girl in a sheer silk dress and one of those new crescent-shaped hats that you wore back on your head so it framed your hairdo and face. They were laughing. She thought of Henry's brother and felt a stab of pain for him. She hoped he didn't see them. He didn't seem to notice.

She wasn't feeling so good herself. When she gave the memo to Henry, she had been certain she was right. She felt no sense of guilt. Not at first, anyway; but it really bothered her later. She believed in Henry, but she didn't want to be thought untrustworthy. It was difficult and troubling. Everything in her background made her value the word she gave to others. There are certain things you just don't do, and, for Henry, she had violated trust others placed in her. She decided not to say anything to him about the incredible news the Director planned to make public tomorrow in New York. It was extremely top secret. They had all been instructed not to breathe a word to anyone. Still, she felt badly torn. She wanted to say something to Henry, and almost blurted out the news when he started venting his frustration over the cases he was investigating. The news ought to make him feel better. The whole thing was over.

Then she realized he didn't know yet—or didn't seem to. That made it harder. They were both silent a long time. It certainly wasn't a happy trip.

Even Great Falls didn't help. Henry loved the falls. The

sheer force with which the Potomac rushed through the gorges, churning over the rocks in a never-ending roar, spinning backward into whirlpools and eddies, and then surging ahead setting off showers of fine spray, always seemed to recharge him. The sound of the waters and the sight of the sheer cliffs surrounded only by woods reminded him of New England. He also thought it the most romantic place in Washington. Nowhere else were the sunsets so dramatic, and so unmarred by any human traces. He clambered about the rocks furiously today, trying to recapture those feelings, and worrying Constance by his recklessness; but it wasn't the same. He couldn't escape his own demons. For the first time, they felt awkward together.

On the way back, he stopped at the Old Angler's Inn. They sat in the darkened bar and watched the remnant of a blood-red summer sun setting through windows facing west across the Potomac. When the pianist played "The Last Time I Saw Paris," they joined in the singing. In New York, when he worked on Wall Street before the war, Henry had become a devotee of Hildegarde's at the Persian Room of The Plaza. Her singing of that song had always touched him. Tonight it held no magic. It seemed sentimental nonsense. He wondered vaguely whether it was his taste or something about himself that had changed.

His moodiness affected Constance strongly. She thought she understood it, but she felt frustrated, hurt, and angry that he was shutting her out. At his apartment, she wanted to give herself to him so completely that he would forget his problems and make the growing unspoken tensions between them disappear.

They made love twice, but the tenderness was missing. He took her with a fierceness and a physical strength that left her exhausted and unsatisfied. This time, the strong smell of their sex made her think of them more as animals than as special people bound together by love. They were lying together, spent and silent, each lost in the same kinds of private unsettling thoughts, when the phone by his Westclox next to the bed jangled sharply, startling them both. It was Thomas.

"Not interrupting you, am I?" he asked.

"No," Henry lied.

"Those witnesses you wanted to talk to," Thomas said slowly.

"Yes."

"You can see them tomorrow if you want. I've got it set up."

"That'd be terrific. What time, where?"

"Strictly unofficial, right?" Thomas answered.

"Yes, of course."

"Okay, just wanted to make sure. They're not used to talking to whites, you understand. They're not very comfortable around Negro cops, either, so we've got to go easy."

"I understand. Whatever you say. However you want to do it. I'll follow your lead."

"Good. Why don't you come by my house, say around noon tomorrow. Saturday's a good time to talk. I'll explain more. Then we'll have that conversation with them."

"Fine. Oh, Thomas—Leon—I've got a friend who has helped me. I mentioned her at lunch the other day. She's—" He glanced over at Constance lying beside him, winked, and she was pleased to see, smiled at her in the old mocking way. "—the one who thinks Northerners like me are worse racists than white Southerners. I told her about you. She says she wants to meet you. Do you mind if I bring her along?"

Thomas gave a deep laugh. "Now that's someone I'd like to meet, Henry. Please bring her with you."

"Swell." Henry listened a moment, then jotted down instructions on a pad he kept by the phone. "See you then. And, Leon, thanks."

Constance was looking at him curiously. "That's the Negro detective? Are you sure, Lieutenant, that you can trust me with him?"

They laughed. For the first time that day they felt better about themselves.

8

Thomas kept glancing out the window.

"Leon, if you don't stop that, I'm going to leave." Saundra was angry. "You invited them here, I didn't, and now you act as if you're ashamed to have them come. There's *nothing* to be ashamed about in this house." She turned sharply and left him alone in the living room.

She's right, Thomas thought. It's ridiculous for this to bother me. Yet it did, and that bothered him most. The minute he hung up, he regretted inviting them here. He was certain Henry and his white girlfriend would look down on his home in Brookland. That made him angry with himself for caring how they felt. At the same time, he was even more resentful for thinking they *would* look down on him. He glanced out the window again, and then wheeled about. I'll be damned if I let this get to me. He sat down and again picked up the morning *Post*.

Several blocks away, Henry shifted into second as they turned from North Capital Street onto Michigan Avenue alongside the grounds of the U.S. Soldiers' Home adjoining Catholic University in Northeast Washington. "Have you ever been in a Negro home?" he asked.

Constance looked up from the road map. "Sometimes you astonish me, Henry," she said. "Do you really think all Southerners are like Bilbo and Rankin? Or that we know nothing about Negroes—the way you do? Of course I've been in Negro homes. All my life. We do have contact, you know. Which is more than I can say for most Northerners."

Henry, feeling rebuked, didn't reply. He shifted down to first to slow for a traffic light.

"You keep going ahead until it becomes Monroe Street,"

she said, studying the map again. "Then we turn left on Thirteenth Street. That should put us in the center of Brookland. Looks like he's near the Dominican College and a seminary."

She noticed they were also near Quincy Street, but didn't mention it. It would only remind him again. She thought about his family. We're so different, and it's more than just personal background. There really is something basically different about Northerners and Southerners. She didn't think Henry was a secret racist, as he said jokingly to Thomas on the phone last night. But she was convinced there was more hypocrisy among Northerners about Negroes. She believed white Southerners understood Negroes far better than anyone of Henry's Boston/Harvard group. As he told her on the way out, the only Negroes he'd ever known were maids or washerwomen. He'd hardly even seen them in Boston when he grew up. Not that the South was like *Gone With the Wind* with Tara and happy darkies, Constance thought. She hated that false syrupy picture. God knows there was enough brutality and injustice and prejudice there to make you blush with shame; but at least there was real contact between the races, and real caring too, though she knew it was easier for her to say that than it was for Negroes.

Constance called out the house numbers as they turned left onto Thirteenth and then right on Newton Street. It was an entirely colored section. She noticed how the children skipping rope on the sidewalk and the few couples sitting on their front stoops, already fanning themselves in the rising heat, stopped to stare as their car slowly passed. From inside the small modest bungalows she could see a brown hand push aside a curtain and white eyes in a dark face peer out to watch them. It's like we're entering foreign territory, she thought.

"That's it, Henry," she said, pointing ahead. "The second house on the right."

They pulled up to the curb, and Henry got out. He started to walk around the car to open Constance's door when they both saw a tall black man walking gravely down the steps toward them. Thomas reached the door before Henry.

"I'm Leon Thomas," he said as he opened the door and looked down at Constance. He didn't offer his hand.

She was struck more by his reserve, air of calm dignity, and the careful, measured way he looked down at her than by his size, which Henry already had well described. "Hello," she said, holding out her hand. "I'm Constance Aiken. Constance, please. I'm really pleased to meet you. I've looked forward to this."

Thomas nodded slightly, still looking directly and impassively at her. Then he turned. "Hello, Henry," he said as he gestured toward his house. "Won't you both come in?"

They followed him up the steps, onto the front porch, and inside. He introduced them to Saundra and their son, James. "Would you like iced tea?" Saundra asked when they were seated on the couch. It faced bookshelves lining one wall. A Philco radio, shaped like the entrance to a cathedral, perched on a small table by a fireplace. They nodded their thanks.

Constance liked her. There was no pretense about her. She was direct and open, with intelligent warm eyes, and a courteous but not obsequious manner. She liked Thomas, too. He seemed shyer than the man Henry had described, but there was something about the way he held himself that gave an impression of strength and depth. He's probably not easy to know, she thought, but he seems well worth any effort to try. She was uncertain about James. He gave off an air of unmistakable anger and hostility. You could see it in the way he stood stiffly, silently staring at but really through them. His face was firmly set, his black eyes smoldered. She wondered how James and Thomas got along and suspected, somehow, that the son was embarrassed about his father. Or maybe just angry about a lot of things. Well, it couldn't be easy. For any of them, and especially for James.

Henry sat beside her. Thomas took the overstuffed chair set diagonally before the fireplace. Henry's eyes quickly took in the room. He noticed two framed sepia photos, each in its own oval frame, standing side by side on a table. They were of an elderly Negro man and woman, both with strong faces peering straight into a camera, obviously long ago. The resemblance to Thomas was unmistakable. Henry wondered if they had been slaves. Could be, he thought, mentally counting the years, but probably not. The Civil War was over, let's see, seventy-five, yes, seventy-seven years ago. Thomas was, oh, about in his late thirties, maybe forty, now. They could have been born slaves, and *their* parents certainly were slaves. It gave Henry a strange feeling. I wonder how he feels about that? He stole a glance at Thomas sitting quietly, then turned as Saundra returned.

She set down a pitcher of iced tea next to a vase of fresh flowers on the coffee table before the sofa, and offered candies she had made. Constance smiled. "That looks like a Carolina recipe, if I'm not mistaken."

Saundra smiled back. "Yes, it is. Please have one."

Constance took the confection and glanced over the row of books of poetry on the shelf before her. "You love poetry, I see," she said to Saundra.

Mrs. Thomas smiled again. "No," she said, nodding in Thomas's direction, "he's the one."

Thomas looked embarrassed. Constance got up, walked to the bookshelf, and pulled out Countee Cullen's *Color*.

"I admire his work," she said, to no one and everyone, "especially the one about Africa. How does it go? 'What is Africa to me:/ Copper sun/ scarlet sea.' " She paused, trying to remember the rest of the verses. Thomas picked up the words: " 'Jungle star or jungle track/ Strong bronzed men or regal black/ Women from whose loins I sprang/ When the birds of Eden sang?' "

Henry stared at Constance, and then at Thomas. Now where the hell did she learn that? And memorize it? And who would have thought this big cop would be spouting poetry? He was flabbergasted. No, he was annoyed. Yes, that was it. He was annoyed at Constance and her knowledge, and, damn it, he was annoyed at Thomas and his erudition. Most of all, he was annoyed that Constance and Thomas obviously liked each other and shared a secret connection. He felt a flash of jealousy; then he felt ashamed, and finally, angry at himself for being so small-minded.

"Have you a minute?" he said to Thomas, breaking the spell cast by Thomas and Constance and Countee Cullen.

"Sure."

Thomas, sensing Henry wanted to speak privately, got up and led the way into the kitchen. They sat down at a table covered with a flowered oilcloth.

"Those eyewitnesses, they're coming here?" Henry asked.

"We're going to meet them in a while. They'll be at a place where some of my friends meet. I'd like you to meet some of them, too."

"Sure. Uh, you said something about a sketch. Do you—"

"Just wait here. I'll be back in a minute."

Thomas left. Henry waited, wondering if this wasn't a waste of time. There were probably a thousand better ways to spend his time now, and here he was making small talk and listening to them recite Negro poetry.

When Thomas came back, he was carrying a large, rolled sheet of what appeared to be artist's paper. "This was done within twenty-four hours after the suspect was seen," he said, and he began to unroll the paper and anchor the corners with ashtrays on the table.

Henry rose and stood back to watch. The large form of a man's face began to appear on the table before him. He stared at it, and nearly shouted. It was stunning, uncanny. This tallied exactly with the terse description of the man Decatur had been traveling with when he phoned ONI from Richmond.

Thomas looked at him quizzically for any reaction. Henry gave none. He looked indifferent, too indifferent, Thomas thought.

"Hair color?" Henry asked quietly.

"Blond."

"Eyes?"

"Don't know. They couldn't remember if they saw the eyes."

"Characteristics?"

"Whoa! Wait a minute, Lieutenant. What's going on? Are you interrogating me? Do you recognize this person? Does he connect in any way?"

Henry steeled himself and set his face more stolidly in a poker mask. He leaned forward as if to study the sketch more closely, then, after a long silence, looked back at Thomas, and shook his head.

"No. No, I'm afraid not. Sorry about playing prosecutor

there. I guess I've been too wound up lately. But, no, I don't get any connection with what I've been working on."

Thomas had been leaning over the sketch, looking up at Henry. He said nothing for a moment, rose to his full height and stepped back from the table. He knew Henry was lying. He had conducted too many interviews, had seen others try to con him too many times, on the streets and in the courtrooms, not to know instinctively, without any doubt, when someone was holding back. He studied Henry carefully, then nodded, giving no other expression.

"I see," he said. "Too bad." He was disappointed, but then, again, he was always being disappointed. He had begun to like this young white man, and felt he might be able to trust him. What he couldn't figure out was why Henry was holding back. What was the point? Maybe he had a good reason. Maybe it would still work out between them. But he was far from sure. He forced himself to suppress the old rush of rage. Getting angry wouldn't do any good now. Besides, there was still a chance Henry might help, and he'd grab every chance he got.

Henry continued to stare at the sketch. He wanted to ask Thomas if he could borrow it to get it copied. He'd even offer Thomas many extra copies. But something held him back. Often, when he wanted something badly enough, he was untroubled by any pangs of conscience or thoughts of what was right or wrong about how he obtained it; and he wanted this sketch very badly. Still, he couldn't bring himself to ask for it and thus admit he was holding out on Thomas. He didn't particularly admire this trait in himself, but usually found a way to rationalize it. He doesn't need to know, he thought, then realized with a pang of guilt what sophistry that was and how hypocritical for him now, especially after his reaction on finally learning all about Decatur.

He was wondering what to say next when Thomas spoke up.

"Look, Henry, I was thinking. I've made several copies of this by hand. I'm going to have them distributed to some friends. You might want to borrow this and get it copied yourself. Maybe something will turn up that could help me, or help you, or help both of us. Here."

He held out the large sketch and began to roll it back up.

"Well, okay, I'll be glad to," Henry said, taking the sketch. Now he felt a wave of guilt at not confiding in Thomas. I'm getting as devious as Hoover, he thought unhappily. I've got as bad a case of the-end-justifies-the-means mentality as any of them.

"Are you two going to be in there forever?" Saundra Thomas said as she stepped inside the kitchen door. "I thought we were going over to Georgia Avenue."

"We are," Thomas said. He checked his watch. "We're finished here."

They all went in Henry's Nash, the Thomases in the back, Constance with Henry in front. James, who had been invited, did not go. He really doesn't like us, Constance thought, noting his sullen "No." He doesn't like them being with us at all.

The club and restaurant on Georgia Avenue near Howard University stayed open so you could always get a drink, food, entertainment, and listen to jazz after hours. On weekends it was crowded nearly all day. It was jammed now, and noisy. When the door opened, Henry and Constance saw a room filled with smoke and dozens of couples, all colored, eating, drinking, and talking animatedly. The din was deafening. At the sight of the young white couple, all conversation stopped. The silence was total. Even the waiters stopped to stare. Only when Thomas gently led Henry and Constance into the room did the noise and movement pick up again. It's as if we're from another world, Henry thought, as he walked behind Thomas's broad back, carrying the rolled-up sketch with him.

Thomas stopped and peered through the smoke, then whispered to his wife and gestured toward a round table in the rear where a group of men were sitting. He motioned for Henry to follow him toward a small red leather booth off to the side. An older man, who appeared to be blind, was sitting there beside a young boy. Both seemed uneasy as Thomas and Henry approached and sat opposite them.

Henry let Thomas begin the conversation. He noticed Thomas never gave him their names, and didn't tell them his, either. Thomas was simple and direct: he told them to describe to Henry everything about the white man they saw with Odessa. He wanted them to answer any of Henry's questions. The "blind" man was nursing a bottle of Senate beer. Thomas motioned to a waiter. He ordered two more bottles and a root beer for the boy. Then they talked. Henry listened intently, took notes on a pad he carried, unfurled the sketch and asked more questions about the man depicted, jotted down more information, asked more questions. No, they had never seen him before. No, they had not seen him since. Yes, they would let Thomas know the moment they did; they'd already told him they would, and they would. Henry looked over at Thomas and nodded.

"Thanks," he said. "This might be helpful." Again he felt, but didn't express, a sense of excitement and frustration. That was Decatur's "Gunther Haupt," no doubt about it. But where the hell was he, and what was to come next?

They left the man and the boy sitting in the booth and walked toward the rear of the room where Saundra and Constance had joined a group of men sitting at a table. Henry could feel the eyes following him as he walked across the room behind Thomas.

He noticed, again with a flash of annoyance, that Constance seemed to be getting along well with the group.

That wasn't the case with him. You could cut their hostility and suspicion toward him with a knife. It wasn't anything they said, or did. It was just there.

Henry felt uneasy, then angry. Goddamn it, he thought, I didn't put your people in chains. My family fought to free you, and many of them died trying to do so. The inner surge of anger didn't make him feel better. He looked across at Constance and remembered what she said the first time they talked about race relations. He had mentioned, proudly, the actions of some of his own family in the Civil War and before. "Yes," she replied, "and I'll bet some of your Yankee sea captain ancestors brought over the slaves in the holds of their ships and then sold them off at auction for the Southern plantations. That's how they got here, you know, Henry. At first you Yankees even tried to use them as slaves in New England. Then you found out that kind of labor wasn't profitable there. That's when you started selling them South." He was annoyed with her, but had to admit she was right. In fact, he liked that about her: she didn't play games; she said what she really thought.

Again Thomas made the introductions. Three of the men were on the Howard faculty, one in the law school, another in the medical school, the third a sociologist, it seemed. The two others apparently were successful Negroes in business, one a realtor, the other in the funeral business. They were polite, but cool. Very cool.

Henry turned on his charm. He was, he thought, at his ingratiating, deprecating, humorous best. It didn't work. They gave off a feeling of resentment—no, more than resentment—a deep kind of bitterness that he had never experienced. I'll bet Constance hadn't, either, he thought. He wondered if Thomas felt that way. He must, Henry thought. He just doesn't show it as much.

For months, Henry had heard top-level discussions about the administration's concern over tensions within the colored population and the new racial strains rising across the country. The "Negro problem," as they put it, was most visible in the South; but in fact it was becoming more serious in every plant and every industrial city.

He knew the Attorney General and the President were troubled by it. He'd sat in during discussions when Mr. Biddle raised the subject as a national security matter and asked for suggestions on combating it. Every private survey they had showed Negroes apathetic to the war. Apparently they regarded it as a white man's conflict. The administration, and the Attorney General, had taken the lead in trying to promote pro-Negro attitudes whenever possible. Increasingly strong public statements were being issued. They called for greater Negro rights. They condemned—gingerly, to be sure, because of the politics of the New Deal and the Democratic President—labor unions for excluding Negroes. They were even helping to promote a new commission about the future of Africa. None of it did much good: the more talk, the more attention it attracted, and the greater friction it created. Racial demagogues in the Congress bleated on about preserving segregation, the innate inferiority of Negroes, and the dangers of America becoming a racially mongrelized society, thanks to the New Deal and the President—and most especially to Eleanor.

White racists weren't the only ones creating problems. Tensions were building on both sides of the racial lines, Henry knew. In the last few days, there was talk about some Negro "march on Washington" being planned for the first few weeks of summer. That set off alarm bells in the administration. It was the last thing they needed now. Henry had been asked to look into this, too. A number of people suspected the Communists were behind it. Henry didn't buy that, but you never knew, either; and after what he'd been going through these past days he was getting to the point where he would believe anything. In any event, these all raised national security and intelligence questions. It was another example of how the war forced things to a head. The possibilities of one explosion after another were all too real.

Until his contact with Thomas at the morgue, and his involvement in the murder cases, Henry's concern about "the Negro problem" basically was academic. It had not touched him personally. Now he listened with growing anger and apprehension at what he heard around the table. He was stunned to hear expressions of skepticism about the worth of the war. He was angered to hear them question whether Germany was the real enemy when there was so much to fight at home. He didn't think of himself as naïve. Far from it. But he realized, after getting over his initial shock, that he had no appreciation of the depth of real feelings; and if these people, obviously the Negro intelligentsia (What was it one of them had scornfully said? "We're not the black bourgeoisie, Mr. Eaton") felt this way, there were real problems ahead.

It was Thomas who took them on, Henry was surprised to hear, Thomas who said there was only one hope for the Negro in America and that was to work for democracy; Thomas who said the country could only survive if it were united; Thomas who said a world with Hitler was a world not worth living in; Thomas who asked them to help Henry and himself.

Henry listened in growing admiration. Seldom had he been so stirred. There was a disturbing and powerful eloquence in Thomas's simple calm way of speaking. He noticed Constance watching Thomas, her face slightly flushed. She seemed almost to be holding her breath. Mrs. Thomas's eyes were shining with emotion.

Thomas didn't hold back anything. He told them how he and Henry had met and how they were now jointly investigating the wave of Negro murders. They needed help. They needed the help of everyone around the table. Not only did they need their help, Thomas said, sitting straight and still as a graven Buddha, he expected it from them. They had a suspect, and a sketch. Word must be passed, everywhere, to be on the lookout for this man. He had brought the small sketches in a folder with him. Now he passed them out. "I want you to get them in the hands of every bootblack and every busboy and every newspaperboy downtown," he said. "I want them circulating on every street corner in Washington."

They looked silently at copies of the sketches as Thomas passed them around. Then they nodded.

Thomas thanked them. "We've got to go," he said, rising. He turned to Henry and Constance. "Are you ready?" They nodded, too, and got up.

On the way back to Henry's apartment on Capitol Hill, after taking the Thomases home, Constance broke a long silence between them. "That big drawing you've got, Henry," she said. "Do you have any idea who it is?"

Henry hesitated. "No," he finally said. "I wish I did. Maybe we'll find out now."

There was something about the way he spoke that troubled her. For the first time, she didn't believe him, and it hurt.

They were lost in their own thoughts for much of the way back. Maybe I'm just too tired, she thought. It has been an exhausting day—days, in fact, she realized. She felt drained, dead inside. Too much emotion too fast, Miss Aiken, she said to herself. Nice Southern girls can't take too much of this.

Henry phoned Arnie Thorson on the "silent" office line as soon as he got back to the apartment. "For Chrissakes, Henry, I've been trying to get you," Arnie said, his voice excited. "Have you heard?"

"Heard what?" Henry said, instantly in a state of alarm.

"Hoover. He called a press conference in New York and

289

said the Bureau has captured all the spies landed from the German subs on Long Island and Florida. Got 'em all. He called the Old Man to tell him that and said they're going to pick up other agents in the United States within twenty-four hours. All of 'em, Henry! The Old Man just informed the President. Big hoorah, you can imagine. Hello? Henry? You there?"

Henry hadn't said a word. He felt a sinking sensation in his stomach. "I'll be right down, Arnie," he said, his voice drained. He looked at Constance watching him with a strange expression on her face.

"Thanks a lot, Charleston." His voice was hard and bitter. "You didn't know anything about what the Director had planned for today, did you?"

"Henry, I—I couldn't say. We were sworn to secrecy, and I thought—" She looked ill, her face white and strained.

"Thanks anyway. That's just the kind of help I can use now."

He paused and looked at her, hard, again. "I'm going now. You want to stay or go home?" He paused again, then said with heavy sarcasm, "Or maybe you want to go back to the Bureau and report."

She felt terribly hurt. "That's not fair, Henry. You're being a real bastard. I—" She stopped. She felt both numb and angry. There was nothing she could say now that would make any difference. "You go ahead," she said finally, her chin stiffly up but her voice almost breaking. "I'm perfectly capable of catching a cab home by myself. And I much prefer to be alone anyway, Lieutenant Eaton." At least I didn't cry, she thought, wrapping that small bit of pride around her, as she picked up her purse and headed stonily for the door.

9

He soaked for two hours without rising, carefully letting out the old cool water and refilling the tub with hot clean water, over and over. It soothed the pain. Once or twice he dozed and started up. He worried that he would fall asleep and drown in the tub. After everything, that would be history's little joke, wouldn't it? He thought of Willi. Too bad he hadn't been able to hide his body better, but the traitorous bastard was gone. He still couldn't believe Willi had been able to hurt him so. Never had he thought Willi was that good. Never had he experienced such pain. Limping back to the apartment Thursday night was sheer agony, and for a moment he had wondered if he would make it. Then he was racked with wave after wave of pain. He had been in anguish all night, and for all of the next day. It still hurt today, but the waters helped. They were restorative. At least nothing was broken as he first feared. He arose from the tub and shook the water from him. Then he dried himself and studied his body in the mirror. His body was black-and-blue and, after the long soaking, his skin was shriveled. I look like the skin of a morel, he thought. He slipped on a bathrobe, every movement causing new throbs of pain. It would be some time before he was able to move well, he realized. Well, he could hole up now. There was no longer any worry about Willi. He could not stop them now.

Slowly, painfully, Gunther moved into the living room and slumped down into a chair. He sat, sunken, for a long while, half dozing off again. Then he turned on the radio.

He listened to the end of "The Shadow." The muffled rasping voice whispering "Who knows what evil lurks in the hearts of men" brought a smile. The Americans were such children.

Just before six o'clock, Gunther heard the announcer tell the audience to stay tuned for Alton Slater and his nightly "Human Side of the News." Seconds later the stentorian voice of Slater boomed out from the radio, even more dramatic now than usual.

"This is Alton Slater. The news tonight is from New York, and it's a big story, Mr. and Mrs. America, an incredible story."

A dramatic pause.

"J. Edgar Hoover, the nation's gangbuster, announced today that the FBI has smashed an amazing Nazi sabotage plot. He and his G-men have captured eight German saboteurs who were put ashore on the Eastern seaboard from two German U-boats. That's right, fellow Americans. Eight Nazi saboteurs landed on the shores of these United States!"

Gunther sat up, the pain momentarily gone. He leaned closer to the radio, turned up the volume, and listened intently.

"The saboteurs were put ashore in two groups—in Florida and on Long Island. Their mission, Mr. Hoover announced, was to cripple American airplane production and other industries vital to the war. They planned to undermine American morale by placing bombs in railroad terminals and crowded department stores. The saboteurs had been trained intensively at a special sabotage school near Berlin. They carried high explosives, time fuses, and delayed-action bombs with them, and huge sums of American money. But Mr. Hoover's FBI, as vigilant in times of war as they are in peace, has got them all. Every last one of them has been rounded up. The ring is smashed. Schikelgruber's plot has failed!"

Gunther let out a roar. He clapped his hands, and then flinched sharply in pain. "It worked!" He half whispered the words aloud. "That old bastard Canaris. It worked!"

He drew himself up out of his chair, walked into the bedroom, and put on his clothes. Then he let himself out of the apartment and slowly walked three blocks to the little newsstand on Pennsylvania Avenue.

Already a knot of people was forming to buy copies of the

Sunday Star's Bulldog edition, just delivered. More and more passersby were attracted by the vendor's repeated cry, "FBI gets Nazi spies . . . FBI gets Nazi spies."

The news drew murmurs from the pedestrians. Gunther waited on line, then handed over his ten cents for the bulky Sunday paper. He stood aside a moment and read the big bold headlines:

FBI CAPTURE OF 8, LANDED BY SUBS, THWARTS SPECTACULAR NAZI PLOT TO SABOTAGE VITAL U.S. WAR PLANTS

TWO-YEAR 'TERROR CAMPAIGN' INVOLVED MASS WRECKAGE OF STRATEGIC INDUSTRIES

He turned to a middle-aged man beside him and shook his head. "Incredible, incredible," he said. The man, grim-faced, nodded back at him. "That'll show those bastards," he muttered, and walked off, clutching his paper.

Gunther made his way back to the apartment, sat down in the living-room chair, and avidly started to read every word of the long front-page story. It was set two columns wide and covered nearly a full page inside. The page-four headline trumpeted:

THE NAZI PLOT THAT FAILED
Special Dispatch to The Star

NEW YORK, June 27. Landed on the Atlantic Coast by Nazi submarines, eight Berlin-trained German sabotage school experts, equipped with $150,000 in cash and explosives for a two-year "terror campaign" against vital American war plants, have been captured, Director J. Edgar Hoover of the Federal Bureau of Investigation disclosed tonight.

The eight men under arrest are all former United States residents, several are former German-American Bund members and two are United States citizens, Mr.

293

Hoover said, while one is a former member of the Michigan National Guard.

One crew of four was landed on Long Island the night of June 13, Mr. Hoover said, and the other four landed at a beach near Jacksonville, Fla., three nights later.

None of the spectacular missions assigned to the Nazi saboteurs was carried out, and all eight men are in custody, Mr. Hoover emphasized, the last having been captured today in Chicago.

"Graduates" of German high command sabotage schools at Berlin, the two crews were landed at night in rubber boats on isolated stretches of the Long Island and Florida beaches, Mr. Hoover said. Besides the vast arsenal of explosives and incendiary equipment they carried, the saboteurs had about $150,000 in United States currency, apparently to be used to bribe their way into strategic spots.

The plan of devastation assigned to the two crews was one of the most amazing and far-reaching of the war and if carried out would have done inestimable damage to airplane production, virtually halted rail transportation in the New York City area and endangered the lives of millions of New Yorkers by blasting its water-supply facilities.

The objectives listed by the FBI included the plants of the Aluminum Co. of America at Alcoa, Tenn., Massena, N.Y., and East St. Louis, Ill.; the Cryolite plant at Philadelphia; Hell Gate Bridge in New York, one of the most heavily traveled river crossings in the country; other New York bridges, including those of the Pennsylvania and Chesapeake & Ohio Railroad; the Ohio River locks near Pittsburgh and water-supply facilities for New York City.

Mr. Hoover said other objectives included water conduits in Westchester County, N.Y.; hydroelectric plants at Niagara Falls, N.Y., and railroad tracks on the famous horseshoe curve near Altoona, Pa.

They planned to plant bombs in locker rooms at railroad stations and in department stores to create panic and break down civilian morale, Mr. Hoover said. . . .

When he finished, Gunther put the paper aside and smiled. It had all been worthwhile. Then he picked it up again and reread the story even more carefully this time. He wanted to make sure it was all there. He paused over one paragraph, trying to see if it contained any hidden meaning:

"Mr. Hoover refused, for obvious reasons, to reveal where or when the FBI received its first information that the Nazi crews were on American soil nor would he tell how the agents were tracked down and clamped in jail, some of them within a week after they landed."

No, he thought, everything was all right. Even the pain didn't feel so bad. He got up, went to a table, and picked up the telephone book.

10

"You should be pleased. A senator says he's going to propose they strike a special medal for the Director."

Henry looked up from the papers, spread out before him on the coffee table, took another swallow of black coffee from his mug, and lighted a cigarette. His eyes were hooded with heavy dark circles, and he appeared pale and drawn from fatigue. He glanced back at the papers.

"There's been nothing like it in American history, they're saying."

He scanned the stories.

"Listen to this: 'The intriguing question of how the FBI learned of the landing of the saboteurs remained unanswered last night as far as the public was concerned, but that agency's success in rounding up the Nazi agents so speedily was taken as another demonstration of the effectiveness of this country's counterespionage system.' And here they say, 'The absence of widespread or effective sabotage in the vast war industries of America has been pointed to as demonstrating the efficiency of anti-spy activities of the FBI.'"

He looked back up. "Maybe they'll make him Emperor."

Constance stared back at him.

"Are you upset because the Bureau got them and you didn't, or is it because I didn't tell you they already had them? I mean, Henry, which side are you on in this? What's *really* bothering you?"

She was tired, too, and looked it. It had been a hard, disturbing night. She had tossed and turned, alternately feeling guilty about not confiding in Henry and furious at him for his reaction to her before she left last night. Something else gnawed at her: what she sensed was his own lack of candor with her all day yesterday. He was holding something back, and she knew it.

At first she wasn't even going to call him; but she realized that was a silly, childish way to act. We're both involved in things so much bigger than ourselves, and we *do* have something special. Constance forced aside thoughts about them being in love. She wouldn't let herself think about that now. Until she met Henry her notion of "love" was more of the Rodgers and Hart brittle, bittersweet version, like their new musical *Pal Joey* that she saw when she worked for *The New Yorker*. That's probably best after all. At least you don't get so hurt, she thought. But if I'm really honest with myself, she mentally argued to herself while churning sleepless last night, I'm still a romantic fool; and I've never felt about anyone the way I have about Henry. When he said to come on over after she called this morning, she was pleased. She wanted to straighten things out.

"And something else, Henry." She studied him and smiled. "You look like hell."

He was sitting on the couch behind the coffee table in his sleeveless undershirt, with his suspenders over his shoulders. He laughed. "I guess I do at that." He smiled back at her. They both began to relax. The closeness, or affection, whatever, was still there.

"I'm really not being a petty jealous bureaucrat about this, Constance. Believe me," he said, turning serious. "Although I must say, if I wanted to play that role there's cause enough. Do you know who Mike Reilly is?"

She thought a second. "The Secret Service? The President's detail, you mean?"

"Yes. Well, I spoke to him today. He's mad as hell. He says he 'unpacked his heart'—those were his words—to Bill Hassett, the President's aide, about your boss and the Bureau in this arrest of the saboteurs. Says he told him he's fed up with Hoover's boys hogging all the credit, as he put it, and plenty sore because the Secret Service always receives the fullest cooperation from Army and Navy intelligence, but never the slightest from the FBI. That's his view. Hassett urged him to take it directly to the President, and he said he would. I know Mr. Biddle feels that way, too. So do I."

He got up from the sofa, ran his hand through his hair, and began to pace restlessly up and down the living room.

"But *that's* not what's bothering me. It's much more serious than that. I'll be damned if this easy capture of all the Nazis adds up. It's just too pat. I *know* there's more to it than that. There's got to be. You remember what that memo said. There was a *third* submarine. *That's* what's eating me. Do you understand?"

He grew deathly still. "Constance, our agent who was killed was aboard that submarine. And so was someone else who came ashore."

He was silent again. He paced some more and let his eyes wander over his collection of naval prints on the wall by the fireplace. She could feel his tension. "That's why I *know* there's something terribly fishy about the great FBI roundup. I've got to find out more about it." He turned and looked at her imploringly.

You *are* a charming bastard when you act that way, Mr. Eaton, Constance thought. She hesitated a moment, then stood up and spoke.

"Henry, I don't want to say much, either." She walked closer to him. "You've got to respect my position and feelings, too. But—" She searched for the right words. "Well, there is something odd. The Bureau didn't track these people down."

He listened intently now, his eyes wary and serious.

"I mean, well, they got the whole bunch when someone called the Bureau—not once, but twice—with the whole story: names, times, places, everything. It was like, well, when I read our report of the phone contacts, and then the interrogation of the informant in a hotel, it make me think it was like someone *wanted* them all to be caught."

Henry was rigid. He stared so hard at her that she felt uncomfortable.

"By God, Constance," he said, letting out his breath, "that's it! That's got to be it!"

He stepped back, exultant. He danced quickly toward her and lifted her into his arms. "That's it, Constance," he said again. He kissed her, ran his hand through her hair, swung her back down to the floor, kissed her again, stroked her rear, ran his hands up and down her dress with growing passion.

"You don't know how much you've helped." He looked at his watch. "Damn, I'd like to take you to bed right now. But I've got to get to the office. Sunday morning or not. How's this for an irony: Along with all the other things we've got to do now, we're also going to have to handle the prosecution of these Nazi saboteurs. Mr. Biddle's asked me to work on that, too. From what he said last night when I talked to him, though, there may not be much of a prosecution. There's a lot of pressure just to have them shot as spies."

He hurried into his bedroom to dress. "You're right," he called back at her, smiling broadly, his eyes sparkling again. "I do look like hell. I'll try to be better next time."

11

Beyond the long concrete bridge crossing the wooded expanse of Rock Creek Park, past the pair of old and weatherbeaten sculpted lions guarding the wide stretch of Connecticut Avenue leading uptown by the zoo, stands a tall hotel. It sits on a high wooded knoll, just off the avenue. For generations, its brick walls and white trim stonework atop its tower with distinctive columned balconies have been a beacon. To its expansive rooms, suites, and apartments have flocked the politically powerful, the influential, and all those who aspire to such stations of Washington greatness, as measured by the fickle standards of the capital. It has housed more United States senators, more members of the United States Supreme Court, and more other assorted dignitaries and worthies by far than any other such address in the city.

In the summer, those favored with the choice Tower Wing apartments retreat to their balconies to take the first wafts of evening breezes stirring above the city.

It is a majestic place to hold court. From there, the sunsets are spectacular. Occasionally, through the sounds of distant traffic, stirrings of animals in the National Zoological Park are heard among the trees far below. Every evening, after dusk, on summer nights early in the war, the inhabitants of this aerie fled from the pressures of their jobs in the rapidly expanding federal anthill and sought the security of their Wardman Park perches. There, they entertained and impressed each other, refought and retold both the battles of the day's bureaucracy and the actual distant military engagements being monitored and marked in the chart rooms and message centers and command posts of official Washington.

Alton Slater was not least among them. Though not official in the literal sense, by virtue of his status as a celebrated journalist he was one of the lions of Washington. Through the backing of his faithful, growing nation-wide audience that had been following his nightly radio commentaries since he became prominent broadcasting from Europe in the early thirties, Slater occupied a special niche in the Washington political hierarchy. He was connected, he was courted, he was favored with inside information—and with the most inside of invitations, from the White House to the best embassies. In turn, as expected, Slater reciprocated. He relished his role of grand host and raconteur to the mighty of Washington. These days, his ninth-floor Tower Wing apartment, with choice balcony facing east overlooking the park, was the scene of constant gatherings.

Tonight was no exception. Charlie the bellhop, small, fastidious in his red uniform, who cheerily brought the breakfast tray with its daily accoutrement of five morning Washington and New York newspapers promptly at seven o'clock each morning, served double duty tonight. He stayed over, for a fee, to escort the assorted ambassadors and admirals and office holders to and from the apartment. They began arriving forty minutes after Slater's Monday-night broadcast. It was shortly before ten o'clock when the last guest left.

While Melissa finished the dishes, Charlie emptied the ashtrays in the living room. He picked up the brandy glasses, put away the bottles in the dry sink in the sunken dining room, and rearranged the wrought-iron furniture on the balcony. When he left, everything was ready for the next round of drinks, conversation, and gossip.

Slater, as was his habit, withdrew to his bedroom. There, with floor-to-ceiling draperies drawn, he sat on the bed and fumbled among the pill bottles standing amid the pile of books and magazines on the night table. He extracted a Tums, poured a glass of water from the silver pitcher also on the night table, took it, reached for the pink bottle of Pepto-Bismol, poured out a thick tablespoon, took that, and then popped a Pep-O-Mint Life Saver. He rose, went to his deep dressing closet, and put on his long, dark blue silk bathrobe. He had bought it in Paris before the war. After tying the robe, he looked at himself in the full-length mirror on the door. He fluffed his short, wiry gray mustache with a comb, vigorously brushed his closely cropped iron-gray hair with an English brush, faced on the back with his initials monogrammed in the sterling silver, leaned closer to the mirror to inspect his ruddy features, and, satisfied, wearing a pleased expression on his short, square features, went back into the living room, pouring himself a Calvados nightcap along the way. Then he plopped down in his favorite chair, reached over and flicked on the Magnavox, put his feet up on the bolster, and, in benign mood, started to listen to a recording of Toscanini conducting the NBC Symphony Orchestra in Verdi's *I Vespri Siciliani*.

There was a knock on the door. That was unusual. Normally, the doorman rang ahead if there was a guest. He checked his watch: 10:55. A second knock sounded.

Annoyed, he got up. Sometimes, people got lost looking for another apartment and knocked to ask directions. Probably that. Maybe a guest who left something.

He walked up the three steps from the living room onto the parquet floors, gleaming with wax, of the foyer. Throwing back his shoulders and lifting his head to peer down through the small rimless glasses that, with his mustache, were his personal trademark, he brusquely opened the heavy door.

"Yes?" he started to say in that peremptory, dramatic voice known to millions.

Then he suddenly choked. The blood drained from his ruddy face and he stumbled back into his apartment, his mouth open, his heart fluttering wildly. He tried to speak and gave only a gurgling sort of sound.

"My *dear* Alton, good evening," said the even, low voice from the doorway, soothing and solicitous in tone. "You are not happy to see me? How disappointing after so long and so hard a journey. Surely you will invite me in?"

Slater continued to stumble back. "You, you—" He choked on the words as he held one hand straight out while the other was clutched to his throat.

"Oh, dear Alton, you are overcome with emotion. I am so pleased. Here, let me pour you a drink. Rob Roy, no? See, I remember. It was your favorite. Or has your taste changed? Dear Alton, I am so worried. You don't look well at all."

Slater stopped and stared, glassy-eyed, as Gunther slid into the room. His face was set in a half-smile and his blue eyes never left Slater. He soundlessly closed the door and stepped forward.

"Out!" Slater roused himself, some of the natural timbre of his voice returning. "You! Out! Get out, now!"

He summoned every bit of strength, stiffened himself, and gestured authoritatively. "I said out!"

"Poor, poor Alton," Gunther said, his eyes still locked onto Slater's, his voice still low and mock gentle, as if he were speaking to a child. "You are upset. I do not want that. *We* do not want that. The Führer does not want that. He sends you his special regards. Think of that, dear Alton, the Führer, *your* Führer, sends you his own personal regards. He thinks of you, Alton. He has great plans for you, Alton."

"No!" Slater shouted the word.

Gunther's eyes turned deadly. He measured Slater as a cobra watches a rabbit and then, in a lightning vicious blow delivered from his left hand, knocked Slater backward and down the three steps into the living room.

"Now, Alton." He hissed out the name and kept his voice low, as he straddled Slater. "You will be quiet. You will be a good little Alton, won't you?"

He reached down and pulled Slater up. Then, with each word, jabbed him sharply and painfully in the chest, forcing him to stumble farther back into the room until Gunther pushed him down in a chair and hovered over him, menacingly. "Sit, Herr Slater!"

His sibilant tone, so low and so still, was more terrifying to Slater than any shouted threats would have been. "Now that's better, much better."

Gunther sounded soothing again. He leaned closer to Slater, who stared dumbly up at him. "Here, dear Alton, I have brought you a special present. You will want to see these before we have our little talk."

Slowly, deliberately, Gunther drew out four photos from

inside the 8-by-10 packet he had brought with him into the apartment.

"They're quite good, really," he said, fingering the glossies, the faintest flick of a tongue tip moving from corner to corner of his mouth, wetting his lips as he talked. "They have a true Leica quality to them, I'm sure you'll agree. Here, see if you don't think so?"

He tried to hand Slater the first picture, but he was slumped, almost frozen in a state of numb shock. "Take it, Herr Slater. I said, take it!"

Mutely, Slater held the print. He moaned almost inaudibly when he saw it. There, standing with a group of German officials now recognizable throughout the world, was a beaming and younger Alton Slater. "Göring has put on his weight since then, no?" Gunther asked gently. "But Goebbels and Himmler, just the same, wouldn't you say?"

Slater turned away. "Not a favorite photo for your album, dear Alton? Perhaps this is the one that will please you more."

He passed over the second. Framed in the background of the picture were the soaring Alps. Standing on a stone balcony before them, just outside two French windows from which the picture was taken, arms happily linked, was an even more pleased Slater. With him were Hitler and his blond mistress, Eva Braun.

"Wonderful likeness. Such healthy air. You look *so* good here. Don't you agree?"

He took back the photo and studied a third. It showed Slater standing attentively before a massive desk where Hitler sat solemnly in full Nazi uniform.

"Now this one, ummmm, let's see. It has a more somber tone. The shading, that's what I like about it. It's so, so—so official, so Germanic, no?"

By now, Slater was resigned to looking at the pictures Gunther handed him. He sat, slumped, glanced at the photos, and silently handed them back. He was quite unprepared for the last one.

"This is my favorite, my dear Alton. I hope it is yours, too," Gunther said as he passed it down.

It was taken in a bedroom, obviously in bright

early-morning sunlight. Lying in a massive four-poster bed, covered with a down quilt, was a beaming Slater. In bed beside him, right arm locked tightly around Slater in affectionate embrace, was a younger, smiling Gunther. "Oh, we were so good together, Alton. I have missed you so."

He took back the picture, rose to his full height, and stepped aside. "You know," he said, in a musing tone, "it is a wonderful thing about photographs, how they capture so much so quickly. And last so long. Forever, really, if you take proper care of them. It's wonderful, too, how you can share these moments with so many others. That's the marvel about photographs and their negatives, dear Alton. You can keep showing them over and over. Of course"—he paused, and his voice took on a tone of sorrow—"there are some people who have no respect for private moments. They would be so cruel as to keep making copies of pictures from negatives and showing them to all sorts of people who really shouldn't see them. Would you believe, Alton, that there are people right here in Washington who are so unscrupulous they wouldn't hesitate to sell copies of these very same pictures they have of you? Right *here*. In *Washington*, Alton. I've even been told they would give them away just to see the reaction they would cause. Tsk, tsk, tsk." He shook his head. "People can be so terrible."

Slater sank deeper into his plush armchair, his mind reeling. The nightmare he had feared, had buried deep in him for years, the one he thought finally safely behind him, had overcome him. His life was ruined. He felt hopelessly, desperately, trapped.

Gunther was still speaking. "That's not the only way people can be cruel, my dear Alton."

He looked straight at Slater. "You know, Alton, you do have the most wonderful voice. Truly distinctive, wonderfully rich. After all these years, I've never forgotten it. I can't tell you how overjoyed I was to turn on the radio and hear you again. And millions, think of that, millions of people recognize that voice, instantly. How proud you must be now."

He smiled. "You will be interested to know we also have some most extraordinary recordings. One of them is historic.

You will surely want to keep it in a safe place. You are just oozing praise for the Führer and he embraces you with his own words. The two of you together. Think of it, two of the best-known voices in the world. What a collector's item! Really, dear Alton, I must say, I was quite jealous when I heard it. But I felt better, so much better, when I heard a recording of some of our delicious encounters. Would you like to hear it?"

Gunther leaned back over the chair, placing one hand on an armrest, while he started to reach in his pocket with the other, all the while watching Slater's reaction with an amused, taunting look.

Slater snapped. He was filled with a consuming mindless hatred such as he would not have believed possible in any human being. His only thought was to kill this inhuman beast leaning over him. "You miserable bastard," he shouted, possessed and shaking with rage, as he leaped out of his chair and tried to grab Gunther by the throat.

Gunther smiled faintly. He had been waiting for this, had wanted it to happen. Hurt as he was, he stepped backward easily and brushed aside Slater's grasp. With his left hand, he grabbed Slater around the throat and lifted him up with seeming effortlessness until Slater's toes dangled on the carpet. He squeezed relentlessly until Slater's face turned red. His eyes began to bulge. Then he pulled Slater toward him and kissed him full on the lips for a long moment. When he finished, he swiftly dropped him back into the chair.

"Now, dear Alton," he said soothingly to the gasping and sobbing wreck of a man before him. "Let us put all that behind us."

He knelt on his left knee, slowly and painfully, and began stroking Slater's head. "I have brought something for you quite special. I have come all the way just for this. It comes with the best compliments of the Führer. You are quite fortunate, Alton. He pays you a great compliment and offers you one of the most glorious moments of your distinguished career. He has a gift for you to present, with my help, to your friend, the President. The President will be pleased, I assure you. After this you will be more popular with him than ever. Now listen to me carefully. Do I have your attention? Good."

12

When he was lean and fit, at the peak of his physical powers, he could play fifty-four holes of golf in the hottest summer weather in Washington, then go to parties, dance until the early hours of the morning, and still be fresh for a long hard day at his desk grappling with naval problems of the First World War. The vigor was still there, though aside from the daily swim in the White House pool he had had built, to the dismay and outrage of his army of critics, he had long since lost his ability to move freely. If anything, his delight in and need for company sharpened as the years passed and the burdens of his office increased. Each day, when he was in the White House he looked forward to this afternoon hour that was now beginning at five-thirty. The baskets of papers requiring his attention were empty, the conferences that never seemed to cease were over, the briefings in the Map Room were completed, the last official appointment on Grace Tully's calendar were kept. Then, with the usual flurry and signal of bells echoing throughout the mansion, he and his entourage returned to his private Oval Study upstairs. This was the break in the day that he relished, the time when he could turn on all his singular charm and, while skillfully mixing cocktails himself, entertain and be entertained by a range of acquaintants, most old, some new. Momentarily, they helped him escape the realities of the war.

Tully checked her calendar for six o'clock today, Thursday, July 2, and pressed the buzzer on her desk.

"You can go in now," she said to Alton Slater, who was standing before her.

"Al-ton, how are you?"

The familiar voice rang out through the room.

"It's very good of you to see me, Mr. President," Slater said, moving into the study. "We all know how terribly busy you are."

"Not at all, not at all. My pleasure."

The accents drew out the words and seemed to make them hang longer in the air. Slater, a professional himself at speaking and always acutely conscious of how others used their words, often wondered if the President always spoke that way. Or had his political career made him alter his style consciously or otherwise? Whatever, he was struck again at the President's theatrical flair and perfect sense of timing and pitch. It must be something to hear him and Churchill talk together for hours.

"Martini, Alton?"

The President jiggled the cocktail shaker on the silver tray beside his desk. He cocked his head to his side and flashed the great grin. His cigarette was standing forth at its high angle, the smoke curling lazily up in the bright sunlit room.

"No, thank you, Mr. President. I came only to present you with a gift."

"Yes," the President said, glancing up curiously at Slater, a slightly bemused look in his blue eyes. "That's what I thought Grace said when she told me you'd asked for a few minutes. Gift? What sort of gift?"

Slater reached inside his suit-coat pocket and stepped closer to the President's desk. "These," he said. He took out a small glassine envelope from inside an ordinary letter envelope and handed it to the President.

"They're from a great admirer of yours, Mr. President, a grateful refugee who arrived only a few days ago from Europe. He's an old acquaintance of mine. I met him years ago in Vienna. He told me to tell you that knowing you will have these brings the greatest joy to his life."

The President took the glassine envelope. It contained six postage stamps. He held up the envelope, quickly examined the stamps, opened a top drawer of his desk, and withdrew a pair of eyebrow tweezers. Slater watched, then turned toward Harry Hopkins, who was standing quietly beside the President's desk.

"Amazing story," Slater said. "The refugee's a stamp collector. He used some of his collection to bribe his way out of Europe, through the Balkans, traveling alone along the Adriatic, and then by freighter to New York."

The President placed a clean sheet of white typing paper on his desk, and started to extract the stamp with his tweezers. His interest was obvious. He had been collecting stamps since childhood, but his hobby had become more than a pastime after his attack of polio twenty-one years ago in 1921. It was a passion. When his illness forced him to give up his regime of robust physical exercise, his enthusiasms intensified for those functions he could perform at his desk. They absorbed him. He delighted in making small model boats of balsa wood. He took inordinate pride in how fast the miniature sloops and schooners fashioned from his hands sailed in the Hudson, near his home at Hyde Park. He became an avid collector of naval books, manuscripts, and pictures; but his stamp collection gave him his greatest joy. For years he sent his aide Louis Howe to represent him at auctions, and enjoyed making purchases himself by mail. In this, too, as in so many other aspects of his complicated life, he was an amateur but an expert.

As he gently pulled the first stamp out, he began questioning Slater.

"You said this man's name was—"

"Rosenzweig, Mr. President. It's Frank Rosenzweig."

The President personally knew, or knew of, many of the world's most noted stamp collectors. He was familiar with the names of most of the great collectors of Europe. He'd never heard of a Frank Rosenzweig.

"Hmmm. Is he Jewish, Alton?"

"I believe so, sir. Yes, I'm sure he is."

"How old a man is he?"

"He's in his mid-thirties now. Tells me he's been collecting all his life. Seems that a distant cousin who had a fabled collection, some of which he apparently inherited, started him off."

The President was looking at him now. "Oh, and who was that?"

"I didn't get the name, Mr. President. You know"—Slater

gave a short deprecating laugh—"I'm not very good on stamps. I never collected them myself."

The President smiled. "Good for the soul, Al-ton," he said expansively. "Good for the soul."

"Yes, Mr. President, I'm sure they are."

"Where did you say this man was from? Austria?"

"Yes. Vienna."

The President was thoughtful. "Ah, yes. I see."

He turned to the stamps and carefully placed them, one by one, on the sheet of paper before him. He became visibly excited.

"By God, Harry! Will you look at that!" Before him was a two-cent blue Missionary stamp of Hawaii. It had been issued in 1850 and 1852, and was exceedingly rare. "A Missionary!" the President exclaimed. "I'll be damned."

He turned his attention eagerly to the second stamp. He drew in his breath, and then tossed back his head, and beamed delightedly. "Well, I'll be . . ."

He appeared overwhelmed. Hopkins drew closer and leaned over the President's chair to look. "It's a 'Post Office' stamp, Harry," he said, his voice rich with enthusiasm. "How do you like that?"

Hopkins looked blank. The President explained why, to stamp collectors, this so-called Post Office stamp of Mauritius now before him was so famous and so rare. The stamp, a one-penny denomination, was issued in 1848. It contained one of the earliest postal "errors." The word *pence* was misspelled as *pense*.

He was as excited as Hopkins could remember seeing him. The next four stamps were from Moldavia, part of the celebrated 1858 series rare virtually from their date of issue. They consistently brought high prices around the world from philatelists. The President was like a child with new treasured toys.

Slater stepped closer to the desk to share in the moment. "Mr. President," he said, "Rosenzweig asked me to tell you that he has some 'Postmaster Provisionals' from America, whatever they are, with him. It would be the greatest honor of his life to be able to present them to you personally."

"Provisionals? He has Provisionals?" The President sounded incredulous.

"That's what he said. 'Provisionals.' He wants you to have them. He told me you represent the hope of the entire world. No one can do enough to thank you."

The President was pleased. "There you are, Harry," he said, in ebullient mood, shifting in his chair. *"Some* people appreciate what we're doing. Maybe we ought to send Mr. Rosenzweig up to the Hill as our good-will emissary. Let him talk to our good Republican friends, and then let's send him over to deal with John L. Lewis. He can't"—the word came out *cahnnt*—"do any worse with them than our people have so far." He tossed back his head again and roared with laughter, pleased at his own little joke, and pleased with himself.

He looked back at Slater. "Of course, I'd be glad to see Mr. Rosenzweig. By all means. Delighted. I'm curious about that collection of his."

He reached over, pushed a button on his desk, and spoke into a voice box connecting him to Grace Tully.

"Grace," he said, "would you arrange for an appointment for a friend of Alton Slater's sometime in the next few days."

"You mean after the holiday weekend, of course, when you get back, Mr. President. You remember you're going to be away at Hyde Park?"

"Yes, yes, of course. Work out the arrangements with Alton. He's leaving now and he'll give you the details on his way out."

He leaned back, gave his best, most seductive smile, and held out his hand. "Al-ton, thanks *so* much. *So* good of you to come. Look forward to the next time."

Slater shook his hand, struck as always with his great strength, mumbled his good-bye, and left.

When the door closed, Hopkins turned to the President. "What the hell are 'Provisionals'?"

"They're something I'd dearly love, dearly, to have for my collection. About a hundred years ago, actually it was primarily in 1845 and 1846, various postmasters, they were principally along the Eastern seaboard, issued their own stamps. That is they issued them in Baltimore and Alexandria and Annapolis, for instance. They also issued them in St. Louis, Missouri, and some smaller communities. Boscawen, New Hampshire. Did you ever hear of Boscawen, New Hampshire? Now there's a Yankee name for you."

The President's in a wonderful mood, Hopkins thought. I ought to try to arrange for him to get rare stamps once a week.

"They also issued them, I believe, in Milbury, Massachusetts. The practice was not widespread. It didn't last long. When the general-issue government stamps came along in 1847 that put an end to the Provisionals. Over the last ninety or so years they've become extremely rare. They're widely sought after. Any of them would make a great addition to my collection."

The President turned back to his new stamps. He picked up his tweezers, plucked the Mauritius from his desk, and held it up to the lamp.

"You know, Harry," he said, as Hopkins leaned over to examine the stamp, "there are several things to be said about all this. Take this Mauritius, for example. What makes it especially rare is the fact that the engraver was stupid. He didn't know how to spell. He erred. Now in most aspects of life, and it's certainly so when it comes to consumer goods, when you buy something that's a lemon, something that's faulty, where the manufacturer has made a mistake, why you march right down to the store and return it. You want no part of it. Not so with stamps."

He turned the stamp to check another angle. Hopkins was interested, not in the stamp, but in the analogy.

"The more error there is on a stamp, the more valuable it is. If the airplane flies upside down, or there's an obvious printing error, or if it's not the color it's supposed to be, well, it becomes not worthless. It becomes not just valuable. Why, it becomes invaluable."

He beamed at Hopkins, who shook his head and smiled.

The President deposited the stamp back on the sheet of paper. "Take those Moldavian stamps," he said, "and throw in this one from Mauritius, too. Rare and wonderful as these are, I think I'll give these to the Smithsonian—providing they are genuine, and I have every reason to believe they are. I'm really most interested in stamps from the United States."

The President turned back to the stamps. He became fully absorbed. Silently, intently, he examined each one as if it were as precious as the Declaration of Independence.

13

Waiting was always the worst part. Henry and Mr. Biddle, as he thought of the Attorney General (somehow the "Old Man" sobriquet didn't fit so courtly and dapper a gentleman), sat on the small sofa at the end of the first-floor lobby staring straight ahead.

They were worn with fatigue, and showed it. The Attorney General's eyes were ringed with what appeared to be permanent gray sacks of puffy flesh. Mine aren't much better, Henry was thinking. It isn't the physical strain that gets to you, he reflected, glancing idly at the huge canvasses of Revolutionary War battle scenes. He could handle that. It's the cumulative pressures that beat you down and make it harder to function; and these past days there had been no letup. No hint of success, either. He had been working around the clock with little to show for it. Thomas, too. They checked each other by phone at the end of each day, as agreed, but neither had anything substantive to report. The German who came with Decatur, "Gunther," had simply disappeared without a trace.

Henry began to wonder if he could be wrong. Finally, under prodding from Arnie Thorson, he briefed the Attorney General about the apparent connection between the murder of the black prostitute and the Norwegian attaché. He explained how the sketch he obtained seemed to match the oral description Decatur gave of his partner on the third submarine. He made the sketch available to Mr. Biddle, with the recommendation that it be duplicated and distributed to all key military installations and security agents, including the Secret Service and the Bureau. That was in process. Still nothing.

Somehow, Henry felt foolish when he briefed the Attorney General. Before, he'd always taken pride in his ability to brief a case. This time, he had been unsure. And, of course, the Bureau didn't buy it. They had captured them all. The Director was being lionized as the greatest of American heroes. Each day's papers brought greater praise for his work, and now they were all caught up over what to do with the saboteurs who had been arrested. The Attorney General asked Henry to assist on this, too. When Bill Hassett called to say the President wanted to meet with Biddle about setting up a trial commission for the saboteurs, the Attorney General asked Henry to accompany him.

"You can go on up now, Mr. Attorney General," the attractive young secretary sitting at the desk across from them in the lobby said. "Grace says he's ready for you."

They got up and followed an old Negro butler, in livery, through an alcove into a corridor where a narrow flight of stairs curled upstairs to the family quarters of the White House. The butler led them to a small elevator, across from the stairs, and pressed the button.

"This should make you feel at home, Henry," the Attorney General said, with a slight smile, as they stepped into the elevator. He gestured toward the oaken panels that formed the elevator walls. "These are cut from rafters in Old South Church in Boston."

Henry nodded. He had never met the President, though of course there were many connections between his and Mr. Roosevelt's family, and he was surprised at his lack of nervousness now. Not that he ever felt in awe of anyone, but he would have expected a sense of excitement about meeting the President, and in his personal quarters no less. He felt none. Oh pride, curiosity, and keen interest, sure; but, strangely, not excitement. It was another sign of strain, he concluded as they walked down the long corridor upstairs and followed the butler into the Oval Study.

"Francis," the President called out, warmly, from behind his desk. "Thanks for coming. Please sit down." He gestured to chairs drawn up before his desk.

Standing off to the side, quiet as ever, were Harry Hopkins and Hassett.

"Mr. President," the Attorney General said gravely and formally, "this is Lieutenant Henry Eaton. I believe you know his father, Archie, from college days."

"I certainly do," the President said, smiling and nodding toward Henry. "When I was editor in chief of the *Crimson*, Archie was the great football hero of our class. Archie made Porcellian, too, and I didn't. Did you know, Lieutenant, that not making Porcellian, where my father and my cousin Theodore belonged, was the greatest disappointment of my life. It doesn't seem so *terribly* important now"—he laughed—"but it certainly did then."

Pleasantries behind him, his tone changed.

"Now, Francis," he said briskly, "I have the papers here ready to sign. These are the ones appointing the military commission to try the spies." He shuffled a set of papers on his desk, then picked up a single sheet and held it up for the Attorney General's examination. "This does not suspend the writ of habeas corpus, but it does deny access to the civil courts of certain described persons." He passed it over to Biddle. "I read that to mean that they must take whatever medicine the commission prescribes. Do you agree?"

"Yes, Mr. President," Biddle said.

The President, pleased, shook his head. "The commission can, of course, impose the penalty of death. Right?"

Again, Biddle nodded his assent.

The President was silent a moment. Then he said, "Hanging would afford an efficacious example to others of like kidney. There's no doubt of their guilt, but we are always too soft in dealing with spies and traitors."

Henry was fascinated at the President's manner and personality. He's a lot tougher than even I suspected, he thought, and he had reason, from the intelligence charter the President had granted Biddle, to know the private Roosevelt was different from the public one.

The President looked at them all, and delivered a short,

sharp question. "What should be done with them?" he asked. "Should they be shot or hanged?"

Hassett, usually so quiet, spoke up. "Hanged by all means," he said. "Shooting's too honorable for them. Hanging will teach a lesson to the Nazis and particularly to American traitors and near traitors."

The President warmed to the conversation. "What about having pictures taken of them hanging?"

"By all means," Hassett said. "You know, I've always thought anyone who ever looked at the photographs of the hanging of the Lincoln conspirators would never forget it—Mrs. Surratt and the rest of them swinging in the hot July sun. That kind of picture's worth more than a million words. It would drive home a lesson the country needs without further delay."

When Hassett said he thought those pictures the more horrible because he'd always believed Mrs. Surratt was probably innocent, the President interrupted.

"I always thought her guilt had been proved," he said sharply. No one disagreed with him.

"Well," he said, "good. Then we agree on the interpretation of the documents."

He looked hard and knowingly at Biddle, who would oversee the prosecution of the saboteurs, and said, "I hope the finding will be unanimous."

"Yes, Mr. President," the Attorney General replied.

"Good, fine. Glad you could come by."

He was in his jovial mood again, Henry noticed, as they stood up. The President shook Biddle's hand and then turned toward Henry and put on his famous charm.

"I'm pleased to meet you, Lieutenant." He held out his hand. "Say hello to your father. I suppose I don't have too many backers at First Boston, but I hope he doesn't think I'm *entirely* a traitor to my class, as the rest of them do."

His eyes twinkled with a faintly malicious gleam. Henry smiled in spite of himself. "I'll tell him what you said, Mr. President. I'm afraid I'm regarded as something of a traitor to the old class myself."

As he leaned across the desk to shake the President's hand, he noticed a single blue postage stamp lying in the center of a white sheet of paper. "If I didn't know better, Mr. President, I'd say that looks like a Missionary."

A quick look of interest crossed the President's face. "You have a good eye, Lieutenant. It is a Missionary. You must be a collector, too."

"Not in your class, Mr. President. I used to do a little collecting, but I thought I recognized that stamp."

The President was pleased. "Quite unusual, really. I was just telling Harry before you came in. Alton Slater, you know, the *com-men-ta-tor*"—he slipped into an almost unconscious and perfect mimicking of Slater's clipped and staccato tone of speaking, watching their smiles as he did— "brought this for me when he dropped by a while ago. Seems they're from a Jewish refugee—a Mr. Rosenzweig—just arrived from Europe who wants to come by and give me some more priceless stamps." He laughed. "Certainly knows the best way to get in my good graces."

"What does he look like?" Henry blurted out the words.

The President was taken aback. Biddle, Hopkins, and Hassett, equally startled by Henry's impertinence, were visibly annoyed.

"I don't know, Lieutenant," the President, more coolly, said. "I've never seen the man."

Henry felt Biddle glowering at him and fell silent. Once again, he felt foolish.

"Well," the President said, breaking the tension, "good of you to come."

They left, stiffly.

Outside, in the waiting limousine standing on the circular driveway at the rear of the executive mansion, the Attorney General turned sharply to Henry. "Well, young man, what was that all about?"

Henry, flustered, stammered a reply.

"Well, sir, I don't know. Nothing really, I guess. It's just that when I heard the President say something about this refugee who wants to present him more stamps, I, well, I—"

"Well?"

"Well, sir, it was just a crazy stray thought, but I found myself thinking about the suspect in Decatur's murder."

He felt foolish as soon as he said the words. The Attorney

General looked at him coldly in unspoken reprimand, then, without a word, stared ahead as the limousine pulled off into the dusk. Henry slumped back in his seat. He was far more weary than when they arrived. They rode in icy silence back to the Justice Department.

14

     Death had no terror for Gunther. In many ways, he welcomed it. He had always thought of himself as destined for something extraordinary. At first, and for many years after, he believed he had been chosen to make his mark in music. Not as a Beethoven, nor as a Wagner, but to be remembered for creating something that would last, and live long after he was gone. His conversion to the Führer's vision of the Germanic future, and his devotion to the Führer both for what he represented personally and for his embodiment of the soul of the German people, were no less total. He glowed with pride over the mission he had been assigned. For a thousand years to come his name would live in history. Now his destiny and that of the Fatherland would be bound together inextricably, his role told and retold until it was etched forever in the minds of Teutonic children yet unborn. He had no doubt now he would succeed. When Slater told him, after he phoned him in the early hours before dawn on Friday, that their appointment with the President had been set for Wednesday morning, July 8, Gunther experienced a state of exultation unlike anything he had felt before. He waited to call, with deliberate cruelty, until he thought Slater probably had fallen into a fitful sleep; then he enjoyed toying with him verbally and hearing him break further.

Slater's voice had croaked into the phone, sounding muffled and distant, not at all like the famous timbre and modulation of his radio tones. Whatever small resolve he had left, whatever momentary spirit of rebellion had stiffened his spine, all dissolved at the sound of Gunther's soothing, mocking, menacing voice.

"How did it go, dearest Alton?" he said in a near whisper.

At first, Slater tried to bluster and hold him off. "Well," he finally managed to say, "it went well," and then was silent.

Gunther let the silence between them build before speaking, even more softly than before. "I said how did it go, my dear Alton?"

Slater stammered his reply. "The President, he, the President was delighted with the stamps. He, he . . ."

Gunther waited, then: "Yes? And?"

"He was grateful, and, uh, we, uh, have an appointment Wednesday morning. He'll—he'll be glad to meet you and receive the other stamps."

Gunther suppressed his emotional reaction. "You have done well, Alton, very well," he said calmly. "Now go to sleep, *mein Liebchen*. I am proud of you, and I miss you, but I do have your pictures and your recordings to keep me company and comfort me."

He hung up.

So, he thought, it worked. He could use the time, too. He had been hurt even more than he realized at first. It was still difficult to walk and his right shoulder was in great pain. He needed to regain his strength.

For the remainder of that day, and for most of the long holiday weekend, he rested in the apartment, nursing himself, soaking more in the tub, painfully kneading and flexing his torn muscles, and eating steaks that "Shrivel" obtained on the thriving black market. He also dyed his hair black, with a preparation Shrivel bought at the drugstore near George Washington University, and practiced applying dark makeup to cover the faint scar on his face. Only once, on Saturday morning, the Fourth of July, did he leave the apartment, and that was just to limp slowly up to the news vendor's stand on Pennsylvania Avenue to buy papers and magazines.

He was amused to listen to all the patriotic music and dramatic readings and announcements pouring out over the radio. It was, as the listeners were told over and over, the first

Independence Day of the war and only the fourth such holiday since 1864 that Americans had been at war. On the newsstand, every full-color magazine carried a picture of the American flag on its cover, something the government had arranged with the magazine publishers. The news was deliberately upbeat, a fact that at least one magazine, *Life*, took issue with, he noted, reading its Fourth of July editorial back in the apartment:

The only battle that U.S. citizens have won so far is the battle of the newspaper headlines. This sham is not entirely the fault of the editors. It's a tough job to write realistic copy when everyone from the President down is shining with sunny optimism. The fact remains that the first news of the dreadful defeat of the Java Sea came to readers of *The New York Times* with a streamer headline: 6 SHIPS HIT BY U.S. SUBMARINES. The battle of the Coral Sea was made to appear a much bigger victory than it actually was. Week before last, great streamers announced that U.S. airmen had bombed the Rumanian oil refineries. When it was discovered that, like every other expedition against the camouflaged objectives, they had bombed the wrong town, the news was buried in the back pages. Donald Nelson keeps telling the nation that it is winning the production battle, and last week the President boasted that the U.S. had turned out 4,000 planes and 1,500 tanks in May. The recent record of American industry and labor, in terms of quantity, is stupendous. But bragging statements about war production are out of balance when they hide from the people grave combat deficiencies in American tanks, guns, fighter planes and other equipment. These deficiencies are well known to the enemy and should not be kept from us. ... on this Fourth of July we face a question as profound as any we have ever faced, as difficult to answer. Like Francis Scott Key, we stand peering into the darkness. Key was unable to tell whether the flag was still flying over the unequal battle of Fort McHenry, and out of his anxious watch our national anthem was born. Today, by the grace of God, we know that that flag flies over our land. But in the darkness of our hearts we cannot see what it means.

Gunther felt something akin to pity for the Americans. They were so unprepared for the reality of war. Their papers gave the impression the war was far away and could never touch them here at home, their public was ecstatic over the easy roundup of the saboteurs and, it was being said, nothing had so captured the imagination of the people since the war began, their Congress was in a rebellious mood over price controls, their President was denouncing selfish "pressure groups," their government departments were openly fighting among themselves, their labor leaders and business executives were ignoring the President's anti-inflation program, and their journals were demanding the government tell them more *bad* news! It was all incredible. Soon, all that would change. He grinned in pleasure and felt another surge of pride over his destiny, then quickly reined in his emotions.

It was important to be absolutely calm and deliberate. Over and over, as he worked to regain his strength, he mentally played out his actions. Surviving was not the question; guaranteeing the success of his mission was. Still, in the unlikely event he emerged from the White House alive, he had to prepare just as methodically for the possibility. The weekend passed. He continued his exercises throughout Monday. Then, in mid-morning on Tuesday, he left the apartment, folded tourist map in hand, and proceeded on one last inspection of any possible escape routes.

Slowly, casually, he again entered the flowing stream of pedestrian traffic and moved with it toward the White House. He circled the grounds, crossed onto the Ellipse, swung down Pennsylvania Avenue toward the Capitol in the distance. All the while, he glanced idly at the adjoining streets and mentally checked the parking lots and alleys and open courtyards tucked away among the office buildings of the Federal Triangle. He imagined hiding places, searched for blind escape routes, guarded against dead ends and physical obstacles, and noted bus and trolley stops where he might slip away among the crowds. He wound his way along the side streets, turned at the corners and strolled back along the other side of the block until he came to Pennsylvania Avenue again.

When he approached Tenth Street he stopped to study his map, then walked north along the west side of the street. This, he couldn't resist. He crossed the shabby shops along E Street and passed the nondescript narrow red brick Petersen House, where Abraham Lincoln had been carried, never to regain consciousness, the night he was shot.

Gunther stopped to watch the line of tourists entering the small narrow house then, on impulse, crossed the street to join the throng waiting to go inside Ford's Theater. He paid his ten cents and shuffled along with the others inside the small dimly lighted building. Gone were the stage and the balconies and even the seats where the audience watched *Our American Cousin* before the comedy was interrupted by the sound of Booth's derringer. It didn't matter. Gunther could play the scene back in his mind. He tried to imagine how Booth felt when he pulled the trigger, and wondered if he experienced ecstasy or fear or doubt—or all these and more. He felt humbled. He was about to enter history's door, too. The crowd silently filed out of the theater. Gunther headed back toward Pennsylvania Avenue and resumed the exploration of the routes he could take tomorrow.

15

The lineup was long over, and the last of the night's arrests were locked away in the rear of the precinct, shouting and cursing as always. In the cubicle beside him a radio was playing loudly. All the fans were turning, but without alleviating the heat and the smell of the station house. Thomas tried to focus on a monthly police report he was supposed to have filed a week ago, but couldn't. The words ran together. He was incapable of dealing with it. Over and over he found himself drawing the sketch of Odessa's killer in his mind, and each time with the same result. Nothing, except a deeper sense of frustration and helplessness. For the fourth time, he turned back to the monthly duty report and tried to come to grips with it. The sharp jangle of the phone on his desk interrupted him.

"Sergeant Thomas here," he said, sitting upright.

At the other end of the line, the voice sounded breathless.

"Sergeant Thomas?"

It was a Negro male speaking. His words ran together, making them difficult to understand.

"Yes, this is Sergeant Thomas."

"Sergeant Thomas, Sergeant Thomas, I seen him, I seen him."

Thomas felt his pulse quicken. He deliberately lowered his voice and spoke evenly and calmly.

"Easy. Take your time. Who is this and what have you seen?"

"The man they say you lookin' for. I seen him."

Thomas bolted forward, his entire body tingling. Forcing his voice to remain in the same calm tone, he asked quietly: "Now hold on, tell me exactly who you saw and where."

"Thirteenth and the Avenue, Sergeant. I seen him go by my paper stand. The man in the drawin', the man they say you lookin' for."

"When?"

Thomas's voice took on an urgency. He gripped the phone tightly and felt the veins on his neck throb. It was all he could do to stay seated.

"Just a minute ago. Right by my stand. Thirteenth and the Avenue. Right here, Sergeant. I seen him."

"Are you sure?" Thomas asked.

"Pretty positive, Sergeant. I believes that's him."

"All right. Stay right there till I get there." Thomas was already standing. "Now who is this?"

"Levi Waters, Sergeant, that's who I is."

"Stay right there," Thomas said emphatically. "Don't do or say anything until I get there."

He raced out of the station house, sketch in hand, and started running from the Second Precinct toward Pennsylvania Avenue. He forced himself to maintain a steady pace, instead of sprinting as he felt impelled. The perspiration quickly turned his starched white shirt limp and wet and began to stain his dark plainclothes suit. His breath was labored and he felt the blood drumming in his temples, not from his physical exertion, he realized, but from the almost uncontrollable excitement he felt. Within six minutes, he reached the avenue. He identified himself to Levi Waters, an old weathered man who had been selling papers and magazines on Pennsylvania Avenue for years, showed him the sketch, and quickly asked questions. Yes, he was certain that was the one he had seen. He showed Thomas the sketch he had been keeping in his pocket for days, and pointed the policeman in the direction he saw the suspect going—due east toward the Capitol.

Thomas drew in his breath, mopped his face with his handkerchief, and began walking. With every step he told himself to keep calm, keep calm, keep calm. He searched the streets from side to side as he walked, scanned every head before him, glanced into every store, and mechanically, instinctively, checked the windows of passing trolley cars and buses. Nothing. A sense of wild frustration began to sweep through Thomas. He'd lost him. Then, as he neared Tenth Street, Thomas's breath froze and his body stiffened. There he was. The hair was dark instead of blond, the hat cast a shadow over much of the face, and he appeared to be more bent over than Thomas would have thought. But it was him. Even in profile, he'd know that face anywhere. No question, that was him, all right.

Gunther turned back onto Pennsylvania Avenue and continued walking toward the Capitol. Thomas, a block away, fell in behind him and began to follow. Half a block away, Gunther sensed someone behind him. It was nothing he saw, just something he felt, and he always trusted his senses.

He was seldom wrong.

He stopped in front of a souvenir shop, with Fourth of July fireworks still displayed in the windows, and glanced in the reflection to see if he could pick up anyone who might be following. No, nothing. He moved on, more slowly now. He attempted to glance peripherally at passing car windows.

Still nothing. He paused, glanced casually around at the buildings, then crossed the broad avenue and started walking in the opposite direction back toward the high stone tower of the Old Post Office Building and the White House.

There, that one. The big Negro, taller than himself, and at least as massively built, he was crossing, too. But how could that be a threat? No uniform, no weapons. Just a big Negro. He quickened his pace slightly. So did the colored man.

Gunther began to feel uneasy. How could this be a problem? Yet all of his senses were signaling trouble to him: he felt that tingling sensation down the small of his back. His breath was shorter and his heartbeat had risen.

He passed the Benjamin Franklin Post Office, passed the massive marble structure fronted with heavy columns that was Washington's City Hall, passed Fourteenth Street and its thick lanes of traffic. Still, that Negro kept stride behind him. He was moving up more quickly now.

As he approached Fifteenth Street and the sprawling white Commerce Department, he made a quick decision. Let's see, he thought. He turned sharply south onto Fifteenth and then quickly entered the Commerce Department. So, the Negro did, too. He stepped up his pace as he moved through the pavilions constructed in Italian Renaissance style. His eye caught a sign that said AQUARIUM with an arrow pointing down a flight of stairs.

Briskly now, Gunther raced down the stairs to the basement. There, the Bureau of Fisheries maintained forty-eight display tanks and three small floor pools, home to about 2,000 native freshwater fish. The fish and frogs and turtles and other marine creatures displayed amid the soft green lights shining from the tanks were one of the most popular lunchtime attractions in Washington. Now, as always, it was crowded.

Gunther pushed his way through the crowds. No doubt now, he was being followed. The big Negro wasn't even trying to hide it: he was pressing forward vigorously toward him. Gunther felt a stir of panic. It couldn't happen now. He couldn't be stopped this way. His eyes desperately roamed around the aquarium. He spotted the department cafeteria, filled with people, and hurried inside. Behind, that big Negro kept closing on him.

Thomas reached the door and started to enter.

"Where you think you're going, black boy?"

A big white General Services Administration guard barred Thomas's path. "Can't you read?" The Guard pointed to a sign by the door. It read: WHITE ONLY. "This isn't your entrance. You got to go around the side."

Thomas, enraged, watched Gunther starting to disappear from view through the glass door.

"Get out of my way you son of a bitch," he shouted. "I'm a District police officer."

He started to reach inside his coat pocket to extract his badge with his right hand, and with his left pushed back the guard.

"The hell you are," the guard shouted back, and started to wrestle with him. A second guard quickly joined them.

Thomas, cursing loudly, lunged forward, struck one guard and knocked him down. More guards arrived. They threw themselves at Thomas and hurled him back. He shouted, "Police officer, you bastards!" broke away briefly, pushed himself forward toward the door, and when unable any longer to see Gunther among the mass of frightened people ahead, in a fit of consuming fury smashed his right fist through the glass door. It shattered. Blood from his hand spurted out and up and onto the uniforms of the guards. Thomas staggered back, spent but still murderously angry. He was subdued, handcuffed, and, still shouting wildly, was taken away. Kicked into a corner during the scuffle, after it was ripped from his hand, lay his District of Columbia Metropolitan Police badge.

The crowd, mute with horror at the violent scene, slowly began to disperse.

Fifteen minutes later Gunther coolly approached the two guards posted, with sullen expressions, before the shattered door. He was deferential and respectful.

"I saw what happened," he said, speaking to the shorter of the guards. "Thank God you were here. No one's safe anymore with *them* around. I just want to tell you how much the rest of *us* appreciate what you did. You did a helluva job.

What was the matter with that nigger, anyway? Was he crazy?"

The guard, flattered, relaxed, shifted his position, and smiled faintly. "Damndest thing," he said. "Just goes to show you, you never know. This guy starts to go in here, and of course they can't. They've got their own entrance. Anyway, he's shouting that he's a D.C. cop, claims he's after someone, and just goes nuts. And I mean nuts! Well—"

He stopped and rubbed his face ruefully, leaned closer to Gunther, who listened with rapt attention, lowered his voice conspiratorially, and said, "Hell of it is, seems he *is* a cop. How do ya like that? Who'd a thought that? And how were we supposed to know? A nigger cop! Can you beat it?"

"You're kidding," Gunther said. "You mean he really *is* a cop?"

"That's right, buddy. No question, he is."

Gunther shook his head in amazement. He looked around as if to make sure no one was listening, and said to the guard quietly, "You know, I don't care who he was. He had no right acting that way. He could have hurt somebody."

"That's what I say," the guard said. *"He's* shouting to us that *we're* obstructing justice. Get that. A nigger telling me I'm obstructing justice when *he's* breaking the law trying to get in a white entrance."

Gunther shook his head again, and looked disgusted. "That's what I say. I thought you guys were very brave. Very brave. He could have hurt someone, and he sure scared the rest of us. Nothing gives him the right to do that. What was he after, anyway?"

The guard shrugged. "Damned if I know. He just kept shouting he was after a suspect and had to get him and we were obstructing justice. Obstructing justice! Us!"

Gunther appeared even more disgusted. He shook his head once more, and started to leave. Then he turned back.

"Say, I've been thinking," he said to the same guard. "I've got a real good buddy at the *Evening Star*. A reporter. They ought to know about this. What *really* happened. You guys deserve credit. People ought to know what kind of crazy niggers are running around with police badges in Washington these days. I mean, I know there's a war on but this is ridiculous. Give me your name and the name of that cop and I'll pass it on to him. They'll do a story on it, I'll betcha. It's about time people begin to wise up around here."

The guard looked reluctant. "I don't know," he started to say, and then turned toward the other guard, who had been listening. "What do you think, Ernie?"

Ernie shrugged. Gunther looked at him expectantly. "Ah, why not?"

The shorter guard spoke up. "The guy's name is Thomas. That's the last name, T-h-o-m-a-s, a D.C. cop. A sergeant. What was his first name, Ernie?"

He checked his notebook. "I think it's Leon."

"Yeah, Leon. Leon Thomas. I'm Charlie Reeves. That's two *es* and *v-e-s*. Reeves. *R-e-e-v-e-s*. This here"—he pointed to his partner—"is Ernie Rivers. Reeves and Rivers, best there is."

He beamed. Gunther had taken out a piece of paper and jotted down the names. "Where'd you say they took the cop?"

Reeves gave a tight, sarcastic laugh. "Where do you think? To Freedman's Hospital. That's where they all belong."

Gunther smiled back. "Thanks. You've been great. I'll see that you get credit."

He nodded, smiled again, and started to walk away. He had taken only a few steps when Reeves shouted at him, "Hey, you!" Gunther froze. He tensed imperceptibly, turned slowly, leaning forward slightly in a crouch, and said, "Yes?"

Reeves called to him. "The middle initial is P, for Peter."

327

16

Proud and ashamed and hurt, Thomas told no one what happened. He didn't call home. He didn't call the Second Precinct. There would be time for that later. For now, he seethed with rage and a helpless sense of failure. Being carted off to Freedman's, the federally supported hospital for all Negroes in the District of Columbia, was a final humiliating indignity. It was fitting, he thought bitterly, while they took X rays, stitched his hand, gave him a sedative, tetanus injections, and dressed his wounds in the emergency room: the hospital for Negroes in the nation's capital was named for a white man, and the land it occupied had been a plantation worked by slaves. His fury over what happened at the Commerce Department cafeteria filled him with a hatred for all whites. He couldn't stop thinking about it. The knowledge that he had been so close to getting Odessa's murderer, and probably the man who killed the other Negroes too, was unbearable. He was haunted by his own doubts. Should he have asked for help from the Metropolitan Police Department? Should he have alerted Lieutenant Eaton? Should he have fired his service revolver when he saw the suspect slipping away? They tormented him and drove him with an irrational determination to continue on alone, find the suspect, and finally end it by taking matters in his own hands. He would dispense justice himself.

When he stepped from the emergency room, the late-afternoon sun struck his eyes. He threw up his left hand to shield himself from the glare. His right hand was swathed in bandages and supported by a sling.

From behind a sycamore tree across the street, Gunther

saw Thomas emerge from the doorway of the emergency room. He had been waiting patiently for nearly an hour since an aide at the information booth in the lobby told him Detective Thomas was still in the emergency room. It would be some time before he was discharged. He took full cover behind the tree and watched as Thomas walked away from the hospital. The policeman was nearly two blocks away, heading down the long hill toward U Street where he could hail a cab, when Gunther slipped out of the playground and began to move after him carefully.

Thomas dismissed his first strange sensation that someone was following him. He turned abruptly around, stared, and saw nothing. For the faintest moment, he imagined he saw the same man in the sketch slipping behind the black iron steps standing before one of the old row houses up the hill. I must be hallucinating from the shots, he thought. Either that or my rage has affected me so that I'm starting to imagine things. Still, uneasy, he turned around again. Nothing. But his instincts signaled otherwise.

He was fully alert now, and wary. He passed an alleyway, and quickly ducked into it, stopped, backed against a wall, and waited. He heard footsteps. They drew closer, and stopped. Thomas stared intently down the alleyway toward the street. Then, framed against the late-afternoon sky, he saw the figure of a man. At first he couldn't make out the face; but he didn't need to; he knew who it was; and now he saw the face. Gunther was smiling. Thomas whirled to face him. Automatically he reached for his .38-caliber service revolver. Suddenly he felt a chill run through his body. Even his sweat felt cold. Numbingly, in a state of shock, he realized his gun hand was useless. In that split second he understood the smile.

Gunther closed incredibly fast. He landed a hard kick on Thomas's bandaged right hand. Thomas cried out in agony and dropped to his knees in excruciating pain. Gunther was upon him. Even then, Thomas fought back. He rained blow after heavy blow with his big left hand on Gunther's side. Gunther grunted and flinched. Then, with an extraordinarily agile movement, Thomas leaned forward and sharply kicked back, striking Gunther full on his already

329

badly damaged left knee. Now Gunther cried out. He fell back, then, summoning all his strength, kicked Thomas on the side of the head, knocking him forward onto the concrete. He landed on his back and swiftly looped his watch chain around Thomas's great bull neck. With all his force, he yanked it tight around the protruding veins and pulled out and back.

It was over in less than a minute. The faint necklace of small red beads began to gleam from Thomas's coal-black skin as Gunther left him sprawled in the shadows of the alleyway.

17

Henry finished the sports pages of the *Washington Post*, reached into his silk bathrobe for a cigarette, lighted it, took a last sip of his coffee, hurriedly flipped through the rest of the paper, and was about to put it aside and head for the shower when his eye caught a one-column headline above the two-paragraph story on the next to the last page:

NEGRO COP FOUND SLAIN

He glanced at it and then sank back heavily onto the sofa, his face white and taut.

"Oh, my God," he said aloud.

The story read:

Detective Sgt. Leon Thomas, 38, of the Metropolitan Police Department was found slain last night in an alley near Freedman's Hospital, police reported. They said there was evidence of a struggle. Thomas, colored, assigned to vice investigations, had been treated at the hospital for injuries to his hand from an accident earlier, according to police.

Thomas, of 1319 Monroe St. N.E., was attending night courses at Howard University. A native of Orangeburg, S.C., Thomas joined the force in 1930. He leaves a wife, Saundra, and two children, James and Harriet.

Henry felt sick. He looked at the story again, then, in a rage, he threw the paper across the room. The pages scattered before his fireplace. He picked up the phone, called the Second Precinct, asked a few quick questions, jotted the responses in his notebook, dressed rapidly, and hurried from his apartment.

The early-morning sun slanting down over East Capitol Street bathed the Capitol dome in faint shades of pink. The grounds were still and lovely, but Henry didn't notice. He drove mechanically across the Hill toward the waterfront and the D.C. morgue, his face set in a grim expression, his hands gripping the wheel tightly. He felt light-headed and empty, and the trip seemed surreal, as if he were floating. He drove mechanically, maneuvering his car through the early-morning traffic, past stalls where watermen were setting out their catches, and against the already heavy flow of cars heading into the capital from across the bridges spanning the Anacostia and Potomac.

Until his brother, Quint, died Henry had never lost anything important to him. His entire life had conditioned him to take success for granted. It was inconceivable he could lose. Now, in only a matter of days, everything he touched seemed to fall apart. He was beginning to feel as if he were incapable, incompetent, doomed to fail. In a strange way, Thomas's death hit him harder even than Quint's. The odds against a combat pilot flying daily missions in the Pacific were high; everyone understood that. But with Thomas it was different. Constance was right: he didn't *know* Negroes, and obviously he didn't delude himself that he *knew* Thomas, either. At first, of course, he dismissed him. He couldn't have cared less. Then he came to have a grudging respect for him, and a sense there was a lot more there than he would ever know. He realized, and the thought came as a shock, that, more than anyone he had ever met, Thomas conveyed a sense of strength; and not just physical strength alone. He had a bedrock integrity; he gave you the feeling that he knew exactly who he was, and always could be relied upon to do what was right. He seemed indestructible. The idea of his death was simply unbelievable.

He pulled up before the morgue and raced inside.

The elevator seemed slower than usual. He fumed as it rose creakingly to the second floor and the autopsy room. Again, the heavy smell hit him like a blow. He felt queasy and nauseated. Dr. Luke was there, his eyes red from crying. So was young James. He stood to the side, his face dark and impassive but with a look of barely suppressed fury about his eyes. Henry remembered, with a sharp pang, Thomas and Constance quoting poetry, and reciting the lines: *We wear the mask that grins and lies.* Jesus, he thought. Look at that boy.

He stepped briskly up to Dr. Luke, all business. "I'd like to see the body," he said.

Dr. Luke glanced toward James and, without waiting for a response, nodded. He silently led Henry toward a stone slab near the front window where a clean white sheet was draped over a corpse. He pulled it back and Henry stared down. The head was bruised, the right hand mangled, and there, around the neck, ran the thin circlet of beads now turned from red into a dark line standing apart from the bluish-black skin. Thomas had found Gunther.

Henry swallowed hard and almost retched. Then he was overcome by a wave of emotion, not of anger or hatred or a thirst for revenge. Those came later. He felt deeply, miserably, unforgivably guilty. *He had no idea what he was up against. If only I had told him what I knew about Gunther. At least he would have been prepared. He'd never have let himself be caught alone. He would have been ready to shoot first. He'd still be alive. I know it. I'm responsible, just as surely as if I planted him alone in that alley.* Each thought stabbed at him like a knife wound. He stood, unseeing, over the body. Then he stepped back and gestured for Dr. Luke to draw up the sheet and cover the body.

He fought not to cry. Nodding silently, he started to

leave. James stepped in front of him, his face purpled with anger. "He should never have got mixed up with people like you," he lashed out bitterly. "People like you killed him. Goddamn you anyway." He struck a blow that Henry sidestepped.

"Now, you wait a minute," he said, stung and angry, holding back James with his extended left arm. "Your father was a remarkable man and he died in the line of duty. I didn't kill your father, and don't ever accuse me of that again. I want you to know that I'm going to find the man who killed him if it takes the rest of my life. And I hope I'm the one that gets to kill him." He brushed James aside and, as Dr. Luke put his arms around the boy, left.

In cold rage, mixed in now with his guilt, he drove swiftly uptown to the Second Precinct. He had never been there. What a miserable, filthy place to work, he thought, as he walked inside. Then he tried to imagine what Thomas must have felt being there engulfed by all the white policemen, the daily humiliations and hatreds. He strode up to the desk sergeant, flashed his Naval Intelligence credentials, and learned that Thomas had been hurt yesterday in an encounter with some guards at the Commerce Department. He noted their names from the report on Thomas's death, thanked the sergeant, who seemed to care little, then hurried down to Commerce.

Henry was capable of intimidating people. He was so assured, and gave off such an air of easy authority, that people naturally deferred to him. Never had he been so commanding as now. Again, he imperiously showed his Intelligence credentials and was shortly seated in a small room. The two guards were summoned before him, their supervisor at their side.

They were cocky at first, as they told what had happened yesterday during the lunch hour at the department's cafeteria doorway. They treated the incident lightly and sounded annoyed at having to explain themselves and recount that dumb colored cop's behavior, but they quickly lost their bluster as Henry coldly, icily, stared at them, his dark eyes hard as diamonds, grimly boring straight into them. They began to stammer and shift uncomfortably. Henry's open air of hostility and contempt and his unmistakable sense of power troubled them greatly. There's something terrorizing about this guy, they both thought to themselves, becoming even more worried. He looked like he'd kill them to get what he wanted. He showed them a sketch. They glanced at each other nervously. Yes, that was the guy. The same one that talked to them later. Henry's eyes sparkled with menace. Yes, they were sure. They squirmed some more. Henry felt murderous toward them. They had caused Thomas's death. They had failed to help him. They had let the German escape. They were bigots. Worse, they were stupid and hopelessly incompetent.

"Thank you," he said in an icy cold voice to their supervisor, as he stood up from the desk. He didn't even glance at the guards. "These men," he said, again addressing their supervisor, "have caused the United States more harm than I can begin to tell you. There is no way to undo the damage they have done. I don't have time to deal with them now, but I suggest that they be instructed on how to recognize and respond to officers of the law, or to officers of the United States government. If you don't, I'll personally take the greatest pleasure in seeing that someone else does in a manner that they will remember the rest of their lives."

He left them shaken and frightened.

Damn, he kept saying to himself as he headed to his office in the Justice Department. If that fucking sketch had been posted around, none of this might have happened. What the hell had happened? They should have had them circulated by now. The more he thought about it, the more furious he became. He upbraided Arnie Thorson about it when he strode into the office.

"Arnie, for Christ's sake what the hell happened to those Wanted posters the Attorney General authorized?"

He was nearly shouting. Thorson, startled, stared at Henry.

"Wait a minute, *Lieutenant,*" he said. "Step back there. We've got our trial starting in three hours, or had you forgotten?"

Henry felt the emotion drain from him. He suddenly was overcome with weariness. "Arnie," he said quietly, a hint of desperation in his voice, "we've *got* to find out about those posters."

Thorson looked concerned. He listened as Henry told him of Thomas's death and his certain encounter with Gunther. "Jeezus." He hissed the word, awestruck. He picked up the phone and called the Bureau of Engraving extension, spoke briefly, then listened a long time. His face fell, then grew red with anger. "Oh, for sweet Christ's sake!" he exploded. "I can't believe that! Now you listen to me! Either you have that done immediately or I'll see that the Attorney General *personally* orders you to have it done—and you'd better have a Goddamned good answer why his orders weren't carried out in the first place."

He slammed down the receiver and turned back to Henry, who had been watching silently, a stricken look on his face.

"You're not going to like this," he said. "Leave it to the bureaucracy. Seems they don't turn these things out just like that, especially these days. There's a war on, you know"—his voice took on a cynical edge—"they tell me you've got to goose the Public Printer to stop one of his top-priority-for-the-war-effort jobs long enough to do a rush Wanted poster. Then an engraving has to be made and then a mat and then an image run off by the hundreds. Then they've got to be bundled and addressed and—"

"You mean they're not done yet?" Henry sat heavily in a chair and bent over, his head in his hands. He felt utterly, hopelessly, defeated. He was too numb even for anger. "Oh, for Christ's sake, I can't believe it."

Thorson looked dismayed. "Seems somehow they didn't get the sense of urgency. Besides, they said, the Bureau already got all the Nazi spies, so what's the big fuss about this ONI *possible* suspect? But they're almost ready to be distributed now."

"That'll help Thomas a lot," Henry said bitterly. He stood back up, his body tense again. "But maybe it'll still be in time to get that dirty son of a bitch." He paused. "For Christ's sake, Arnie," he said, his voice rising again, "let's get those bastards moving on it!"

He checked his watch. It was only a quarter to ten in the morning. It seemed years since he read about Thomas's death. Now he had to prepare for the opening statements of

the secret trial of the saboteurs. It was scheduled to begin
shortly behind closed and heavily guarded doors just down
their fifth-floor corridor at the Justice Department.

18

The sound of many wailing sirens rang up and
down the avenue. They could be heard for miles around.
Everywhere, people stopped and stared. Moving rapidly
toward the Justice Department, from the ancient sweltering
District of Columbia jail where the temperature rose to 110
degrees by mid-afternoon, led and followed by a long
motorcycle-police escort, was a procession unlike any ever
seen in the capital.

Behind the uniformed motorcycle cops was a car filled
with FBI agents. Their eyes grimly scanned the streets.
Next came an Army scout car. It carried two mounted
machine guns manned by soldiers in full battle dress,
including steel-pot helmets. Two more soldiers were
stationed behind the machine gunners. They held tommy
guns. Around them were several jeeps with heavily armed
Military Policemen. The MPs, also in full battle dress,
stood tensely, brandishing their weapons. A thrill of
excitement and fear swept through the watching morning
rush-hour crowds. The jeeps moved before, alongside, and
behind two unmarked black police vans. The heavy twin
rear doors to the vans were shut and locked. An armed
soldier stood on the rear platform of each van.

As the leading wedge of the procession approached the
Justice Department and began noisily to turn into the inner
courtyard, sirens still blaring, someone in the crowd shouted
"There go the spies!"

Pedestrian lines broke. People began to run toward the
Justice Department where a knot of scrambling, pushing,

cursing reporters and photographers had been awaiting this moment for hours. Waiting anxiously with them was a large gathering of civilians and off-duty servicemen and women. They had all been drawn to the gates by constant breathless radio reports and big front-page newspaper headlines announcing the start of the trial of the saboteurs that morning. They pressed forward, expectant and excited, as the procession ended inside the courtyard.

The jeeps and the motorcycles encircled the vans. The scout car swung to a halt, its machine guns trained on the crowds. The FBI agents hurried from their car with drawn revolvers and formed a line alongside each van. MPs ran from their jeeps. They formed battle lines. Other soldiers quickly clanged shut the huge iron gates to the courtyard, keeping out the reporters, photographers, and general public. As flashbulbs popped, the doors to the vans swung open. The eight handcuffed saboteurs in prison denims were quickly escorted into the building and out of sight.

Back in the crowd, Gunther watched. Then, with the rest, he turned and began slowly to walk away. He felt a sense of perfect peace. Even his pain did not bother him. He welcomed it. It was his own private mark of martyrdom, proof that his suffering had not been in vain. He was triumphant. His hour had come. He limped badly for a few blocks from the Justice Department to Lafayette Park in front of the White House, his right shoulder slumping as the throb beats of pain raced through him. Even these afflictions were as they should be, he had thought that morning when he left the apartment. They change my appearance. They make me seem naturally older and more bent over.

He arrived in the park at exactly 9:30. He moved up to the high black iron fence surrounding Andrew Jackson's statue and waited. Their appointment was for 10:00. A few minutes later, he saw Slater walking stiffly, reluctantly, toward him.

Gunther reached inside his shabby suit-coat pocket—just right for a poor refugee, he had thought earlier when he inspected himself in the mirror back at the apartment—to make sure the glassine envelope with the "Postmaster Provisionals" was secure. He nodded at Slater, whose normally ruddy face was dead white. Nudging his elbow, he walked with him toward the White House just across Pennsylvania Avenue.

"How are you, Mr. Slater," said the guard inside the concrete post behind the iron fence and gate at the visitors' entrance.

"Fine, thanks," Slater said. His voice was low. It lacked its normal range and timbre.

Slater pointed to Gunther, standing politely and meekly beside him, a battered gray fedora matching his cheap faded gray pin-stripe suit.

"This is Mr. Rosenzweig. We have an appointment for ten o'clock. Grace set it up."

"Sure thing, Mr. Slater," the guard said.

Gunther handed over his Austrian passport for identification. The guard took it, checked the picture, and picked up the phone. Moments later he handed the passport back.

"Go right on in, gentlemen," he said, as he pressed the buzzer opening the first of two small iron gates.

Gunther beamed gratefully at him. "Thank you so much," he said.

He followed Slater through the first gate, waited with him until the second buzzer was pressed to open the next, and then limped slowly along the curling black pavement walkway leading to the West Wing of the White House.

Gunther looked at the simple clean lines of the building, its white walls and columns washed in the soft morning sunlight. He felt himself transported into a state of reverence. It was like approaching a cathedral. All his life, all his training from the seminary on, had pointed to this moment. He felt blessed and humble. A divine hand had protected and led him to this place of his destiny.

The Marine guard, in scarlet blouse and deep blue trousers, half snapped to attention and opened the door to the West Wing. They entered. An old Negro butler, with a faint gray mustache and a mop of white curly hair, bowed gravely and pushed open the door leading to the lobby. They walked in and stopped before a young woman receptionist sitting behind a large desk.

"Hello, Mr. Slater," she said, smiling, speaking in the friendly even accents of the Midwest.

Slater looked at her for a long moment before speaking. "This is Mr. Rosenzweig," he finally said, his voice low. "We have an appointment for ten o'clock."

She nodded cheerfully. He must be sick, she thought. She'd never heard him sound so listless. "Yes, of course. Please have a seat." She picked up the phone.

The butler led them to an overstuffed leather sofa beneath a huge canvas, *The Battle of Lake Erie*. After they were seated, he took their hats and placed them on an immense round table made of polished Philippine hardwood standing in the middle of the lobby. Then he shuffled back to his post by the door beyond the receptionist's desk.

It was still. No one spoke. They could hear the seconds ticking away on the tall mahogany grandfather clock standing by the door. Slater desperately tried to control himself. He fought back the urge to stand and shout, or just to run. Gunther had settled into what seemed a trancelike state of pleasure. Once, on the pretext of checking the time himself, he drew out his watch and caressed the chain.

Down the hallway, and around the Cabinet room, seated behind his desk inside the Oval Office, the President hung up his phone and turned to Harry Hopkins, who was standing beside him.

"Harry," he said, "Grace says Alton Slater and that refugee with the stamps are waiting in the lobby. I don't really want to see that man."

The President paused and looked sharply across at Hopkins. "I've been thinking about it. There's something odd about this. I've never heard of a 'Rosenzweig Collection.' My guess is he stole those stamps. Either that or he bought them with blood money from real refugees and now he wants to ingratiate himself with me. It all strikes me as *rather* gamey. I'll bet he's been dealing in the black market, and probably making a profit from the Germans. You know, the Nazis are great stamp collectors. Did you know that?"

Hopkins shook his head to indicate he did not know.

"Well, they are. Whenever they occupy a country, they go stamp hunting. They confiscate every collection they can get their hands on. They like to 'liberate' treasures. Coins, art, sculpture. They go for the great Jewish collections, such as

339

the Rothschilds', first. Stamps are always high on their list. This Rosenzweig's probably been dealing with them. It's a big business these days." He waved his hand in a gesture of dismissal.

"Slater's a fool. He should have spotted that man's *ca-naard*"—the Roosevelt accent was fully at work, Hopkins dryly noted—"and he's let himself be used. I started to say something to him the other day, but decided not to. Slater's very useful. He influences a helluva lot of people every night. We need him."

Hopkins listened silently.

"Do me a favor, will you, Harry? Go out and say hello for me. Tell them I've been called away to an *ur-gent*"—he drew out the word—"meeting about the *wah*. Terribly sorry and all that. Appreciate their coming by. So good of them."

He smiled up at Hopkins, pleased with himself.

Hopkins nodded and began to cross the thick carpet. He was at the door when the President called out to him. He had that crafty expression that Hopkins knew so well, but others seldom saw. "Oh, and Harry," his voice sang out, "if he *does* have the 'Provisionals,' be sure you get them for me, will you?"

Hopkins smiled and left. He walked down the corridor, past the guards posted every few feet, and through a glass doorway into the lobby.

Slater and Gunther rose to greet him. Slater felt faint. Gunther's body tingled.

"Hello, Alton," Hopkins said, holding out a limp hand to be shaken.

Slater took it and stammered an introduction. "Harry, Mr. Hopkins, uh, this is, uh, Frank Rosenzweig, the man I mentioned to you and the President last week. He, uh, he—"

"Yes," Hopkins said, all business. "How do you do, Mr. Rosenzweig. Good of you to come."

Gunther shook his hand and felt a race of emotion as he did.

Hopkins stepped back and addressed them both. "Alton. Mr. Rosenzweig." He gave a slight bow. "The President asked me personally to tell you how much he appreciates your coming by."

A strange expression crossed Gunther's face. His eyebrows

knitted together. His smile was gone. He looked closely at Hopkins.

"He's terribly sorry he can't see you." He shook his head regretfully. "But he's been called away to an urgent meeting on the war. He wanted to be sure you understood how much he regrets not seeing you. And"—he spoke directly to Gunther—"he said to tell you specifically, Mr. Rosenzweig, how pleased he was with the stamps. Not just with the gift, which pleased him greatly, but for the sentiments you expressed to him through Mr. Slater." A brief smile crossed Hopkins's sickly-looking face. "I can tell you, he was deeply touched."

He paused, became all business again. "I'll be certain to see he personally gets the stamps you brought for him today," he said, half extending his hand slightly toward Gunther, and at the same time glancing quickly at the grandfather clock.

Gunther said nothing. He didn't move a muscle. He seemed frozen in place. His eyes had a glazed look. His first impulse, after the initial shock, was to push this weak fool aside and race through the doors toward the Oval Office. Sickeningly, he realized such recklessness would be in vain if the President really was away. His heart beat furiously. For a mad moment he was afraid they could hear it. He fought to regain his composure but was locked in tormenting indecision. He still said nothing.

Hopkins looked at him with a curious expression. "Mr. Rosenzweig," he said. "Mr. Rosenzweig." When he got no response, he turned to Slater. "Does he not understand English?"

Slater looked pathetically eager to please. "Oh, yes, he understands. Don't you, Mr. Rosenzweig?"

Gunther fumbled into his pocket. He withdrew the glassine envelope and handed it silently to Hopkins. Then he reached out and touched Hopkins with his left hand. "Mr. Hopkins, Mr. Hopkins," he said, stepping closer and stammering, "perhaps we can come back and just shake the President's hand. I would be, it would be—"

"Well, yes, of course, I understand, Mr. Rosenzweig," Hopkins said, slipping the stamps into his pocket. "I'll see what I can do, but you realize, I know, how terribly busy the President is. But I'll certainly do everything I can. I'm sure we can work something out. And he does appreciate your kindness. I know he'd be very pleased to meet you."

Slater had brightened considerably. He grabbed Hopkins's hand and shook it vigorously.

"Harry, thanks so much." His voice had regained its deep dramatic tones. "We're grateful." He turned and took Gunther's elbow and began to usher him out of the lobby.

"Yes," Gunther finally said, as he limped toward the door, now held open by the butler. "Thank you—and thank the President. It will be such an honor to meet him. I—"

"I'll tell him, Mr. Rosenzweig," Hopkins said as he started to walk away. "Alton, good to see you, as always."

They walked silently and slowly back down the driveway, out through the two iron gates, and crossed Pennsylvania Avenue into Lafayette Park. Neither looked at the other. When they reached the northwest corner, near the monumental statue of Friedrich Wilhelm Ludolf Gerhard Augustin, Baron von Steuben, the Prussian who trained America's Revolutionary Army and was General Washington's military aide, Slater stopped. He kept his voice deliberately emotionless. "Well, that's that," he said flatly, without any hint of relief or gloating.

Gunther turned and moved to within an inch of Slater's face. His eyes were cold and hard and his voice was ominous. "Maybe," he said with quiet menace. Slater shivered. "Maybe. But I think not."

Gunther shifted even closer. "Go about your business as usual. I'll be in touch. And, Alton"—he stared with deadly malevolence into Slater's eyes—"I'll be watching you and thinking about you all the time. I'm counting on you to make certain I get that little personal introduction to your great friend. You *do* understand, don't you, dear Alton?"

Slater watched, standing deathly still and shaking inside, as Gunther limped painfully away through the park and out of sight.

Gunther had lost his sense of shock. He was both wary and enraged as he carefully and deliberately walked back to the apartment, stopping every now and then to see if he was being followed. He was not. But he felt in turmoil, on bayonet's edge. Too many things had gone wrong. He kept ticking them off mentally. That dumb bastard of a Norwegian. Who would have expected that? And that black cop? Where the hell did he come from? How could *he* have been following me, and why? What did he know? What was wrong? And, the President, was he really away or did they suspect something? But how could that be? Slater? No. Impossible. Willi! Damn him anyway. It was Willi, it had to be! Everything would be all right if it weren't for that traitor. What did he tell them? What did they know? Who were they? Damn that miserable bastard. They should have spotted him back at the farm. I should have killed him then instead of that stupid mail clerk Steiner I killed for him. Willi was the problem. The way things were going, Willi could even win in the end. Damn him! Willi, Willi, Willi. His face had begun to color a deep angry red and his lips moved soundlessly as he walked. A distinguished-looking man with gray hair glanced at him curiously as they passed on the street. Gunther was startled by his loss of control. He forced a neutral expression onto his face. For the first time, Gunther had a feeling of dread.

19

"You aren't exactly a barrel of mirth tonight, are you?"

Marjorie Stith looked across the large round dining table at Constance and Henry, as they glumly toyed with their food. Constance poked at her meat course but didn't really eat it, and Henry seemed sullen, withdrawn, and tense.

"Are you not feeling well, my dear?" she asked, addressing Constance directly. Marjorie's voice had taken on that slightly cutting and patronizing tone that let everyone know she was displeased without actually saying so.

Constance, flustered, looked up. "Oh, no. I'm fine, thank

343

you." Her eyes seemed to have lost their brightness. They were shadowed and streaked with red. Marjorie suspected she had been crying.

"Just a little tired, I guess." Her smile belied her words. It was forced and wan.

Marjorie turned to the dinner companion on her right. "Francis," she said, "if Henry's any example, you must be working your young men too hard."

The Attorney General glanced at Henry. "Getting ready for the trial today has given us all a great many extra hours, Marjorie," he said, "and Henry has been working especially hard in helping us prepare for it. But"—he paused and smiled slightly—"I hope he doesn't think I've been a Simon Legree."

Henry spoke up. "No, sir, I can assure you that's not the case." He tried to sound light, but his smile, like Constance's, was strained.

Marjorie frowned and gave a tight little laugh. "Of course, of course," she said. "Do tell us more, Francis, or as much as you can."

It was all they had talked about, and Marjorie had been delighted earlier over cocktails when Biddle told her guests that if the saboteurs were found guilty, the President wanted them hanged publicly in Washington as the Lincoln conspirators had been. They all listened raptly. His brief recounting of the President's remarks brought murmurs of assent. One British diplomat gave a loud "Here, here!"

She was so lucky, Marjorie had thought as she listened, to have her little "summer bachelors in wartime Washington" dinner party on this particular night, but, damn, underneath the surface gaiety of the evening somehow there was an air of grimness and sadness. It was ruining everything. Constance and Henry must be having a silly lovers' spat. Their mood was rubbing off on everyone. And it wasn't just them: Alton was a *real* pill. She'd never known him to be so morose and silent. He was so bad she'd accused him earlier in the library of being a spoilsport—and he hadn't even denied it! "I'm worried about the war and I'm not feeling at all well this evening," he responded, shortly, then lapsed back into a long silence. Well, he *doesn't* look well, she thought, but he *could* try to be more cheerful. After all, this was an occasion, and he had no right to ruin it. She was truly concerned about Constance, though.

Marjorie had grown terribly fond of Constance, and felt protective of her. Constance was a grand girl; she didn't want to see her hurt. After dinner, when the men retired to the library for brandy and cigars, Marjorie took Constance to the powder room and tried to draw her out. She failed. Constance seemed awfully troubled and preoccupied. Marjorie tried to tease her about how the heat wave was affecting everyone, even young lovers; but she failed to get much of a response there, too, and gave up.

God, I'm glad I'm through with all of *that* kind of romantic nonsense, Marjorie thought, but it can hurt, I know.

Constance was touched by Marjorie's rather heavy-handed attempt to cheer her up, but she couldn't talk about how she felt. She didn't want to *think* about it, either, though that was the only thought that filled her mind.

The news of Thomas's death affected her deeply and personally. She felt a sadness and a loss and a sense of tragedy that she couldn't put into words; but it was more than that. She felt a distance from Henry, a drawing apart, a tinge of distrust and disappointment—he *hasn't* been entirely straight with me, and I'm certain he wasn't with Thomas, either, she kept thinking—yet she desperately didn't want to feel that way about him. About them. It was tearing her up inside. They were close. So quickly and intuitively they sensed each other's moods and thoughts, and God knows we've touched each other in ways that are special beyond any previous experience. Now something seemed to be slipping away from them. She thought it was bound up somehow with Thomas's death, or maybe Thomas's death was just the symptom. Maybe it was the war. Everyone seemed to be getting hard and bitter. People at her office, people she knew, they were all different. She was beginning to think she couldn't trust anyone anymore. Henry seemed—well, ruthless, brutal even when he talked now, and he hadn't done much of *that* lately. She understood what he was going through, or thought she did. But damn it! It was hard for her,

345

too, and he didn't seem to appreciate that, or have time for her. She was starting to hate Washington again. Too many things were happening that made her feel, what?, used or useless, or both. Sometimes she thought she'd much rather be a nurse in the service overseas, horrible though that probably was most of the time. At least then she'd be making a small difference.

They had driven to Marjorie's in uncomfortable silence, both reluctant to say what they were thinking. Henry couldn't bring himself to share with Constance his sense of guilt about Thomas. He was ashamed; he didn't want her to think the worse of him. It was too complicated and too personal and too searing. He still couldn't sort all that out for himself. It would take a long time for him to unravel those emotions, if he ever did, he thought. What made it worse—unbearably, frustratingly, worse—was his knowledge that the German was still loose somewhere in Washington. He was filled with rage and fear alike. It wasn't over yet. God knows what would come next. He suddenly wished he could talk to Thomas about it, and realized, with a sense of late shock, that he didn't just feel guilty about Thomas. He missed him. There were so many things he wanted to know about him, and he had come to feel a sense of absolute confidence in him. Thomas had been reassuring. Now nothing was sure. At least the Wanted posters finally had been finished! What a disaster that had been. And it wasn't until after dark when they were all dispatched. By then, Henry was exhausted. The last thing in the world he wanted was to go to one of Marjorie Stith's dinner parties, but there seemed no way out. It was too late to renege, especially since the Attorney General was going to be there.

While the women withdrew after dinner, Henry followed Slater into the library with the rest of the men. They talked about the war. Henry confided to Slater that he didn't want to sit out the war in Washington. He was anxious to leave Naval Intelligence and get to the Pacific, maybe serving in one of the new PT boat units or on a ship of the line. Anything, really, so long as it was combat duty. Slater had been listening distractedly, obviously uninterested, further infuriating Henry, but he seemed to come alive when he learned that Henry was in Naval Intelligence.

"What do you do in Naval Intelligence, Henry?" Slater asked.

Henry hesitated. "Oh, they've been keeping me busy with various matters and various investigations," Henry said vaguely. "You might say I'm part of the permanent Washington bureaucracy now. That's why I'm itching to get out of Washington and into combat."

Slater sunk back into one of his silences. "Oh," he said. He finished his highball and excused himself.

"Elias," he said to Marjorie's butler, "where can I find Mrs. Stith?"

"She's in the living room with the ladies, Mr. Slater."

Slater nodded. "Tell her I'm leaving, please, and want to say good night." He waited in the foyer until Marjorie appeared. Slater took her hands and kissed her gently on the cheek. "I'm going, my dear," he said. "I feel rotten."

He does look terrible, Marjorie thought, and suddenly felt concerned. "Are you sure you're all right?"

"Yes, thanks. Just a summer cold."

"Well, I'll call you in the morning. If you're not better then I'm going to insist that you call Dr. Lawrence—or I will."

Slater shook his head gravely and said good night. He told his driver, who had been waiting outside on the circular driveway, to take him back to the Wardman Park.

Once inside his apartment, Slater walked directly to his study, took off his suit coat, slipped on his robe, sat down at his big rolltop desk, and began to write, in longhand, in ink, on his personal stationery.

"My Dear Lieutenant Eaton," he began. "I don't know if you speak German, but in Germany they have an expression that encompasses the quickest and surest escape, what they call 'selbstmord.' It means 'self-murder,' and I am writing you now . . ."

He bent over the paper, his concentration total, and filled page after page. The only sound in his apartment was the faint scratching of his pen on paper. When he finished five pages, Slater slowly and deliberately reread what he had written. He read it once more. Satisfied, he changed nothing. He folded the pages, put them in an envelope, sealed it, and wrote Henry's name and address on the outside. Then he picked up the phone on his desk and asked the night clerk to come to his apartment. While he waited, he opened a small wall safe in his bedroom and took out two one-hundred-dollar bills. When the clerk appeared, Slater gave him the envelope. He told him he wanted Charlie the bellhop to deliver it personally to Lieutenant Eaton at dawn the next morning. It was urgent, he stressed. He gave the night clerk the two hundred-dollar bills, one for himself and one for Charlie. The clerk, murmuring his gratitude, took the envelope and the money and left.

Slater returned to his desk. He picked up his pen and began writing again. First, he wrote a short note to Marjorie Stith. Next he wrote an even shorter one addressed to Franklin Delano Roosevelt. Again he called the clerk, and again instructed him to have these two letters delivered later in the morning. He thanked the clerk and went back to his desk. For the next few hours he wrote and rewrote a final broadcast script.

It was almost dawn when Slater finished. He had no feeling of fatigue. He got up from his desk, pushed back the chair so it was neatly in place, walked into his living room, straightened the magazines on the coffee table, poured himself a Calvados, and carried it to the large French windows opening onto his balcony. He opened them and stepped outside.

The city lay soft and still below him. He sipped his drink, savoring the taste, and let his eyes run over the hazy landscape of a Washington still swathed in shadows. As the skies brightened and the first streaks of yellow slanted across the eastern horizon, he saw a hawk circle lazily over the thick woods of Rock Creek Park; then, suddenly, it dipped low in a dive for prey and disappeared from sight amid the stretch of forest.

Slater sighed, took a deep breath of the early-morning air, finished his drink, and hurled the heavy crystal glass out over the balcony. He watched it fall. A shaft of sunlight glistened for a brief second from the crystal and then it, too, disappeared. He turned, walked back into the apartment, through the living room, and into his bedroom. From the top drawer of his dresser, tucked deep under his socks, Alton Slater removed a .45-caliber Army-issue pistol. He carried it into his bathroom, took down a towel, wrapped it around his head, knelt over the tub, put the pistol to his right temple, and pulled the trigger.

20

He could hear the phone ringing as he walked up the steps to his apartment on the Hill. As so often happened when he was in a hurry, Henry fumbled for his keys. He kept trying the wrong one; but the persistent sound of the phone continued anyway. He raced toward it in the dark and grabbed the receiver.

"Eaton here."

"Henry"—he recognized Arnie Thorson's voice, and stiffened at the agitated tone—"where the hell have you been?"

"Stith's. Marjorie Stith's house. Hell, I left word with the duty officer, and the Old Man was there, too."

"Oh, for Christ's sake." Arnie sounded disgusted. "They didn't have it. Jesus, can't we get anything right?"

Henry interrupted him. "Arnie. Have they found him?"

"No."

Henry was silent. He felt, again, frustrated, angry and weary, all at once. "Well, what's up then, Arnie?" he said, with just a trace of annoyance in his voice.

"Here's the thing, Henry," Thorson said. "Something very odd's going on." He paused. "It's about that guy Rosenzweig and his stamps. You remember, the refugee from Europe that the President told you and the Old Man was going to give him some invaluable stamps at the White House?"

"Yes."

"Well, on a hunch from the President and from him to Hopkins and on to us, we started to check out this guy. No one has a fix on him. No one can make him. His name doesn't turn up anywhere."

"That's interesting, I guess, but so what, Arnie? There must be tens of thousands of refugees we don't have anything on."

"Yeah, but not like this one. The guys at the Smithsonian's philatelic division—the stamp guys—say they never heard of a Rosenzweig or a 'Rosenzweig Collection.' But what's really interesting is they said it's inconceivable one collector could have all those rare stamps in one batch. Just can't be. There's gotta be something funny about it."

Henry was growing impatient. He had too many other things to worry about than a bogus stamp collector.

"So I say again: So what, Arnie? Why don't you ask Alton Slater about this guy if it's so interesting. He's the one who introduced him to the President."

A dead silence. Then Arnie spoke, slowly and testily. "That's the whole point, Henry. That's why we've been trying to get you." He paused again. "You know Slater, don't you?"

"Hell, I just had dinner with him, Arnie. He was at Stith's tonight. I don't know him well, but, yes, I've met him. And I talked with him again tonight. So what?"

"The 'so what' is that we want you to interview Slater personally first thing in the morning, and it's got to be done with, with uh"—Arnie fumbled for the right word—"with, ummm, discretion. Slater's big, very big, and this conversation has to be very informal and very private. But it's, it's also"—he groped again to express himself—"well, it's absolutely crucial, Henry."

He was quiet a moment. Henry could feel the growing tension in Arnie's voice. "Now, here's the thing, Henry, and I think you'd better be sitting down. The Old Man sent for the FBI files on Slater. Whatever Hoover had. It was almost a direct order. Well—and get this!—we got them—and how. Turns out that Hoover had a big file on Slater's early years. You sitting down?"

"I'm down."

"Slater was a Nazi sympathizer and—"

"Oh, bullshit, Arnie! That's more of Hoover and his imagination. I don't like Slater. Correction. I can't stand him. He's a pompous little ass, but if he's a Nazi, I'm a nun. I just don't buy that. You should have heard him talk about Hitler and patriotism tonight. I mean—"

"Henry." Arnie sounded soothing. "No one's saying Slater's a Nazi, just that years ago, when he was younger, he was attracted to them. Lots of people I knew in the Midwest belonged to America First. I heard plenty of people then who said they admired what Hitler and Mussolini were doing. I'll bet you did, too. It seems Slater was one of them. But here's the thing: Hoover knew this and was practically blackmailing the poor bastard with that information. As you know, Slater's always praising Hoover and the Bureau—'The G-men'—on his broadcasts. Next to Winchell, no radio commentator has been a bigger cheerleader for the Bureau. Anyway, talk to him first thing in the morning, ask him for more details on this Rosenzweig guy, feel him out about his early years—he *was* in Germany, you know—report back immediately to the Old Man."

"Yes, of course. And, Arnie—" Henry hesitated. "Thanks."

Henry hung up and went right to bed, but he didn't sleep well. He kept having a series of disconnected fragments of dreams, all of them disturbing, all of them somehow involving endless races over strange terrain, but unlike anything he'd experienced in his track days: the faster he tried to run, the farther he fell behind, the greater the physical effort and strain, the more the feeling of defeat. He never could picture just who, or what, ran far ahead of him. At one point he bolted up, and was startled to find his heart pounding, his tongue swollen, his face and neck damp from perspiration just as if he really had been running; then he fell back into a state of half-sleep and more dreams.

The ringing noise in his head seemed part of the dream, until the sound finally cut through and jolted him awake. He groped for the phone by his bed, and looked at his clock. It was 6:12 in the morning.

"Hullo, what is it?" he said heavily.

"Lieutenant Eaton?" It was a young man's voice.

"Yes." He sat straight up in bed, fully awake.

"Lieutenant, this is Corporal James Shelby at the White House."

"Yes."

"Your office gave me your home phone."

"Yes."

"Well, I got this drawing in front of me and a note that says if anyone sees this guy to give you a call. And—"

"You've seen him?" Henry shouted. He jumped out of bed and held the phone tensely.

"Well, yeah, Lieutenant, I—"

"For Christ's sakes, Corporal, get it out. When did you see him? Where? Was he alone? And what—"

"Excuse me, sir." The corporal interrupted. "That's what I'm trying to tell you. It was yesterday—"

"Yesterday! Why the hell didn't you call sooner, man. Those sketches were delivered late yesterday afternoon! What the hell—"

Corporal Shelby held his ground. "Well, yes, sir, I know, that's what I'm trying to tell you. I don't come on duty until six o'clock each morning and as soon as I saw the drawing I knew I'd seen that guy here yesterday at the White House and I called you right away, sir."

Henry spoke quietly into the phone. "Yes, of course, of course, Corporal. Now take your time and tell me exactly what you saw."

"Well, sir, this guy came in—and I'm certain it was the same one—with that man from the radio. You know, Mr. Slater. George let them through. I was just standing there."

"Slater? Alton Slater? You're sure? Was the other man a Mr. Rosenzweig?"

"Yes, sir, it was Mr. Slater. He comes here all the time. And I think the other one was something like that Mr. Rosen—whatever you said—but I'm not sure about that, sir."

"Corporal." Henry spoke crisply. "Now I want you to make a full report on everything you saw and heard, and have the other guard make one, too. Everything, understand? Who's your superior officer?"

"Colonel Breverton, sir."

"All right. I want you to give Colonel Breverton your report and then have him call me immediately." Henry started to hang up. "Oh, and Corporal."

"Yes, sir."

"You did just right. I'll personally see that you're commended."

Henry scrambled to dress, put his revolver in his shoulder holster, snapped the button on the holster, and hurried out of his apartment. Now he was really running, and this was no dream.

He jumped into his Nash, and quickly drove off. Just as he was leaving, he noticed a hotel bellhop walking down his street, checking the numbers on the town houses. He was carrying an envelope. Helluva time to be delivering a letter, Henry thought, then, his mind racing, he put his foot down on the accelerator and lurched forward faster. He jumped the red light at the corner and sped off toward Rock Creek Park.

21

Sleep was never a problem for Gunther. He could nap at will and always awake refreshed; but this night was different. There was no sleep. He was unable even to rest. Hour after hour he tossed and turned, coiled and uncoiled his body, and tried to make his mind a blank. It was no use.

Shortly after dawn, he reached a decision. He would force Slater, at knifepoint if necessary, to get him back in the White House. Today. Immediately. He would not be denied. Slater could do it if he tried.

Gunther cursed, got out of bed, stumbled painfully to the phone, and dialed Slater's number. The line was busy. He cursed again and began to dress.

A few minutes later he dialed again. Still busy. *Damn him.* "Who's he talking to? What the hell is going on?"

Gunther realized he had spoken aloud. He shook himself. This was ridiculous. He had to get a grip on himself. But he was losing his iron control and with it his confidence, something that had never happened to him before. I'm just tired, he thought. That's it. He went into the small kitchen and made coffee. He waited until it perked and poured himself a cup before calling Slater's number again. Still busy! Now he felt a sense of acute alarm, and something else: a ripple of fear. Suddenly he felt chilled. He felt his flesh rise.

"Damn!" Again, he spoke aloud, and again he was angry at himself for his loss of control.

He went back into the kitchen and slipped the knife into his sock. Once more he called Slater. The buzzing busy signal infuriated him—and made him even more apprehensive. He left the apartment and began the long walk uptown along Connecticut Avenue to the Wardman Park.

It was already suffocating and the day had barely begun. God this place is terrible, he thought. He was filled with an inexpressible hatred for the Americans and everything connected with them. As he limped slowly along, he tried to nurse his hatred and rekindle his confidence, but it wasn't working. He couldn't shake a feeling of nervousness and deep unease. He felt very alone.

He was perspiring heavily as he crossed the long bridge over Rock Creek Park, but he didn't feel warm; he felt clammy and cold. He could see the tower of the Wardman Park rising from atop the high hill ahead, its lines shimmering in the early-morning heat waves; and he could see something else: a tangle of cars and flashing lights.

Gunther came closer. He drew in his breath. The place was surrounded by police cars with squad radios blaring. An ambulance, its red emergency light circling slowly overhead, stood just outside the front doors. Nearby, parked at odd angles in the driveway, were cars with large PRESS stickers on their windshields. Gunther sucked in his breath. He slumped slightly, his eyes wary for any sign of recognition, as he stepped inside the lobby. It was a scene of bedlam. Reporters with notepads were shouting questions at D.C. policemen while news photographers snapped shot after shot with their Speed Graphics. Each flashbulb made a popping sound. No one paid attention to Gunther. He stopped beside a photographer putting another plate into his Speed Graphic and tapped him on the shoulder.

"What the hell's going on?" he asked.

The photographer, a middle-aged man with rimless glasses, pale blue eyes, gray hair, and a thin pencil-line mustache, turned around sharply. He looked contemptuously at Gunther.

"Where the hell have you been, buddy?" he snarled. "Haven't you heard? Alton Slater just killed himself."

Gunther, stunned, took a step backward. His face blanched. He experienced a tremor of sheer panic. For the first time, he felt trapped. He had to get away. He turned, moved rapidly out of the lobby, through the doors, and then began stumbling in a half-sprint, half-jog, toward Rock Creek Park.

Henry saw Gunther before his car pulled into the driveway of the Wardman Park. He spotted him moving quickly away from the apartment. There was no question about it. It was he, for sure. He slammed the car to a stop and leaped from it, not even bothering to turn off the engine or close the door. He pulled out his revolver and began running.

Gunther was several hundred yards ahead of him, already across Connecticut Avenue and heading toward the woodland of the park. He was moving as rapidly as he could. But he was slow, terribly slow; the injuries inflicted by Willi and Thomas had seriously affected him. He cursed himself furiously as he moved.

At first, he didn't realize he was being pursued. He was startled—and almost stopped dead at the sight—when he glanced over his shoulder and saw a young American, pistol in hand, sprinting at great speed after him. He lunged forward desperately and tried to summon all his reserves of physical energy, but the harder he pushed himself in the heavy summer air, the farther behind he seemed to fall. The young American was gaining on him relentlessly. Gunther began to limp. For the first time in his memory, he felt physically weak.

He turned into the grounds of the zoo, ran, stumbled, nearly fell, lumbered ahead, and, exhausted, found himself before the largest structure in the National Zoological Park—a huge open iron birdhouse set among trees and waterfalls. It soared a full story above the ground, and was filled with a collection of brilliantly hued birds: macaws, scarlet ibis, birds of paradise, toucans, parrots.

Henry slowed as he saw Gunther stop. He raised his .38 and moved ahead, his face grim and hard.

Gunther whirled. He put his back against the cage to steady himself. His lip curled and he growled an unintelligible snarl. He pulled out his watch chain, tensed it in his hands, and crouched as he awaited the American. Behind him he heard what sounded like hundreds of birds squawking at once. A wave of terror passed through him. He gagged slightly and felt a harsh knot of vomit catch in his throat. He turned slightly and started to shout at the birds in German. As he did, Henry fired his revolver. The bullet struck Gunther in the Adam's apple. The sharp crackling sound of the pistol reverberated through the grounds and touched off an avalanche of noise from within the birdhouse. Gunther's hands flew to his throat. His chain fell to the ground. Henry fired again, and again the crackling sound set off a shrill of noise from the birdhouse and a rumble and echo of other strange noises from all directions of the zoo. The second bullet struck Gunther just below the left eye.

22

By three o'clock that afternoon, things had calmed down at the D.C. Police Department press room. Baxter ("Bax") Riley dictated lots of good stuff on Alton Slater's suicide—the guy knew he was dying of cancer of the esophagus, they said; well, who could blame him, how the hell could a famous radio announcer last without his voice?—and all he had on the shooting of the robbery suspect at the zoo. He still couldn't answer his city editor's questions about who the guy was. They thought he was a hard-up refugee trying to burgle some of those old ladies' apartments on Connecticut Avenue, but there was no ID, so how the hell could you know for sure? Anyway, he had a real exclusive now to break and it was a helluva lot better story. He smiled as he picked up the phone in a private office off the press room that he used for confidential calls like this. Wait'll that little prick Nelson of the *Post* sees this one, he thought.

Riley had worked for the *Evening Star* for twenty-four years and for each one of those years he had the same job—police reporter. His 245 pounds of corpulence and his square, pudgy face and small eyes gleaming behind thick glasses had earned him the nickname "Sheriff" among his newspaper colleagues and police cronies. Every day at this hour, fifteen minutes before the final deadline for stories to make the last red-streak edition that would hit the streets at five o'clock, Sheriff went through the same routine. He called the City Desk and offered his late-breaking news.

"Remember that big story Nelson had about all the colored shootings?" Even though he was alone, with the door closed, he whispered into the phone. "Yeah, that's right. Well, I got this one exclusive and it's on our time. Yeah, exclusive. Well, Waddleduck says they've arrested a cab driver who's confessed to shooting eight jigaboos in the back of the head in the last four weeks. No. He's white. Waddleduck says the cabbie is some kind of a religious nut. He carries a Bible beside him on the front seat of the cab. Says God ordered him to destroy nigger males. Says it's right in the Bible. How the hell do I know *where* in the Bible? Naw. Yeah. Yeah. That's right, exclusive. Okay, gimme Muldoon on rewrite and I'll unload it now. Oh, hey, wait a minute. What'd you do with that zoo story I gave you?"

He listened, then grew angry. "For crying out loud, what's the point of busting my ass if you're going to put my stuff on leftover?" He listened silently again. "Okay, okay. I'll give you a short overnight on it. Now gimme Muldoon. I'm ready with this one. And remember, I got this one exclusive."

When he finished dictating his notes to the rewrite man, Sheriff stretched, smiled, and then got up and went back into the press room. He couldn't resist. He walked over to Nelson of the *Post*, who was sitting alone at a long table where they all played cards after deadline.

"Hey, Nelson," he said expansively, throwing a meaty hand around the reporter's shoulders. "Guess what?"

Nelson, instantly suspicious, looked up quizzically, but said nothing.

"That great story of yours about all the colored nobodies that got shot?" Sheriff paused and watched Nelson's consciously impassive face.

"Well," he continued, "you can file that one away. I just gave my desk an exclusive. They got the guy who did it. And I got it in the last edition. Exclusive!"

The muscles in Nelson's face twitched. His eyes narrowed, but he still said nothing.

Sheriff leaned over. "Helluva story," he said. "Got religion and everything. Crazy cabbie who carries a Bible confessed to killing 'em all. Says God ordered him to do it."

"Shit, Sheriff," Nelson said sharply. "You been had. I know all about that. That's a phony. My sources in homicide tell me he shot the last one after reading about the others in the *Post*. They don't believe he killed them all. He just wants to get credit in the papers. He wants to be famous."

Sheriff rose to his full height, puffed out his chest, and looked disdainful. "Yeah, sure, Nelson, sure. That's what I'd say if I got beat. Well, let me tell you, little buddy, the guy's arrested, and the guy's confessed, and they got no other suspects, and you can read it all in the *Star* now."

Sheriff turned and sauntered out of the press room. He had three more hours before he had to file the short overnight they wanted on that shooting at the zoo.

23

Four white faces stood out sharply amid a sea of colored. In the back, in the last pew by the door, was Nelson of the *Post*. Across the aisle from him, at the very end of the pew by the wall, spotlighted in the rays of sunlight filtering through a stained-glass window directly above, was a big D.C. policeman. He looked unhappy and uncomfortable.

Just one white cop out of the whole force, Henry thought bitterly. It was probably that Southern cop Thomas said he liked.

Henry felt conspicuous in his formal white naval officer's uniform. He debated whether to wear it, and decided he wanted to show that at least someone of rank openly paid tribute. He sat beside Constance, on the aisle, halfway down the congregation. They arrived separately at Ebenezer Baptist Church, a plain old red brick structure standing at the foot of Georgia Avenue below Howard University, and reacted stiffly and uneasily when they saw each other. There was so much to say and yet no way to express it. They didn't try. Instinctively, they kept silent as they walked together into the church. They were intensely aware of the glances, both curious and openly hostile, they drew as they walked down the aisle. Once they took their seats, they stared straight ahead, lost in their own thoughts, as they waited for the service to begin.

He glanced around the church. On his right, several pews ahead, Henry spotted a heavy Negro woman—Mama Nellie, he instantly recognized, remembering Thomas's description. She began to sob softly as the organist played the strains of the spiritual "Go Down Moses." Beside her a slight man with a thin black mustache, his yellowish skin giving him an Oriental look, openly struggled to control himself. He swallowed repeatedly as if to choke back tears. Seated in two of the front rows were Thomas's angry friends from Howard, the ones he and Constance met that Saturday afternoon. Their faces were frozen. They sat up rigidly. In the first row, on the aisle, before banks of carnations surrounding the open coffin, were Thomas's widow and son and daughter. They were all dressed in black. Mrs. Thomas wore a veil. Their faces seemed set in solemn masks. There were no tears. Stoics, Henry thought; then he remembered, again, those lines Thomas had quoted from one of the poems from slavery days: *We wear the mask that grins and lies* . . .

They still do, Thomas, he thought, your people still do.

He tried to avoid looking at the coffin but found himself unable to take his eyes from Thomas's features. They were clearly visible among the white satin lining of the casket and the banks of white flowers around it.

Henry felt a sharp sense of loss—and more anger and guilt, too. I never began to understand him, he thought, and I'll probably spend the rest of my life wishing I had acted differently. Once more, he berated himself for failing to alert Thomas to what he would face if he met the German. He half muttered to himself. It was all so unnecessary. If only I had . . .

He caught himself. If only *Slater* had acted differently. God, what a tragedy of needless errors and misjudgments, maybe Slater most of all. That letter he wrote me was pathetic. He wasn't a Nazi, just a screwed-up guy with a superiority complex. His real problem was he couldn't live with the knowledge that his homosexuality would be exposed. The poor miserable bastard. Henry felt a flash of rage. If only Slater had come to us. We would have protected his secret. For God's sake, he wasn't the only homo in Washington. The ranks of the government were filled with them, and in high places, too. We could even have used him. And if he *had* told us about the German, Thomas wouldn't be lying there in that coffin. Probably even Decatur would still be alive. Great God, what a waste. He sighed heavily.

Constance, her eyes red, looked up hard at him, and she

sighed, too. She felt numb and weak. She bit hard on her lower lip and swallowed quickly.

The service began shortly after eleven o'clock. It was emotional. The choir, in bright red velvet robes, sang "Shall We Gather at the River." Their voices filled the now-stifling church and seemed to hang, trembling, in the hot summer air. They drew out the verses—*"S-h-a-l-l w-e g-a-t-h-e-r a-t t-h-e r-i-v-e-r—"* in a way that Constance found excruciatingly poignant and sad. She choked and began to cry.

An old white-haired preacher took the pulpit. He boomed out words about a time to live and a time to die, then recited examples from the Bible to make his points. As his voice rose dramatically and a sheen of perspiration showed on his dark face, the congregation began responding with a chorus of "amens" that grew louder and louder as he preached.

"Jeremiah was imprisoned because he spoke out about the political institutions of his time." Amen!

"Paul, in jail, converted his own jailer." Amen!

"Jesus preached a social gospel for this world as well as the one to come." Amen! That's right! Amen!

Constance was struck by the political context of the passages and the increasingly emotional response to them. The minister preached on. He recalled the story of Jesus driving the money-changers from the Temple.

"Jesus was angry when he did that," he shouted, "but no one in Negro churches ever gets angry."

He raised his right hand and made a fist, drawing forth a wave of sound from the congregation. "I would to God somebody would get angry. There's nothing wrong with anger so long as you keep your hand under control. I see this segregation and discrimination. I see people living in shacks, living in poverty. I see the politicians sitting back, looking on, doing nothing. I see the Negro treated like an animal. I see the good people cut down in the bloom of life."

He swept his arms over the casket. "I am angry. Yes, I would to God we'd get angry."

There was a stirring in the church and a feeling of heavy emotion. It was almost frightening in its intensity, Constance thought. The minister slowly sat down.

Total silence now, even more charged with emotion.

The choir sang "Balm in Gilead." The congregation stood and swayed as one. Somehow the physical movement and the sound of the voices washed away some of the tension.

A slim, elegantly dressed man with imposing and stern features stepped forward from the first row. He walked around the casket, stood directly in the center over it, turned around, and faced the congregation. Constance recognized him as one of the many men they had met with Thomas. Quietly, and with grave dignity, he delivered a personal eulogy to Thomas, "that good man whose life is gone but whose spirit is still with us." His words were generous and touching, but both Henry and Constance found them tinged with bitterness. He spoke with an unmistakable undercurrent of hostility toward whites. He finished by reading, at Mrs. Thomas's request, some of Thomas's favorite lines, from Countee Cullen:

> Lord, I fashion dark gods, too
> Daring even to give to You
> Dark despairing features . . .
> Lord, forgive me if my need
> Sometimes shapes a human creed.

The choir sang again, and again their voices washed over the congregation soothingly and brought forth more sounds from the people in the pews. It was over.

Constance and Henry felt drained as they filed silently out of the church. The noon heat hit them with physical force, drawing their breath and making everything seem heavy and slow. They turned, awkwardly, to each other, and felt the tension between them grow. Neither said anything. After a long silence, Henry shifted his feet, licked his lips, and spoke.

"I've got some news, Magnolia," he said in an unusually husky voice.

Constance looked up at him oddly. She shaded her eyes to see him better.

"They've granted my request for a transfer." He sounded more brisk and official now. "They're even giving me a promotion. To Lieutenant Commander." He laughed, but hard, not pleasantly. "So I guess they expect me to earn it."

He looked away as he spoke. "I'll be leaving for the South Pacific soon."

He paused and looked straight at her, his eyes dark and impenetrable. "You know"—his voice had just the slightest hint of a catch in it—"how I feel, how I want to get away. I've had it with Washington. Well, now that this is all over, I'm finally getting what I want. So I guess this is . . ." He stopped, groping for the right word.

Constance had been listening to him tensely. Suddenly, she relaxed. She gave a wry smile, and shook her head slowly. "I have something to tell you, too," she said in a strangely pitched voice. "I thought it was going to be too hard, but now, somehow, it's not."

He looked at her with a peculiar expression. She smiled again, more with an air of resignation now.

"I'm leaving, too," she said. "Aren't we something? I can't stand any more of what I've been doing. I *hate* everything that's been happening. I hate what it's doing to you—and to me. I've got to get away, and I'm going to."

They both were silent a moment. Constance fought back an impulse to cry. No, damn it, she thought, I *won't* do that. Henry felt his stomach churning. His mouth was dry and parched.

"Anyway," Constance said, striking, and almost achieving it, the old light teasing pose, "thanks to Marjorie, I'm going to London. I'm going to be Averell Harriman's personal secretary. I didn't know how to tell you. Obviously, it doesn't make any difference now, does it?"

She laughed tightly. He tried to smile, but couldn't.

"What the hell, Mr. Commander, who are we to worry about ourselves? There's a war on, isn't there? So we'll just have to wait till it's over, then see who we are."

"Yes." He didn't know what else to say.

They were silent again. For a brief but intense moment, each looked searchingly into the other's face. Without another word, both feeling hurt and dead inside, still terribly in love, and terribly disappointed that it was ending this way, they turned and went their separate ways.

EPILOGUE

WASHINGTON, SATURDAY, AUGUST 8, 1942. A blinding rain lashed the streets, breaking the long depressing heat wave. The city was still oppressively steamy when four black cars moved away from the private entrance to the White House. The license plates on all the cars had been changed. Instead of the low numbered plates they normally carried, they all bore higher numerals. It was 1:34 P.M. The streets were deserted. Inside, the passengers sat silently, as if mesmerized by the drumbeat of rain on their vehicles and the sound of the windshield wipers rhythmically clicking and squeaking away. They stared out the streaked wet windows at the bent trees and sodden shrubbery on the south grounds. The procession passed through the open iron gates onto East Executive Avenue, then moved slowly toward the Potomac and the parkway to Maryland.

In the second car, seated beside his personal secretary, Grace Tully, and his cousin Margaret ("Aunt Daisy") Suckley, and across from two Secret Service agents in jump seats, was the President. Aunt Daisy held his Scottie, Fala, in her lap. The President checked his watch, cocked back his head, and called out to the agent sitting beside the driver in the front, "All right, Mike, let's turn on my 'newspaper.' "

Reilly smiled, as he always did at the President's little joke, and snapped on the radio.

The announcer sounded breathless as he read INS news bulletins that had just clattered into the studio over the teletype machines:

"The White House has just announced that six of the eight accused Nazi saboteurs have been executed." They all listened intently. The President arched his eyebrows slightly and smiled.

"The first went to death in the electric chair at the District of Columbia jail at noon. It became obvious shortly before noon that the executions would come soon. Army officials and the District of Columbia coroner and a clergyman entered the jail. Newsmen inside the jail were forbidden to make telephone calls. Then came the White House announcement that six of the accused saboteurs had been electrocuted at noon . . ."

The President turned to Aunt Daisy. "They should have been hanged," he said.

"Oh, Franklin," she answered, stroking Fala.

They all continued to listen.

"Here is the text of the White House announcement on the execution of the Nazi saboteurs: Quote, The President completed his review of the findings and sentences of the Military Commission appointed by him on July second, 1942, which tried the eight Nazi saboteurs. The President approved the judgment of the Military Commission that all of the prisoners were guilty and that they be given the death sentence by electrocution. However, there was a unanimous recommendation by the Commission, concurred in by the Attorney General and the Judge Advocate General of the Army, that the sentence of two of the prisoners be commuted to life imprisonment because of their assistance to the government of the United States in the apprehension and conviction of the others. The record in all eight cases will be sealed until the end of the war. Unquote."

The President, who had been leaning forward to catch every word, relaxed. "The seal on that particular record will last a lot longer than that," he said quietly, to no one in particular, sounding as if he were speaking to himself.

Aunt Daisy looked at him quizzically but knew, from long acquaintance, that he was not going to say more. She continued patting Fala. Tully and the agents showed no reaction.

"All right, Mike," the President called out, his voice like a bell now. He was smiling broadly and appeared delighted. "That's enough."

Reilly turned off the radio.

The President turned to his companions, his mood expansive. "I still think they should have recommended hanging," he said. "Then I could have released the pictures to the public." Aunt Daisy made a disapproving face.

"No, Daisy," the President said, responding to her look, "we're always too soft in dealing with spies and traitors."

He faced back to the front.

"All right, Mike," he sang out again, "on to Shangri-la."

The heavy rain continued. Their caravan wound through the Maryland countryside, passing through the center of small villages and towns, always stopping to observe traffic lights so as not to attract undue attention, and began climbing high into the Catoctin Mountains toward the secret retreat the President, the most secretive of leaders, mischievously called "Shangri-la."

Two hours after their trip began, they passed through gates heavily guarded by Marines. They moved along the roadway toward seven rustic cabins clustered around the largest one occupied by the President.

His guests—Dorothy and Sam Rosenman and Ada and Archie MacLeish would share the presidential cabin with him and Aunt Daisy this weekend—found him to be in an unusually ebullient mood. They attributed it to the good news about the Nazi saboteurs and the landing just the day before of the Marines on the island of Guadalcanal in the South Pacific. What they didn't know, and as usual the President delighted in their lack of knowledge, was that he had also just given the final authorization for the Tube Alloys project which now was to be known as the Manhattan Engineering District Project.

The President loved his informal secluded weekends at Shangri-la. They had a reinvigorating effect, and, with the strict wartime secrecy that shrouded his every movement, he felt wonderfully free there from press and public clamor and attention. Yet through a direct phone line to the White House switchboard, he could also be in instant personal touch with leaders around the world. And, always, as on this trip, high civilian and military aides bearing maps and top secret plans accompanied him.

His favorite place was the lovely screened-in porch with a

stone floor. It sat on the edge of the woods and overlooked a valley which could be seen through an opening cut especially for him in the deep forest. Sometimes he would sit there for hours, working on papers or his stamp collection, or just studying the countryside and the various types of trees that gave him pleasure. He enjoyed sharing the view with special guests; but today, the rain was pouring so hard they couldn't use the porch.

He didn't seem to mind, though. None of them remembered him being in such high spirits. He wheeled his chair vigorously around the paneled cottage, inspecting to see where the new prints he had sent up from Washington had been hung. Pleased, he complimented Isaac, the Filipino in charge of the cabin, for his artistry in the new arrangements. Guests gathered around him before the big stone fireplace. He began the late-afternoon ritual in which he took such great pride—the mixing of martinis in a silver cocktail shaker, performed, as always, with the precision of a chemist, and the equally important task, after much twirling in a bucket of ice, of providing frosted stemmed glasses in which to drink them.

The President was a great storyteller. They all always enjoyed listening to him hold court. Normally, his stories had a gentle edge and ended with a round of easy laughter. But not those he told today. The ones he told now with such relish all had a grim, bloody, and violent cast to them. They were gruesome stories about murders and plots and forgeries.

He was sitting in an easy chair in the living-dining room, his specially designed new aluminum wheel chair beside him. Over his shoulder, and somehow bracketing his big torso, they could see the American and Presidential flags posted on either side of the fireplace.

His stories, the setting, the sound of the rain beating on the cabin all combined to give the scene an intensity and sense of tragic drama such as they never recalled in his presence before. Some of the women shivered as they listened to him.

He told the story of a wealthy Chicago widow who died while traveling in Moscow. When the casket finally was brought back to her grieving children in Chicago, they opened it to take one last look at "Dear Mama" and found instead the body of a Russian general. He told about a famous English general who was killed in the Battle of New Orleans. His body was placed in a barrel of rum and lashed to the deck of a ship to be brought back to England for burial. But when his family inquired about the state of the body on arrival, they were told, "It would have been all right, but some of the crew got thirsty and used an auger on the way over." He told a story of a barber during the last desperate days of the siege of Paris in 1870. The people were starving but somehow the barber managed to provide excellent "veal" to the local butcher. Everyone said they'd never tasted such delicious meat. Then it turned out several of the barber's customers had been missing for weeks. The President paused dramatically and then graphically told how the "veal" was butchered and delivered.

"How awful," one of the women said.

The President laughed uproariously.

He's really quite bloodthirsty, another of his guests thought.

Aunt Daisy asked about the Nazi saboteurs executed that day and wondered where they would be buried. He told her in unmarked graves in Washington. Then she said: "Well, Franklin, you have to say the FBI did a marvelous job in capturing them."

The President laughed again. "Y-es," he said, drawing out the word, "Ed-gar the Hoo is taking all the credit, and the intelligence boys are mad as hell. And so is Mike here." He gestured toward Reilly, standing quietly and solemnly in the corner of the cottage off to the side of the fireplace.

The President paused and looked at them conspiratorially. "But there's a little bit more to all of it than that. Just a little bit more."

He threw back his head and laughed again. Then he finished his drink, checked his watch, and began wheeling himself quickly toward his study.

"Carry on, everyone," he said over his shoulder, as he left the living room. "I've got some wonderful new stamps, some 'Postmaster Provisionals,' and I want to inspect them more closely."

ABOUT THE AUTHORS

Haynes Johnson and Howard Simons have closely observed the workings of Washington for many years as colleagues on *The Washington Post*. Simons presently oversees the Nieman Fellows at Harvard University as curator of the Nieman Foundation for Journalism. He was an award-winning science writer and from 1971 to 1984 served as managing editor of the *Post*, directing coverage of such stories as the Watergate scandal. Johnson, a Pulitzer Prize winner in journalism, as was his father before him, has been a reporter, columnist, editor, and T.V. commentator. He has taught at Princeton University, is the author of a number of books, and regularly appears on the "Washington Week in Review" television program broadcast nationally over PBS. This is their first novel.